Heroes of Reighja

THE TALE OF ACHYUT
THE GALLANT

Jim Gill

Jim Gill Books

jimgillbooks@gmail.com
www.jimgillbooks.com

Cover design by Kimberly Lý   (www.kimber-ly.com)
Edited by Sonya Costa   (www.drplottwist.com)

ISBN (Hardcover)   979-8-9888188-0-9
ISBN (ebook)   979-8-9888188-1-6

Printed in the United States of America
First Printing, 2023

Dedication

to Marianne Kent Young (Oma), my beloved grandmother, teacher, and friend, who passed from this world in September 2021.

Midnight. Silence upon the forest floor.
Erie is the stillness of withered shrubs and naked trees and breathless wind and birds and boars and dreaming bears and bees.
Heaven's stars are fast asleep above the mountain's peak.
Even the moon has slipped away and dulled the night's mirthful mystique.
Kneeling before a single stone, tears fall from my sunken face.
The mountain's protector is sleeping too with holiness and grace.

Birthed by love and baptized by water she lived better than most of us even try;
Matriarch of my clan, steadfast as her mountain, knowledgeable and wise and warm as a sunrise, she showed the world strength and compassion until she said goodbye.
Although our lives all differ, we won't outlive our bonds, as one day, whether we're ready or not, we'll face the great beyond.

Regrets from my past billow forth from my head, like thunderclouds heavy with rain; drowning my heart and filling my mind with loneliness, dread and pain.
Secular minds and scientific finds cannot prove the existence of life after death.
Humans, past, present, and prospect, will seek life through faith or must accept we are no more after we draw our final breath.
Yearning to believe that optimistic lie, moonlight breaks through the starless sky.
Wrapped in the wind's gentle embrace, she wipes the tears from my face.
From the deep desolate dark I hear an owl, kind and wise, perched atop the Protector's home, who lets me know I'm not alone.

Because of our love for each other and the cherished memories we retain, if we wish, and wish very strongly, perhaps we'll meet again.

iii

Acknowledgements

First and foremost, thank you to my parents, Liz and Craig, for supporting me in whatever endeavors I pursue, whether it be writing, animal training, or moving all around the country seeking new adventures and following my passions. I would have never accomplished so much without your guidance, support, kindness, and affirmations.

Thank you to all of my immediate family, my siblings, Katie and Emrys, my grandmother, Patty, and all of my uncles, aunts, cousins and extended family for listening whenever I needed someone to talk with, for believing in me to see this project's completion, for filling my life with fun and wonderful memories to draw inspiration from, and for helping me challenge myself; both physically and mentally to become the man I am today.

Thank you to all of my friends, whom I consider family, who have stayed by my side from the earliest days of elementary school through our graduations from Murrah High School. From board game nights to social events and celebrating holidays together, you've always made me feel loved and free to be my goofy self.

Thank you to everyone I've met at Hendrix College, who helped me develop my own opinions and ideas about the world and reinforced the idea of who I strive to be.

Thank you to my EDM family, and every raver I've met, strangers who showed me nothing but kindness and love, and restored my faith in humanity and myself during some of my darkest moments of coming into adulthood and having to face the world.

Thank you to all of my co-workers who made the more mundane days enjoyable and allowed me to ramble on about my books and my goals for hours at a time.

Thank you to all of my teachers, both in school and out in the world, who taught me lessons I'll never forget and provided me with creative insights and new ways to approach problems.

Thank you to everyone who helped me create 'Heroes of Reighja' and be able to share this world with everyone; my mentor and brother, Jordan Hampton, my editor, Sonya Costa, my cover artist, Kim Lý, and my photographer, Cassie Flynn.

Last and certainly not least, thank **YOU** for supporting my dream. I wish all of you the very best in whatever endeavors you choose to pursue and am excited to see how bright your light will shine.

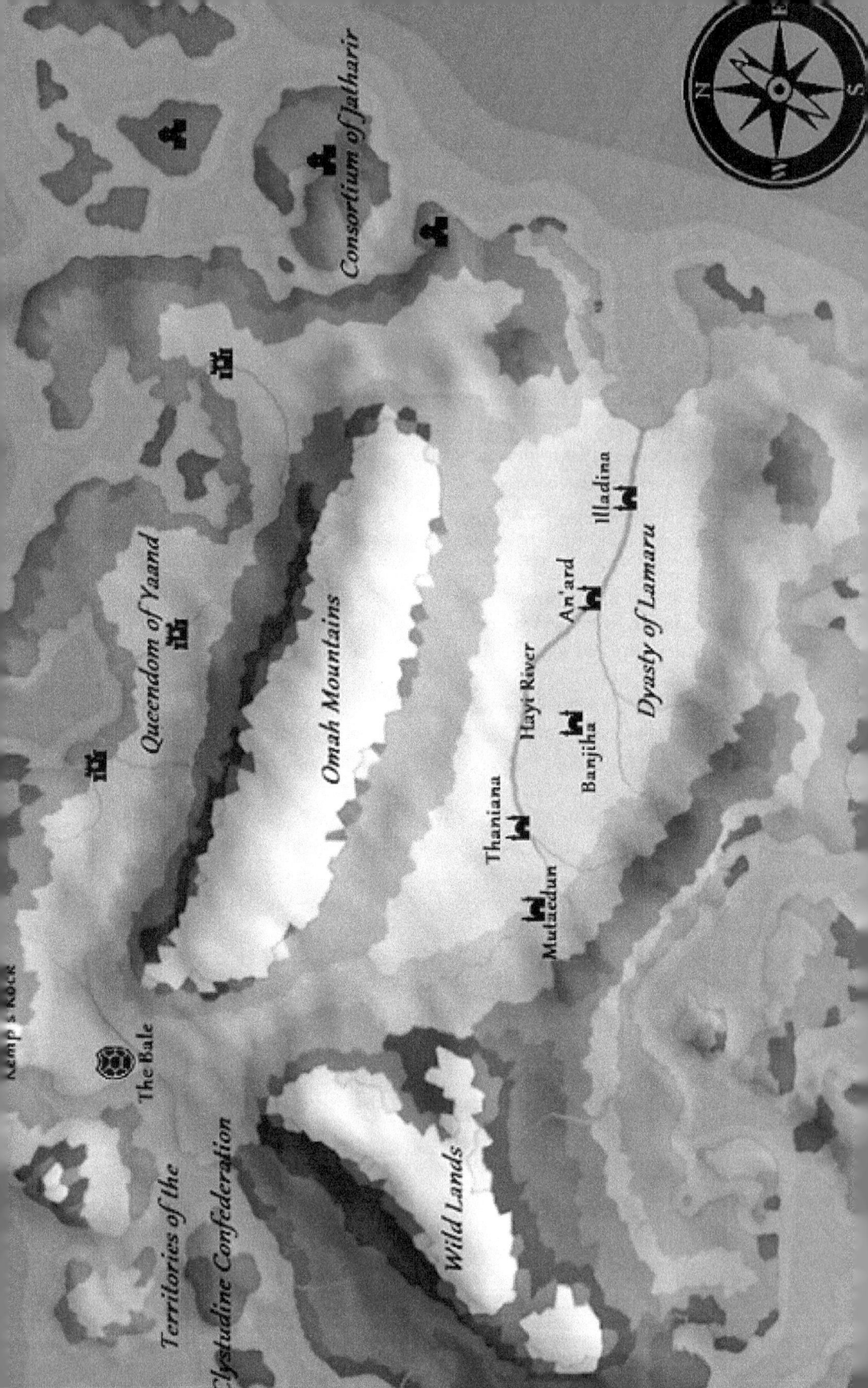

Contents

Part I

1

A Prince's Mischief

Year 149 A.D. (After Demotion); present day

"You're not getting away this time! Naemin! Get back here, you brat!" Amira roared as she chased her brother through the empty halls of the sandstone palace.

"Nuhir Amira! Wait! You shouldn't be running through the halls! What if we're caught? This is unbecoming behavior!" pleaded a second, exasperated girl with sandy blonde hair who chased after the royal children. "Please consider how I'm supposed to explain this to the Padishah if we're seen!"

"You won't have to explain anything because we won't get caught, I promise!" Amira called back to her best friend and retainer, Saffi. "I've had enough of his ridiculous antics! This time, *he'll* explain to everyone what he's done!" She skidded around a corner and sprinted into the central, square courtyard brightened by the desert sun. She blocked the light from her eyes and squinted—a predator searching for her prey.

"There you are, you little twerp," Amira muttered as she saw him. "That's the last time you sneak into my room while I'm busy."

Prince Naemin's dark curly hair bounced around as he laughed and skipped down the long, winding path fringed with flowers and blooming cacti to the heavy, wooden doors of the lone building in the center of the courtyard. He hadn't had this much fun in ages! Yet sooner than he hoped, the sound of heavy footsteps caught his ear.

"*Eep!*" he squealed.

His older sister gained ground.

He raced toward the building as fast as his little legs could move. *I just have to make it inside, just make it inside!* he thought, over and over, as he squeezed through the doors left ajar and wove his way past the citizens of the kingdom and castle staff, who shuffled around the atrium of the library.

Heheheh, sis won't risk yelling and running around here. I'll stay hidden until she gets bored. He praised his genius and sprinted up the stone, spiral staircase at the back of the building.

Amira watched her brother disappear into the library and slowed to a brisk walk. *Ooohh, that sneaky brat! I can't risk being chewed out by Mother... again.* She leaned against the library's stone walls and caught her breath, running her fingers through her long dark hair and tying it in a loose ponytail. She took a cloth handkerchief from her pocket and wiped the beads of sweat off her caramel skin. Now no one could tell she had spent the last half hour chasing her brother through the palace.

"I have to admit, he's smarter than I gave him credit for, using your status as the Nuhir against you," mused Saffi as she finally caught up.

"Don't give him too much credit. He stole the idea from General Gil while the two of them played board games. He—" Amira held her tongue.

The two girls bowed as a pair of Magi dressed in red robes approached. Saffi held the door for them; they bowed in return, then stepped inside.

"He didn't even consider being the next ruler would have its drawbacks until Sir Gil pointed them out," Amira finished.

"He still put that knowledge into practice," Saffi retorted.

"Whose side are you on?" Amira stuck out her tongue. "Just teasing. Either way, he messed up. He's trapped in there. Let's go."

She took a deep breath, assumed a more regal demeanor, and strutted through the carved doors with all the elegance and confidence of one who would one day lead the Dynasty of Lamaru, yet in her mind she slandered her brother with childish insults.

Lined with four long rows of floor-to-ceiling shelves, the library's ground floor brimmed with the murmurs of its occupants and the gentle scratching of pages turning. Between the middle rows of countless tomes and historias, students and Magi scribbled with chalk against stone slates or sorted stacks of parchment at hundreds of desks and kiosks.

"If I were my brother, I'd hide somewhere with a good view of the entrance, but not somewhere I could be easily seen or caught," Amira reasoned, examining the enormous expanse of the esteemed establishment.

Saffi peered up at the wooden walkways overhead. "My guess is he's on the second floor. He wouldn't have time to climb any higher. He's probably watching us from behind the railing."

"Good thinking," Amira nodded. "You take the left; I'll take the right."

They sauntered further into the library, scanning the railings overhanging the first floor. Movement caught Saffi's eyes. A flash of yellow, presumably Naemin's kurta, dashed out of view behind a bookshelf.

"I think he's up there," Saffi murmured. They hurried across the floor with inconspicuous intent and prowled up the staircase.

Amira stopped right before they reached the landing. "Hang on, let me check something." She closed her eyes and touched a small emerald embedded in an amulet she wore around her neck.

"*Rakshif Goti*; Prince Naemin of Lamaru." The stone emitted a soft, warm light. Glowing green footprints, only visible to her, appeared on the ground. They led to Naemin's previous hiding spot, then looped around and continued up the stairs. *Sneaky. Maybe he is smarter than I assumed, but only a bit, and he still isn't getting out of this.*

Amira and Saffi proceeded up the stairs. Again, Amira stopped a few steps short of the landing and muttered her incantation. Naemin's footprints lit up the floor, but this time, they did not double back. He was still here.

"Saffi, stay here and wait. I'll flush him out, then you grab him when he tries to escape."

Saffi nodded.

Amira strode up the landing and veered away from his footsteps. She had no doubt he was watching her. She casually rounded a bookshelf then quickly retraced her steps. Movement caught the corner of her eyes. She crept further down the aisle beside where he hid then peered around the corner.

Her brat of a brother snickered to himself as he knelt behind the bookshelves, watching where she should pass by next, unaware he was being hunted. She skulked as close as she dared then sprinted toward him as fast as she could.

Naemin heard footsteps and glanced behind him. His sister's grin was all teeth. Amira loomed over him, angry as a dragon whose hoard had been disturbed.

"Aaahh!!" He stood up, barely escaping her grasping talons, and raced toward the stairs, right into her trap. Saffi blocked his escape, her grip as equally foreboding as Amira's. Naemin skidded to a halt, turned on his heel, and sprinted down a second, long row of bookshelves.

He swallowed, his eyes growing wide with fear—a dead end. "I'msorry-I'msorry-I'msorry!"

The two girls cornered him. "Sorry isn't good enough," Amira stated. "You're coming with us, and you're going to tell Mother you broke your promise and snuck into my room. Again."

Naemin bit his lip. The Padishah would be furious if he interrupted her meetings, especially for such misbehavior. His eyes darted between his sister and her retainer. He had no other choice.

I've got to break though! He mustered up his courage and ran.

Saffi stretched out her arms to grab him, but Naemin dodged her initial assault. He ducked. They swiped again. Amira stepped back and widened her stance, preparing to take both of them to the floor, but he dipped lower to the ground and dove between her legs, knocking his sister off balance. Joyous thoughts filled his head as Saffi lunged and tripped over Amira. He was free! ... or so he thought.

At the last possible moment, Amira wrapped her claws around his ankle. Naemin stumbled and slammed into a bookshelf. A large, leatherbound book fell, hit him on the head, and forced him to the floor. Tears welled up in his eyes. He held his head in his hands and curled up into a ball.

"Ouch-ouch-ouch-ouch-ouch!" he moaned as streams of tears became rivers that rolled down his red face.

"Ah shit." Amira cursed under her breath as she examined the large bump forming on Naemin's head. *Now I'm the one who'll get in trouble, even if he does tell Mother what happened.* She took a deep breath and exhaled. "Hey, hey, it's okay, little bro," she said, her tone much gentler than before. "It's just a little bump, I promise. It's not that noticeable."

Saffi coughed. Amira glared at her retainer. Her further reassurance failed to quell her brother's screams and sobs. She had to think quickly lest she risk the library staff finding them and telling the Padishah before she had a chance to remedy the situation. Her eyes shifted to the fallen book beside her wailing brother.

"The Definitive Expedition of Prince Achyut of Lamaru," Amira read aloud. She smiled. The instrument of her potential demise would now be her salvation. Her brother loved stories, especially those about princes on adventures.

"Naemin, sweetie, would you stop crying if I told you a story? It's about a prince, just like you, and his adventures. Doesn't that sound nice?"

With a sniffle, Naemin nodded, pulled out his handkerchief and blew his nose. His tears dwindled to a slow trickle. Although his eyes remained red and puffy, they focused on the book in his sister's hands as she sat beside him.

Amira opened the book but frowned as she flipped through its pages.

"Huh? It's written in Magesep runes but these aren't the ones the General taught me in my minna lessons. I only recognize a few per page."

"Y-you mean you can't read it?" Naemin's lower lip quivered. The waterworks would soon follow.

"I know someone who can," Amira answered. "We'll go see Father and he'll read it to us."

Naemin smiled. Saffi sighed in relief. Another crisis averted.

"Come here you." Amira picked up her brother and the book. "First we need to do something about that bump."

"I'll stop by the infirmary and get some healing salve and a few snacks," volunteered Saffi.

"Perfect," answered Amira. The three of them made their way back down the stairs.

"Father should be nearly done with his morning sparring. We'll meet you outside the southern training grounds. Then we can listen to him read this story in the bluebell garden. That's your favorite, right little bro?"

Naemin blew his nose and nodded.

They stepped out into the courtyard and parted ways with Saffi. Amira pointed out pretty flowers and cool bugs and did everything to buy time and keep her brother from crying. When she had delayed long enough, she picked up Naemin and set off through the palace once more.

"I'm sorry I snuck into your room, even after I said I wouldn't," mumbled the young prince after a few minutes of silence. "I was bored and wanted to play. You keep so many interesting widgets in there."

"I accept your apology, though that doesn't excuse your actions. My leadership and politics course is stressful enough. I don't want to come back to my room to find all my things scattered across the floor."

Naemin opened his mouth to protest, but his sister shot him a glance that said 'no excuses'.

"You're right," he sighed in defeat, "And my head wouldn't hurt if I hadn't gone in there... It's just, we haven't played together in so long."

He hugged his sister. "I liked running through the palace with you, even if you were mad. I miss playing with you."

"Naemin, I can't play with you like that anymore in the palace, only when we go on excursions with the exploration team. I'm sixteen now. I'm a big girl. I have to take my studies seriously if I'm to one day take the throne. Think about your actions from my perspective. Can you imagine how annoying it would be if I borrowed one of your coloring books, and every time I gave it back, I colored in a random portion of whatever picture you were working on?"

"I guess I would get annoyed if that happened over and over again."

"And if the person promised they'd stop but kept doing it anyway?"

"Oh. Then I'd probably be a little angry. But coloring is fun! Studying is so boring! All you do is learn things that you get tested on and then forget because you have to learn more things. What's the point?"

"The point is to learn about your environment and better yourself, to build a wealth of knowledge you can use to solve problems. Look, you're only eight and you spend most of your time in the palace. You haven't sat in on any of Mother's council meetings. There's so much that goes into maintaining our kingdom and keeping our people happy. If we don't lead well, we could very easily ruin their lives."

"I guess that makes sense. But that's Mom's job, not yours."

"But it will be my job someday. I have to practice while I have the time. I promise you'll understand how useful studying is once you've had more worldly experience, even if it's sometimes boring." She booped his nose and he giggled.

They stopped outside the training grounds and waited for Saffi who held a bottle of white salve in one hand and a basket of fresh fruit and flatbread in the other.

Amira slathered the salve on Naemin's bump which disappeared in a few, short minutes. "There. Good as new." She ruffled his hair, then the three of them walked onto the training grounds, greeted by the clamorous echoes of clashing metal from the weapons of the two most recognizable men in the palace: the Sword and Axe of Illadina.

The Sword of Illadina was none other than Amira and Naemin's father, King Jordan. A tall and well-kept man with dark curly hair, rich ebon skin, knowing eyes, and a mind filled with countless stories from his own wondrous adventures. His silver tongue and debonair had won the hearts of many, but none more so than Nuhir Lila, now Padishah of Lamaru. During their long and happy marriage, he proved himself quite apt as co-leader of the kingdom and took to the royal responsibilities as easily as a young drake spat fire.

His mahogany robes fluttered in the desert breeze as he parried his opponent's strikes with the fabled fluid movements and tenacity that earned him his title. Yet his adversary, unphased by the King's legendary skill, powered through with his own relentless assault. Every strike bounced off his sable armor.

General Gil, the Axe of Illadina, was a mountain of a man with warm blue eyes, slate-gray hair, and broad shoulders, dressed in custom, heavy armor, covered in scratches and dents, but nonetheless impenetrable. In his younger years, Gil had become a distinguished mercenary, whose company had earned a reputation across all of Reighja for completing jobs the average sellsword deemed outrageous and impossible. Yet internal schisms fractured the company and its inviolable reputation faded to legend. As fortune would have it, the Axe took the position of King Jordan's retainer, earning the rank of General and the prestige of being Amira and Naemin's mentor and tutor in any and every subject imaginable.

Gil arc'd his axe over his head and down upon his long-time friend and liege with the strength that could fell a tree in single swoop. Jordan stepped aside, closed the gap between them, and forced Gil back on the defensive, lest the Axe risk being tagged by his slender blade. Gil swiveled his axe in his hands and used the flat edge to block the King's flurry of blows. He regained his footing and parried the King's next attack, retaliating with his own cadence and shifting the rhythm of battle back under his control.

Amira watched in awe as they traded blow for blow and parried each other's attacks. Their battles were a spectacle to behold, each man a master of his craft, and together they had trained the best generation of paragons Lamaru had seen in ages.

With a sudden sly and precise movement, King Jordan bound Gil's axe and knocked his legs out from beneath him. The mountain of a man toppled and lay prone on the ground. The King pointed his sword at his friend's throat.

"A point for me." Jordan smiled. "I win again." He offered Gil his hand and helped him to his feet.

Gil swept the sand off his armor and slicked back his hair. "Damn. I almost had you this time."

"That's what you said last time, and the time before that, and the time before then if I'm not mistaken," Jordan retorted with a confident smirk. "But you are making me work harder each time we spar." He glanced over Gil's shoulder. "Well now, look who's come to join us." He waved at his two children and Saffi. "Good morning, my dears. Unfortunately, there is little more to watch of our session." His eyes fell on the book in Amira's hand. "But I surmise you came for another reason. What do you have here?"

"It's a book!" replied Naemin.

Jordan smiled. "Why, yes, it is."

"We came across this book in the library," answered Amira. "I thought it would be a good story for Naemin, but it's written in a different set of Magesep runes than what I'm used to. I can barely understand any of them. We were hoping you could read it to us in the bluebell gardens." She handed him the book.

"Ah, this is a historical record of one of your ancestors, many years ago, in our kingdom's golden age, just before the Collapse."

"Before the Collapse?!" Naemin gasped.

"That's right." Gil crossed his arms over his chest. "One hundred and forty-nine years ago, our kingdom was heralded by sprawling cities, ethereal technologies and widgets, and an unending sum of harnessed minna. We were the peak of the four Pillar Civilizations of Reighja."

Amira giggled. "I know you're old, Sir Gil, but you aren't that old."

"Maybe I am, maybe I'm not," Gil retorted with a smile. "But I have read countless books on the subject and studied the remaining maps and lasting works of art."

"Was it really that great?" Naemin's eyes swept between his mentor and his father.

"It was," answered King Jordan with a sad smile on his lips. "It pains me to acknowledge it, but the Dynasty of Lamaru is a shadow of its former self. The Collapse brought years of famine, crime, and decay, and culminated in the humiliating and inglorious demotion from our longstanding status as a Pillar Civilization."

"And, of course, there's the Withered." Amira shuddered. "Those disgusting, horrid chimeras give me the shivers."

Saffi nodded. "I dread the day we have to face them in combat."

"And I pray that day never comes," added Jordan. "If it does arrive, protect each other and remember your training. A royal's most valuable comrade is their retainer, and you and Amira already make a wonderful team."

"Thank you, Your Grace." Saffi placed her hand over her heart and bowed.

"Hey, hey, what about me?" Naemin tugged on his father's robes.

"You and Jiian will make a fine team as well, once you're a little older and trained sufficiently."

"Why do I have to be older to have any fun?" the young prince pouted.

"Because you have yet to show your mother and I you're able to protect Jiian, the same as he is able to protect you." Jordan ruffled his son's hair. "But you are free to read up on your history and practice your minna runes till your heart's content."

"I'd prefer to have you read me this story. Pleeeassse?" pleaded Naemin.

"I will, although the text itself is quite the dry read and the ending is one of many unsolved mysteries instead of a happily ever after."

"But you're great at telling stories! You can make any book into a wonderful story!" praised Naemin. "And If I don't like the ending, I'll come up with a better, happier one!"

Jordan laughed.

"Prince Naemin," interrupted Gil, "I have no doubt you could write a satisfactory ending to this tale, but please remember even sad stories are important. Failure, rather than success, is often the better teacher. Our failures give us opportunities to learn and grow, to empathize with others and make amends for the future."

"Indeed." Jordan nodded. "A lot can be learned from facing and overcoming difficult situations, as you'll soon learn from this story. This is also an excellent opportunity to teach you all about our past through the lens of our kin. Let's be on our way."

Naemin, Amira, and Saffi followed Jordan and Gil to the bluebell garden—a small courtyard filled with hundreds of blue flowers, which chimed like tiny bells when disturbed. Naemin and Amira spent hours at a time flicking the flowers in the garden. It did them no harm and each made a different sound depending on their size. They composed their own songs and melodies and played them for their parents, although his sister had been too preoccupied with boring adult stuff to join him as of late.

"Father, why is this book written in nonstandard Magesep runes? Does it contain family secrets or clues to the mystery surrounding the Collapse?" asked Amira as they strolled down the path, surrounded by bluebells, to a quiet sitting area with rocking chairs and large, comfy benches covered with soft, plush cushions.

"That would be enticing, wouldn't it?" Jordan sat on a bench. He picked up Naemin and held him in his lap. "But, unfortunately, no family secrets or ancient riddles. All of our ancestor's records are written in a different dialect because these words hold more power than standard minna runes, both figuratively and literally. If one is to delve into history's secrets, they must be able to readily accept the past, the good and bad. The runes react to a person's mental state and reconfigure themselves into a recognizable form when the reader is calm and focused, ready to push the limits of their mental capacity and imagination; an unorthodox approach, but this prerequisite allows the reader to look into the past with unclouded eyes."

Amira sat quietly next to her father. *I never knew books could be so judgy. How dare it underestimate my cognitive prowess. I have a very open mind and phenomenal imagination.*

Saffi sat beside Amira. Gil reclined in a lone rocking chair.

A sly smile crossed Jordan's lips. "But I digress, before we start, we need to give this story a proper title, something that grips the audience." He thought to himself for a moment. "How about *The Tale of Achyut the Gallant?*"

Naemin, Saffi, and Amira nodded and looked on in approval.

"Perfect." King Jordan opened the book, skimmed the first few paragraphs, and transformed the historical text in his mind. He cleared his throat and began:

"The bright blue sky was completely clear with not a single cloud in sight." As he spoke, the words on the pages glowed and the image of a massive ship sailing across a vast ocean sprung up between its pages...

2

Quid Pro Quo

Year 1 B.C. (Before the Collapse)

The bright blue sky was completely clear with not a single cloud in sight. The salty sea breeze filled Achyut's nostrils as he stood shirtless in the crow's nest on the frontmost mast of the magnificent and reliable ship: the Prospector. The endless sea stretched out around him. The noontime sun kissed his dark copper skin. His umbral dreadlocks drifted in the wind, adorned with golden beads and minna stones. He raised his arms up and out and embraced the sprawling continent, growing larger and larger on the eastern horizon. He pursed his lips together and sang a jovial tune.

Yar har ho, yo ho har, I'll search for treasures near and far.
Yo ho har, yar har ho, led by the ocean's wind we go!
A maiden here, a trinket there, a pirate's life without a care.
We fight, we drink, we live, so freeee; a pirate's life for you and mee!

He held his bansuri—a long, wooden, enchanted flute–to his lips and sang the words again in his head adding the bright, wafting, trill of his accompaniment. *No, no, no. This isn't right at all. I need something brighter,*

14

with a sway that matches the swatch of the waves. He closed his eyes and played, the new notes much more to his liking. Captured by the melodious trill, he shook his hips and tapped his feet until his simple movements gave way to joyous dancing in the small space. Yet just as he lost himself in music and imagination, a familiar voice hollered from below.

"Achyut! Get down here! We're landing in the Bale soon. The Captain wants to have a word with you before we arrive!"

Achyut peered over the edge of the crow's nest and rolled his eyes. A woman in a crimson qipao dress stood beneath the ladder with her arms crossed over her chest. She wore fingerless, elbow-length, black gloves adorned with crimson armor and thigh-high boots similarly reinforced with plating that covered her knees, shins, and calves. Mona had jet black hair which complimented the bloom of her warm brown skin. A strand of hair had freed itself from her stiff, fish-braid ponytail and curled around the scarlet eyepatch over her left eye. She glared at Achyut with her right.

"I know you're up there. You've slacked around enough today!" Mona grumbled, her voice as rough and strong as a viscous maelstrom, the complete antithesis of her intriguing outfit.

While Mona's garments revealed more than those of the other women in the crew, and even more so compared to those so closely associated with the royal family, the Dynasty of Lamaru had no such laws prohibiting what its people could wear and anyone who looked at Mona with disgust or lewd intentions found themselves with her fist in their face or their neck nearly caressed by the blade of her two-handed aruval strapped across her back.

"Achyut!" Mona howled once more.

"I heard you the first time! I'll be down in a minute, geez," retorted Achyut.

Mona didn't try to come off as imposing and irritated, and with a stick shoved where it shouldn't be; it was just her nature. Still, it could get tiresome. He had been bossed around enough by his older sibling and parents back home.

Achyut leaped from the crow's nest. The wind whipped around his beige dhoti, light and airy strips of cloth wrapped around his hips and thighs and tucked into a dark leather waistband adored with blue gemstones.

This time I'll get it right, he thought to himself as he clenched his bansuri in hand. He fell past the deck of the ship, the cold azure waves growing closer and closer.

"*Hashira de Nile, Goti!*" he shouted seconds before he hit the water. His flute glowed a brilliant blue. A column of water sprang up from the sea and pressed against his feet as if a solid surface, keeping pace alongside the vessel. The column grew taller and taller until Achyut hovered over the main deck of the ship. He crossed his arms over his chest in a stance to mirror Mona's.

"Aye, first mate Mona, the captain wished to have a word with me?"

"Don't call me that," she retorted in her oh-so-familiar no-nonsense tone. "Besides, aren't you a little too old to be playing pirate?"

"Hey, you're the one who dressed for the occasion," he shot back brazenly as he tapped his cheek where Mona's eyepatch rested against her skin.

"If I wasn't your retainer, I'd slug you here and now." She glared at him, a faint smile on her lips.

Achyut hopped onto the deck and returned a much friendlier smile. "Yeah well, your job is to keep me safe and uninjured. Besides, you taught me too well for you to get a punch on me. I'd dodge each and every attempt, guaranteed."

"I'll take that wager. I could use a warm-up for tonight, and we should have enough time for a sparring match or two before we reach the Bale."

"Ugh, we've already sparred for three hours today."

"So? Your techniques could use three more hours of practice."

Achyut's smile shifted into a sly grin. "I'll make you a deal: I'll spar with you again tonight if you promise to double your next dotara practice."

Mona groaned. "Seriously? I hate that thing. It's too light and I always break the strings when we play."

"Come on," Achyut begged. "You've gotten really good at it! We can have another music night! I'll even let you take center stage."

"That sounds more like a punishment than a reward."

"Oh? I guess your technique could use three more hours of practice."

"Shut it, you." Mona swatted at Achyut who sidestepped away and stuck out his tongue.

"Told you I'd dodge! Race you to the helm!"

"Oh, you're on!" Mona smiled as they sprinted across the ship's main deck.

Built like a citadel, the entire ship was covered in metal-like plating harvested from ironwood trees. Its rounded hull could flatten to travel across the rolling hills, grasslands, and chaparral deserts of the continent of Reighja, the Prospector's destination. The bow of the ship showcased a figurehead of a large animal with its maw agape. The tip of the bow also housed a minna orb– a large open metal frame that could absorb spells or magical energy and launch them at targets far away. A massive brass gong sat on top of the deck behind the first minna orb along with two more orbs on both sides of the ship, and three more mounted on the raised stern of the vessel. The Prospector was so large it had four distinct sets of portholes and a long, rounded air-filled frame on either side of the hull, connected by a series of metal ribs that acted as buoys.

Three sturdy masts rose from the center of the ship, each adorned with clean cloth sails that lazily spun, their blades embossed with the crest of Lamaru's royal family. The helm of the ship overhung the main deck, connected by two long sets of stairs.

Achyut and Mona raced up the starboard-side staircase and around a massive telescope fixed to the helm, where Captain Tanoy, a gentleman in his late fifties or sixties or even seventies, maneuvered the majestic vessel with the skill of a lifetime of experience. He wore a glossy, viridian knee-length kurta and cream-colored dhoti. Atop his fading, wispy, silver hair perched a black tricorn hat with the symbol of the royal family embossed on the left side.

"Hah! Take that bansuri boy!" chided Mona as she slapped the helm and struck a triumphant pose. "Captain Tanoy, Prince Achyut will be along shortly. He's just a tad too slow."

"Vaulting up the stairs using minna is cheating!" complained Achyut as he reached the helm, his breaths labored.

Mona snorted. "Is not. If you practiced your minna harnessing you could do the same."

Tanoy smiled at their antics. "At least he's making an honest effort. I saw you practicing your new cantrip." He chuckled to himself. "Gave the crew half a fright when they saw you jump off the crow's nest... again."

"They should know a man who harnesses water minna will always be drawn to its magnificent sources." Prince Achyut grinned mischievously. "Got any more spells you can teach me, Cap?"

"Perhaps on a later date. We've more important things to discuss. Take a seat on one of the barrels there, both of you."

Achyut and Mona did as instructed.

"We'll be arriving in the Bale soon, Clystudine territory. I don't believe you've met them. They're reptilian folk—a foot or two taller than us on average, with strong, sturdy shells, two sets of yellowish eyes and a long, flat tail for swimming. My old sailing buddy, Rakriliox, is one of five leaders of their newly united nation, the Clystudine Confederation. Because of their renewed status as a Pillar Civilization of Reighja, and as we are in the company of royalty from Lamaru, our simple stop for supplies is now something of an official matter."

Achyut smiled. He loved being a prince of Lamaru, especially one not in line to take the throne. While his older sibling Rakiba resided at the palace, studying and worrying about silly politics and such, he was out on the open sea, exploring the world, playing music at festivals, and meeting many, many important lords and, more importantly, their daughters.

"Prince Achyut," Tanoy commanded in a stern voice that shook him from his daydreams. "You are the first ambassador to the Clystudine Confederation from the Dynasty of Lamaru. As such, it is on you and Lady Mona to make a good first impression for our nation. I trust you've kept to your studies on Clystudine etiquette and society?"

"Yes, sir," responded Achyut with simple confidence. "I've memorized their greetings, table manners, social hierarchy, customs, and even a few jokes. Since they speak the common tongue of Reighja, learning the foundation of their culture was a simple task.

"Good lad. Lady Mona, are you prepared for the trial of strength at this evening's dinner?"

"If those shellbacks want to see power, I'm happy to show it to them." Mona smiled wolfishly. "I'll take on whatever champion they choose so they can see the strength of Lamaru. Besides, being on this boat for so long has me feeling antsy. This'll be a perfect way to work off some excess energy."

"Just make sure you don't kill whatever champion they send against you," teased Achyut. "We want to showcase the strength of our nation's warriors, not start a continental conflict."

"Yeah, yeah, I'll hold back when they're ready to give up," replied Mona, almost disappointed.

"Well then, I'm pleasantly convinced with both of your responses," Tanoy interjected. "We'll reach the docks in two or three hours. Please inform the rest of our crew and conduct whatever preparations to be ready at such time."

Achyut and Mona followed their orders, then went below deck and sparred for an hour before they departed to their quarters and freshened up for their arrival.

The Prospector sailed into a calm bay surrounded by small rocky islands with colorful corals underneath the waves and even more dazzling fish swimming around them. Small, rounded huts and domed buildings made of black onyx, coral, and stone lay scattered across the ocean floor with lawns of cut seagrass and kelp that rolled lazily in the tide. Hundreds of the turtle-like Clystudine swam and walked under the ship. All glanced up at the strange vessel as it approached a crude and hastily-made wooden dock. The Clystudines had little use for ships, the exception being a few large, flat-bottom barges beached further down the shore.

Achyut and Mona stood on the bow of the ship, their mouths agape at the strange beauty in front of them. Sights like these made Reighja special. No matter where anyone traveled, there was always something new to see.

Prince Achyut straightened his light blue kurta and dark blue vest, embroidered with gold stitching and gold buttons. He smoothed out his clean, dark-brown dhoti and fixed his matching tricorn hat, then made sure his bansuri was strapped onto his back in the same way Mona carried her sword.

The sailors lowered the anchor and threw down ropes that moored the ship in place. Clystudine sailors caught and wrapped the lines around the shaky, wooden stilts and muttered simple cantrips to keep the lines magically tied. The gangplank was lowered and Captain Tanoy, Prince Achyut, and Lady Mona, strode down to meet their entourage.

A hulking individual sauntered toward them and spread his arms in a welcoming gesture. His long, flat tail swished back and forth as he walked. He wore a simple orange cloak that hung over his shoulders and around his hard shell, clasped around his lanky leathery neck with a polished white scallop. His own shell was covered in paint, depicting pictures of hunted nafsiyat whales, inked islands he explored and claimed, a symbol of marriage, and many more symbols of Rakriliox's military and political accomplishments for his people.

"Captain Tanoy, it has been so long since I've seen you. You haven't aged a day!" Rakriliox spoke in a rough, grainy voice as he held out his tree trunk of an arm for the captain to shake.

"Aye, Rakriliox, you don't look so bad for someone over a hundred and forty!" Tanoy grasped Rakriliox's arm, careful to avoid his thick, knife-like talons. "And congratulations on your marriage! And on your new position as Enlightened One of the Bale. You've sure been busy."

"Yes, yes." Rakriliox nodded. "My wife and I wish you could have made it to the ceremony, either one for that matter, but I see you've been busy. Would you introduce me to your compatriots?"

"This is Prince Achyut from the Dynasty of Lamaru and his retainer, Lady Mona."

"A pleasure to meet you, Enlightened Rakriliox of the Bale. May your mind and shell remain ever strong." Achyut grasped Rakriliox's other arm and bowed.

Rakriliox smiled. "Thank you, Prince Achyut. I hope this is to be the beginning of a wonderful relationship between your country and ours. Already you are much more charming than the neighboring humans of Yaand." He glanced curiously at Mona and studied her: muscles, sword, outfit, and all. "This is your champion for tonight's festivities?"

"Yes, Enlightened One," replied Achyut. "Lady Mona from the city of Thaniana. Her blade and wit are unmatched by anyone in her home region. They hold a similar contest of strength between their greatest warriors each year. Mona was the former reigning champion before she came into my service as my retainer."

Mona did not speak but crossed her arms over her chest in an 'X' and bowed.

"This shall be a merry night indeed. You humans of Lamaru are well known for your ability to harness minna. In fact, minna stones and crystals from your region are extremely valuable in these parts, and I am curious to see their combat-focused applications, especially from such a small combatant." Rakriliox gestured to a taller and much bulkier Clystudine off to his right. "This is Griskrus, my loyal bodyguard and champion. He hails from Coral Bay, south of here. As you can see from his shell pigments, he is a deadly and seasoned warrior."

Griskrus was dressed in bits of armor that covered his callous skin. His shell was adorned with hundreds of pigments and tally marks from hunts, challenges, and other achievements. Prince Achyut noticed the head of an emerald dragon painted in the upper left quadrant of his plastrodon. A spiked bone club double the size of Mona's sword hung from a braided kelp sash that wrapped around his shell. Griskrus did not speak but crossed his arms over his shell, exactly as Mona did, and bowed to Achyut.

"I'm just as curious to see how a powerful Clystudine warrior fights." Achyut nodded to Griskrus. He looked up at Rakriliox and smiled. "Though, surely you agree, there are more important factors than size alone, in combat and in other matters."

Rakriliox threw back his head and laughed, or the equivalent for Clystudines. He let out a deep, monotone honk that pulsed in the air like a foghorn's wail. "Indeed, Prince Achyut, but it is a factor nonetheless. Come, come, let us save further banter for the dinner table. Bring your entire crew. We have more than enough space in our hall and green pastures where your mounts can rest."

Rakriliox led his visitors through the streets, paved with bleached corals, shells, and smoothed stones and lit by lanterns made from dried pufferfish mounted on wooden poles. Houses made of stone, wood, and onyx, structured similarly to their underwater counterparts, clustered together and resembled nests of eggs, stacking three or four floors high. They passed through an open-air market where natives bought and sold goods at wooden stalls, each with a colored, cloth flag waving in the wind which displayed the name of the merchant and nature of their goods.

The procession crossed over a sandstone bridge embossed with shells and corals. Curious, Achyut glanced over its edge and into the deep, trough-like dugout filled with black sand below. White specks lay nestled among the dark grains, organized into small clusters around slender pedestals, each capped with a gemstone that pulsed either red or blue light. A Clystudine caretaker watched over every clutch, occasionally rearranging or rotating the eggs.

"What are all those little white things?" asked Achyut. "They look just like—"

"Eggs in our hatcheries," Rakriliox completed. "Our kind lay groups of eggs, fifty to one hundred, cared not just by the parents, but nursery aids too. The clutches are divided into whatever ratio of males and females the parents' desire."

"They already know how many eggs will be boys or girls?"

Rakriliox nodded. "Sex is determined by the temperature of the sand around it. Lower temperatures produce males. Higher temperatures produce females. Not all of the eggs successfully hatch, so the parents divide them proportionately into whatever outcome they desire and hope for the best. I understand you humans have a much more... random way of producing your young. A strange thing to be sure, but our method is likely strange to you."

Achyut smiled, further intrigued by their new northern neighbors, and he and Rakriliox exchanged questions and answers about each other's species and cultures. They walked through the strange and wonderful city until they arrived at the foothills of the Bale's central mound. A towering, ovular colosseum stood on top of the hill, with a base of sandstone and a roof of charred timber bound by woven kelp, supported by many decorative columns, each carved from a single, massive bone. Rakriliox led the procession to the main entrance and inside the building.

Achyut, Mona, and Tanoy looked around the interior of the assembly hall. The sun shone brightly through a rounded hole in the roof. A wide staircase descended into an open area that mimicked the shape of the outer structure, wide enough to fit twenty adult humans, side-by-side, with their arms outstretched. The floor was covered in fresh sand and clay. Six doors on each side led to the lower chambers. A wood railing surrounded the entire arena with long tables that jutted out from its posts. At the far end of the room, a beautifully carved table surrounded by chairs stood atop a raised platform. Achyut thought these seats looked much more comfortable than the stone chairs for the rest of the throng, instead crafted from kelp mats woven together.

"This is where we bring all of our guests so we may partake in drink and food, pleasant company, and learn of each other's strengths through friendly combat. This way of greeting one another is a tradition passed down from the first Clystudine tribes long ago during the Dark Age of Dragons."

"I'm honored to be part of such a momentous occasion," replied Achyut. He rested his hands on the wooden railing. "Where, um, where should I go?"

Rakriliox pointed to the table at the far end of the hall.

"As my honored guests, you and Captain Tanoy shall join me and the other leaders of the Confederation who are able to make tonight's celebration. Our champions will join us after their best of three duals. We have so many festivities planned for tonight, including the best orchestra in the Bale and a reenactment of our slaying of the first dragon, when my ancestors claimed their freedom. Please follow me."

Achyut did as instructed, grinning in pure joy. This was the type of thing he loved as a prince.

While crew and Clystudine filled the Hall, Rakriliox introduced Prince Achyut and Captain Tanoy to the other leaders of the Confederation, who regaled their grand plans to expand and nurture Clystudine territory. Achyut listened attentively as he took his seat on Rakriliox's right. Captain Tanoy sat on Rakriliox's left. Once every seat in the Hall was filled, Mona and Griskrus descended the stairs and stood on opposite sides of the long arena while Rakriliox gave a speech and introduced his guests. He then granted Mona and Griskrus permission to begin the first duel.

"Well then, let's not keep our lords waiting." Mona grinned. She hefted the aruval off her back and held the great sword in her right hand. Sparks crackled from the billhook on its tip. They spread like spider lighting on a humid summer's night as they traveled up the blade to the hilt but did not electrocute Mona. A mote of white fire blazed in the palm of her left hand and burned its way up her arm. Although the flames licked at her black gloves, Mona's skin remained unburned as embers dripped onto the sand below.

She brought her sword over her shoulder and sprinted toward Griskrus who held his spiked bone club in the air and slammed it against the ground. The sand rushed into the air as if cracked by an invisible whip and a wave of magical energy raced toward Mona.

A lance made of fire erupted from her left hand. She plunged the lance into the ground and vaulted over the shockwave. Her aruval became encased in orange, crackling electricity as she dropped and struck at Griskrus's head but the Clystudine raised his charrwood shield and blocked. He took a single step back and hefted his club in an upward strike. Mona kicked off from the rounded tip of the giant club and backflipped in the air. She landed on the far side of the arena.

Griskrus charged.

Twenty small motes of fire appeared and hovered in a grid pattern above the ground in front of Mona. Griskrus weaved his way through the first three rows but unbeknownst to him, the tip of his shield tapped one of the motes. Suddenly, it exploded in a brilliant ball of crimson fire that set off chain after chain of explosions as smoke filled the ring.

The Prospector's crew cheered. Mona smirked, but as the smoke cleared, she and the crowd realized Griskrus had not been hurt at all. He simply retreated inside his tough shell. Mona summoned a second mass of white flames and hurled them straight toward Griskrus.

Achyut closed his eyes and coughed as smoke once more filled the room. Even if it dissipated quickly, the sensation still felt unpleasant. Yet when the air cleared a second time, Achyut's focus shifted from the battle to the forty or so humans who had emerged from the side doors dressed in orange clothes, held together with white scallop shells, and began serving food.

"I didn't know there were any human citizens in the Clystudine Confederation. I assumed we were the only humans around for miles," Achyut commented as he glanced up at a beautiful young woman with long, blonde hair who served him grilled fish and shrimp on a bed of greens.

"Well, they are human, but they aren't citizens of the Confederation. All of them are indentured servants or slaves of a sort. When my staff told me you were visiting, I grew giddy in anticipation of your arrival." He raised his cup to his lips and drank. "You see, we've had trouble keeping them healthy since we obtained them from a disputed border territory with the neighboring queendom of Yaand. Those bastards to the east built a settlement right on top of a lake clearly stated to be ours in the treaty which ended our last conflict. Still, they encroached on and stole our lands, harassed and maimed our border patrols, and bribed the Consortium of Jatharir to hike up their prices on goods or not send merchant ships at all!" Rakriliox's voice grew louder and louder with each scathing comment, his talons dug trenches into his wooden cup. He closed his two sets of amber eyes and took a deep breath. "But I digress, I was merely hoping you could give me a few pointers as to how to keep them alive and well."

Achyut was stunned. "You want me... to give you pointers on how to keep your slaves... healthy? You want me to tell you the correct way to keep human prisoners like cattle and domesticated animals?" He did everything he could to hide the anger in his voice, yet he wasn't entirely sure he succeeded.

However, Rakriliox either didn't notice or didn't care. "That is correct," he replied in the same matter-of-fact tone Mona used when she wanted to irritate him.

Achyut was speechless. The Pillar Civilizations banned slavery long ago. That was one of the tenets of maintaining a shared and peaceful Reighja. *This isn't right,* he thought. *It's immoral to own another person. It's barbaric and degrading and about as ludicrous as judging another solely by the color of their skin or hair or ability to harness minna!*

An old man with a white beard and bald head refilled Achyut's chalice with wine and his wooden cup with water, then bowed and left without a word, not daring to make eye contact with him or Griskrus.

Achyut stared at the cup. *How can he chain people against their will and force them to do his bidding?* He glanced around the hall at the other members of the crew. Most of them were entirely focused on the duel, but the ones who took notice of the slaves also bore uneasy expressions.

A Clystudine soldier yelled at a cowering slave and demanded she bring him the correct food. Another soldier basked in the breeze brought by two giant fans. The slaves' arms shook with exhaustion; their expressions sullen and pained.

How does he justify such a heinous act? What kind of apathetic, self-aggrandizing, greedy, evil beings would do that? Achyut's nails dug into his palms. He took slow, steady breaths to ease his nerves. *Calm down, Achyut. Remember, you are a guest here. This must be approached with a clear head and firm negotiations... but I will put a stop to this.*

Mona rushed at Griskrus and slammed her blade against his armored exterior. She knew one good crack would force him out. Suddenly, an arm reached from his shell, wrapped around her toned leg, and flung her across the arena.

Griskrus pushed his shell round and round with his arms, then pushed his tail out and used his momentum to stand back on his hind legs.

Mona slammed against the wall and laughed. It had been much too long since she had a proper fight and the strength and scale of her opponent only made her passion burn all the brighter. She dusted herself off as Griskrus charged her once more.

"How can you justify keeping slaves at all?" Prince Achyut slammed his fist against the table.

"I do not understand why this displeases you, Prince Achyut," Rakriliox said in honest bewilderment. "Yes, they are humans, but they are not your kin. They do not share your culture, your talent for minna, or even worship the same divine being as your kingdom. You are of different lineages. They are as distant from you as you are to me. We took back what was ours and they were our spoils. This is the way of nature. A shark doesn't fight for the rights of its prey, it eats them."

"A shark is not sentient nor intelligent enough to know that enslaving others is morally wrong," Achyut shot back.

"That is a tenet of your culture, not of ours," Rakriliox replied calmly, "Slaves are the same as cattle or pets or beasts of burden. Their feelings and intelligence only matter so much. As long as they fulfill their purpose in our society, we treat them well and they live well enough. They have families and can buy or sell goods and even be educated, to an extent."

"My apologies, Enlightened One," Achyut said through gritted teeth. "I cannot condone this course of action. My duties as a prince and my moral code will not stand idle. I am in no position to make demands of you, but should Mona defeat your champion, I will enact my right as the victor, and you will give them all to me."

"I commend your knowledge of our laws, Prince Achyut, but the Pact of the Champions can only be enacted between two Clystudine government officials. This is merely a contest of strength and sport to allow our nations to study each other's combat techniques."

Achyut glared at Rakriliox. He had to think of something he could do to free these people from their bondage. "If you will not give them to me by the laws of your culture, I'll buy them off you. Name your price. The Dynasty of Lamaru has untold riches. I would gladly give my weight in minna stones to buy the freedom of these people."

"A tempting offer, my friend, but they are not for sale. You humans are soft and small and can fit into spaces we cannot because of our hard shells. Your hands are more dexterous than our sharp talons. These differences alone make your species a valuable resource in our society."

A ball of orange lightning encased Mona and shielded her from Griskrus' club yet it quickly cracked then shattered. Mona rushed her opponent. She parried one of his swipes and forced him back on the defensive but Griskrus blocked with his shell and shield and struck again. Mona rolled out of the way, standing with seconds to spare, barely blocking his next attack with her aruval.

"You're tough, for a human." Griskrus grunted as he swung his club around his body and attempted to smack Mona with his armored tail.

"Flattery won't get you anywhere," she replied as she vaulted off the wall of the arena and regained her balance not a moment too late. Her electric shield materialized once more as Griskrus tried and failed to shield-bash her into the wall.

Rakriliox bore a devious grin. "If you are so intent on seeing your course of justice through, I can think of one small favor. As you surely know, our kind, along with every species of maiamorph across Reighja, were the end result of experiments conducted by dragons long, long ago in an attempt to create a ritual they could use to hide themselves among your kind. If you wish to call out a species for unethical treatment of others, they should be your target, not us."

Rakriliox's eyes grew distant as he remembered the horror stories his parents told him and his siblings; scouting parties scooped up as an afternoon snack, entire towns raided, their inhabitants stolen away and used as test subjects, the remains of his kin left to rot on the open road.

"We give our slaves food and shelter. They left us to the whims of nature and kidnapped our young and old whenever it suited their selfish needs. There is but one absolute principle in every Clystudine subculture: those wretched beasts should be brought to justice for the pain they caused and their crimes against my ancestors. As it so happens, two dragons have stolen land in the northern mountains of our territory— around a ceremonial peak named Kemp's Rock— a black tungsten dragon named Magri and an ice elemental dragon named Vitra. I will not sell my slaves for minna stone or coin, but if you and your crew join our force to drive off these wretched obscenities and help us reclaim our lands, all of the slaves from the raided settlement of Yaand will be yours.

Achyut bit his lip. To kill a dragon was impossible. To drive one away was improbable, but not outside the realm of possibility. His parents would be worried sick and he would get the tongue-lashing of a lifetime if they ever found out he went out of his way to fight a dragon, let alone two, but he couldn't stop thinking of the slaves. They deserved to be free. It was not their fault to be born in Yaand, and he would not let them suffer for it.

"I'll do it." Achyut glared at Rakriliox. "We'll help you drive off those dragons and you'll release all of your slaves into my care."

"All of the slaves from the raided settlement," Rakriliox corrected in a stern tone. "If you wish to free more slaves, you will have to do something else for myself and the leaders of the Confederation."

"It's been fun, but it's time I end this!" Mona held her aruval above her head. A dagger of lightning grew from the tip of the billhook as she hacked and slashed toward Griskrus. He effortlessly parried all of her blows, but when he tried to block with his shield, Mona knew she had won. She reversed her grip on her sword and plunged the dagger into the shield which pierced through as easily as a pickaxe chipped stone. Mona held the hilt and yanked as hard as she could. She tore the shield from Griskrus' grasp and began her final assault.

A fierce wall of flames sprang up behind Griskrus and thwarted his retreat. Mona closed the gap between them. There wasn't enough room for him to wind up a powerful swing without risking his arms or legs being struck by her sword. He couldn't risk retreating into his shell, not while they dueled at such close range. He was running out of options.

Mona's left arm became a phoenix of fire. It knocked Griskrus's club out of the way. Griskrus staggered backward, smacked his shell against the solid wall of flames, and lost his balance. Once more, Mona reversed her grip on her weapon and hooked the tip around the lower edge of his shell. She dispelled the wall of flame and pulled with all her might. Griskrus toppled over like a great oak tree whose roots had been all but severed by the hurricane that was Mona. He fell prone onto his back and struggled to stand. Mona sprinted to his side and pressed her aruval against his long neck.

"I yield!" Griskrus croaked.

The crowd whooped and cheered at the fierce spectacle of strength. Captain Tanoy leaped from his chair and sang Mona's praises. Achyut wanted to join him. He wanted to yell and clap for Mona's victory but instead he sat silently in his seat. Tanoy and Mona and the rest of the crew had no idea he had just volunteered them to be dragon bait.

3

The Battle of Kemp's Rock

Far in the northern mountains of Reighja, near a narrow inland sea, deep within a sprawling network of caverns and tunnels under the tallest mountain, an ancient dragon woke. No creature of the world knew his original name, for it had been erased by the flow of time, and all, be they dragon, human, or maiamorph, only knew him as Magri, the oldest being of Reighja, who spent most of his days alone in his caves reminiscing of centuries gone by, when dragons rightfully ruled the continents. He cracked open his amber eyes and stretched, lazily swinging his flat, triangular head from side to side. He sharpened his two curved horns, each nearly as long as a fire eel, against the walls of his grotto and combed his magnificent bronze barbels, mustatache, and mane. The gargantuan alloy dragon, his scales long and spiked, reinforced with raw tungsten, whomped toward the entrance of his abode.

Magri spread his black leathery wings and pushed himself off the rock outcropping and into the fjord at the base of the steep cliffs surrounded by waterfalls gushing out of countless lakes hidden in the mountains above. He closed his eyes and sat in the cool water, warming his giant wings. He grumbled, as older dragons do, and looked up as a small cerulean shape blotted out the sun.

The other dragon descended in a slow spiral, landed on the shallow banks, and waded in to meet him.

"Hello Magri," the cerulean dragon spoke in a deep, monotone voice. "Have you given further thought to my proposition?"

"I have, Vitra, though the rest of our kind would seek to disband such an alliance, by force if necessary. My spies inform me you seek to also gain the aid of the emerald dragon clan that lives on the western isles."

"Of course I seek their aid. An alliance of Elemental, Gemstone, and Alloy dragons would become the strongest force on all of Reighja. We would have complete control of the western seaboard and our influence would only continue to spread from there."

"The final entente before our dispersal has forbidden this kind of propinquity. We are no longer involved in the affairs of Reighja's Pillar Civilizations."

"Yet whispers of other alliances carving up the continents have reached my ears. They could very well soon come for your mountains, mine as well."

"And if they do, my champions are ready. No dragon is foolish enough to destroy another. Even a young and fit drake as yourself would be quickly disposed of should you break our ancient laws."

"I have a more pressing reason for disturbing your great rest," Vitra retorted, not the least bit discontented with Magri's circumambulating response. "The entrance to the tomb has been discovered."

Magri's eyes flashed to meet Vitra's. "To posture so nonchalantly while proclaiming such a revelation, you are either unaware of such power or a scheming fool who seeks it as his own."

"I am well aware of her ability to transpose souls across the great divide and the curse she laid with her dying breath. Any of our kin who enter her domain will rest with her for eternity. Yet unlike you or I, the coalition of humans and maiamorphs who found her tomb possess no such knowledge and double as our key to taking her power safeguarded since time immemorial."

"It is a tempting proposition." Magri stared at the bright blue sky. "I will not deny your offer, but I cannot accept it either. Our time for meddling in the continent's affairs has passed. Our ancestors permanently changed the ecology, the species, even the landscape, and that attention brought us ruin from the humans and other creatures unhappy with our will. If we were to fail, or such power proves uncontrollable, we would only succeed in reigniting the ire which brought us to the brink of extinction."

"That is precisely the reason we must forge a strong alliance and pool our resources, to ensure such failure is impossible. We can still reclaim our glory. The humans are different now, splintered into factions that fight among themselves. The maiamorph clans have long gone their separate ways or have grown weak by interbreeding with the humans. They no longer pose a unified threat. Once we subdue one faction, the others will fall in line. It is simply a matter of choosing our first target."

"Come into my cavern. I've grown tired of the sun and wish to rest underground. Tell me more of your ambitious plans." Magri folded his wings against the row of spikes that lined his spine. He stood. Powerful swells surged from his sides, smashed against the stone bluffs, and uprooted the smallest trees along the shore. He climbed the steep cliff face and vanished into the maw of his dark tunnels that led to the base of the mountain.

Vitra smiled. This would be easier than he anticipated.

***

The next morning, Prince Achyut and his crew set out alongside the largest army that had ever gathered under one banner, a strange and humbling sight that neither Achyut nor any member of the Prospector's crew had ever seen or could remember. Open war had not occurred between the four Pillar Civilizations for hundreds of years. Reighja was a place of peace, at least for those sheltered by the chaparrals and central deserts of the Dynasty of Lamaru.

The first day of travel proved unusually quiet. Mona flat out refused to talk with Achyut. Captain Tanoy kept his answers brief and concise, obliged to answer the prince but not in so many words. None of the crew approached him as well. Whether from fear or anger Achyut didn't know, although he could certainly understand if they felt a bit of both.

Why can't they see the moral necessity of my choice? he mused to himself as he putted around the ship. *Gold and reward and prestige are important, but we cannot relinquish our obligations to each other. We must free these slaves from their shackles. Yes, one or two of us might die, but the lives of the many outweigh the lives of the few, don't they?* He sat on his bed and pondered this moral quandary. *At least, that's what everyone in my family always said.*

He thought about his parents, back at the Palace in Illadina, ruling the kingdom, helping its citizens prosper; it always commanded all of their attention. *I hope they'll understand. I hope they'll be proud of me. I have to keep my promise, to them and myself. I am a prince of Lamaru. It is my duty to help those in need, to fight for those who cannot and purge this world of its evils.* He looked out the porthole at the setting sun. A wide grin spread across his lips as he closed his eyes and snuggled into his fluffy mattress.

I'll become a hero, just like them: Nuhir Rakiba the Indomitable and Prince Achyut the Gallant. We'll be heralded as paladins of virtue! Songs and praises will ring throughout the land about our grand undertakings. I can see it now. Tomorrow will be better.

The next morning, he woke and joined Mona and the crew for breakfast yet their somber moods did little to cull his enthusiasm and excitement for the upcoming battle. Again, he found himself in the crow's nest, accompanied by his bansuri, as the lyrics to a new ballad bounced around his brain:

Across ole Reighja's northern sea, our forces march for all to see.

The stoney cliffs that guide our way, to fjords and pine trees on display.

Ancient beasts have stolen land but we will force them to disband.

The pirates of Lamaru, the warriors of the Bay, will fight to reclaim what was lost, and drive the dragons away.

The snowflakes fall and steal my eyes for never have I seen such skies.

They top the mighty mountains, with crowns of purest white, but snow and ice won't freeze our hearts we're striking out tonight.

Our vessel sails onward, with fire eels by our side. Atop these giant crimson fish the Clystudine do ride.

The pirates of Lamaru, the warriors of the Bay, will fight to reclaim what was lost, and drive the dragons away.

The leathery, laden nosorogs that roam the central plains, tamed and raised by Clystudine, their armor bests both cold and flame.

The mighty mounts that house their wares, their weapons and supplies, could eat an irrivir intact. I'm glad they're on our side.

Man and mount and Clystudine all rally to one banner, anticipating victory with shouts and cheer and clamor.

The pirates of Lamaru, the warriors of the Bay, will fight to reclaim what was lost, and drive the dragons away."

The melodious trill of Achyut's bansuri echoed across the deck of the Prospector. One by one, the crew looked up to the crow's nest with hopeful smiles. Miniature sailors, Clystudine, nosorogs, and fire eels fought back two miniature dragons amid a winter storm. By midday, Achyut's music and illusions turned even the sourest of moods. Nearly all of the crew had decided this was not only a feasible mission, but a winnable battle, and returned to their preparations with renewed fervor. All except for Mona, who held her tongue and refused to even consider underestimating the daunting task that lay before them.

Achyut slid down the ladder, lauded by the crew, and approached Mona with a hopeful smile, who turned around to look at something else. She stood by him, as her duty as his retainer, but wouldn't dispel her silent fury until her prudent mind was convinced they weren't sailing to their deaths.

"Come on, Mona, please, just let me know you hear me," Achyut begged.

"I hear you."

"And you're still mad?"

"Yes."

"Well, how long are you going to be mad? It's not like I wanted to get caught up in some raid on a dragon's lair but what was I supposed to do? Those people are slaves and we have a moral right to help them."

Mona turned and glared at Achyut. Her charcoal eyes could erupt into flames at any moment.

Achyut gulped and looked away.

"I understand your moral compass, but this is something that should have been first consulted with myself and the captain at least," she hissed. "You've endangered the lives of all the crew, not to mention our own. I don't care what your initial motives were! If you wanted to help them, we should have continued on our journey back to Lamaru where we could have sent proper aid to help the slaves and adequately deal with this situation. Morale alone doesn't win battles. Tactics and strength do."

"I'm sorry that I thought it was more pertinent to help these people now. I was taught to fight the evils of the world, not run away and come back when it's more convenient," Achyut retorted.

Mona sighed and rubbed her eyes, quickly becoming exasperated trying to reason with the young prince. Only three years her junior, yet sometimes she felt his maturity had scarcely hit puberty. She hoped one day he'd learn better foresight and prayed she'd live long enough to see it. His heart was in the right place, of that she had no doubt, but his impatience and constant inability to think ahead knew no bounds.

"That's not the point and I'm tired of trying to convince you otherwise." Mona turned her back to him and watched a fire eel surface a few feet away. More often than not, his antics left her thankful she had no siblings of her own.

"Are you worried about the dragons seeking vengeance against us?" asked Achyut. "They won't be able to ascertain we're from Lamaru. We'll use the spare sails and it's not like we're the only country that uses these ships. The merchants of Jatharir have twice as many as our own fleet."

"The young prince is right," called Rakriliox as he sauntered up from below deck. "Lady Mona, I will personally guarantee the safety of this vessel and your crew and will compensate you for any damages incurred. We have a few surprises for those dastardly dragons and while I would love to skin them and shave their teeth into swords, our objective is not to kill but to disperse. Thankfully, we are not headed to their main lair, which they would defend tooth and claw. Think of this as raiding their holiday home."

Mona glared at him.

"If the two of you would please come with me," Rakriliox continued, "I will inform you, your captain, and my generals of our plan."

Mona sighed and crossed her arms over her chest. She silently followed Achyut and Rakriliox to the helm of the ship where Captain Tanoy and nine Clystudine warriors, armored from head to tail, stood around a wooden table.

Rakriliox placed a small, golden box with minna stones embedded on five of its six faces on the table and muttered an incantation. A beautifully recreated, three-dimensional replica of the bay at the end of the fjord appeared. Hundreds of waterfalls flowed over the steep stone cliffs into the clear, blue water which the Clystudines had deepened as they prepared to construct a new underwater city.

"Huh, it's like a CNA from Lamaru," mused Achyut as he poked at the stone cliffs. Small distortions in the map appeared wherever he touched.

"A what?" asked one of the Clystudine generals.

"A CNA. Continental Navigation Assistant. It's a widget, that's what we call our smaller bits of minna-powered technology, that synchronizes with a pair of eyeglasses to help explorers map an area. Anything seen through the glasses gets stored on memory plates in the CNA that can be used in other rituals to create self-drawing maps, scale models, and all sorts of useful applications."

"And this is commonplace in your kingdom?" asked another general, his voice filled with awe.

Achyut nodded. "The ritual and building process takes about a month to complete but when we're producing a hundred or so at a time it doesn't really matter."

The Clystudine leaders let out gasps and various statements of disbelief. This was their first creation of the sort and it had taken their magicians and sorcerers an entire year to perfect.

"You see?" Rakriliox smirked. "Their understanding and harness of minna is unmatched. The technology on this vessel alone could usher in a new age for our species."

"And we'll be checking every system and chest on this ship to make sure it stays here before we depart," Tanoy teased the Clystudine leader. "However, if you're willing to make me an offer... well, we'll see."

Rakriliox laughed and nodded. "Yes, yes, old friend. I'd never plunder this fine vessel. I've not forgotten she's saved my life nearly as many times as she has saved yours. But I digress, let us return to the moment at hand."

Rakriliox detailed his plan to the other generals and leaders who all added their own input and suggestions. They agreed that they would send individual battalions to set off clustered barrels of explosive jelly on the far side of the mountain and sequentially collapse the caverns to flush the dragons out of the waterfall entrance. The Prospector would wait and ambush the elemental dragon while the Clystudine warriors drew the attention of the black tungsten dragon. While the bulk of their forces fought, four separate legions would storm the caves and prevent the dragons from returning. They would also be in charge of securing the area when the battle was won so that whatever loot remained could be taken back and split among the Confederation.

The nine generals jumped onto the backs of fire eels and departed to inform their troops of the plan. Captain Tanoy informed the crew of the Prospector. The ship's Magi charged their minna foci and pre-channeled their tomes with spells, ready to be released in an instant. They activated the minna orbs which spun slowly, storing kinetic energy until a spell was thrown into its center and unleashed. Those less trained in the art and science of harnessing minna loaded cannons, ballistas, and set up shelters around their armaments as they waited for the Clystudine army to get into position.

After three hours of preparation, the crew of the Prospector heard a loud explosion, then another and another. Each grew louder and louder until fire peered over the edge of the mountaintop, scraped the sky with its burning claws, and shook the very mountain itself. A horrible shriek split the air and a massive, dark shape darted out of the rocky opening. It hid the sun with its head alone and night seemed to fall as the black tungsten dragon spread its leathery wings and flew high above the stony peak.

Magri's copper eyes glowed like bonfires against the dark grays and black of his body and wings. His limbs and tail dwarfed the thickest, sturdiest ironwood trees. Jagged scales, the color of a starless sky protected every inch of skin from his head to his tail. The ancient dragon spotted a line of trebuchets flinging chunks of earth and stone into the air which smashed against his armored body. He would have none of it. He tucked his wings against his ridged spine and dropped out of the sky faster than a meteor. He struck the ground with the same force and crushed ten of the twelve siege weapons. Limbs and tail sprung forth, tore down the remaining two, then tore into the hundreds of Clystudine warriors who swarmed him.

A second shape flew out from the mountain cavern, smaller than Magri but just as deadly. A pair of azure wings carried the cerulean dragon, who tucked his legs close against his body. His spine was lined with a single row of frozen spikes that sparkled like diamonds and ran the length from his triangular head to the tip of his long, powerful, spaded tail. He spun and flipped in the air, dodging volleys of arrows and bolts. His sapphire eyes glared at the Clystudine hordes below as he roared with a sound that shook the earth, opening his mouth and letting loose a hail of icy bullets. Hundreds of jagged icicles formed from his wingtips and fell, impaling nosorog, Clystudine, and fire eel alike. This was the elemental dragon, Vitra, and the target of the Prospector's mission.

"All hands man the minna orbs, we've a dragon to defeat! Fire at will!" Tanoy ordered from the helm of the ship. He slung the vessel around and broadsided Vitra high above. Twenty or so spells detonated on the dragon's flank. Boulders made of minna slammed against his sides. Cyclones sucked away the air beneath his wings, and lances of fire left scorch marks against his pristine blue scales.

The Prospector immediately had Vitra's attention.

"You dare to strike at me, Vitra the Eternal Winter?!" the dragon roared as he descended upon the Prospector yet the Magi kept him at bay as they harnessed and launched hundreds of powerful spells.

Vitra swooped and soared and dodged much of their assault. He gathered ice into a giant sphere and dropped it onto the ship below. Boulders made of earth minna erupted out of minna orbs and smashed the dragon's ice until it fell to the deck as harmless, powdered snow.

Vitra snarled with rage. He let loose another hailstorm which strafed across the ship. A curtain of fire stretched from stern to bow protecting the ship and crew. A bronze cyclone appeared on the Prospector's starboard side and sucked away any of Vitra's stray shots.

Furious, irritated, and positively piqued, icicles the size of fishing boats formed at his wingtips, and Vitra smiled devilishly as the crew of the vessel made its first major mistake. He dropped two more icicles as a maelstrom appeared over the ship to suck away his first volley. However, just as the icy spears made contact, the whirlpool fizzled out and the ice crashed through the top three decks. The crew had little time to react as more and more ice broke through their defenses and shattered one of the ship's three masts.

"Fools! You dare harness water against me? Ice is my domain! I am in control here!" Vitra laughed maniacally as two more icicles pierced through two minna orbs before they could release their defensive spells. They detonated with colorful explosions that shook the ship from side to side.

Mona grabbed Achyut's hand. They raced across the deck, dodging ice and debris as it flung all around them.

"Prince Achyut, I suggest we get below deck and allow Captain Tanoy to handle this situation. If you're unable to harness minna against that beast, there's only so much I can do to protect you."

"No!" Achyut shook his head. "We've got to buy the Magi more time to re-coordinate our defenses. Otherwise, we'll risk further destruction. I got us into this mess. I'm going to get us out."

"Prince Achyut, I insist! Listen to me for once! There's nothing we can do to damage that thing!"

"Ah, silly Mona, we don't need to damage it." He reached behind his back and drew his bansuri, smirking as he spun it in his hand, "We'll be the distraction. Come on!" Without a moment of hesitation, Achyut sprinted to the first of the Prospector's masts. His flute glowed as he held it above his head and snapped his wrist as if it were a whip. A length of rope shot forth from its end and wrapped around the top yard of the sail. Once the rope was secured, it retracted and pulled Achyut off the deck and up to the crow's nest.

Mona vaulted into the air with her own fire and landed on the yard above the prince. She drew her aruval which crackled with electricity.

Prince Achyut put his flute to his lips and played.

High above the ship, Vitra laughed as he pelted the Prospector with ice. Although the crew managed to block some of his attacks, it wasn't long until the top three decks were full of holes. Then something strange happened, something Vitra thought impossible. His entire volley missed. All of his ice splashed harmlessly into the water off the port side of the ship.

Perplexed, Vitra launched two more giant icicles. Although they seemed to strike the ship, the sound of splashing water gave away the illusion at play. The faintest sound of a flute's trill hit his ears. A human stood atop the crow's nest and played a joyous tune in defiance of his wrath. He snarled at the source of his misfortune. The human would die. He opened his gaping maw and pelted him with ice, but another human in red summoned shields of lightning and fire and blocked his assault. Once was lucky. The second time he grew annoyed. The third time they deflected his onslaught warranted a new tactic.

Fine! If I can't harm them with minna, I'll grab them and swallow them whole! Vitra swooped closer and closer to the ship. The human male played on in an effort to ruin Vitra's accuracy, but he was doomed from the start. Vitra was big. His palms could crush ten men at once. He didn't need to hit his target directly, merely be close enough.

As Vitra approached, the man stopped playing. He and the woman jumped off the mast in a feeble attempt to flee. The woman evaded his claws, but Vitra laughed as he soared back into the sky.

"W-what the hell are you doing? Let go of me you wretched, scaly lizard!" Achyut yelled as he thrashed in Vitra's grasp.

"Not until you answer my questions, then perhaps I'll let you go," replied Vitra, who had no intention of letting him live. "Who are you? What purpose do you have for attacking me unprovoked?"

"I'm but a simple pirate, paid by the Clystudine Confederation for our assistance in reclaiming their stolen land from you dragons!"

"Liar!" Vitra yelled and shook him back and forth. "You harness minna too well to be simple pirates. Your ship and crew are too well equipped! If you won't tell me the truth, I'll force it out of you!" Vitra's eyes glowed with an eerie white light.

Achyut cried out in anguish as his head started spinning. His skull throbbed with sharp frozen pain. He felt as if an icicle slowly bored into his brain.

A deep, dark voice consumed his own thoughts. *So, you are Prince Achyut from the Dynasty of Lamaru... your decision to aid these fools was unwise. You and your descendants will pay the ultimate price... death!*

The pain became worse and worse. Achyut screamed. His senses grew hazy and faded away. Vitra yelped in surprise. Achyut regained consciousness and the icy pain suddenly vanished.

Bewildered, Achyut searched for his salvation and sighed in relief as Mona stood on Vitra's back, her aruval plunged into a gap between his scales. She gripped its hilt and sent another shockwave of minna through her blade and into the dragon, who swatted at her with his long, spaded tail. Mona drew her sword from the wound and raced up his back. Again, she impaled the sword past his scales. Again, it crackled with orange lightning, so much that the blade cracked. Her assault struck a nerve in Vitra's shoulder and forced his talons open. Mona dove off Vitra's back after Achyut.

Far below on the deck of the Prospector, Captain Tanoy watched in vain through the lens of the telescope. He bit his lip as the dragon released the prince and held his tongue until the two were clear of the blast radius.

"Everyone! Fire everything we've got! Don't let up until that dragon is far over the horizon!" Every spell and cantrip imaginable roared out of the functioning minna orbs.

Vitra was poisoned, blinded, burnt, shocked, stabbed, stoned, sliced, and had the wind knocked from beneath his wings. He roared in pain as flecks of blue blood coated his wings and scales. These arrogant humans were not to be trifled with...yet.

He soared into the sky and cursed the humans from Lamaru. "One day, Prince Achyut! One day I'll have my revenge! Whether it be against you or your descendants or your entire people, I care not, but you will pay for your insolence!"

"You'll try and fail, dragon!" Achyut called back, his fist above his head as he and Mona fell through the sky. "Lamaru is strong, her people stronger still! The deserts themselves will soon bow to our use of minna! We will transform—"

Mona's hand covered his mouth. "That's enough for today. He's leaving. No need to antagonize him further. Our job is done."

"I—" Achyut started, but Mona shot him a glance that said 'If you even think about sassing me, your parents will absolutely hear about this.'

Achyut closed his mouth in defeat. He drew up a column of water from the sea below that caught the both of them and they made their way back to the Prospector in silence.

On the far side of the inland sea, the Clystudine soldiers rallied their strength as one army against Magri. Like a thousand tiny insects, they slashed and bashed their swords and clubs against the dragon's body. Others resorted to pickaxes and chisels to chip away at the dragon's scale, made from the ores of the earth. Yet with every swipe of his talons and tail, Magri killed several Clystudine warriors and knocked hundreds more into the air but their shells and armor were strong and their resolve stronger still. They launched volley after volley of explosive tipped arrows at his wings in effort to wound his leathery skin and make it impossible for him to fly away. This was a battle of attrition and stamina and although the dragon was fearsome indeed, the sheer numbers of Clystudine pressed on and gained the advantage.

Magri's roar shook the mountains themselves. Any further damage to his already tattered wings would render them useless, so he tucked them close to his body and shielded himself with his tail while he gathered every ounce of energy. Mistaking this for a sign of weakness, the Clystudine army drew in closer and redoubled their assault.

"You will die!" Magri harnessed every particle of minna in his body and let loose a wicked blast, incinerating the closest warriors.

"Fall back, fall back!" cried the Clystudine leaders as Magri scorched the earth around them. Black dragonfire dripped from his mouth—hot plasma from a fallen star— melted boulders and reduced trees to sticks of charcoal. The fire consumed anything and everything, granting the ancient dragon a few precious seconds to spread his wings and push off into the sky.

They only won because of the element of surprise, Magri reasoned to himself. They never would have won, had he known they were coming, and this would not be the last time he dealt with the lesser species. As he flew off to his home in the mountains further north, he recalled Vitra's offer to form an alliance of Elemental, Gemstone, and Alloy dragons. Perhaps Vitra was right. It was time the species of Reighja remembered their place in the hierarchy of the world. He too would have his revenge.

Shouts and cheers rose up from the Clystudine warriors. The dragons had retreated, the spoils of the cave belonged to the Confederation, and their land was freed from the talons of the ancient beasts once more.

Tears came to Rakriliox's eyes as the triumphant shouts of his warriors and the crew of the Prospector filled the air with the sounds of victory. It had been a hard-pressed battle, though he knew every soldier who gave their life did so with veritable resolve to free their land from the dragons of old. In his heart, he knew the Clystudine Confederation would mature and prosper, the likes of which neither their ancestors nor Reighja as a whole had ever seen before. Most importantly, however, his wife and their newly hatched sons would be safe.

4

The Oracle

The trip back to the Bale was filled with celebration. The crew of the Prospector had lost none of their own and the damage to their ship could be fixed in a matter of days. One by one they apologized to Prince Achyut. They had thought him a fool for accepting this mission but now that it was over and they reaped their rewards, they grew giddy with the thought of what legends would be told of the Dragonslayers of Lamaru. Of course, they hadn't slain either dragon, but that was the kind of detail to downplay in tales of the gallant paragons of the Padishah, knights of Lamaru, and defenders of humanity.

Upon their arrival in the Bale, Rakriliox departed for the city's administrative center. He returned with a rolled-up scroll, heavy enough to be used as a club.

"Prince Achyut, here is the slave manifest from Yaand's raided settlement, just as I've promised. You and your crew were magnificent. It was an honor not soon forgotten to fight alongside you." Rakriliox smiled and handed Achyut the heavy scroll.

Achyut bowed, broke the wax seal, and unrolled the scroll which dropped out of his hands and rolled across the deck of the Prospector.

"How many are there? This list must be at least three hundred names long!" Achyut fumbled to reroll the lengthy scroll. He'd enchant it later to make the document easier to store and read.

"Three hundred and sixty-nine," Rakriliox corrected. "All now in your care. I hope this has satiated your lust for morality."

Achyut frowned. *It's all nice and well that we freed so many, but this is only the tip of the iceberg. The other Clystudine leaders have also raided entire settlements and taken not just the men, but the women and children too. I have to do better. I have to do more for them.*

"Additionally," Rakriliox continued, "thanks to the influx of resources we've obtained from the dragons' lair, I've decided to triple your supplies at no extra cost to Captain Tanoy. The Prospector is an impressive ship, yet you have many more mouths to feed and your journey through the mountain pass will be long and cramped. I would feel liable should harm befall your crew while you stopped and gathered additional resources."

"Aye, cramped it will be, all the way down the Hayi River." Captain Tanoy nodded. "Even when we reach Illadina, your problems will be far from over, Prince Achyut. The Padishah and King will be extremely curious as to why so many have joined the Dynasty of Lamaru. We'll be sure to dampen the details for your sake." He winked at Achyut.

"I'd appreciate that, Captain Tanoy." Achyut nodded. "But these people have next to nothing. They'll need proper education and resources to lead prosperous lives in Lamaru."

"If you were to alleviate your parent's burden of collecting all of the necessary information to pursue this endeavor, I'm positive they'd praise your actions instead of berating you about the dangers you brought upon yourself," Tanoy suggested.

"Now that's a fanciful dream," Mona's words dripped with sarcasm. "He still endangered his life and the life of the crew. They won't let him off the hook that easily."

"That's true," Achyut agreed in a sullen tone. "I'll need every tactic and tool to get out of trouble, regardless of our victory. Oh, there's so much work to be done: gathering personal information, filling out the official registry, ascertaining elemental flairs and minna affinities... what a mess."

"I've been meaning to ask you about that," interrupted Rakriliox. "As I understand, every individual from Lamaru shows a natural aptitude for one of the six primal facets of minna. I've ascertained your ability to harness water minna." He glanced at Mona. "But you, Lady Mona, seem to harness both fire and electrical minna with ease."

"My elemental flair is fire but I come from a long line of Magi who specialized in harnessing electrical minna. Any good Magi knows how to harness a wide variety of spells for combat and mundane uses," she answered.

"Fascinating indeed," mused Rakriliox. "I was under the impression each human could only harness cantrips of whichever element they had an innate affinity for. So, Prince Achyut, what other elemental cantrips are you capable of?"

"Well, you see, I..." Achyut blushed and laughed. "I'm, uh, I'm still working on that part."

Rakriliox smiled. "It is of no matter. With such capable protection, you can afford to be languorous with your abilities."

"I wouldn't go that far," retorted Achyut. "I've simply specialized differently from most in my family. Music and charisma are my weapons and they've yet to fail me."

"And I pray a time never comes when they do," replied Rakriliox. "Now, if you will excuse me, there is much I must discuss with the other leaders of the Confederation. Thank you, all of you, your names will not be forgotten in the Bale." Rakriliox bowed his head and walked off the side of the deck. He swam ashore and joined a group of Clystudine who walked into the city.

Over the span of the next four days, Captain Tanoy shuffled all nonessential crew off of the ship so repairs could be made as efficiently as possible. Achyut and Mona watched from the ramshackle dock as Clystudine smiths and woodworkers prepared the vessel for its voyage inland. They unlocked the keel and swung it up against the side of the ship, hoisting the Prospector onto wooden stilts and bringing it ashore so the bottoms of the side buoys could be removed and the ironwood rollers and treds could be lowered and allow the ship to cross the flat, continental terrain.

In their downtime, Achyut and Mona begrudgingly double-checked the manifest of all the slaves and their families and scribed any pertinent information that would help them start their new lives in Lamaru. None of the slaves wished to stay within the Clystudine Confederation. Their reptilian conquerors treated them well enough, but all agreed a cage was a cage, whether gilded and comfortable or held together with wrought iron and twine. Furthermore, none of the slaves wished to return to the Queendom of Yaand, feeling abandoned by their former leader, and surmising their capture concluded some sick social experiment to test the consequences of imposing upon the Confederation's lands.

Although Achyut enjoyed the constant praise and adoration from his new audience, he quickly grew weary and bored cataloging the freed slaves' information. Time and time again, he introduced himself and Mona to the long list of people, learned their names, and abated their fears while Mona ascertained every bit of useful information and stored it on a secondary scroll.

"I can't believe this is only the first day. We've only gone through a hundred names," he moaned as he flipped through the pages of Mona's manuscript. "There's got to a better way than to do all this by hand, right?" He yawned as the sun dipped lower into the sky.

Mona snatched back her work and continued writing. "None with the widgets we have available," she replied. "And hopefully this little exercise in patience and adult responsibilities will improve your foresight for future matters. I'm still unhappy with the stunt you pulled. Things could have gone a lot worse. Next!"

"Except they didn't, so there's no point in staying mad," Achyut retorted. "This should definitely be handled with minna." He sighed as a family of three— a young man with black hair, a younger woman with blonde hair, and a sleeping infant, all of whom wore cloth scraps stitched together— strode forward.

"Names, previous occupation, medical abnormalities, and education if possible?" Mona asked. She had since decided Achyut's method of striking up a friendly conversation was the reason why it took them so long to obtain the necessary information. However, even if she asked all the questions, he still had to sit with her and not wander off or cavort with the lovely maidens of the group.

"I am Gerald Miller. This is my wife, Sonyia, and our child, Jennifer. I worked at the town grainery and as a driver in our trading caravan to the capital city of Yaand. My wife stayed at home as a seamstress before we were captured. Let me just say, thank you from the bottom of my heart, Prince Achyut, your kindness in both freeing us and helping us restart our lives will never be forgotten."

"Of course." Achyut smiled at the three of them. "As one of noble birth, it is my duty to help those who have fallen victim to the cruel whims of fate. So many things happen in our lives that are out of our control, I'm merely providing the opportunity to help you regain what you've lost."

"Thank you, Prince Achyut, truly, thank you." Sonyia wiped tears from her eyes and smiled at her husband and sleeping daughter.

"Medical abnormalities and education, if possible," Mona repeated.

"Oh, yes, yes, my apologies. I'm sure it must be exhausting gathering this information from all of us," replied Gerald. "My wife and I are allergic to camu berries, but it's not a severe reaction, just a bit of a rash and bloating. Neither of us have any formal tutelage."

"We both picked up our trades from our parents," added Sonyia. "But if there's any chance our little one could attend a formal school...."

"Now, my dear, don't go asking for too much. These fine people have already given us countless blessings," Gerald reminded her in a hushed tone.

"Well, Lamaru does have a public education system, and not just for the children of nobles. In fact, those considered 'commoners' by Yaand's standards are simply citizens of Lamaru," Achyut interjected. "I was always taught that an educated populace is the best counter to a ruler's ego. Better still, if the problems of miscommunication or misunderstandings can be mitigated by having a people who are able to express themselves and understand each other's expressions, there's less of a chance for something to go awry. Once we reach Illadina, the capital city, I'll make sure all of you have the chance to be formally educated, should you wish for it." Achyut flashed them a dazzling smile.

Gerald and Sonyia looked as if they were about to weep tears of joy.

Mona wrote down their information, stamped their wrists as proof they had been seen, and hurried them along.

"Don't go making promises you won't be able to keep," Mona warned him before their next freedmen approached. "Once we return to Illadina, you'll have to resume a more princely decorum. None of this freedom fighter and pirate nonsense."

"Relax, Mona, it'll be fine. Mom and Dad will be pleased I've a noble task to occupy my time: a project to work on that betters a life other than my own. They always said it was unbecoming of a royal who only wished to explore and that I needed a more princely enterprise, even if I'm second in line for the throne. Now you and I have all these people and their needs to tend too." He flashed her the same dazzling smile.

Mona rolled her eyes. "Next!" she called out for the umpteenth time.

Prince Achyut looked down at the scroll and groaned. They still had twenty-three people to meet and that was just today's quota. It would take at least two more days before everyone was accounted for. *At least the repairs will take the same amount of time. It's not like I have anything else to do,* he thought to himself as the next person in line walked up and silently sat in front of Mona and himself.

Her face and body were hidden under a tattered, gray cloak and only a few strands of long, copper hair poked out beneath her hood.

"Name, previous occupation, medical abnormalities, and education if possible."

"U-um my name is K-Katria, with a 'k', K-konners, also with a 'k'. I don't really have an occupation...or any medical problems... or education," she mumbled and fiddled with her hands.

Achyut and Mona stared at her in confusion, which only made the girl more nervous.

"How did you make a living before being captured by the Clystudines?" asked Achyut.

"Also, miss, you'll need to remove your hood so I can see your face. No one gets on the Prospector without us knowing who they are," commanded Mona.

"Ah, okay, I'm sorry. I just didn't want to be a problem. I'm no one important," replied the girl.

"In my experience, those who believe themselves the least important often turn out to be some of the most important people in the world. Come now, there's nothing to fear. We're here to help you start a new life." Achyut flashed her a brilliant smile.

Katria bit her lip and slowly removed her hood as instructed.

Achyut took in the details of her face. He thought her a pretty, young maiden by all standards, with a fair complexion and freckles dotting the bridge of her nose. She had a cute, round face with peach-colored lips, yet the black circles around her cold, distant eyes left her looking tired and sullen and gave the impression she had not slept in days. He peered deeper into her eyes as if a simple look could discern her problems and solve them immediately, for it was a prince's duty to help maidens in distress, yet his steady gaze had the opposite effect.

Katria grew even more wary. She rocked back and forth on the barrel and looked away from the prince.

Mona too took in the oddity that was Katria, but she dismissed the girl's personal problems; they weren't her business anyway. Instead, she grew concerned about the prince's safety. Nervousness and an inability to answer simple questions often demonstrated precursor behaviors of those under stress or with ulterior motives. Katria devoted herself to hiding her face and anyone acting so strangely put Mona on edge.

"I, um, I did various odd jobs for the village," Katria murmured as she fiddled with her hands. "I gardened a bit and um, cleaned for people, but if I had to describe my main occupation, you could call me an oracle of sorts."

Her answer intrigued Achyut even more than her appearance. Few claimed to have any knowledge of divining fate, and those who did were often charlatans and frauds.

"Very well," Mona replied, unphased by her odd answer. She pressed the stamp against an ink-soaked sponge and offered it to Katria. The woman held out her arm. Mona stood up and reached over the wooden table. She grasped her arm and stamped her wrist.

"Alright, Miss, you're free to go. Make sure that stamp stays clean. It's your ticket onto the Prospector when we depart. Next!"

"T-thank you..." Katria mumbled and hastily threw her hood back over her head then hurried away as fast as she could.

Achyut watched the strange girl depart. *She's got nice legs, a bit odd though,* he thought to himself as she scampered into the crowds going about their daily work. "Hey, Mona, I was thinking,"

"Don't even try it. You're not going anywhere."

"Oh, come on, I didn't even finish!"

"I'm not going to let you chase after some strange girl while I sit here and document all of the people *you* wished to save. Swords and spells are only half of the heroics."

Achyut waited until Mona stamped the next group before he continued their conversation. "Who goes around claiming they are an oracle? Maybe she's a soulseeker."

"Highly unlikely. Only those descended from the Eleven Families are able to harness that form of minna."

"But it's not impossible. There was that one soulseeker some fifty or so years ago. Sure, she had already been hospitalized and only lasted a month or so, but both Grandma and Grandpa confirmed it was true. Maybe there's some truth to what she claims. It could also be a different altrusynaptic act, something we haven't seen before."

"Regardless, she wanted to be left alone. Don't go around harassing the poor girl. If she wants something, she'll ask for it."

Although Achyut had more to say, Mona returned to the task at hand. Still, he couldn't shake the image of the self-proclaimed oracle out of his mind.

Over the next day and a half, Achyut spent every moment of his downtime walking through the freed slaves' tents and asking everyone what they knew about the young woman.

"She's the quiet sort. Keeps to herself most of the time, only talks when absolutely necessary," answered an old man tending a fire. "I've never seen her with a partner of any sort, though a few of my drinking buddies saw her playing with the stray cats after dark."

"She's always been a bit of an oddity, even before the Clystudines ransacked the village," added a woman folding laundry. "She lived in a small cottage at the edge of town, very out of the way, the road was nearly overtaken by brambles and thorns," she dropped her voice down to a whisper. "Though, between you and me, I heard she used to live in Yaand's palace. Not sure how she ended up here. Maybe she did something the Queen didn't like?"

"She's really quiet but amazingly good at finding things! Yeah! I lost my favorite doll for a month and she found in about fifteen minutes! I lost my toy sword in the woods and she found it for me the next day. It was so dark, I don't know how she ever found it," answered a group of children playing with a ball.

Once or twice, Achyut found Katria and tried to strike up a conversation, either about her past or her insights as an oracle, but they barely exchanged thirty words before she took the first opportunity to walk away, which only annoyed him further. If anyone had the power to make her life easier, it was him.

On the eve before their departure, Rakriliox threw the liveliest celebration the Bale had ever seen with thanks and praise aplenty for the Prospector's aid. Achyut wore his best clothes and reveled in his princely status. He embraced the laud and praise of all, danced with anyone who asked, and played his bansuri with a cheerful Clystudine accompaniment.

After Rakriliox's final speech, Achyut left the grand hall and basked in the brisk autumn air. He hummed to himself as he walked around the Bale. It was a lovely little place to live, though he felt ready to return to the palace at Illadina. Out of the corner of his eyes, he saw a copper-hair woman in an old gray cloak, sitting alone on the end of the dock. He cleared his throat as he approached, not wanting to catch her off guard.

Katria turned around, let out a small 'eep', and tightened her cloak around her body as he joined her.

"Good evening, Miss Katria, and quite a merry one at that. Are you enjoying the festivities?"

"Yes, I suppose," she replied. An awkward silence fell between them.

"And tomorrow we set sail to Lamaru. Tell me, have you ever seen the deserts and chaparrals of southern Reighja?"

"N-no." She glanced up at him then hurriedly looked away.

"You've stayed in Yaand and the Bale your entire life?"

"Y-yes," she answered, keeping her eyes transfixed on the dock.

"Have you ever wished to travel?" Achyut sat on the edge of the dock, swinging his legs over the open water and gazing out at the sea beyond.

"U-um, I've always been interested in seeing new lands, but I never thought I'd be able to visit them." She fiddled with her hands beneath her cloak. "I'm not strong enough to travel alone."

"You don't have to travel alone." Achyut smiled at her. "I'm sure there are plenty among us, myself included, who would love to help you experience our beautiful world. What about other lands interests you?"

"L-lots of things; cultures, food, everything."

"I love trying foods from across the continent. Do you like to cook?"

"Sort of."

Achyut did his best not to sigh. He closed his eyes and exhaled calmly. "Did you cook for yourself when you lived in Yaand?"

Katria nodded without a word. Once more their conversation had turned dreadfully simple. He wished she would at least attempt an effort.

"I-I'm sorry. I must be going. I have a lot to do before we depart." Katria yanked her hood over her head and jumped up, attempting to sidle past him, but Achyut stood and stepped with her down the dock.

"I've never met a person so insistent on avoiding conversation. If I may be blunt, do you find me repulsive? If so, I swear I'll leave you be."

"No, that's not it at all," Katria mumbled.

"Do I unknowingly evoke painful memories of someone you used to find dear?"

Katria shook her head 'no'.

"Are you daunted by my royal heritage? Does my status as a prince make you believe I think less of you as an individual? I can assure you that is not the case."

Katria peeked at him from beneath her hood. "N-no that's not it either."

Achyut stalled his footsteps and leaned against a worn wooden piling. "Then perhaps you just despise conversation and wish to be left alone?"

Katria paused. "No, please, I, um, I rather enjoy hearing you talk. I'm just not used to talking with others. It's not a good idea for people to get close to me."

"And why's that?" Achyut asked, intrigued by her answer.

"B-because of my curse. Because of my powers as an oracle."

"And what's the nature of this curse?"

Still partially hidden beneath her hood, Katria lifted her face and met his gaze. "Those who befriend me will always be plagued with misfortune and ruin."

"I see. I've always thought one's mindset was more powerful than any curse. Your focus determines your reality. If you expect bad things to happen, then you'll only notice when bad things happen. I know if you search long and hard enough, you'll discover the right ritual or countermeasure to remove your affliction. Minna can solve any problem."

"I appreciate your optimism, but a shift in mindset will never solve my problem. Am I free to leave, Prince Achyut?"

"You were never shackled to stay, fair maiden."

Katria opened her mouth to speak but the courage to respond failed her. The prince drifted toward her. *Run. Vanish into the night and never see him again.* She thought to herself. *It's the only way to keep him safe.* But her feet remained glued to the dock.

"Once we reach Illadina, we'll talk with the best Magi around and figure out a solution. Until then, I can only help you if you'll let me." Achyut slowly lifted his arm and gently pulled back her hood, resting his left hand on her shoulder. Just like her cloak, it felt warm and reassuring.

"So please, try to open up, if only a little." He smiled and placed his right hand over his heart. "I swear I mean you no harm."

Katria examined his face, his features more handsome than she remembered when they first met. He had a strong jaw and a cute nose that seemed a little too small for his stature. His eyes were dark and mysterious yet held no malice.

"Why are you doing this?" she demanded. "What are you trying to gain? Why bother being nice to someone who will only bring you pain?"

"Because I don't believe you'll bring me pain. Because you seem like a good person who could use a friend and because it's the right thing to do."

"Because... because it's the right thing to do?"

Achyut nodded. "You talk about the future as if it is some grim, inevitable thing, but I was always taught to talk about the future with laughter and a smile. Nothing is promised so let's enjoy our journey. There's no limit for friendships or falling in love. All that matters is that we are alive now and when our time ends, we can pass into the next world with no regrets and a satisfied soul."

Katria sighed and turned away, staring over the open ocean, across the dark horizon and up at the gentle light of the moon and stars above. "I wish I could share in your optimism, truly I do. It seems like a lovely way to view the world."

"And what's stopping you besides your own thoughts?"

Katria fell silent and looked at her feet.

"I understand how easy it is to grow comfortable in your solitude, to push people away and protect yourself, but if you extinguish every flame of hope, what's the point of living? Burying your heart won't heal it."

Katria looked up at him, the faintest flicker of a smile on her lips. Tears welled up in her cold eyes and rolled down her face in a steady stream. She threw her arms around his chest and clung to him as she wept. "Thank you, Prince Achyut. I can't remember the last time anyone was genuinely kind to me and... it's been too long since I've shown kindness to myself" *Too long since I've told myself my life was worth any value.* Katria's cheeks turned pink and puffy.

"I'm so tired of being alone. All my life I've only wanted to be loved and needed by others and to give them my love in return, even if it's all a lie, even if only for a moment. Yet every time they end up hurt and they end up hurt because of me, because of my curse! Nothing ever changes! I can't, I won't go through that again! I'm so tired of hurting those who show me kindness. I don't want to hurt anyone else!"

Achyut, unsure of what to say or do, quietly stood and hugged her back. He wasn't sure how long they stood on the dock and he silently prayed no one saw him. Still, his heart ached for the poor girl, for no one should have to live that way. Her tears subsided and her despondent, mousey demeanor gave way to the smallest sliver of confidence and hope. When she pulled away, he offered her his handkerchief. She accepted, wiped the tears and snot from her face then offered his handkerchief back.

"Um, you can keep it. I've got a spare."

"Please," she insisted and held out her hand once more.

"No, really, I insist. It's yours. Keep it. Consider it a, uh, a token of my friendship and a promise I mean you no harm." He closed his hand around hers, his handkerchief in her palm.

Katria bit her lower lip. "Still, I'd like to give you something to repay your kindness."

"You don't have to give me anything." Achyut paused. "But perhaps, in return, you could tell me more about your powers as an oracle?"

Katria nodded, wiped her face once more, and cleared her throat. "I, um, well, I can see the origin and history of any inanimate object just by holding it. The events sort of flow through my mind's eye, like turning the pages of a book. I see when the object was first made and a general overview of what it has seen. The longer I hold an object, the more detailed its history becomes and the more information I can glean from it."

Achyut stared at her, his mouth agape.

"Um, please don't stare at me. It makes me uncomfortable." Katria blushed and moved to raise her hood once more, but Achyut clasped her hands in his own and smiled brilliantly.

"That's amazing! Such an incredible and useful talent! We have something similar in my culture called soulsharing, which allows individuals to see the truths, ideals, and memories another holds dear. I know I have the capacity to harness such minna, but I've yet to unlock that power myself."

His statement brought a fresh wave of tears to Katria's eyes. "Y-you have powers like mine? You mean I'm not alone? I'm not some oddball freak?"

"Yes, I promise, you aren't alone. There are lots of people in Lamaru capable of harnessing mental minna. Perhaps this is a little sudden, but could you give me a demonstration of this power? If it isn't too much of a burden, I'd love to see it for myself."

Katria nodded and wiped her eyes again. "What object's history should I divine?"

Achyut reached over his shoulder and freed his bansuri, his prized gift given to him by his mother on his birthday and carved from rare wood. If Katria's talent was true, he was sure she would be able to uncover that much. He handed her his flute. She held it gingerly in her hands and ran her fingers over the smooth wood.

"It's beautiful." She took a step back. "Okay, give me a moment." She closed her eyes and slowed her breathing.

Prince Achyut looked on, half expecting the wind to gale or the water beneath the dock to quake but nothing happened. Nothing that would make him aware of any magic or powerful abilities.

"Is it working?"

"Give me a moment." Katria giggled shyly and smiled. It was a very cute, girlish giggle, and Katria looked quite pretty when she did.

Now that's a smile worth protecting. Achyut found himself smiling back at the young woman.

"Here we go." Katria exhaled and opened her eyes.

Achyut's jaw dropped. If he thought the black circles were ominous before, now her entire eyes were such, including the whites of her sclera and her dark, amber irises but Achyut wasn't afraid in the slightest. He was used to this strange change whenever anyone from his ancient lineage practiced soulsharing. With the right training, Katria could become a powerful Magi indeed.

"You... you received this as a gift, many moons ago. It was from your mother I believe, on your sixteenth birthday. Oh, you were an adorable child! And to think how much trouble you caused your dear parents... you took this instrument and played it wherever you went. When you learned to harness minna, you had stones worked into the wood." She rolled the bansuri in her hands and touched a blue stone flattened and pressed against the grain. "Though, that's not it's only power. There is another enchantment here, one that allows you to create illusions whenever you play. The wood itself has another innate property. Fireproof? Yes, this is carved from timber of hellswood."

Achyut was speechless.

"You lost it once, in your early twenties during a battle against a giant stone scorpion but the woman with you, the one in the red dress, found it after the beast retreated underground. Oh, you were so happy. You hugged her and cried tears of joy. Hmm... I see another of the flute's memories; it's a late-autumn night under the light of a full moon, very much like tonight. Who's that girl? She's rather pret— hey, I thought you wanted a demonstration." Katria pouted as Achyut snatched the flute from her hands.

"I believe you, I swear on my bansuri itself," Achyut answered quickly. "I just always kept it on my person and there are a few memories I'd prefer you not to see from its point of view."

"Oh!" Katria nodded, a hint of rosy blush on her cheeks. "I apologize. I'm not privy to choose what information I see. It just sort of flows out of the item."

"Still, what an incredible talent you possess! To think what historical secrets could be revealed, what timeless mysteries could be solved!"

"What dark secrets would be shared, what horrid plots and ploys revealed, to have people hurt you out of fear of what you might know." Katria's eyes grew cold and distant as her pessimistic demeanor returned. "Tell me, Prince Achyut, if your walls had ears and eyes and lips what would they hear and see and say? What unbecoming thoughts and actions would be revealed? "

Achyut's smile disappeared. He hadn't thought of that. How many times had he broken his parents' rules and snuck out of the palace? How many things had he said and done in private that he wished he could take back? How different would his life be if the world knew all of his secrets? How different would he be if he knew the world's secrets?

"This is not a wondrous power," Katria continued, "This is a curse. Having all the knowledge in the world means nothing to me if I'm hated by all and unable to protect myself."

"Then perhaps a change of company will do you good." Achyut smiled at her, warm and genuine. "I vow to not let others use your gift against you or for personal gain, myself included, and to protect you from those who would do you harm, yourself included."

Katria's eyes faded from black back to amber. "P-prince Achyut, you mustn't say such things... to promise me something like that... Please don't lead me on. I've grown so tired of empty promises and false hopes."

"I'm not leading you on, fair maiden. I am a man and a prince of my word and it wounds my heart to know how you've suffered. I would like to be the first to make amends for how this cruel world has wronged you, if you would permit me so."

"B-but my curse. As my friend, you'll only know pain and suffering."

"I told you I don't put stock in curses of any sort. If a ritual or spell is cast, it can be uncast, no matter how complex or lofty the consequences."

The tears in Katria's eyes rolled into a steady stream. She sniffled and rubbed her eyes but for the first time since she could remember, she didn't cry tears of sadness. No, these were strange tears of joy; joy that she was fortunate enough to meet someone so kind, someone who would put all this effort into helping someone as miserable and worthless as her.

She leaped into Achyut's arms and hugged him again, somewhat to the prince's surprise, but he returned her warm embrace. They stayed in the moonlight for a moment more so Katria could wipe her face and regain her composure before returning to the festivities. Afterall, to be standing alone in the night with a crying maiden was not good for a prince's image, regardless of the context.

5

The Journey Home

Katria rubbed her eyes as sunlight drifted through the front flap of her tent. For the first time since she could remember, she had a good night's rest and woke up smiling. She sat up, stretched, and studied her reflection in the cracked mirror on the barrel beside her cot, frowning at her disheveled appearance and the stagnant moldy smell emanating from her cloak.

Ugh. Have I really not noticed the smell? Maybe it just never bothered me before. Is this how everyone sees me? She looked at the mirror again. *Even him?* Her cheeks turned red as she thought of Prince Achyut and the fond memories of last night wafted through her mind like the smell of good food and a warm hearth after an endless, cold, bitter winter.

"No. Katria, pull yourself together." She dipped her hands in the cold water from the barrel and splashed her face. "No thoughts like that. He was being nice. No need to get carried away." The stamp on the back of her hand caught her eye. Immediately, she was aware of the sound of people tearing down tents and gathering their things. She poked her head out the front flap. Two-thirds of the tents were already gone.

"That's right! Today's the day!" Panic rushed over her as she frantically tore down her tent and folded it into a sack. She grabbed her few belongings and stuffed them into her makeshift bag. Her gaze fell on Achyut's handkerchief on the barrel beside her cot. It was a simple gift, but also the first she had received in a long time and it deserved to be handled with care. The soft square of cloth fit perfectly in her cloak's front pocket. She ladled and drank spoonfuls of water then folded her cot under her arm, picked up her bundle, and hurried toward the dock.

The massive ship, with its clean white sails and splendid grandeur, filled her with mixed emotions. On one hand, she'd be free from her Clystudine captors and able to speak with Achyut again. On the other, her venture into the great unknown, cramped aboard a ship with so many strangers, terrified her.

I can't back out now. I have nowhere else to go. I just have to stay quiet and out of everyone's way. Under the protection of her cloak, she scuttled to the back of the long, slow-moving line and studied the ship from afar. *But why is my heart beating so fast?*

Eventually, she reached the front, where Prince Achyut, Mona, and another man in a long green shirt and cream-colored trousers checked stamps and marked names off a long scroll.

"Good morning, Katria. I hope you slept well." Achyut smiled as he checked her hand.

"I, um, yes, thank you," she muttered.

"If you don't mind, would you come back to the main deck once you've been assigned your bunk and stowed away your things? There's something I'd like to show you that I know you'll enjoy."

"Um, ah, s-sure," she stammered out before she was bustled along by the family behind her. A crew member took her tent and belongings, amid her failed protests, as she moved further up in line. She decided she would ask about it later when she accidentally bumped into another of the crew.

"Oops, careful there. Are you by yourself, Miss?" asked a burly man with short black hair and covered in tattoos. He had the same style pants as the man in the green shirt but no shirt himself.

"Um, ah, yes." She pulled her cloak around her.

"You'll head down these stairs here. Two decks down and take a left at the first intersection. Pick whichever bunk is available. It'll be a bit cramped, so the room is for sleeping only. Next!" he called out as the next person in line shoved Katria aside. It didn't bother her though—she was used to being unnoticed and preferred it that way.

She followed the man's instructions and found an unclaimed, lower bunk in the corner of the large, square room filled with other women. Most of them laughed and talked among themselves, getting to know their bunk neighbors. Katria sat on the strange bed. She smoothed out the simple white sheets and pushed her hand against the white cloth pillow; it was far softer than anything she was used to.

"Hi there! I guess you're my new bunkmate, huh?" A small girl dropped down from the bunk above hers. She wore tattered clothes and her sandy blonde hair was tied in two messy pigtails.

"Eep!" Katria squeaked and drew her cloak around her.

The young girl frowned. "Hey, you don't have to be scared of me. I'm not a scary person, I promise! I'm Reena! Reena Shizuka." She smiled and offered her hand.

"U-um hello. I'm Katria. Katria Konners." She timidly shook Reena's hand.

"Katria, that's a very pretty name! Are you here by yourself?"

Katria nodded.

"I'm by myself too. Well, I've got my best friend, but he's over in the boy's cabin. I think you and I should be friends! We can be each other's travel buddies!"

"Um, ah, I don't mean to be rude but perhaps you should find another friend."

"Why?" Reena frowned. "Did I do something wrong? Do you not like me?"

"No, I just prefer to be alone. It's better that way."

"Better? Why? I think it's better to be friends. I'll change your mind while we travel!"

"I, uh, that's very kind of you but—"

"So! What's your favorite color? Or favorite food? Or favorite animal?"

"Excuse me, I have to meet someone." Katria stood and hurried out the room. She gripped her cloak as she waded through the crowds of people on the main deck of the Prospector. Her muscles clenched and her breath hastened, having never been so close to so many people, yet nearly everyone on board wanted to witness the moment the great ship set sail. She gasped and winced reflexively as someone tapped her shoulder.

"Found ya," sang Achyut.

"H-how did you know it was me? There are so many people here, I thought I'd never find you."

"From your cloak. It sticks out like a diamond among stones. Plus, it's a lot easier to see people from up there." He pointed at the crow's nest on the repaired mast. "Now if you'll follow me, we'll get you out of this crowd." He offered his hand.

She stared at it then slowly reached out for him.

Immediately, Katria noticed the *thump-thump-thump* of her heart. Her face felt overbearingly hot, yet her palms felt cold and clammy. Her mind raced but her body refused to listen. She couldn't remember the last time she had held hands with anyone, much less someone as handsome and kind as the prince. *The Prince.* His title weighed on her conscience. He was a man of prestige and propriety, someone who history would remember in song and reverence and accolades aplenty. *Who am I but a freed slave? Worse, a cursed slave. I'll only damper his glow, cast him into misfortune and misery, and sully the name of the roy—*

"I won't force you to hold my hand," Achyut uttered in a calm and gentle tone. "I just don't want you to feel lost in an unfamiliar place. I promised I'd help you."

The sun broke through the gray clouds of Katria's mind and the turbulent storm of her thoughts dissipated into a gentle rain. As she slid her hand into his, a tender warmth permeated her soul. "Okay, I'm ready."

"Good. You'll love this." Achyut smiled and led her through the gathering crowds, to the bow of the ship to a roped off area and a hastily painted sign that read "CREW ONLY BEYOND THIS POINT". He ducked under the rope and held it up for Katria. She hesitated but followed, relieved and relaxed at the lack of people surrounding her.

"I thought you might like the view from here better, especially with less people crowded around."

"That's very kind of you." Katria held the ship's railing, silently thankful for its support. Far away from the crowds and alone with the prince, her knees felt weak and her legs wobbled like jelly. Instead of the strange sensations of her body, she refocused her mind on the sights of the Bale. The tall buildings and hulking Clystudines appeared much less threatening from this distance. The city looked quite peaceful.

She listened as Prince Achyut rambled on about the ship and how it worked and how he thought of it as his second home. A tinge of sadness and envy crept up inside her. *How nice it must be to think of someplace as a second home.* She cast her eyes downward. *I don't even have one. Of course, that's the way of the world, some for all and none for some.*

"Hey, stop thinking about depressing things." He touched her shoulder. Her heart raced.

"Wh-what?" She shook herself from her stupor and glanced up at him.

"Whenever you think of something sad, you look downward and to the left."

"Have you been watching me so carefully?" Her face blushed a deep shade of pink.

"It sounds risqué when you phrase it like that." Achyut chuckled. "I've got a talent for reading people. I think it's linked to my ability to soulshare. I hoped you'd see this as a jovial occasion— a chance to start over."

"It's difficult to shake years of old habits and melancholy thoughts."

"I don't expect you to change overnight, but if you don't mind, I'd like to help you from slipping into bad brain."

"Bad brain?"

"Mhmm." Achyut nodded. "It's something my older sibling, Rakiba, taught me. They say when we're depressed or jaded or exhausted and feel like we're drowning in sorrow or anxiety, a lot of the time it's easier to just swim deeper and deeper into those feelings than try to pull ourselves out, and we think even less about ourselves than what is objectively true. Sometimes our thoughts lead us to ignore even simple tasks like eating or taking a shower. It's the beginning of the endless spiral of self-destruction. That's what they call bad brain and it's up to us to find something or someone to help us stay afloat and weather the storm until it passes. Even if we hurt now, that pain won't last forever and it will go away or at least dull itself in time."

"So, what do you do when you find yourself slipping?"

"The first thing I do is take a nap— a quick and easy way to shut off my brain and distance myself from whatever ails me. I'll also write music or sing or play my bansuri. I find comfort in sad, slow melodies. Rakiba goes on a run with their partner. Everyone has to find their own thing, but it never hurts to have friends to help pull you back out."

Katria slowly smiled then jumped as a loud 'bong' of the gong reverberated behind them.

"All hands on deck! Shift the windsails west by southwest. Lower rollers!" ordered Captain Tanoy from the helm. In the belly of the ship, the crew pulled levers and twisted knobs that cranked and turned a million gears and lowered the ironwood treads.

Achyut grinned as the ship's hull lifted off the ground. "Looks like it's time to go! Hold on tight!" The blades of the windsails caught and the ship lurched forward. Katria lost her grip, stumbled back, and fell into Achyut's strong arms.

She looked up at his dark hair and smiling face. "Oh my... ahh, m-my apologies! I didn't think our start would be so rough." Her face felt red-hot as she awkwardly pulled herself from his gentle grasp, yet that simple moment had branded itself into her mind. She returned her gaze to the land that stretched out in front of them, unable to look Achyut in the eyes.

Soon the Clystudine cities fell behind them, replaced by the Omah Mountains in the distance, capped with snow and pine trees as the Prospector gathered speed and rolled across the open plains. Giant birds and small wyverns flew overhead. Herds of wild nosorogs looked up and moo'ed as they shuffled out of the ship's course.

"Oh, this is wonderful," Katria sighed. "I've never seen anything like this before."

"Isn't it though? Neither land nor sea can hold us back! Look out world, we're coming for you!"

Slowly and surely, the freed slaves went below deck. Achyut and Katria lost track of how long they stood on the bow. The sun slipped lower and lower in the sky and past the horizon when they heard a woman's voice behind them.

"Aye, Prince Achyut, Miss Katria." Mona sauntered onto the bow with a yellow and white bundle of cloth in her hands.

"Aye, first mate Mona, what news from the captain?" Achyut replied in his best pirate impression.

Katria giggled.

"I told you to knock it off," Mona grumbled.

"Ah, come now, what's a little fun before we sail home? Tis the time of adventure and merriment!"

"Yeah, sure, whatever." She turned toward Katria, still dressed in her gray cloak. "Actually, I was only looking for you."

"Me? Oh, I, um, hope I haven't caused you any trouble." Katria fiddled with her hands beneath her cloak.

"What? No, it's nothing like that. You don't have to wear this if you don't want to, but it doesn't fit me anymore and I figured anything would be better than your shoddy cloak." Mona unfurled the bundle of cloth: a sleeveless yellow qipao dress with a white floral pattern. "You'll also burn alive under that thing once we reach the southern basin."

Katria gasped. She had never seen such exquisite clothes before, much less had any been offered to her. It was much more revealing than anything she had ever worn but after the kindness these two had shown her, she felt it would be rude not to accept.

Mona stepped closer and held the dress against Katria. "Yep. Seems about your size."

"Is it really okay for me to have this?" Katria asked.

"Of course." Mona smiled.

"I think it'd look great on you," added Achyut.

Katria blushed.

"The crew and I already handed out a bunch of older but still wearable clothes," continued Mona. "I hoped to find you first and give you something you might feel more comfortable in, but I didn't and this is one of the few pieces we have left."

Katria stared at the cloth bundle. Gratitude bubbled inside her chest and burst out like an erupting volcano. "I-I... thank you, Lady Mona. Thank you, thank you, thank you! I promise I'll always take good care of it!" She bowed over and over again.

"H-hey, no need for all that. Hahaah-ah." A tinge of pink crept into Mona cheeks. "I just wanted to make sure you were comfortable during our long journey home. It's the decent thing to do. You're welcome to shower in my quarters first. Figured you'd like the privacy."

"A warm shower... I haven't sho—" Katria stopped and held her tongue. Again, the putrid smell of her cloak assaulted her nostrils. *When was the last time I took a shower? I must look pitiful. A smelly, grimy waste of–* Her eyes fell to the floorboards.

Achyut rested his hand on her shoulder. "It's okay. There's nothing to be ashamed of."

Katria took a deep breath, gathering every ounce of courage to not run away and hide. "Um, I'm sorry, how do I get there?"

"Take the stairs below deck and turn right at the first intersection. The library will be the first two doors on your left, my room is the first on the right."

"Thank you again, Lady Mona. I deeply appreciate everything you've done, for all of us. Katria bowed again and clutched the dress close to her heart as she hurried off.

Mona sighed. "Geez... poor girl, seems like she wasn't ever shown any decency...She's like the runt of a litter of dire wolf pups."

"Yeah, but she's got a good heart." Achyut grinned at his friend. "Thanks for offering that dress by the way. Her cloak smelled like mold."

"That cloak's been abused more than her." Mona chuckled. "Still, I advise caution on your behalf. You are a prince of Lamaru, and although you may consider her a friend, it'll be up to you to teach her our customs, should she remain in our company once we return to Illadina."

"That means she'll have to know some form of martial combat." Achyut frowned. He couldn't ever imagine Katria being able to hurt anyone.

"Leave that part to me." Mona crossed her arms over her chest. "This little wolf pup will be more bite than bark once I'm through with her."

Achyut stifled a chuckle. "I'm not sure she's got much bark to begin with."

***

Katria hurried through the massive ship, happily bewildered at such a wonderful gift. She ran her hands over the yellow fabric. It was the softest cloth she had ever felt. She followed Mona's instructions and entered her quarters, amazed at the collection of swords and shields and other weapons displayed on three of the four walls.

She entered the bathroom and hung her cloak on an empty peg on the wall then stepped into the tiled shower. The warm water felt like heaven on her bare skin, so much so she simply sat under its spray for the first twenty minutes. She examined a shelf full of different shaped bottles and tested each of the sweet-smelling soaps and shampoos. She laughed as suds and bubbles tickled her skin and lathered extensively, scraping off the many years of grime that clung to her hair and body.

After an hour or so, she turned off the hot water, stepped out of the shower, and wrapped a soft white towel around her waist. It was the fluffiest towel she had ever felt. She caught her reflection in the mirror and smiled. She felt like a brand-new woman! Her eyes fell onto a strange, cylindrical device on a shelf at the base of the mirror. She picked it up and flicked a lever. A small 'eep' escaped her lips as the machine whirred to life and emitted a gentle, warm breeze. *Is this some sort of device to dry one's hair? What did Prince Achyut call it? A widget?* She examined the device a moment longer and decided it was suitable for her purposes. She found a hairbrush and went to work.

After she styled her hair to her liking, she picked up the dress, slipped it on, and fastened its buttons. Mona was right: it fit perfectly. She studied her reflection in the mirror and frowned. The dress was lovely but much more snug and sensuous than she felt comfortable in. She noticed a second piece of white fabric hidden under the dress and unfolded the soft, opaque, white shawl which covered her shoulders and draped down past her waist. Mona had thought of everything!

She stepped out of Mona's room and followed the sound of music and laughter back to the main deck of the ship. Night had fallen and the crew and freedmen sang and danced and ate in the flickering firelight. She heard the melodious trill of a wooden flute. Prince Achyut played with the crew's accompaniment as others clapped their hands and sang in time with his newest tune.

"Yar har ho, yo ho har, We'll search for treasures near and far.
Yo ho har, Yar har ho, led by the ocean's wind we go,
A maiden here, a trinket there, a pirate's life without a care.
We fight, we drink, we live, so free, a pirate's life for you and mee!
Far across the ocean blue, with bright and cloudless skies;
We'll hop from island shore to shore with adventure in our eyes! Oh!
Yar har ho, yo ho har, from the merchants to the old bazaar
Yo ho har, Yar har ho, hear our songs and voices grow!
If you sail the ocean blue then you can join our fearless crew!
We fight, we drink, we live, so free, a pirate's life for you and mee!"

Katria tore her eyes from the spectacle and spied Mona in the midst of an arm wrestle against the burly, tattooed man who greeted her when she first came aboard. She watched as Mona yelled, grit her teeth, and slammed the man's arm against the wooden barrel. Shouts and cheers rose up from her spectators. Someone placed a handled mug in front of her. Mona raised the mug and gulped it down, met by another round of acclaim and applause.

"Hah! I told you I'd win! Seven drinks in and I'm still undefeated! Who's next? Come on, I'll take on any one of yous!" She searched the crowd for her next victim, but her eyes landed on Katria instead. She couldn't help but smile.

"Actually, boys, I'll be back in a moment." Mona stood and made her way through the crowd. "Well now, look at you all dolled up! I half wondered if you drowned in the shower!"

"Oh, I um, I didn't mean to take so long, it's just that—"

"Look, whatever your reason, it's fine with me. A girl's got to have spa time to herself, you know? From what Achyut told me, you deserved every minute of it."

"Thank you, Lady Mona. It was the best experience I've had in a long time. Honestly, I can't remember the last time I was this clean, and this dress fits perfectly."

"I do have the best eye when it comes to fashion." Mona chortled. "And please, just Mona. I don't care for formalities unless they're necessary, just think of me as your big sister."

"My big sister?" Katria repeated. "I, well—"

"Or you don't have to if it makes you uncomfortable," Mona quickly added.

"No, it's not that at all." Katria shook her head. "I've always wanted a big sister. I never had any siblings nor knew either of my parents, but I often dreamed of having a big sister who would teach me all sorts of fun and useful skills."

"Then I'll be your first instructor, and I've already thought of your first lesson. Have you ever danced before?"

"Not really."

"Doesn't matter. I'll show you a popular one in Lamaru. Come on, class is in session. We're burning moonlight!"

Before Katria could protest, Mona took her hands in her own and showed her the basic steps. In a matter of minutes, the two danced across the deck of the Prospector. More and more people joined them. Achyut and his fellow musicians amended their clamorous tune into a melodious rounded waltz. Katria gazed into the accompanying crowd as partners smiled and laughed and danced with one another. Quiet tears brimmed from her amber eyes.

"No crying tonight." Mona frowned. "This is a happy occasion."

"I am happy." Katria wiped her eyes on Achyut's handkerchief. "Tonight has been wonderful. This outfit, the music, learning to dance, this is the kind of thing I wished to learn when I was a little girl. Tonight feels like something out of a dream."

"Well, let's hope you never wake up." Mona spun Katria under her arm. Katria laughed as she and Mona twirled round and round, their dresses swaying like flower petals in the wind.

"Mind if I cut in?" Achyut held Katria's outstretched hand and spun her away from Mona and under his arms, his chest pressed against her back, as they waltzed in a slow circle around the deck. He twirled her under his opposite arm, catching her in a warm embrace. Achyut smiled and stared into Katria's eyes, which shone more brilliantly than the stars above.

Katria could do nothing but smile. For one night in her long, miserable existence she forgot about her curse and powers. She didn't dwell on the pains of the past or whatever strain the future would bring and danced in the firelight under the moon. Even after the music died down and nearly everyone retired for the evening, Katria and Reena talked long into the night.

"You looked so happy dancing with Lady Mona and even more so with Prince Achyut," teased Reena.

"Ah!" Katria covered her face with her pillow. "Reena, don't say such things."

"Why not?" Reena snickered. "You both looked like you came right out of a fairytale!"

"Reena, I told you to stop, it's too embarrassing."

"I mean it! I think the two of you—Hey, what are you doing with that? Ah!" Reena covered her face as Katria whacked her with her pillow.

"I told you to stop teasing me!" Katria grinned as she smacked her again.

Reena giggled and reached for her own pillow, only to be smacked again. She slipped on Katria's sheets and fell to the floor with a loud thud. Katria playfully thwacked her again.

"Okay, you win, you win! I'll stop teasing you."

"Good. I hope you've learned your lesson about testing people's boundaries."

"You girls be quiet! People are trying to sleep!" hissed a woman from across the room.

Katria and Reena tried and failed to hold back another onslaught of giggles. They whispered until sunlight drifted through the portholes and Reena climbed back into her bed. Katria hugged her pillow and closed her eyes.

"Hey, Katria, are you still awake?" murmured Reena from the top bunk.

"Not for much longer," replied Katria.

"Oh. Nevermind then."

"It's alright, you can tell me."

"Would you be my big sister, just like Mona said she'd be yours? Please?"

From her time as a prisoner in Yaand's palace throughout her stay in the Bale as a Clystudine slave, Katria's answer to any such question had always been a short and simple no. Anyone she loved would always get hurt. That was the way the world worked... before she met Achyut and Mona, and before her first wondrous night aboard the Prospector.

"Of course, Reena. I'll do my best." They both fell into a deep slumber, eagerly awaiting whatever surprises the next day would bring.

6

Bonds

"Wakey, wakey, sleepyhead! Today is day one of your martial training." A familiar voice roused Katria from her rest, yet she did her best to ignore it. "Come on, you've already slept past noon. I hope you don't expect to sleep this late every day."

Something poked Katria's side. She rolled over and cracked one eye open. Mona stood over her, two wooden swords under her arm.

"Ah! Lady Mona, err, Mona, what can I do for you?" she asked, immediately awake.

"You can get up and join me on deck. We've got sparring practice. It's my job to make sure you can defend yourself. I'll see you in fifteen minutes." She dropped a sword on Katria's bed and left without another word.

In fifteen minutes, Katria stood at the stern of the ship, clad in leather armor, with the wooden sword in hand. She groaned at the bright sun overhead as Mona explained the basic guards and parries practiced by Lamaru's paragons.

"Now let's see if you've been paying attention. Ready?" Mona lifted her sword above her head.

"Wait, wait!" Katria clamped her eyes shut and cowered behind her blade. "Can we take things a bit slower? I've never even held a real sword."

"That's why I'm teaching you to defend yourself. Practicing against a live target is the best way to learn."

"Can we go over them again first? Please?"

Mona sighed. "Fine, but just once more."

Two hours later, Katria sat on a cot mentally battered, physically bruised, and bathed in sweat from Mona's training. *That was horrible. I just want to go back to bed. I never want to hold another sword ever again.* She rubbed her eyes and sighed.

"Not too bad for someone without any experience. Here, drink this." Mona sat beside her and offered a vial of blue liquid. "You'll feel better in no time at all."

Katria hesitantly took the vial and gulped it down. "It's so sour!" Her face scrunched up in discomfort. "And the texture, it feels like I swallowed a lump of slimy jelly." Yet almost immediately, her muscles relaxed, her breathing became regular and even her bruises lost some of their dark coloration. "Woah, what is that?"

"Dragon's blood." Mona grinned. "Not real dragon's blood, but it's one hell of an after-training stimulant. Just don't do anything strenuous for the rest of the day. I don't want to overwork your body."

"I believe that ship has already sailed," Katria grumbled.

Mona laughed. "This is only day one. I'll have you fighting like a pro by the time we reach Illadina."

Katria's stomach lurched, either from the dragon's blood or the realization this would be part of her daily routine, probably both. "Is there any other way to satisfy Lamaru's custom?"

"How about we teach you to harness minna? With your abilities as an oracle, it might be easier than swinging around a sword." The sweet sound of Achyut's voice rang in Katria's ears.

She and Mona looked up. Achyut swaggered down the stairs, hands behind his head, followed closely behind by Reena. He wore a confident grin, beige dhoti, and nothing else. Reena wore a pink knit cap and a bright yellow sundress, similar to Katria's. Her eyes lit up like stars at the sight of Katria and Mona and she raced across the deck to meet them.

"Katria! Prince Achyut just showed a bunch of us the irrivir! I didn't even know there were any animals here, this ship has everything! Have you seen them yet? They're giant brown birds, you can even ride them! Hey, are you even listening to me? Why's your face all red? Are you feeling okay?"

"I'm fine Reena, just tired," Katria stammered out, focused entirely on the ship's floorboards. Her heart raced; its thump-thump-thump pounded in her chest and ears as she dared not look up at the shirtless prince.

"That might be a good idea," Mona answered Achyut, then smiled knowingly. "Actually, Katria, I've been meaning to ask you about your powers and Prince Achyut said you worked as a confidant to the Queen of Yaand?"

Katria wrapped her arms around her stomach, her eyes still glued to the floorboards. "'Confidant' is a bit of an overstatement. I lived in the palace, yes, and I also would occasionally use my powers to aid the Queen but... but I always felt more like a prisoner than her aid." Her eyes darkened. "I'm cursed with the ability to divine an object's history simply by touching it, including larger structures like walls. The castle staff hated me for what I could do, and felt threatened that the Queen could use my power to expose any of their misdeeds or malcontent. I avoided them whenever I could, spending my time alone in the flower gardens or listening to the birds chirp around a nearby babbling brook."

"I hate those castle jerks for making you so sad," Renna pouted. "But was everyone that way? I hope there was at least someone you could talk to."

"I did have a few friends, although their names and faces have faded from my memory. One of the gardeners taught me how to grow all sorts of plants before he passed away from illness. The apothecarist showed me how to make simple potions before he was killed on a business trip. I remember a knight in black armor and his lover, a maiden from the local sika maiamorph clan. They used to bring me flowers from their travels, and I learned to use my powers to 'see' where they came from, the only positive use of my curse, and the closest I could get to visiting such faraway places. Their visits always made me smile, until one day the Queen banished them both. I never knew what they did, nor did I ever see them again."

"How did you end up all the way in the Bale?" asked Mona.

"Eventually the castle staff chased me away and told the Queen I was mauled in the forest. I wandered from town to town, doing odd jobs and such. One day a caravan passed through where I was staying, on their way to a new settlement, and any who moved there was offered land and a home. I had nowhere to go and the option seemed as good as any." She looked down at her cloak and smiled, freshly cleaned and scented with some of Mona's perfume. "I met an older couple on their way to retire by the lakeside. They gave me this cloak and taught me enough skills to properly care for myself. When the Clystudines attacked, they were deemed too weak to be of use and well... I never saw them again either. I'm sorry, I don't mean to sullen such a beautiful afternoon with my horrendous past."

"You won't ruin the afternoon, I promise," replied Mona. "And thank you for sharing. I apologize if I've caused you any discomfort bringing up such painful memories."

Katria shook her head. "The last five years of living in the Bale have dulled my pain and my memories. *Maybe further than I'd like to admit.* She thought to herself as her eyes caught the wooden sword hastily discarded after her sparring session. "But now I have the chance at a fresh new start." She looked up at Mona and smiled, then shifted her gaze to Reena and finally Achyut. "And maybe one day I can forget my past entirely and live the life I choose."

"And we'll be with you every step of the way," added Achyut with a friendly wink, "Prince's promise."

"Yeah, we'll all live happily ever after!" proclaimed Reena.

"Yeah, sure." Mona stood and picked up Katria's sword. "Good work today, Katria. I have high expectations for your progress. Now, if you'll excuse me, I've got more work to attend to."

"Awe, wait Mona, why are you leaving?" pouted Reena. "I thought we were gonna talk about our happy future together!"

"Mona doesn't do mushy talk," teased Achyut. "The former Champion of Thaniana would never be caught discussing something so sensitive as their 'happily ever after'.

"Shut it." The color of Mona's face perfectly mirrored her dress. She turned in an instant and kicked Achyut in the shin, who fell onto the deck in a mixed expression of pain and satisfaction.

"Worth it," he groaned. Reena broke into a fit of giggles.

"Hmm, I could have sworn you recently said you could dodge each and every one of my punches, my mistake," taunted Mona, a slight smirk on her lips.

"That was a kick. It doesn't count," replied Achyut.

Mona rolled her eyes and sighed. "When you're done lying around, take Katria to the apothecary and find out her and Reena's elemental flairs. You can spend the next couple hours teaching them basic minna theory."

"You two have the strangest relationship," Katria mused aloud as she helped Achyut to his feet and Mona departed down the starboard stairs.

"It is a bit unorthodox for a retainer to be so 'hands-on' in fulfilling her duties to keep me safe and provide counsel, but our strengths and differences complement each other well. She ensures I don't stray too far from commonsense and keeps my reflexes sharp, for the most part, and I in turn remind her to be a normal human every once in a while."

"I dunno, it seems like you get the worse end of the deal," added Reena as the three of them set off down the portside stairs and below the ship's main deck.

"She takes her job very seriously, and for that I am eternally grateful. I wouldn't be the man I am today if not for her strong and steady hand. For all the mental strain and fatigue I cause her, she reciprocates on me physically. Thus, our relationship remains perfectly balanced, as all things should be."

A strange, unsettling feeling churned Katria's stomach and made her chest feel tight. "Are the two of you... you know," she paused, seeking the right words and the courage to speak. "Oh how do I put this... romantically involved?"

Achyut doubled over in laughter, loud and boisterous. "Oh, gods no," he could barely speak through his guffaw. "We would have killed each other a thousand times over! No, no, no. I do love her, but our relationship is strictly professional and platonic. She's more like a sister or close cousin or aunt even."

"I see," Katria answered, hoping she hid the wave of strange relief that washed over her. *What is wrong with me today? I never had this much trouble keeping my emotions under control in the Bale. I already promised myself not to get carried away.*

"And here we are." Achyut opened the door to a small chamber, its walls lined with bottles of all shapes and sizes, managed by a Magi with short blue hair, dressed in white robes.

"Good afternoon, Prince Achyut." The Magi bowed his head. "How may I assist you today?"

Prince Achyut informed him of their mission, the both of them grabbing the necessary equipment. The Magi pricked Katria and Reena's fingers, adding a few drops of blood to separate vials, each containing a clear crystal. He placed the vials in a ritual circle, recited a simple incantation, and added a clear, viscous liquid to both vials. The circle pulsed with faint orange light.

Katria's crystal turned bright red and Reena's turned a pale green.

"Fire and earth," Achyut remarked. "At least finding your teachers will be an easy task. Katria, you'll double up with Mona for minna and sparring practice. Reena, I'll help you understand basic minna theory, but if you want an earth specialist, Joseph is one of the best."

"He's the nice man who takes care of the irrivir, right?" asked Reena.

Achyut nodded. "And now for my favorite part of harnessing minna, learning theory and Magesep runes! To the library!" Achyut wrapped his hands around their arms and pulled them out of the room and back down the long hall.

"Prince Achyut, please, slow down," begged Katria. "I'm still sore from my training."

"Yeah, even I'm having trouble keeping up," complained Reena.

Achyut slowed his pace and let go of their arms. "My apologies, both of you. I just get so excited teaching others how to harness minna. It's one of the few topics I could read about for endless hours."

Once they reached the ship's library, Katria and Reena took their seats at a long wooden table as Achyut scribbled countless diagrams, strange words, and runes until his chalkboard had been entirely covered. Darting back and forth between bookshelves, he stacked seemingly random books into a tower and dropped them onto the table with a weighty *thud*.

"Okay, so," Achyut began, bouncing up and down on his heels. "I don't want this to be daunting so I'll try to keep my explanations short and sweet. I'll explain in further detail once you both start to grasp the basics." He pointed to his largest diagram, a hexagon with lines connecting every point to each other.

"Any spell, ritual, curse or widget functions because of the intertwined nature of the six primordial facets of minna: fire, water, earth, air, binding and shatter. Each combination of two primordial facets creates a Facet of Creation, the blueprint forces that determine how tangible facets of minna will interact with each other." He turned to his chalkboard and began writing.

"For example, pure fire minna combines with binding or shatter minna to form the facets *Potentia* or *Freya*, respectively. *Potentia* is a facet that coalesces minna and creates charges. Let's say, to create an orb of fire or store electrical energy. *Freya* is its opposite; this facet expels whatever fire minna is currently stored or gathered in an area and produces cold. Fire also combines with earth, water, and air to create the facets *Tashki*, the aspect of forging and purification, *Pressura*, the aspect of condensation, and *Lux*, the emanation of light."

Achyut waited as Katria and Reena frantically scribbled down everything he said and drew.

"However, there are two exceptions to the fifteen combinations. The four tangible facets, fire, water, earth, and air, can also combine with either binding or shatter to create the Facets of *Sensu* or *Namal*—life and death. While more complex facets are created by combining the Facets of Creation with each other or another primal facet, *Sensu* and *Namal* can only be drawn out and harvested from acts that create or destroy life. Thus, both are simultaneously the most abundant facets and the hardest to obtain." Achyut flipped through the pages of the first book in his tower and showed them a page with twenty-seven glyphs.

"When anyone first learns a cantrip, minna can only be harnessed with the proper gesticulation and articulation. However, instead of common Pleb, the spell must be said in Magesep, the ancient language of the first humans on Reighja. Once a Magi has sufficiently trained their mind, they no longer have to verbalize incantations. I won't make you memorize a Magesep dictionary, but knowing these runes is the first step to creating or modifying any spell or cantrip."

For the next couple hours, Achyut lectured Katria and Reena about the intricacies of harnessing minna, only stopping to answer their occasional questions. If not for his pupils' insistent hunger, Katria and Reena knew he could have talked all night and far into the next day.

After a delicious dinner of korma and naan, Katria hurried back to the stern deck, eager to begin her minna training.

Mona sat atop a pile of wooden crates, her legs crossed as she meticulously studied an ancient tome. She looked up at the sound of Katria's footsteps and closed the hefty book, grabbed her rucksack, then stretched and slid off the barrel to meet her student. "Ready to begin? We've got a lot of ground to cover tonight. We'll start with a few basic fire cantrips, then focus on your divination abilities. I couldn't find any record of a power like yours in our list of altrusynaptic acts, so we'll end our sessions by writing down everything you've ever experienced when divining an object's history."

"Everything? That could take hours."

"Hours, days, we'll likely reach Illadina before we finish, but we've barely invented the wheel when it comes to understanding how your powers work. At least with harnessing fire minna, you've got the best teacher around." Mona reached into her rucksack and pulled out a pair of long white gloves, handing them to Katria.

"Put these on. Until you understand how to hold fire minna in your hands, you'd burn your hands off if not properly protected."

"Burn my hands off?" Katria's eyes grew to the size of dinner plates. "Mona, what kind of spells are you planning on teaching me tonight?"

"Nothing to fancy. Blinding Flame, Towering Inferno, Searing Shield, just the basics."

"Basics?" *I'm going to die tonight. I'll be killed in a horrendous explosion, engulfed by bonfires until not even ashes remain.* Katria thought as Mona explained the gesticulation and articulation for Blinding Flame, which created a flash of dazzling light and coated Katria's hands in intense heat, perfect for a distraction and sneak attack, which Mona thought suited Katria's quiet demeanor. She gave Katria a set of protective eyewear and stood on the far side of the ship.

"Let's see it!"

Katria stared at her gloved hands. Her mind suddenly went blank, forgetting everything Mona and Achyut had taught her over the course of the day. "I... I... I can't do it, Mona. What if I mess up and hurt myself? What if I hurt you?"

"No way in hell you'd hurt me, even if you detonated the spell at point-blank range!"

"Detonated?!" Newfound horror coated Katria's face.

"You're protected. And I wouldn't have you try if I thought you'd fail."

Katria bit her lip. Her hands shook as she rotated them to the proper positions. The incantation formed on her lips yet she suddenly lost the courage to speak. A tiny ball of orange fire formed in her hands.

"Come on! You've got to trust me, and yourself!" Mona shouted.

"*Caecus... Caecus lux e*—I can't do it!" A flash of light and heat erupted from her hands and expanded outward, blasting the nearest barrels off the deck and rocking the ship from side to side.

I'm dead. I knew it. I knew I would die tonight. Katria suddenly felt hot. Sweat poured over her skin and dripped from her hair. Then as soon the sensation started, it faded. Mona stood across from her, hand outstretched as the heat dissipated and the lights flickered away."

"I've seen worse." Mona closed her hand into a fist and suddenly the night turned quiet. Dazed and confused, Katria glanced around the deck. She had tripped over a single barrel, knocking it over and falling onto the deck. The gentle sway of the ship subsided as it crossed over the nearest dunes.

"What, what happened?" Katria asked in bewilderment.

"You made the equivalent of a few torches and started screaming. I nullified your spell," Mona stated blankly.

"That's it?" Katria hung her head in defeat. "I'm so pathetic. You must be so disappointed in me."

"Why would I be disappointed? I'm the one who asked you to try."

"I... I don't know, I just assumed you'd be angry. Whenever I messed up for the Queen of Yaand or the Clystudines, I'd be punished."

"I promise, you won't be punished for honing your power."

"Are... you sure? I don't think I'd ever be able to repay such kindness and patience."

"I never said you had to repay it. I enjoy teaching others and watching them grow stronger, in whatever field they choose to follow."

"You make a fantastic teacher and a wonderful big sister. I'm sure you'd be a wonderful mother as well."

"Me? A mother? Ha! That's way too far in the future for me to even consider. I've got so much to do before I even think about settling down. Besides, I still have to make sure Prince Achyut doesn't do anything too reckless. He's handful enough until I can find someone else to help keep him in check."

"That's true," Katria smiled faintly.

"But since you brought it up, what about you? Have you ever considered settling down?"

"I'm afraid it's never been much of an option for me, not with my curse. I've given up on pursuing romance."

"But is it something you'd want?" Mona pressed further.

"Well, yes." Katria looked up at the bright stars in the night. Sadness and longing crept into her smile. "It's always been something I've dreamed of. I'd love to start my own family. Perhaps it's because I never had one growing up, perhaps it's because I want to make them smile the way I couldn't, but it's a fleeting dream, just like the stars that vanish in the morning sun."

"I don't think it's impossible. You just have to work at it. The only way to break your curse is to overcome it. It's a liability, sure, but everyone has some sort of weakness. That's what it truly means to get stronger; not erasing your problems entirely but learning how to work around them."

"Thank you, Mona, for helping my train, for these pep talks, for everything. Truly, I'm blessed to call you my big sister."

Mona smiled. "Instead of getting all mushy, channel that energy and attitude into your training. Afterall, I still expect you to wake up bright and early for our sparring lessons tomorrow."

Katria bit her lip uncomfortably. "I guess I shouldn't complain. I'll just have to do my best each and every day."

"That's the right attitude." Mona nodded. "Let's go again. I've got a good feeling you'll get it right this time."

***

It was well past midnight by the time Mona and Katria finished their lesson. For the first time in her life, although her body ached more than ever before, Katria felt satisfided with the progress she made in understanding her powers, both in harnessing fire minna and breaking down individual aspects of her divination into smaller more manageable pieces. She hugged Mona and bade her goodnight to enjoy the quiet, peaceful night and gentle breeze on her own.

It was the first time she had been alone since joining the Prospector's crew. She stretched and closed her eyes, enjoying her private contemplation, when the soft trill of a flute caught her ears. *Prince Achyut? I wonder why he's up so late.* She followed the tranquil melody to the base of the central mast and climbed the ladder that led up to the crow's nest. Yet she stopped halfway up.

Achyut's voice accompanied his bansuri and the words he sung made her heart skip a beat.

"I must have loved in every age, a kindred soul on life's grand stage.

From standing on the dock alone to sailing toward a brand new home.

From palace walls to ocean blue I searched the world for someone I once knew.

A lonely prince seeking glory and pride, has found a friend he can confide in.

A gentle soul with skin so fair with amber eyes and copper hair.

A kind heart cursed by life's cruel ways, a maiden prays for peaceful days.

Do I know you from before? What is this feeling I can't ignore?

A kindred soul on life's grand stage, I know we've met before this age.

"Hmmm. Is it too obvious? What if I changed these words here? Yeah, that reads a lot better. Now to start the second verse."

"Good evening, Prince Achyut." Katria poked her head into the crow's nest.

"Ah!" Achyut fumbled his chalk and slate in the small space. "Katria, you startled me. What are you doing up so late?"

"Mona and I finished my training some time ago, but the night was so lovely, I decided to enjoy it a bit longer." She climbed up the last few rungs of the ladder and sat in the crow's nest beside him. "I heard the most enchanting melody from up here and decided to investigate." She glanced at the slate on the floor. "Are those the words to a new melody you're composing?"

Achyut grabbed for the slate and set it out of her reach. "They are, although the song isn't quite ready yet. There are still a few details I've yet to work out. I'm writing it for someone special."

"Oh?" A tinge of pink rose in Katria's cheeks. "What kind of songs do you compose at this hour?"

"Anything that comes to mind, really. I write my best songs late into the night, whether they be about good experiences or bad, my dreams, my relationships. There's something magical about this time of night, when the rest of the world is asleep. Some call it the djinn's hour."

"That's frightening. Aren't djinn's supposed to be malevolent spirits?"

"Spirits, yes, but not all are evil. They are beings of rich emotions, wanderers searching for something in our plane. While there are stories about djinn seeking power, there are also those who are looking for a lost romantic partner or simply lonely spirits in the night."

She frowned. "I can understand that last part."

"Looking for a romantic partner or being lonely?"

"Both, I suppose." She fiddled with her hands in her lap. "Do you ever feel the same?"

"I do, although not in a way most people can relate to. Always being in the public eye means always being on guard for those who wish to harm me or use my position or their relationship with me for personal gain. I don't envy Rakiba, who's slated to take the throne. They rarely have a moment to relax or be themselves. I'm quite blessed I'm able to go on these expeditions. The crew treat me as one of their own, not a prince. At home, I don't get that choice."

Katria nodded. "Once someone finds out about my powers, I always become a tool for them to get information, valuing my insight over my existence. Once my usefulness has ended, I'm cast aside and left alone out of fear from the repercussions of my curse."

"Their loss, for missing out on getting to know such a kind and wonderful person."

The faintest smile formed on Katria's lips. "And those who only see you as a prince miss the opportunity to revel in your music and spontaneity. Although, there is one thing I've been wondering since I've met you."

"Ask away, fair maiden."

"Why did you choose to go on such a dangerous adventure?" Katria looked down at her knees. "Surely, you must have had everything back home."

"It just felt like the right thing to do." Achyut smiled and looked up at the stars.

Katria studied him; his bright smile and relaxed posture could have fooled anyone, anyone who didn't look into his eyes, nearly hidden in the darkness. They were sad, like how she imagined her own often appeared, but there was something else there, a fierce determination and unyielding spirit. Fire that could never be extinguished. Light that would never fade. It drew her to him more than his station, more than his looks or wealth or abilities, more than anything she had ever experienced.

"I truly admire your strength, Prince Achyut. It's something I've never had, but if you ever chose to let down your guard, I would be honored if you could see me as someone you could confide in."

"Even on my worst days? Being a prince is a heavy burden; to make choices that weigh lives against each other is something no reasonable person should ever have to do."

"Especially on your worst days, that's when I, when anyone I'd guess, needs support from people who love them."

Achyut returned her unwavering gaze. "I believe you, and I apologize for not answering your sincere question to the best of my ability." He thought for a moment. "I left my lavish home for a dream I never had, hoping to find something I could one day believe in."

"A dream you never had?"

"That's right. You see, my older sibling, Rakiba is a tactical genius and great warrior. They've routed bandits, slain monsters, and vanquished all manner of threats to the kingdom. My parents' legacy will be a titanic ritual, a century's worth of preparation to terraform the inhabitable parts of the desert into fertile land. Even Mona is a former Champion of Thaniana, the greatest honor of the region."

"Everyone around me has found their calling or accomplished honorable and memorable feats. I haven't done anything, but by joining expeditions, I hoped I could find a dream to follow along the way. I don't want to be remembered as the spoiled younger brother of a great leader. I want to prove to the world, and myself, that I'm worthy of my station."

"I, um, I hope I'm not overstepping your boundaries, but I honestly love your ambitious nature. Your kindness and aspiring attitude toward life may very well be my favorite qualities about you. Just sitting here, talking with you, I find myself wanting to follow in your footsteps."

"Your words leave my heart aflutter and revive my weary spirit, fair maiden. Let's make a promise, here and now, to strive for a better future and choose to live the lives we want, to throw caution to the wind and live every day as our last!"

"You shouldn't say such things." Katria giggled and shook her head. "Someone might overhear us talking. I don't want to get into trouble because rumors start spreading."

"And what if those rumors turn out to be true?" he teased.

"Then Mona will make sure I don't survive her training program."

Achyut grinned and chuckled which only grew and grew until he laughed like a madman. "Oh, my goodness. You know, you aren't wrong?" He rubbed his eyes, on the verge of gleeful tears.

Katria beamed at him.

"You'll just have to surpass her gruesome training and show that your intentions of stealing me away are pure of heart."

"You tease far too much for your station, sir. Maybe I will steal you away!" She gasped, covering her mouth with her hands. Her face blushed deep crimson, utterly embarrassed at her own boldness.

"Is that a confession?" Achyut asked with a mischievous grin.

"Um, no. Not at all," she stammered out. Her mind erupted with consequences of her curse; memories of friends and those she loved who had been taken away or hurt or killed, all because she cared for them. "I'm sorry, Prince Achyut, it's late and I must be so tired I'm saying nonsense. Goodnight." Without another word, she hurried back down the ladder and darted like a djinn across the empty ship back to the safety and warmth of her bed. She hugged her pillow tightly and cried herself to sleep.

For the next few days, Katria avoided Achyut entirely and focused solely on her training with Mona. She trained for hours and hours, both with her wooden sword and at harnessing basic fire minna, until her body became exhausted and demanded sleep. Every so often, she confided in Reena, who swore to keep her big sister's secrets and helped her understand and accept her growing feelings for the prince.

After a week of training until exhaustion and distracting herself by listening to a plethora of Captain Tanoy's adventures, Katria could once more comfortably distance herself from her feelings, the passionate flames in her heart reduced to warm coals.

"Katria, might I seek a moment of your time?" Achyut asked one night before dinner.

"Of course, Prince Achyut," Katria answered politely, yet she turned away from the prince.

"I want to apologize for my brazen comments that night in the crow's nest. I was inconsiderate of your feelings and took my teasing too far. I want you to be comfortable around me. I enjoy feeling close to you, sharing stories, and being in your presence. I'd like us to be friends again."

"Thank you. I accept your apology and I'd like that very much." *Even if we can't be friends. Even if I'll have to leave you behind once we reach Lamaru.* She wanted to turn around and hug him, to let him know how deeply she cared but knew the moment she accepted him into her life, the worse his would become.

"Thank goodness." Achyut sighed and smiled. "Then will you join me in the library after dinner? I'd love to help you with your minna lessons and cultural studies."

"I'd love that too." Katria blushed and nodded. They parted ways, both hiding a faint smile.

7

A Promise Eternal

Over the next two months, Katria found herself gravitating back toward Prince Achyut, spending hours together in the ship's library. She loved learning about the arcane arts, about his country, his life, and the hundred or so random topics of which he taught. Most of all, she loved being close to him. Every day she found herself growing more and more infatuated by the handsome prince, yet from the back of her mind, a quiet voice constantly reminded her of the impending danger from forming attachments. It took every ounce of willpower to not fall for him. She felt guilty for taking up so much of the prince's time, although he assured her it was no problem at all, but the voice in her head persisted and Katria's worry and anxiety spread like a kudzu vine.

On an ordinary day, after an hour of being whacked by wooden swords, Katria sat beside Prince Achyut and Mona listening to a riveting tale from Captain Tanoy's past.

"And then the great white nafsiyat whale, fierce as a demon and strong as one too, leaped up from beneath the waves and crushed one of our smaller ships beneath its weight. The crew swam for their lives but half were gobbled up befo—" Tanoy stopped and peered across the dusty land.

"But then what? Captain, what happened next?" Katria pleaded.

"Aye, my apologies, something caught my attention." He pointed at a steady stream of smoke at the foothills of a nearby mountain. "Prince Achyut, what do you make of that?"

Achyut strode over to the mounted telescope and looked. "There's someone out there, an old woman at the base of a campfire. She's covered in blankets and waving a bright red cloth. She looks far too old to be traveling by herself and her carriage is flipped on its side. The front wheels are shattered. I think she needs help."

"I don't like this." Mona crossed her arms over her chest. "Too many reports of brigands hiding in the mountain pass and using the surrounding caves to lure in and ambush travelers."

"If there are reports of thieves and brigands that's all the more reason to help her," Achyut retorted. "Come on, it'll only take an hour or so. We can spare a bit of time." Achyut turned to Captain Tanoy. "Captain, have Joseph hitch an irrivir and skiff. We won't be gone long."

"Aye, Prince Achyut, though exercise caution. I fear Mona might be onto something. I've got a bad feeling in the pit of me stomach."

Prince Achyut and Mona found Joseph, the burly man covered in tattoos, who took care of the irrivir on the ship. He led one of the massive, flightless birds out of its pen, placed a saddle on its back, and harnessed it to a flat-bottomed skiff. On the far side of the cargo hold, Achyut and Mona turned a pair of large wooden wheels connected to the pulley system that opened the hold on the stern of the ship and lowered it to the ground. Joseph led the bird out of the ship. It ruffled its feathers and stretched its wings as it basked in the warm sun. Joseph hoisted himself onto the bird's back. Mona and Achyut boarded the skiff.

"Wait! Wait! I'm coming with you!" Katria called as she dashed down the stairs and out the stern of the ship. She wore a mishmash of cloth armor over her dress with a shortsword strapped to her waist, leaning against Achyut's arm as she caught her breath. "I'm coming too," she panted.

"Are you sure?" Achyut held her, his eyes full of worry. "It could be dangerous. I don't want you to get hurt."

"So, you're okay with *us* getting hurt? Thanks!" Mona shouted from the skiff.

Joseph snickered. Achyut shot them a glance.

"I'd feel safer if I'm with you." Katria's cheeks flushed pink. "And if she's in trouble, I want to help. I can use my talent to verify the truth." "I hadn't thought of that and it would be incredibly helpful." Achyut smiled at her. "Okay, you can come along too, just stay close to me. If something goes wrong, I'll protect you."

"Yes, of course. That was my intention." Katria giggled as she clung to his arm and joined the others in the skiff.

"Ya!" Joseph flicked the irrivir's reins and the bird took off across the desert floor. Its large, flat feet slapped against the sand and in no time at all the rocky foothills of the Omah Mountains towered above them. Mona kept her eyes on the old woman through a spyglass. She stopped waving her flag as the skiff grew closer and waited for their arrival.

"Hello ma'am," Prince Achyut called as the skiff approached her carriage. "We saw your smoke and flag from our ship! Are you in need of assistance?"

The woman didn't reply, but only continued waiting for them.

"Joseph, check the surrounding area. Make sure no one is hiding nearby." Mona commanded as the skiff slowed to a halt.

"Yes, Lady Mona." He jumped off the bird's back and knelt on the ground. He closed his eyes, and placed his palm on the earth. Invisible waves of minna poured through his hand and spread across the ground like a growing puddle. Plants and animals broke apart the waves and reflected their silhouettes back to Joseph's mind.

"I can only trace our group, the woman, and a few jaracuts hiding in the nearby bushes. No other humans or maiamorphs are hiding on the ground or in the surrounding caves."

"I guess that's good enough. Still..." Mona's eyes flitted around their surroundings. She hefted her aruval off her back and held it at guard, gathering minna that sparked and crackled in her off hand.

Prince Achyut approached the woman, followed by Mona, Katria, and Joseph.

"Why hello, young ones," the woman called out weakly from the side of the campfire. She sat very still with a large blanket across her lap. "Thank the gods you saw my fire. I thought no one would pass by and I'd die here all alone."

"We're happy to help, ma'am. I am Prince Achyut from the Dynasty of Lamaru. These are my friends: Mona, Katria, and Joseph. What ill has befallen you?"

"My husband and I were headed to the Queendom of Yaand when we were attacked by bandits crossing through the mountain pass! We tried to outrun them, but our carriage got caught on the rocks. I was flung from its side and landed in a crevice near here. I broke my leg. They spooked my tapi and she ran off. Then the ruffians grabbed my husband, ransacked our carriage, and ran away. That was six hours ago. Oh, my poor husband!" She held her face in her hands and wept.

"I'm so sorry to hear that," replied Prince Achyut. "But you're more than welcome to travel with us. We've got spare cots and the proper medical widgets to set your leg."

"No, no!" the woman cried. "I have to make it to Yaand! I have a very important mission to accomplish."

"And what is that mission?" asked Mona.

"I have a special minna focus to deliver to the Queen. My husband and I are tinkers from Thaniana." She brought out a small amulet from underneath the blanket. "Thankfully, I grabbed it when they attacked."

"What Guild do you belong to? Someone with such lofty customers must have the reputation to match," Mona interrogated the old woman further.

While Mona asked question after question, Katria conducted her own investigation. Unlike people, objects always told the truth. She wandered off unnoticed, a skill she mastered in her long years of solitude, and quietly examined the wreckage. She closed her eyes and touched various parts of the carriage, discerning their origins and pasts.

The carriage had been attacked by bandits or thieves, yet she couldn't see how long ago. She opened her eyes and touched a small piece of rope. It had in fact been used to harness a tapi—a strong four-legged beast, smaller than a nosorog, with a short, spaded trunk, tusks and a dark-brown and cream-striped pelt.

In all regards, the woman's story seemed to be true, yet Katria remained dubious. She crouched, examined the underside of the carriage, and smiled at her discovery: crumbs. There were hardly any of them— bits and pieces of bread or rations— but that didn't matter. A single crumb was more than enough to find out where it came from. She closed her eyes and concentrated.

"I understand this is a very important delivery to you and your Guild but you are in no shape to continue on your journey. We'll drop you off at the gates of Thaniana and you can tell the Guild what happened." Achyut sighed and rubbed his eyes as the old woman made up excuse after excuse to have them bring her supplies, fix her carriage, and allow her on her way. She insisted her husband and tapi were alive and she needed the resources to find them.

Mona glared at the stubborn old woman. "Listen, you old hag, if you continue to be obstinate, we'll be on our way. We've no obligation to hel—"

"Prince Achyut?" Katria called as she stumbled from the wreckage of the wagon. She looked frighteningly pale. "I'm feeling rather faint, would you mind taking me back to the Prospector?" She leaned against him and grasped his arm.

"Katria, what happened?" He held her close and studied her face. Her eyes were wide and alert as she dug her nails into her dress. *Something's wrong*, he thought.

"I think it was something I ate," she groaned and clutched her stomach. "It must have been at breakfast. I don't think those sausages were cooked all the way through. Please, let's go. We can bring this kind woman whatever she needs."

The woman glanced at Katria.

Achyut looked at her in confusion. "But you didn't eat any sausages for breakfast, just a few pieces of toast with jam and a handful of fruits."

Katria stared at Achyut as if she wanted to punch him.

"The girl's onto us! Get them!" cried the old woman as she threw the blanket aside and hurled a dagger at Achyut's chest. Mona blocked the dagger with her sword.

"They're hiding in the trees!" Katria yelled as seven bandits sliced their ropes and dropped from the trees and cliffs above, all armed with clubs, swords, and knives. Achyut and Joseph drew their swords. Mona summoned an electric minna shield and blocked their initial attack then turned and parried a second blow. Her gloves and boots swelled with fire as she dueled four of the brigands.

The fifth bandit kicked Joseph in the stomach and off the rock where he stood. Joseph grabbed his leg as he fell and brought him down with him. They tumbled to the base of the hill losing their weapons in the process. Joseph stood first and cracked his knuckles menacingly. He rushed the bandit with his fists and teeth clenched.

The sixth and seventh bandits attacked Prince Achyut, who defended himself well with his sword, but not well enough, as a swift kick to his ribs threw him from his feet.

"Prince Achyut! Help!" Katria yelled as the woman held her in a chokehold with a dagger to her neck.

"Boris, come with me!" the old woman shouted. A burly bandit dressed in black disengaged from Mona and landed by the old woman's side. "The rest of you take out his guard! Come on, little prince, come save you dear woman!" She laughed and kicked aside a wooden door, painted like rocks, and dragged Katria into the cavern behind it.

"Go! Save Katria!" Mona called as she blocked and parried the bandits' strikes. The two bandits who attacked Achyut ran at her from behind only to be blasted off the side of the cliff with a white-hot explosion. "We'll be right behind you!"

Achyut rushed into the dimly lit cave, his sword in his right hand, his bansuri in his left.

Boris the bandit squatted on a ledge above the mouth of the cave, hidden in darkness. He silently drew a dagger from his belt.

Achyut walked further into the musty cavern which separated into four tunnels. He heard Katria's screams from further down one of the tunnels on his left but before he could give chase, movement caught his eye in the reflection of his sword.

The dagger hit Achyut's watershield inches from his chest and clattered to the ground. Boris jumped down from the ledge and rushed the young prince, blocking the way out, holding a mace in one hand and a second dagger in the other. Achyut blocked the bandit's swipes with both his sword and bansuri. Their grunts and groans and the clanging of their clashing weapons filled the cavern with an eerie ballet of battle.

"Any chance you'd be willing to talk this out? I'll pay you double if you help me save Katria."

Boris said nothing and slashed at him again.

"Yeah, I didn't think so." Achyut summoned a rope from the end of his bansuri which wrapped around a ledge and pulled him high into the air. He released the rope and plunged toward Boris with his sword, but the man was quicker than he expected and evaded his attack. Achyut raised his sword above his head and held his bansuri in a front guard as Boris closed the gap between them. Achyut stood and steadied his breath. Once more, they came face to face.

"You seem like a decent fellow, I'd hate to kill you. Tell you what, I'll pay you triple. Final offer."

Boris swung again. The Prince parried his mace and stepped aside as Boris launched his dagger toward his exposed leg. Achyut summoned a second watershield. The dagger clattered against the cavern floor but Boris charged ahead, knocked Achyut's sword aside, and flung his foe from his feet. Achyut slammed into the stone wall.

"Boring conversation anyway," he coughed.

Again the bandit advanced, but the young prince summoned a second rope which tied itself around a metal torch mounted above one of the tunnel entrances and pulled him across the cavern floor to safety. Boris's mace smashed against the cavern floor where he had been seconds ago.

Achyut heard Katria's screams. He had to finish this quickly, but Boris's constant attacks snatched away any chance he had to harness enough minna for a more powerful cantrip or play his bansuri.

He looked around the cave and tunnels for anything to turn the tide of battle. He grinned wolfishly. He had to act before Boris caught onto his plan, so he did the only thing he could to buy time and rushed the bandit like a madman. He closed the gap between them and abandoned all guards or blocks.

Achyut's rabid swings kept the bandit on edge as he fought through his increasing pains and pushed Boris to the entrance of the rightmost tunnel, filled with crates and barrels and supplies. He summoned a third rope and whipped his bansuri around like a lasso. Boris dodged out of the way, just as Achyut hoped. The rope wrapped around a large barrel. Achyut pulled as hard as he could. The barrel slammed into Boris and threw him against the side of the tunnel. Achyut roped a small crate and smashed it against the bandit's head. Boris dropped to the floor. He rubbed his head, stood, and rushed Achyut again, but the prince had stolen back the few precious seconds he needed. He summoned four large icicles that pierced and dislodged the stone above the mouth of the tunnel. Boris stared at him. The rubble fell and sealed him on the other side.

Achyut leaned against the cave wall and caught his breath. He stood in a shallow pool of his own blood, the price of his gamble, but one he was willing to pay double—no, triple—to save Katria. He summoned a small orb of water and cleaned and closed his wounds the best he could, although his work was rather sloppy. *I thought studying minna theory was enough.* He bit his lip and winced in pain. *Guess I need a bit more practice. Oh well.*

He picked up one of Boris's daggers and tucked it in his belt behind his back then hurried down the tunnel toward Katria's last shouts. He ran and ran and skidded to a halt at the end of the empty tunnel.

Where did they go? I know I heard her voice from here. There must be another secret entrance. Sure enough, as he retraced his steps, he found his old handkerchief, caught behind a round boulder. He sheathed his sword and pushed the fake stone aside then continued down the dimly lit tunnel.

"I don't know how you figured out my trap, but I'll make sure the young prince pays handsomely for your return." The old woman kicked the ladder leading down the hole aside. She lit several torches and a large brass flambeau then hoisted it to the roof of the cave and tied its rope.

"Now you be a good little wench and stay in your cage while I prepare for his arrival."

"You'll never get away with this! He'll save me! We'll have the entire crew chase you down until you've paid for your crimes!" Katria kicked the woman's shin.

The woman howled in pain and grabbed Katria by the throat. She drew her dagger and pressed the point to Katria's neck. A small bead of blood formed at its tip.

"I disagree. If he wants to see you live, he'll comply. When Boris knocks him out and brings him here, your crew will pay anything to get their prince back. You're nothing but my contingency plan. And on the off chance Boris fails, if you try to warn the prince or if he doesn't heed my demands, I'll gut you like a fish. Either way, your life doesn't matter." She threw Katria against the floor, slammed the iron gate shut, and returned to her preparations.

Katria stayed quiet, huddled against the cavern wall, a small silver key clutched in her hands. She watched the old woman, waiting for a sufficient distraction, when the sound of echoing footsteps up above caught her ears.

Prince Achyut was coming to save her!

A small whirlpool materialized at the base of the hole. Achyut jumped down, bansuri and sword in hand as the old woman hurled a dagger at his chest. He blocked her first, second, and third daggers then lunged toward her, hatred in his eyes. She threw a fourth dagger which sliced through the rope that suspended the large brass flambeau above the room. It crashed toward Achyut who flung himself out of the way.

"Shit!" He cursed as he dropped his sword.

The woman sprinted toward him and kicked it across the cavern. Achyut moved his bansuri to his lips.

The woman brandished a fifth dagger. "If that flute gets even halfway to your lips, I'll gut your lady friend and make you watch. Drop it, boy. Be reasonable. Let's have a little talk, you and I. There's no reason either of us has to end up dead."

Achyut lowered the bansuri but still held it at guard. He looked over his shoulder at Katria. She flashed something shiny in her hands. *She has the key! I just have to keep this old hag talking.*

"Alright, you win. Tell me your demands." He held one hand up in surrender.

"First, drop the flute." The woman revealed a sixth dagger and aimed it at Katria. "This one won't kill, but it will definitely hurt." She glared at him.

Achyut bit his lip and frowned. He dropped his bansuri at his feet.

"That's a good little prince. Now you and I are going to go outside, and if your crew is still alive, you'll tell them to surrender as well. We'll take your skiff back to your ship and you'll have the crew lower down whatever valuables and food you have. Got it?"

"I understand. Release Katria to me and I'll do as you say."

"Oh no no no no," The woman laughed. "This little bird is going to stay in her cage as my insurance policy."

"How do I know you'll release her once you've gotten what you want?"

"You'll just have to trust me on that."

"You don't seem like the trusting type. I've got a better idea. You release her to me now and we'll be on our way. You get to live. and I won't send Lamaru's army to hunt you down."

"Seems like an awful lot of trouble for such a small group of bandits," the woman twirled the daggers in her hands, "And you don't seem to be in a good bargaining position, boy."

Achyut glared at her.

Katria silently reached for the lock. She palmed the key in her hand and clicked it open.

The old woman heard the sound and spun around but not before Achyut drew Boris's dagger and lunged at her. She blocked his strike, caught his wrist and twisted. Achyut cried in pain and dropped the dagger. The woman knocked him off balance and forced him to the floor.

"No!" Katria screamed. She rushed out of the cage and reached for Achyut, as if her words alone could pull back the woman's hand.

The old woman plunged the first blade into the prince's leg and twisted. Achyut screamed in pain. She raised the second above her head.

Rage filled Katria's heart. She grabbed a torch and smashed it over the bandit leader's head. The wood splintered as she collapsed, limp and lifeless on the ground.

Achyut pulled the dagger out of his leg and dropped it, his breath heavy as he staggered to the cavern wall. Katria rushed to his side and lowered him to the ground. Achyut tried to seal the wound, but the cut was too deep for his simple cantrip to work.

"You're bleeding! You're bleeding because of me!" Katria wrapped her shawl around his wound and applied pressure as best she could. "I knew it! I knew I would bring you ruin!"

"I'm bleeding because of that old bitch." Achyut ripped long strands of cloth from his kurta. "You saved me." He handed the strips to Katria who wrapped and tied each piece around his wound. After the seventh wrap, the wound no longer bled through. Achyut sighed in relief.

Katria hid her face. "You're hurt because you came to save me. You're hurt because of my curse." She wrapped her arms around her knees and hugged them to her chest.

"Of course I came to save you! We would have walked right into that ambush if not for your early warning. You saved us and just now you've saved me again! And don't you dare blame yourself for us investigating in the first place."

"But don't you understand? Things will only get worse from here on out. I should have never come with you on your journey. I'm so sorry. I never wished to bring you harm. You and Mona are such wonderful people."

"Katria? Katria, look at me," Achyut demanded.

She raised her puffy eyes to his.

"You are not a burden and will never be a burden. I'm happy you came on this journey with us. I love spending time with you. I love being near you and learning about your life. I love your willingness to learn; your curiosity and your kindness. And you're stronger than you realize. You keep growing stronger, day by day. Even if you don't see it, I do, and I'll say it over and over again, until you believe in yourself the way I believe in you."

"You shouldn't say such kind things." Her heart raced, adrenaline entwined with emotions she promised herself she'd never feel. "A girl might get the wrong idea and think you were confessing your feelings."

"I am. Do you feel the same?"

Katria blushed, her cheeks dark crimson. She bit her lip and looked away. "I've never been as happy as this time I've spent with you. You make me feel safe. You're brave, and strong, and smart, and I love how much you care about everyone. I've learned so much by your side; about minna, about the world, about myself. When I'm with you, I want to be better. I want to protect you. You make me feel like the luckiest girl in the world and I want to do the same for you. And... I can't deny you're the most charming and handsome man I've ever met."

She turned to him, pain and longing in her eyes. "I want you to be happy and that's precisely the reason we can't be together. I won't let my curse bring you misfortune. I won't let my curse—"

His hands on her shoulders, Achyut pulled her close and kissed her soft, sweet lips. Katria melted. She wrapped her arms around his neck and kissed him back, the two of them locked in a warm embrace. Achyut gently pulled away, peering into her amber eyes, as he tucked a strand of copper hair behind her ears. She returned his amorous gaze with bewilderment and avid desire.

"Wha... what was that for?" Her lips quivered, already missing the taste and feel of his.

"I want to be with you. Whatever misfortune your curse brings, we'll face it together. I want to make you happy and see you smile. I'd rather face a thousand curses than not have you by my side."

"Prince Achyut... I—" She held his face in her hands and leaned in once more.

"Prince Achyut? Katria? Are you down there?" Mona called from the larger cavern above.

"We're here and relatively unharmed," Achyut called back. "My leg is a little messed up though. I'm not sure I can climb up."

Mona sighed. "As long as the two of you are safe, that's all that matters. Joseph's making a rope and sling out of binding minna. We'll lower it down and haul you two up. Just give us a few minutes!"

"Take all the time you need." Achyut called back to Mona. He cupped Katria's face in his hands and smiled. Katria blushed and met his gaze.

"Prince Achyut, please, never let me go."

"I never intended to." He kissed her soft, sweet lips once more and she reciprocated with the veritable passion that gripped her heart.

She broke their prolonged and gentle kiss and buried her face in his chest. "Promise me."

"I promise; for as long as I live and well after that." He held her close as they waited for their escape.

End Part I

8

Interlude

Year 149 A.D. (After Demotion); present day

"Oh, how romantic!" Amira clasped her hands together and swooned. "They must have really loved each other! I can't wait till I find someone like that. He'll be brave and handsome and witty and—" She broke into a fit of giggles.

"Let's not be too hasty. You're still very young," replied King Jordan, a tinge of discomfort in his voice. "There'll be plenty of time for that sort of thing when you're much, much older."

"Bleh!" Naemin stuck out his tongue in disgust. "I didn't know this story had gross, mushy stuff involved! Dad, can we skip the mushy bits? I wanna hear more about swords and minna and sandships!"

"Absolutely not!" reprimanded Amira. "The romantic elements are the best part of this story! You're just too young to understand how wonderful they are."

"Nu-uh! They're stupid and boring and gross and a waste of time, but I guess that's why you like them!"

Amira's nostrils flared. "Why, you little..."

"Calm down, kids," King Jordan intervened. "Naemin, that was very rude. Apologize to your sister, now."

Naemin crossed his arms over his chest and huffed in annoyance.

"Now." King Jordan closed the hefty book. He glared steadily at his son. Naemin bit his lip. He knew this was his last chance to get out of trouble unscathed.

"I-I'm sorry, sis. You're not boring or gross or a waste of time."

"Hmph. Little twerp…"

"Amira…"

"Fine, fine. I accept your apology."

Jordan sighed. "There, that wasn't so hard. Now, if you two behave, we can continue our story after lunch and your minna harnessing lessons. I won't skip over any bits of the story, including the mushy parts, but I won't be too vivid with my details either."

"When do we get to the part about the Collapse?" asked Naemin excitedly.

"In due time, as with all things, but what I'm telling you now is just as integral for you to understand Prince Achyut's story."

"Integral?"

"It means something is necessary or essential," added Amira.

"But how is Prince Achyut linked to the Collapse? And how does Katria fit into all of this? It seems like she's only in his story to add in mushy stuff."

"Well, she did just save his life and Achyut's love for Katria and their relationship is a force that drives his behavior and shapes his ideals. In fact, examining a character's development, applying empathy, and trying to understand their motives are all crucial aspects of active story-telling, and accepting life itself, even more so than ferocious battles or passionate romance.

"You see, many historians believe the mystery surrounding Prince Achyut and Katria is linked to the Collapse, although we have little proof to verify this theory, and understanding him as a person may help us uncover the truth. That is why this record and why so many others are written: to allow us to look back and view events through the eyes of those who lived in such times. We can learn so much from our past and use that knowledge as a tool to guide our future. But for the present, let's break for lunch. Your mother will wish to join our little reading circle for the next part of our story. She's studied the Battle for Banjiha and the terraforming ritual quite extensively."

"Ooooh!" chorused Naemin, Amira, and Saffi. The afternoon's anticipation bubbled up inside all three of them.

General Gil stood up and stretched. "Well then, the sooner we depart for lunch, the sooner we can begin your training and the sooner we can continue this riveting tale."

"Precisely," agreed King Jordan. "And perhaps you'd like to narrate the next few chapters, my old friend? I'd like to see how well your storytelling has improved from our own lessons and conversations."

"It would be an honor, my liege."

"Father, may I examine that book? I promise I'll join you and the others for lunch in a moment," asked Amira as Naemin and Gil departed.

"Of course my dear." Jordan handed the book to his daughter.

Amira thanked him as he left and set the book on a thatched ottoman. She knelt in front of it, closed her eyes, cleared her mind and opened the historical text. Flipping page after page after page, she sighed as a frown spread across her lips.

"I don't understand, Saffi. I've got an open mind. I'm mentally prepared to learn about the past, yet I still can't make out any words from these runes."

"Maybe King Jordan was joking about them transforming into an understandable state. They could just be written differently on purpose."

"I don't think so. You saw how vivid those pictures were, the ship, the dragons, Katria and Achyut in the cave. I definitely believe some sort of illusion was at work, and since father didn't harness any minna, the only source could have been from the book itself."

"That makes sense," Saffi admitted, just as perplexed as her friend.

"Then what am I lacking? I've studied everything from politics to biology, minna theory to fashion. I know what I'm doing. Out of all of Lamaru's history, what makes Prince Achyut's tale any different?"

Part II

9

Changing of the Guard

Year 1 B.C. (before the Collapse)

Dear Nuhir Rakiba,

It's been so long since your last letter, I hope you and Amarak are both in good health. I'm pleased to announce our return to Illadina a month ahead of schedule, with countless adventures to share: meeting the leaders of Clystudine Confederation, freeing over three hundred slaves, routing bandits, and ousting two dragons from the northern mountains. I didn't even know dragons still roamed across Reighja!

Additionally, I cannot wait to introduce you to Katria Konners, an oracle and former adviser to the Queen of Yaand, whose divination abilities equate to those of a soulseeker! Most importantly, she's the most mesmerizing woman I've ever met. She's quiet, reserved, kind, caring, and a wonderful singer (although much too embarrassed to perform in front of anyone else). We talk for hours and hours every day. She and Mona have become fast friends and watching her train tirelessly has helped me redouble my efforts. I feel like a new man in her presence, more uplifted and sagacious than ever before. I'm sure you'll adore her as much as I do.

Per your last letter, I'm filled with grief learning your previous retainer has laid down their sword; I was quite excited to meet them upon our return. Still, I can think of countless individuals willing and able to serve the next heir to Lamaru. Second, how are our parents' and their preparations for the terraforming ritual? I miss them dearly, but with our early return, and a large addition to our crew, we have plenty of fresh hands looking for jobs, if such labor is still needed. Lastly, have you any news from the supposed soulseeker in Banjiha? For two non-royal individuals to show such aptitude (both Katria and Lilith), fate must have something grand in store for us! I look forward to hearing from you soon and seeing you, Mother, and Father, sooner than expected.

Your loving little brother, Prince Achyut

PS. Both Mona and Tanoy send their best wishes.

Prince Achyut stood on the bow of the Prospector, his dreadlocks drifting in the warm, afternoon breeze, as he reread his letter for the umpteenth time, finally rolling it into a cylindrical, tin canister. Its cap tightly secured, he slid his fingers down the line of embedded minna stones. Suddenly, the container shrank to the size of his thumb. He tied a strip of woven fabric around two pins that stuck out from the center and turned around as the serenade of Katria's voice filled his ears, a small brown bird perched atop her head.

"My dear, you know I love the sound of your singing, which would surely drive a siren mad, but I'd rather not be late for sparring practice, otherwise Mona will have me running laps around the ship... again."

"Awwe, just one more, please?" Katria whined, frowning as she gazed upon her beloved.

"Alright, just one more," Achyut sighed and smiled. "You know I can't refuse your angelic face."

Katria beamed brighter than the setting sun. "We'll be quick, I promise." She returned her attention to the little bird. "La–da–dee, la–da–dee~" The bird mimicked her tone.

"La–dee–da–dee–da–dee–doh~" she continued, and still the bird matched her perfectly. "La–dee–da–dee–doh~". They finished their duet and Katria offered her finger as a perch. The bird happily obliged. "I would have been much less lonely if I had you as my companion in Yaand, little one." The bird chirped their song once more and Katria giggled at its enthusiasm. "Now you have a very important job to do: make sure this letter reaches Nuhir Rakiba in Banjiha." She offered her hand to Achyut.

"I've no doubt she'll find her way," Achyut said as he slipped the fabric over the bird's neck, the metal tube resting against her feathered chest. "Loyal swifts are Lamaru's best. Their ability to navigate long distances is unmatched by anything I've ever seen." He scratched her neck with one finger. "Take Nuhir Rakiba's response and find us in An'ard."

The bird chirped in understanding.

"Safe travels!" Katria threw her arms above her head, vaulting the bird into the air, who spread her crescent wings and soared into the sky. She flapped higher and higher, catching Reighja's prevailing winds and gliding along its warm currents to Lamaru's central region of Banjiha.

The little loyal swift flew straight and true, eating small, airborne insects, sleeping on windborne wings, safe in the sky from ground predators, and too meager of a meal for the larger birds and wyverns of Reighja. The desert stretched on and on below, an endless sea of yellow sand, broken up by rocky islands and the occasional green and blue of a lonely oasis. She chirped with pride and accomplishment as red clay walls formed on the horizon, growing taller and closer as she circled the city, her sharp eyes dotting back and forth, searching clusters of buildings, wind-towers, and the narrow streets between them, finally landing on a bell-tower at the edge of a crowded, stone plaza.

Her eyes swept across the groups—humans, maiamorphs in their humanoid form and maiamorphs in their animalistic form—attending colorful stalls and going about their daily lives. Groups of urosi—hulking, stalwart, bear-like creatures—carried crates of goods and raw materials. Giant hawks and ravens flew overhead. A smiling, furred woman with orange and black stripes and triangular ears sold large slabs of cooked meat. A man sold trinkets, souvenirs, watches, and wares hanging from his antlers. Whether from a coffee shop window or a simple stroll downtown, the city was filled with the wonderful, dazzling majesty of life in every form. Finally, the swift found her recipient and flew down to meet a great, golden dire wolf; running up and down the stalls with a child on its back.

The swift chirped and whistled as the wolf slowed and then stopped, before landing on its massive head, right between two floppy ears.

"Hey, why did you stop, doggy?" Asked the child, who pulled back her messy, black hair and scratched a patch of scales intermingled with her skin. She gasped, her slender, serpentine pupils widening in excitement, "Look, Nadia! There's a bird on its head! And it's carrying something!" She called to her older sister buying food two stalls down.

"I can see that, Netheli," answered Nadia, her arms laden with delectable baked sweets. She turned to the wolf. "Do you have to deliver this to your friend?"

"Woof!" he replied and knelt to the ground, so Netheli could climb off his back.

"Awwe, that's no fun, but thank you for playing with me!" Netheli hugged the golden wolf, wagging his tail in reply. "We'll have to play again soon!"

"Come on, Netheli, let's go find momma and enjoy these sweets." Nadia took her sister's hand and the pair wandered off into the crowd.

The dire wolf trotted across the stone plaza, the little swift perched atop his head, to the opposite end of the bell tower, where the central embassy of Banjiha stood. He strolled up its ramada and through the main entrance, pausing to collect his daily treat from the reception desk, and up the first two flights of stairs. Hearing his master's voice down the hall, he pushed open the door to the conference room, where three figures all fought for the future of Lamaru.

"We have an unexpected visitor," announced the towering, blonde man with piercing golden eyes, dressed in white paragon's armor.

"Who let this dog in?" grumbled the woman behind a palm desk, dressed in a colorful sarong and ill-fitting buttoned jacket. A white turban with colorful feathers hid her blonde hair and denoted her status as the newly appointed Grand Vizier of Banjiha. "Uriel, please lock the door. These constant distractions are growing irksome."

The wolf growled and trotted over to his master, resting his head in their lap.

"Amarak apologizes for the intrusion, Grand Vizier Lilith," answered the third, striking individual, with rich, dark skin and umbral dreadlocks, whose unyielding confidence and charm repealed Lilith and Uriel's somber auras. "You've returned earlier than expected. Did you have fun playing with Netheli and Nadia?" Rakiba asked, eyeing the loyal swift atop Amarak's head and offering their finger as a perch. The bird hopped onto their finger and they retrieved the metal canister. They slid their finger over the minna stones, which expanded to fit their grip, and pocketed it. The swift chirped and returned to Amarak's head, both bird and wolf settling down in the corner for a nap.

"Now then, back to business." Rakiba flashed Lilith and Uriel a dazzling smile.

"There is no 'back to business'," answered Lilith, her tone as frozen as a glacier in a blizzard. "I have already told you, Nuhir Rakiba, that under the late Grand Vizier's orders, I am to finish his term and succeed his position. My first directive, with full votes from my council and ministers, is to secede from the Dynasty of Lamaru and create an autonomous state. You failed to protect us from recent maiamorph attacks while your tax policies take everything we own for your terraforming ritual, with no guarantee of success or shared return. The people have spoken. Your reign is over."

"Grand Vizier Lilith," Rakiba began carefully, "The terraforming ritual is for everyone in our kingdom and as Banjiha is the most wealthy of the six provinces, you are expected to contribute proportionally. No region is being forced to impoverish its citizens for this magnanimous occasion. Your citizens also stand to gain the most arable land and freshwater, as your region contains the fewest tributaries from the Hayi

River. Banjiha's wealth and usable land will more than quadruple if you help us now, instead of planning this secession. I have word from the Padishah the ritual will be ready in a mere three months. Is that not reason enough to pause these talks and retable them after the ritual's completion?"

"I will not bow to empty promises from a fading crown," answered Lilith in an unwavering voice. "I know what you're trying to do, Nuhir Rakiba. Three months is enough time to gather your forces and lay siege to my city, bleeding us dry until we surrender. I will not give you that advantage. I will not put *my* people at risk. I am happy to negotiate trade relations, but I will not step down nor be pushed aside. From one soulseeker to another, I suggest you leave."

Rakiba narrowed their eyes, returning Lilith's resolute gaze. "Your succession is not my only cause for concern. I stand firm against your policy to displace all of Banjiha's maiamorph citizens and the Watchers report that your arrangements are not as affable as you claim. There are rumors in the streets that extremists in your favor plan to use more violent methods than relocation. I will not allow you to harm any of *my* citizens."

"First of all, the maiamorph savages you so wish to protect will be given resources and leave without incident. I do not, nor have I ever endorsed violent altercations. The actions of a few extremists have been punished accordingly. Banjiha has voted on a new age, an age of humanity, one not defiled by maiamorph half-breeds. Second, you are a fool to trust those religious freaks, who seek humanity's re-enslavement under their false dragon gods. I will not say it again; let us be, and we will not turn to bloodshed, but any declaration of war will be met with adequate force. Our meeting is over, Nuhir Rakiba. For your personal safety, I suggest you board your ship and leave."

Uriel placed his hand on the hilt of his greatsword.

Rakiba towered over Lilith, their eyes shifting to the color of a starless sky. "Your apathy and hatred toward my people is appalling. Now you threaten me under your guise of peaceful negotiations? From one soulseeker to another, I will unveil your true intentions here and now."

Lilith laughed, her own eyes shifting to the color of coal at the bottom of a desolate mine. "If you want to know why myself and so many others refuse to live with such uncivilized sub-humans, be my guest, you of all people understand the persuasiveness behind our power."

***

Rakiba stood in the middle of a jungle surrounded by towering palm trees, a passenger who saw Lilith's memories through her own eyes. They laughed and played and swung through the trees with her younger brother, whom Rakiba recognized as Uriel. Suddenly, a woman screamed near the base of the tree. Lilith and Rakiba leaped down from the highest branches. Uriel followed.

Their tent had been slashed to limp, wispy fabric in the wind, the warm fire stomped down to cold ashes. All of their supplies lay scattered across the ground; broken jars, crushed vegetables, and stains of what was previously fruit. Three fearsome urosi surrounded their parents and trapped them against a large boulder.

"Please! Take whatever food you want!" begged the old human man. Rakiba had never seen him before but instantly recognized him as Lilith's father.

"All you have are bread and vegetables," pouted one of the fearsome bear-like creatures.

"We've been so starved, we need something more meaty!" added another.

"And we have two sources of fresh meat right in front of us," added their chief who licked his lips hungrily.

"We'll hunt something for you, I promise!" pleaded Lilith's mother.

"I appreciate the offer, but a human in the paw is worth two in the bush," replied the chief. He lunged toward them and swiped with his massive paws. The others followed suit. Bones snapped. Lilith's parents crumpled to the ground. Blood swelled and dripped from the claw marks on their necks.

"No–!" Lilith covered Uriel's mouth seconds before he screamed. The urosi chief stood and spun around, his eyes searching for the source of the sound. Lilith grabbed Uriel's hand, scampering to the far side of the tree trunk as he glanced up at its branches. He sniffed but smelled and saw nothing, so he returned to the meal at paw with the others.

Lilith, Uriel, and Rakiba wept silent tears as the three urosi savages tore into their parents. Then the memory faded.

"I'm sorry for your loss at such horrid individuals," Rakiba spoke through Lilith's mind, *"But is one incident so bad as to condemn an entire race? Would anyone still be alive if I worked using your methods? If I condemned all of Banjiha for the act of a single criminal?"*

"One incident? Oh you naive fool, I've witnessed the savage nature of sub-humans time and time again. I'll show you another memory. Years passed. Uriel and I barely survived, but we fought against the world and made our way here. Through hard work and grueling days, he became a paragon of the city, praised for his survival skills and knowledge. As such, he was often given assignments in the field, and I was left alone." Lilith's voice echoed through Rakiba's mind.

The scene changed. They sat alone in the corner of a dark bar with a bowl of soup and a cup of water in front of her. Rakiba looked down at their reflection, now a much older but still recognizable Lilith.

"What's a cute thing like you doing out so late without a man on your arm?" Lilith and Rakiba looked up. Three maiamorphs, one avian, one foxtail, and one lotor stood in front of their table. All three held empty mugs and reeked of alcohol. Lilith ignored them and slurped down her soup.

"Hey pretty face, I'm talking to you!" The foxtail stumbled forward and leaned on her table. He tilted her head up with a single sharp claw. "It's rude to disrespect such fine gentlemen like ourselves."

"Maybe she's one of those humans who thinks she's better than us!" called the lotor. "Well, do ya?"

"I'm not in the mood for any of this. Please leave me alone." Lilith set her spoon aside and drew a dagger from beneath her cloak. She gripped the hilt and stared at the foxtail.

"Oh? Boys, I think this little treat is threatening us!"

"Cute girls like you shouldn't play with knives!" crowed the avian.

"I'll give you ten seconds to put that away then we can start fresh. Ten, nine, eight…."

Lilith glanced over her shoulder. The barkeep was nowhere in sight. She didn't know if he had stepped outside to smoke or was using the bathroom, or had simply given up for the evening. She was on her own.

"One."

Lilith lunged at the foxtail with the dagger. Blood dripped from the open wound on his arm as he yelped in pain. His lotor friend punched her in the face. The foxtail tried to grab her but she picked up her hot soup and threw it in his face. He tumbled to the floor and screamed as he wiped the steaming soup from his fur. Lilith jumped over him and sprinted toward the exit but the avian grabbed the back of her cloak. She gasped as it choked her. Within moments, he was at her back, and she was on the floor. Lilith sliced at his foot. The avian cursed loudly. The lotor kicked the blade out of her hand and before she knew it, he and the avian had pinned her against the floor, her wrists bound above her head. The foxtail wiped his fur clean. He glared at Lilith as she struggled.

"I was going to be gentle, but it seems you like to play rough. He towered over her and grinned with malicious intent.

"No! Get away from me! Someone, help! Help me!" she screamed, and he laughed as he pulled down his trousers.

"No one is going to help you, little bitch. You humans talk big but you're nothing when it counts. I'll make you pay for disrespecting us."

Pain and sadness and hatred welled up inside Rakiba. They knew those emotions belonged to Lilith, but felt them as their own nonetheless. They closed their eyes and accepted their fate; helpless, scared, and alone.

The next sound they heard was the twang of a bow and a shriek of pain from the avian. Splotches of warm blood dripped onto their skin.

"Hey! Who the hell are you—aarrggh!" cried the foxtail.

Lilith screamed. A silver sword had pierced his chest. His eyes rolled to the back of his skull as a man threw his corpse aside. She watched as the lotor scampered away. A bronze cyclone erupted from the young man's hand and slammed the lotor into the wall. Before he could stand, the man brought his sword over his shoulder and sliced cleanly through his head.

The bar became as silent as a grave. The man cleaned his sword and approached them. Lilith struggled. She wondered what this assassin wanted and what he would do with her in this compromising position. He drew a knife from his belt. *Rescued only to be cast back into the fire.*

"Easy now, you're in shock." He carefully cut through her bonds. "I promise you're safe now. My name is Gunith. I'm one of Banjiha's paragons. I'll get you a wet cloth to wipe off the blood and escort you home. Nothing will hurt you anymore, I promise." Lilith didn't respond. Gunith did as he said and helped her to her feet then walked her to her home. She hid her face and cried.

"Gunith checked on me the next day. He offered what aid he could and gave me information about the city's support groups. He even gave me the bounty on those three criminals. I asked if he would come back the next day and the next day he did. I asked him again. A year later we were married. He was promoted to captain of the city guard and sent on a mission to rout a herd of minotaurs hunting in Banjiha's outlying villages. Do you remember?"

Rakiba grimaced, remembering all too well. They remembered the eulogy given and the city-wide procession. It had been their mission to aid Gunith's paragons, yet their ship had been horribly damaged sailing into a nest of giant pitcher scorpions and forced to make emergency repairs in Thaniana. They arrived too late; Gunith and his paragons had been slaughtered.

"That's right. Once more half-humans ruined my life, and this time, the Crown did nothing to help us. We asked for your aid and you abandoned

us. Still, I told my story. I kindled my pain into the fierce flame of resolve that burns in my heart. I shared pain with others like me, wronged for no reason but being alive. Under my leadership, we vowed to create a paradise for humans alone, but you were blind to our cause. The only way to save ourselves, the only way to find peace, is to rid our world of the monsters who wronged me and countless others and cast aside a leadership who failed to protect our own. That sentiment echoes across all of Banjiha."

***

Rakiba shuddered as Lilith's mind pulled away. They felt their own arms and legs, standing once more in Lilith's office. Only minutes had passed, yet Rakiba had lived through each of Lilith's memories and felt her emotions as their own.

"Now you understand my way of thinking, my hatred for those sub-humans, and my disdain for the Crown." Lilith smiled, relaxing in her chair. "Was there anything else you wished to discuss, Nuhir Rakiba?"

Rakiba ground their teeth, completely caught off-guard by Lilith's mastery of her abilities. "No. Good day, Grand Vizier Lilith, Vizier Uriel." Rakiba bowed. "Come, Amarak, let's return to the ship."

Rakiba, Amarak, and the swift atop his head stepped outside the main embassy and into the shining sun, yet dark clouds engulfed Rakiba's heart. They ambled down a narrow road, back toward the port outside the main city. Amarak growled and looked up at his master.

"I know bud, and I have a feeling things are about to get worse. She showed me exactly what she wanted me to see. I couldn't even pull away to search our negotiations for deceit. Every instinct in my body is telling me this 'peaceful resettlement' as she says, is a facade for something much more sinister. The resurgence of guerilla raids by out-lying maiamorph clans, the unexpected death of the late Grand Vizier, Lilith's sudden rise to power, it's all moving too quickly for anyone to find a connection, if one exists."

"Woof!" Amarak barked loud and powerful.

"We can't. Her words have not spurred violence. They're protected under Lamaru's law, no matter how asinine they may be. With no evidence to convict her, her political rise is legitimate. Even if it were otherwise, I've not enough time nor resources to prevent her first wave of deportations." Their eyes fell to the loyal swift sleeping on Amarak's head. "I can only send a message."

Rakiba looked up at the setting sun and considered their options. They felt the weight of the tin canister in their pocket and smiled. *Ah Achyut, to be unburdened by duties of a Nuhir and free to explore this world's beauty. Sometimes I envy your position. I hope you've more good news and stories to help me weather this storm. You've always found a way to make me smile.* They took a deep breath and exhaled. *I see no other way. So be it.* Rakiba knelt to the ground and ripped off a piece of their jade cape, a green glow emitting from their fingers as they wrote a coded message in Magesep and offered it to Amarak.

"Take this. You and your friend head back to the ship. I'll take my skiff back to the Salvation after Lilith's speech tomorrow. I have to know what she's telling our people."

Amarak whimpered and pawed at his master's shoulder.

"It's okay, buddy. We still have allies within the city. I know a safe place to stay the night."

Amarak laid down at Rakiba's feet.

"No, you can't stay. You'd draw too much attention."

Amarak snorted.

"Yes you would, what with that soft fluffy fur and those big floppy ears." Rakiba scratched the fur behind his ears. Amarak's tail wagged in approval.

"I'll see you in a couple days, then we can finally go home, okay?"

Amarak barked in approval.

"Good boy." Rakiba stood and lovingly thumped his side before turning and walking back into the city, taking every side road and back alley until they arrived at the gates of their old teacher's estate. They rang the doorbell and waited.

"Good afternoon, sir, may I help you?" A woman opened the door, dressed in a bright green sundress, which complemented her emerald eyes and meticulously combed, black fur, evidence of her maiamorph heritage, yet, aside from two triangular black ears and her sweeping black tail, her sylphlike proportions remained humanoid.

"Good afternoon," Rakiba bowed, "I am Nuhir Rakiba. I apologize for the sudden intrusion, but is Semoru Joruka here?"

"Oh! My apologies, Your Majesty, we weren't expecting any visitors, least of all one from the royal family." She curtsied and led them inside." My name is Masami, Semoru's wife. If you'd follow me, he's upstairs in his study. Rakiba followed the foxtail maiamorph, glancing at the innumerable family portraits and rich heritage that covered every inch of the available wall.

The Joruka family had lived in the city of Banjiha since its founding and were well known for careers in education and politics. All in the Joruka family were formally educated and often left for Illadina when they came of age. Many served as confidants and advisors for the royal family, such as Semuro's father, an exceptional Magi who had trained Rakiba from a young age. Although Rakiba and Semuro had not seen each other in years, the two remained friends, writing letters back and forth and reminiscing about simpler days.

Masami knocked twice and opened the door. "Semuro, darling, we have an unexpected guest and a very notable one at that."

Countless tomes, scrolls, and small ritual altars, covered the expansive table that filled most of the room, where a lanky man with red hair and glasses too big for his face poured over research notes, scientific articles, and the latest news from Illadina's terraforming ritual. He looked up, his glasses nearly sliding off the bridge of his nose, and gasped in excitement.

"Rakiba? Rakiba it is you! Oh, my friend, it's been far too long!" He stood and crossed the room, wrapping his left hand around Masami's waist and offering his right.

"Hello, Semoru." Rakiba shook his hand. "I'm glad to see you too and congratulations on your marriage and on your position as head of theoretical minna studies at the university."

"Oh thank you, Your Majesty. I do enjoy my minna research and Masami is the love of my life. No man could be happier. But look at you! The next heir to Lamaru, you've certainly dressed the part, except for your cape, but we can have that fixed in an instant, I've just the widget." He turned around and sped to a cabinet, pulling and pushing drawers open and closed until he found a small black box and a bit of cloth. "I wish you would have told me you were coming in your last letter, I could have cleaned the place a little more."

"If I had known I was coming sooner, I would have written to you, but the circumstances of my visit are rather complicated," answered Rakiba.

"It's about the new Grand Vizier, isn't it. That Lilith has been stirring up the masses with unsettling fervor." Semoru stuffed the bit of cloth into the black box, along with a few drops of colored dye, then traced over the tear in Rakiba's cape. The widget sewed the cloth and cape perfectly, the seam nearly unseeable by the naked eye.

"Keen as always, my friend." Rakiba nodded. "Both her words and actions worry the Padishah and King. I'm only here for another night, but if it's not any trouble, I'd prefer to stay with you while I attempt negotiations."

"Of course. I'm happy to assist in whatever way we can. And we'll have a grand dinner tonight in your honor! I've so much to tell you since your last letter, and you'll have to meet our little pups when they get home from school."

"Thank you, Semoru, both for your kindness and hospitality." Rakiba bowed.

"The pleasure is mine. Here, let me show you to your room." Semoru led Rakiba back down the stairs to a large guest room, chatting about this and that along the way.

After a hearty feast, Rakiba lay in bed, reading Achyut's letter. *Little brother, the stones you have taking on a dragon, let alone two! I commend you for saving so many lives and gaining the support of the Clystudines, but pray your gall will not attract malicious repercussions. I thought I taught you that playing with dragons only brings fire. Mother and Father will not be happy... Oh? This Katria must be a sorceress to cast such a spell upon your heart. For you of all people to settle into a relationship before me.* Rakiba chuckled to themselves. *I am disgraced.* They placed Achyut's letter on the nightstand beside their bed. *Perhaps it's best I not tell him of Lilith's ambitions. He deserves to revel in his happiness.* Rakiba stretched and closed their eyes. *Yes, he deserves it more than anyone.*

They woke before the sun and donned a simple cloak and clothes, hiding their dreadlocks beneath their hood, taking every precaution to conceal their identity before they left for the central embassy. As the sun rose higher into the sky, more and more humans flooded the narrow streets, all on their way to hear Lilith's inaugural speech and her plans as Grand Vizier of the region of Banjiha. Rakiba reached the grand plaza, now cleared of the colorful stalls and good-natured chaos of yesterday, and steadily made their way to the front of the crowd, just as the clock tower on the opposite side struck noon.

***

Lilith stood on the second floor of Banjiha's main embassy. It had been two weeks since their successful coup and every government official who had foolishly remained loyal to the fading crown of Lamaru had been captured and detained or found themselves the victim of a tragic 'accident'. Yet she and her leaders knew they had to act quickly and spread their version of the truth to ensure the people's support before word of her takeover escaped from the city. She smiled as she gazed out a window at the crowds of people gathered in the plaza to hear her triumphant speech and plans for their new nation, one where all humans could prosper when the sound of footsteps pulled her from her own thoughts.

The crest of the region had been scuffed off Uriel's ceremonial armor and replaced with Lilith's symbol of freedom. He wore a greatsword and scabbard on his belt and used a beautiful and deadly lance as a walking stick, not for his aid but as a show of power. Those who defied their rule would face the consequences.

"Sovereign-elect Lilith, dear sister, I've received word that every port and city gate was successfully secured. There has been no unauthorized movement in or out of the city since we seized control."

"Then it is done." Lilith sighed. "The city is ours to do with as we please, the rest of the region will soon follow. Thank you, Uriel." She bowed her head. Uriel shifted uncomfortably. He opened his mouth as if to speak but instead closed it again.

"Is there more you wish to say?" Lilith gazed curiously at her younger brother. He was not one to hesitate or mince words.

"I... I do not doubt your powers, dear sister, nor your leadership or skills. The amassing crowds are a testament to that. You have honed your abilities as a soulseeker and proven your conviction time and time again. I trust you completely, but I don't understand why you choose to displace the maiamorph population instead of killing those monsters outright. I worry that once they arrive in Thaniana and Illadina, they will come back as soldiers for the Crown, led by that irksome royal and their mutt."

"Potentially, although the maiamorphs have no combat training, not like you or I, but there is a greater reason, one I must make clear to every human of Banjiha. I must ensure the population sees our revolution as one without terror or bloodshed, regardless of our true intentions. If we openly give the Crown reason to fight, they will react accordingly, and we will lose on numbers alone. If we begin down a violent path, the people who once supported our ideals and now heed our calls will see us as terrorists, devouring their lives, efforts, and culture. We will lose everything even before the forces of the Crown attack. We must show them we can show mercy, even if it is merely a facade and publicity stunt. We must provoke them into making the first move, to show our people their naturally violent vocations. Then all humans will see our rule as kind and just and support our glorious new nation of their own accord.

"The ideals of our nation must grip the people's souls and spark the same fire that burns in our hearts. If it comes to war, it will not be by our hands. Thus, even if we are slain, we will be remembered as martyrs and revolutionaries. Our most devout followers will continue our work and build the future we desire. Even if we fail here, our dreams will be realized. A free state for humans alone will one day be recognized as a Pillar Civilization of Reighja."

"Thank you, sister." Uriel bowed. "You truly have the gift of a silver tongue."

"A silver tongue is only half the work. We must continually craft a narrative that writes us as the heroes and rightfully paints those abominations and the Crown as the enemy. We'll stage a few more attacks by maiamorphs and blame their trade caravans for the shortage of commodities. The people have grown so used to comfort, they'll be irascible within the week. After we shower them with luxurious goods, we'll have the numbers to make our dream a reality."

"Then do I assume correctly that it is not by chance you chose the anniversary of the founding of Banjiha for your speech?"

Lilith smiled. "There is no better day to reclaim our heritage and share our story with the people."

Twelve bells sounded from the top of the tower on the far end of the plaza.

Lilith tied back her long, blonde hair, walked over to her desk, and donned her own ceremonial helmet, mentally preparing herself to greet her people and deliver her masterplan to purge the city of the half-human filth and take her rightful place as the new leader of her freed country.

Uriel buckled the black cape to Lilith's shoulder pauldron. She examined her reflection in the mirror and smiled then walked across the room and opened a glass case in which a single sword rested, the Mammothbane; an ancient sword and powerful relic wielded by those in the Eruber family, one of the Eleven Families of Lamaru and the first settlers of the Banjiha region.

"The blade that once slaughtered the maiamorph savages of the region. Finally, it rests in the hands of one fit to wield it." Lilith smiled as she touched the sparkling amethyst embedded just below the base of the blade. "The Eye of Eruber is uncracked. Fate is with us, Uriel."

They walked downstairs and onto the ramada of the embassy, met with thunderous applause from Lilith's leaders and the crowd as she approached her pulpit. She traced her fingers along a ring of yellow minna stones embedded in the wood.

"My friends, my family, my followers," her voice echoed throughout the plaza and filled their ears, confident and powerful, enhanced by minna. "Thank you for joining me today, on the anniversary of the founding of our great city, long ago by my ancestors of the Eruber family. We stand on the precipice of a new age and a government led by the people it represents to fight against the poisoning of our great city by the irresponsible representatives of the old regime. We will fight this infection that threatens our lives and the lives of our descendants and the children of tomorrow as one body with one purpose; to bring forth the radical reformation of the political, cultural, and economic lives which we rightfully deserve!

"The province and the city of Banjiha were once a great place of commerce and art. If Illadina was the head of Lamaru, where pompous noblemen and weak leadership think, Banjiha is the arms and legs! You good people, and your forefathers and mothers worked tirelessly to provide meals and shelter for your families only to have it stripped away, to be taxed and taken by the Crown for this supposed terraforming ritual. I see no problem with our land! I see no problem with our water, yet those of Illadina wish to replace our lives and homes with palaces and monuments to their own narcissism! We have a right to be heard! We have a right to exist! My soldiers, my brother, and I are willing to sacrifice our lives, though I pray that the jaded crown sees reason and does not choose the path of bloodshed.

"You and the late Grand Vizier Mithin, peace be with him, have chosen my leadership with your words and actions. I vow to abolish the liberalistic, vain, and greedy lifestyles of Illadina's noblemen and create in its place a folk community, rooted in the soil of our city, and bound together by the bond of common blood. While in theory, this is a simple concept, it is based on a cornerstone principle of tremendous consequence. Our new nation will be the first to realize and act on this cornerstone principle; that of all the hardships we must face, the noblest and most sacred duty of each species is to preserve the purity of the blood with which it was founded.

"Yet we have failed to recognize our crucial error, one which cannot be so easily remedied without hard work and commitment. We will cultivate our crop of children with the utmost care and a pivotal understanding of the importance of conserving our blood, free from intermixture with the lesser beast folk, born unnaturally of this world by the cursed talons of the ancient dragons. We must act as our wise neighbors to the north, the newly unified Clystudine Confederation, a Pillar Civilization, and cleanse our lands of impurities and those who choose to stand beside the failed crown!

"We were the ones who ended the Age of Dragons! Humankind reclaimed their dignity, their land, yet it is with great sorrow I must announce that there are those among us who wish to live with the dragons' unnatural abominations and openly covet their return to our society and our place as slaves beneath their wings! The Watchers, with their blasphemous desires, support a regime that steals our resources and flagrantly opens our borders to half-blooded beastmen! Their path is one of ruin and from today onward, their Order will also be banished from inside these walls! It is not our duty to understand the minds of those who wish for humanity's enslavement but rather to recognize that we will only be punished should they have their way! This is why I have called you, this is why you all have gathered from across the provinces of Lamaru! We recognize the importance of conserving our blood and keeping our cities in our own human hands!"

The crowd erupted in a second storm of applause. Men and women let loose screams of joy and admiration at their new leader's passion and conviction. The masses wholeheartedly clung to her words and openly thanked their ancestors and gods that they would be the ones to usher in this new age; to live for this glorious moment and create a new world. Rakiba's stomach twisted into a knot.

"We are those born from nature, and we will follow nature's course!" Lilith's words quickly quieted the ruckus from the crowd. All in the plaza basked in her radiance. "We will not choose our leaders by royal blood, or ancestry, name, or wealth, but by ability and merit alone! Those who show wisdom and a call to serve will be appointed to positions of political leadership in our newly reclaimed nation! Every human will be allowed and encouraged to seek their natural vocations!

"I understand there are those of you who fear losing your status and position, who have profited from the failed systems of old. I do not seek to take that away from you. No, my aims are to only ensure equality of opportunity for all countrymen and women. All will have the opportunity to climb the social strata and prove that with hard work and conviction, anyone may achieve their dreams and heart's desires! We will save the lives of millions, damned by the old society. We will free the indentured and downtrodden, the outcasts and castaways from their shackles and educate them to be proud of their human ancestry and status as citizens of the greatest country in all of Reighja, no, the world!"

Uriel smiled as cheers shook the plaza once more. Now came the final revelation that would secure the people's loyalty to their state. The linchpin of their success, taken from the failed systems of old and reforged into something new and strong.

"Many of you have heard this rumor, but today I will confirm to all that I am a soulseeker, one of common birth who has liberated powers locked away by royal lineage after the supposed destruction of the Eruber family. Yet my mother was a seamstress and my father a widget tinkerer. I understand the struggles of a life born without prestige and privilege. I've listened to your pleas and fought for your rights. Look at us now; brothers and sisters, husbands and wives, humans united in a common goal, under a common banner to reclaim Banjiha's lost glory and usher in our newly christened epoch!"

10

Outcasts

Rakiba lay restless, unable to sleep as they processed Lilith's words, the roaring crowd, and the dawning expressions of shock and terror as maiamorph citizens realized the hour of their exodus had come.

There has to be something more I can do, Rakiba thought as they turned on their side. *I cannot allow Lilith to do as she pleases, yet I am bound to act amicably and conspicuously, lest I risk legitimizing the peoples' distrust of the Crown.*

A clock chimed six times somewhere downstairs, just as the first rays of sun peeked over the red walls of the city, yet the scorching smell of smoke and sudden shouts and wails quashed the hope and beauty of a new day. Rakiba leaped from their bed and hurried to the window. Crowds of humans had gathered, slamming a makeshift battering ram against the gates of the estate while two robed Magi weakened the iron with repeated motes of fire and splashes of water.

The thump-thump-thump of rapid pounding on the bedroom door shook Rakiba from their stupor. They dove to the floor and grabbed the hilt of their sword as Semoru launched into the room.

"Rakiba! Lilith's followers have lost all semblance of sanity! They're storming the streets, tearing families from their homes, and snatching up anything of value! Peaceful transition my ass! Riots have broken out across the city. I need to get you out of here."

"What about you and Masami? Your children and your staff? As Nuhir to Lamaru, it's my duty to protect you."

"And as your host and friend, it's my duty to protect you. Come with me." Rakiba hastily dressed and followed him down the hall. "I understand your desire to help, but empathy and logic are wasted on those blinded by rage and bigotry. I can sneak you out the back through a hidden passage in the wine cellar. Above all else, you have to make it to Illadina. Only you can–" Someone banged on the mansion's front doors, accompanied by the harsh voice of a city guard.

"Semoru Joruka, Professor of Theoretical Minna Studies at the University of Central Banjiha, by order of Sovereign-elect Lilith, head of the newly seceded Banjihan Autocracy, I demand that you open these doors immediately!"

Semoru gulped. He motioned Rakiba to stay silent and pointed toward the kitchen then hurried to confront the guard. "I don't know what you mean, sir. My allegiance is to Padishah Angem and King Debesh as Banjiha is the central province of the Dynasty of Lamaru."

"There's been a change in power, Professor Joruka. Under our glorious leader, Banjiha is now its own country, freed from the shackles of Lamaru and her failed regime. Now, open these doors!"

Semoru glanced over his shoulder at the frightened and furious and bamboozled looks of his gathered staff and family, yet thankfully, Rakiba had fled. "If I do as you say, will you swear to me on your new, glorious leader that no harm will come to all in my residence?"

"I swear to you," replied the guard. "My job is not to incite violence, but to relocate you and your kind out of the city per the Sovereign's orders."

"And all our possessions? Our property? My job at the University?"

"All repossessed by the state. This is your final warning. Do as instructed or I will be mandated to use force!"

Semoru opened the doors. Four armored paragons marched into the house. The emblem of the royal family had been scuffed from their armor, replaced with one he didn't recognize. The captain of the guard unrolled a scroll of parchment and read aloud the Sovereign-elect's first decree.

"All jobs, property, possessions, and wealth, held by former maiamorph citizens and their human allies are to be consolidated and redistributed so that all of humanity may step into our glorious new era on equal footing. All individuals of maiamorph ancestry, and any who willingly associate with them, are to be escorted to the docks for relocation. Said individuals are allowed any number of personal items, as long as they carry them on their own."

"We'll do as you say, just please give us time to pack our things."

"You have ten minutes." The captain of the guard waved his hand over his wristwatch and a timer started counting down.

Semoru and his staff grabbed emergency provisions: blankets, preserved food, and spare clothing, all stored in woven brackets. He filled another with whatever small widgets and trinkets they could sell along with the contents of the estate's safes. As Masami helped their children pack bags of favorite toys and books, she caught the stern and disapproving glare of one of the guards. She bared her fangs and flattened her ears, meeting his gaze until he gave way, mumbling profanities under his breath and leaving to oversee the rest of the estate's staff.

The ten minutes passed faster than Semoru's family would have liked, and they were ordered out the doors. The former paragons escorted them through a mob, shouting obscenities and insults to the city's main road where hundreds made the long walk to the dock.

How many of us will safely leave the city? Semoru thought as he led his family and staff outside the city walls, recognizing many of the sullen faces marching alongside him. *So many here hold positions of prominence. I guess our mistreatment could cause schisms in Lilith's populace, but how many lacking luck and prestige will be left to fend for themselves?*

They reached a tributary of the Hayi River without incident and joined the long line of former citizens of Banjiha and boarded the small ship destined for Illadina.

***

Rakiba sprinted through the backstreets of Banjiha to an out-of-the-way townhouse near the city's southern wall, where a skiff had been carefully hidden the last time the royal family visited Banjiha, their irrivir cared for by the couple who ran a hair and nail salon next door. Rakiba knocked on the door and waited.

A small snake poked its head out of an indent in the wall, glancing up at Rakiba before disappearing inside. They heard various latches and locks being undone, and a small child with messy black hair and serpentine pupils barely opened the door.

"Where's your doggy? Is he okay?" Netheli mumbled.

"He's safe and sound with the rest of my friends," Rakiba answered. "Are your mothers home? I need to speak with them immediately."

"They're gone, along with all of our neighbors and friends," answered Nadia, who ushered Rakiba inside and slammed the door behind them, hastily redoing the locks and latches. "Please, you have to help us." Her body shook, her eyes wide and alert. "We're the only ones left."

"Nadia, Netheli, I won't let them hurt you, but I need to know everything you can tell me. What do you mean, 'they're gone'?"

"They've all been taken away, imprisoned somewhere in the city. We barely escaped on our own. They challenged Lilith's legislation and went to speak out against her treatment of maiamorphs, but the entire protest was rounded up and arrested, charged with destroying public property and inciting violence. Then the former city paragons forced everyone out of their homes. We've been hiding under the floorboards all morning."

Netheli tugged at Rakiba's cape. "Can we go with you? I'd feel safer with you and doggy."

"Yes, of course, both of you will come with me to Illadina, and I'll do everything in my power to help your parents. Is the skiff still in the back?"

Nadia nodded. "And we've already packed our bags." She led Rakiba and Netheli out the backdoor, where a large, brown irrivir squawked and flapped its prickly wings. It dug its talons into the ground, eager to leave the unfurling chaos and find a more peaceful place to nap. The two naga children climbed into the skiff and shifted their bodies to resemble two little garden snakes instead of their natural or humanoid forms. Rakiba took the reins and led the irrivir out the back gate. They jumped on his back, thudded his stirrups, and the round, flightless bird took off running down the empty alleyways and streets.

"Halt! Who goes there!" called a woman in paragon's armor, as the skiff rounded its final corner and skidded to a stop just inside the city's southern gate. She drew her sword and held up her hand, engulfed by blue fire.

"By order of Sovereign-elect Lilith, you are to return to your home until these riots are disbanded and... Nuhir Rakiba?" The guard stood motionless as Rakiba approached, the two naga children safely hidden in the skiff. "Wha...what are you doing here?" Her face contorted in confusion and disbelief.

"My business is my own," Rakiba answered, "and as I am not a citizen of your new nation, please let me pass without incident. I am returning to my ship and leaving peacefully."

"I'm sorry, Nuhir Rakiba, you should have left when you had the chance." She bit her lip and tightened her grip on her shaking sword, blocking their path.

Rakiba sighed and dismounted, their arms raised high and away from their own blade. "You don't have to do this." They stared down the guard, calm and unflinching. "We can resolve this without conflict or violence. I don't want any of my people to hurt each other."

"Don't come any closer!" The guard raised her trembling sword. "You should have thought of that before you abandoned us to those maiamorph savages! Before you let your people die!"

"I am so sorry you feel like I abandoned you. I'm sorry for not being quick enough, for being unable to save your friends and family and for failing as your leader. Yet, destroying the lives of innocent citizens, of bakers and blacksmiths, teachers and gardeners, firefighters and friends, will not bring them back nor will it bring you closure. Instead, help me forge a path of peace. Do not let the loud voices of a few overturn the compassion and empathy of the many."

"Don't try to trick me with your guilded words! I've bore witness to the crimes of those savages! They only care about their clans, not our city, not our society! It's us or them!" she spat. "We are creating a new golden age for humans! I have my orders. If you do not comply, I will take you into custody."

"What crime have I committed?" asked Rakiba.

"The Sovereign-elect will decide your malfeasance and punishment."

A loud, boisterous laugh boomed from the roof of a nearby building. "We told you, Nuhir Rakiba, the people's minds are made up; their hearts follow a different path than those loyal to the jaded crown."

Rakiba looked up as Uriel jumped off the roof and landed on a sudden ring of fire appearing above the street. He summoned another ring and another, as he spoke, until he stood on the ground beside the guard.

"I thank you for your part in creating the Banjiha Eye Network, although, I doubt you could have foreseen it being used to find you. I would have died of embarrassment had you successfully fled the city after refusing our kind offer to let you leave. But here you are, out in the streets and harassing my paragons." Uriel drew his greatsword and pointed it at Rakiba's chest. "I'd expect nothing less from the royal lapdog. You will surrender your weapon and come with me to the embassy."

Thundering footsteps echoed all around as Uriel's paragons flooded out from adjacent streets, surrounding them in moments.

"And if I refuse?" Rakiba asked plainly.

"Then we will bring you there ourselves. Make the smart choice and give up. You cannot hide within the city; the Eye Network will find you. All of the gates are guarded by my paragons. You have no hope left. Surrender is your only option."

The ground rumbled beneath Rakiba's feet as a stone column erupted from the street and rose to the height of the nearest building. They leaped from the column which shattered in an instant, running and jumping from rooftop to rooftop.

"Get them!" Uriel howled and summoned a javelin of fire. He vaulted up to the nearest roof, chasing Rakiba as his paragons followed suit on the ground. A mass of barely visible silver threads swatted at Rakiba over and over again as the Magi below did everything in their ability to capture Lamaru's next heir. A gust of frigid air nearly froze Rakiba in their tracks, but they encased themselves in earthen armor and powered through the blizzard. A whirlpool opened up beneath their feet but Rakiba's armor restructured itself into a bridge to cross an otherwise impassable gap. A wall of fire sprang up along the edge of a building and the bridge reshaped itself into a tunnel protected from the burning heat.

Bursts of emerald light pulsed from Rakiba's sword. Stone replicas built themselves up on either side. Each of the five Rakibas took off in a different direction and forced their pursuers to split into smaller groups.

Uriel vaulted to the top of the nearest building, purple smoke congealing into mist in his right hand. He closed his eyes and held his hand in front of him. Mist swirled around each of the Rakibas, only for an instant, yet still enough time for him to track his prey.

Uriel smiled and took off toward the city's red wall.

Rakiba stopped to catch their breath and saw a mass of dark haze outside the city wall. Pinpricks of orange and red light pierced through the blue leaves of ironwood trees, releasing a toxic smoke that suffocated its residents. *They're burning the ironwood forests? What could Lilith hope to achieve, except provoking the nearby avian clans? No, that's exactly it. If the maiamorphs deal the first blow, Lilith's forces will only claim self-defense, sowing further chaos and confusion. It's just as Semoru said, logic and empathy cannot save–* They turned on their heel and drew their sword, blocking Uriel's strike inches from their side.

"Royal scum." Uriel lunged forward, his sword sweeping down upon Rakiba's shoulders. Rakiba parried his strike, thrusting at a chink in Uriel's armor but the captain of Banjiha's paragons blocked and shoved the flat edge of his greatsword against Rakiba's weapon and chest, knocking them from their feet. Rakiba rolled and skittered away, regaining thier balance and guarding thier side, just as Uriel nearly landed an incapacitating blow.

A mass of stone engulfed Rakiba's hand. They grabbed Uriel's blade, bringing their own sword around to strike, but Uriel shoved his shoulder into Rakiba's chest and the sword bounced harmlessly off his armor. He pushed Rakiba further away, pursuing his opponent with a stream of fire, but a bulwark of stone deflected his spell. Uriel's greatsword glowed purple as he slashed through Rakiba's barrier. Rakiba yelped as a second stream of fire burned their hand. Their sword clattered against the edge of the city wall, precariously perched before it tipped and fell into the desert below.

"You are beaten. Surrender!" Uriel proclaimed.

"You will face justice by my hand, I swear as Nuhir of Lamaru." Rakiba stepped off the edge of the wall. Confounded, Uriel hurried to the edge and cursed as a giant raven with crimson wingtips gripped Rakiba in its talons and carried them to safety.

"Thank the gods, Kinnari. You have no idea how thankful I am to see you. I was beginning to wonder if you got my message."

"We sent a swift to Illadina explaining the situation, just as you asked," Kinnari cawed in a shrill voice. "They I decided to come and rescue you."

"Good job." Rakiba sighed and smiled, although we aren't out of danger yet. Head toward the ironwood forest. We might be able to–"

"Nuhir Rakiba, I appreciate your willingness to aid my kin, but our top priority is getting you safely to Illadina. Aquilo and Eravil began evacuating our flock last night, should Lilith's hubris and bigotry threaten us. Should they turn to violence, the Blue and Gold Feather

Squawdrons will cover our retreat. They've bested roc wyverns and pitcher scorpions, they can handle a few misguided humans," added Kinnari, pride in her voice for the well-earned reputation of the legendary avian warriors.

Kinnari swooped low to the ground, dropping Rakiba on the deck of the Queen's Salvation, where the crew hurried to meet them. Amarak leaped onto his master, knocking him to the ground and licking his face.

"I'm okay, I'm okay, I promise," Rakiba reassured his friend. They scratched Amarak's head and stood, just as a middle-aged woman with short black hair dressed in a violet captain's jacket approached them. She had long lines around her cheeks and cold, calculating eyes yet the sight of Rakiba, relatively unharmed, brought her visible relief.

"Nuhir Rakiba, thank the Padishah you're safe. We tried to find you through Banjiha's Eye Network but were locked out of the system. Minna barriers have surrounded the city, as if they were preparing for a siege. Care to explain what the hell is happening?"

"The newly elected Grand Vizier, Lilith, has declared Banjiha as an independent nation and banished all citizens of maiamorph ancestry and their allies from the city. I fear it is only a matter of time before the entire region is under her control. Countless lives will be destroyed in her misguided attempt to create a safe haven for humans alone. We have to stop her. It's the only way to–"

"Captain! Three sandships approaching from the southwest!" Kinnari called from the crow's nest, now in her humanoid form, her black wings folded against her back, her clover hair in a neat ponytail.

Iyushi, Rakiba, and Amarak, sprinted to the ship's helm just as three colorful explosions shook the sky around them.

"Warning shots? Dammit!" Iyushi punched the ship's railing. "Windsails shift north by northeast! Put everything we've got into the arcane engine!"

Rakiba stared at the city walls and burning ironwood forest as the Queen's Salvation turned and fled. *Semoru, Masami, Nadia, Netheli...*

everyone, I'm so sorry I couldn't do more. Please hold on. We will return and I swear Lilth and Uriel will face judgment.

Amarak whimpered and licked Rakiba's hand.

"I know, buddy. We can only hope our message reaches Mother and Father in time."

A month after Lilith's rise to power, the lively chaos and majesty that once filled the streets of Banjiha had been snuffed out, replaced by a quiet and eerie normalcy. The wondrous sights in the streets were dreams of bygone days. The great cacophony of calls, chirps, whistles, roars, growls, and barks was replaced by the monotone drone of human voices. The magic of the city was gone. Even the avians, proud and fierce warriors, were beaten into submission and driven from their forests. All the maiamorphs, riff-raff, and unnatural creatures had been pushed out of the city and only humans remained… or so Lilith and her loyal followers thought.

Parents hid their adopted children for fear they would be taken away. Friends separated from families spent day after day hiding in houses, unable to exist outside, scared to even look through the window at the bright sun overhead. Lovers pretended their soulmate had abandoned them and they were finally free to mingle with the more intelligent, sophisticated, and civilized of their own kind. Although pockets of resistance still existed throughout the city, they remained sparse and disorganized at best.

11

Dragons & Dreams

"Ugh, this one doesn't work either," Achyut groaned and smudged out his sequence of Magesep runes, erasing the last hour of his work from the chalkboard. "I need the puddle to form in any orientation, not just flat on the ground. If I add the *mawja* facet here and inverse the *hikagara* glyph, I can get it to stay vertical, but then I have to create a branching path for the spell, and this already consumes too many minna charges," he mumbled to himself, scribbling and erasing another set of glyphs. "And I have to find a way to stop the ripples. No point in creating all this if I can't see the other person. What to do, what to do."

Katria looked up from her scrapbook, giggling as Achyut stuck out his tongue and scratched his temple with a piece of white chalk. "Darling, half your face will be covered in chalk if you keep scratching like that. I've never seen you focus like this before. It's actually kind of adorable."

"The inner machinations of spellcraft are an enigma. Like putting together a puzzle where every time I place a new piece, the overall picture changes. Add one piece and I create a majestic mountain range, the next and I create a portrait of my parents wearing silly hats."

"And what sort of picture are you trying to create?" Katria asked as she arranged her newly pressed flowers, collected from their last stop to let the irrivir stretch their legs."

"If done correctly, the caster could create a whirlpool with their focus that shows reflections of themselves or their environment to another Magi's focus, far away. Then the two could share visual information over great distances. Imagine if you were in Yaand and I in Illadina and we could see each other, potentially even converse, if I can crack the runic code."

"Seeing each other and conversing over such distances does sound incredible, although I'd prefer to never return to Yaand." Katria looked down at her flower arrangement. "I have everything I could ever want right here."

Achyut ambled to her side and kissed the top of her head, wrapping his arms around her shoulders. "I only said that as an example. If the world followed my design, I'd never ever leave your side."

"What a wonderful world that would be." Katria wrapped her arms around his and rested her head against his chest.

"You two are so sweet, I might get diabetes." Mona sighed as she and Reena entered the library. Once we reach Illadina, you'll have to refrain from such public displays of affection. There's a time and a place for everything."

"Then it's a good thing we're still a few months away," retorted Achyut as he assaulted Katria's neck with kisses. Katria's face flushed the color of beetroot.

Mona snorted and rolled her eyes. "Whatever, get it out of your system."

"Yeah! Because tonight we're stealing Katria from you!" Reena shouted in excitement.

"Huh? Was that tonight?" Katria asked as she gained the slightest hint of composure.

"Don't tell me you forgot," Reena groaned. "Maybe you are spending too much time with him."

"And it's up to us to fix that," added Mona.

"Hey, don't I get a say in all this?" complained Achyut as Reena and Mona wrestled Katria from his grasp.

"Nope!" Reena sang, "She already promised and you look really, really busy, especially with all that chalk on your face."

"We were just about to take a break," argued Achyut.

"Then you can wash yourself up and go hang out with Captain Tanoy or Joseph," suggested Mona. "You can't neglect your other relationships just to spend time with Katria."

"I–" Achyut tried to protest but Reena grabbed Katria's scrapbook and the three of them hurried out of the room.

"These flowers are so pretty, did you collect all of them?" Reena asked, flipping through the pages of the scrapbook as the three of them walked down a long hallway.

Katria nodded. "All from across Reighja. They hold my few precious memories and the rare moments I've been truly happy. Each time I touch one, I can see the landscape in my mind, feel the wind drifting through my hair, smell their sweet scents, and feel the sun's warmth on my skin. But I digress, was all that really necessary?" she whined. "I would have been happy to spend time with you and Achyut."

"Trust me, a bit of alone time is healthy for relationships, especially sailing in such limited space for such a long voyage," answered Mona as she led Katria and Reena down a long hallway. "Once we reach Illadina, there will be times when Achyut is occupied with royal duties. If you develop codependency now, it will only make the moments you're separated that much more difficult."

"I guess that makes sense," Katria murmured. "So, what did you have in mind for this evening?"

"We have all sorts of fun things planned!" Reena grinned. "Did you know this ship has an art studio? It's full of paints and pottery wheels and all sorts of craft stations! Then we can play some board games and eat snacks and end the night with a pajama party playing truth or dare!"

"That does sound exciting." Katria smiled.

"And here we are." Mona opened the door to a large studio with four white tables evenly spaced in the middle. Paints and canvases and mounds of clay lined the back wall, along with countless brushes and a variety of sculpting tools. Bowls of fruit, swords, vases, and other objects had been artistically placed on a long table on the left wall, surrounded by artists' benches. Three pottery wheels took up the right wall, along with a large sink and drying racks. Katria and Reena gasped in delight at the sheer number of materials and colors stockpiled for such frivolities.

"We can start at whatever station you'd like and work our way around the room. I'm happy to give you a crash course in how to use everything here," offered Mona. "I don't expect you to master it all tonight, but we can cover the basics and you can start thinking about what projects you want to complete over the rest of our voyage."

"Wow! This is all so cool!" cried Reena, running around the room examining everything from the tools to the first few artworks hung on the wall. "How come you didn't show us this sooner?" she pouted.

"Someone who will not be named tried to harness unstable minna to add some flair to their pottery and nearly burned down the entire studio. We only recently finished renovating it."

"Was it Prince Achyut?" Reena asked bluntly.

"I told you that person wouldn't be named," Mona said, shaking her head 'yes'.

Katria and Reena giggled.

For the next few hours, they drew pictures, painted, carved, and Mona instructed them how to properly use a potter's wheel. She showed them her half-finished mural, a rendition of the Prospector's battle against Vitra and Magri, and helped them develop compositions. By the time the sun set, their aprons had become abstract art of their own design, painted with colors and clay stains and wood shavings.

"It's perfect!" Reena smiled at her painting of a black and white nafsiyat whale in the ocean.

"Why is it surrounded by colorful socks?" asked Mona.

"Those are fish!" Reena pouted. "Katria, they look like fish, don't they?"

"If I squint my eyes they look exactly like fish," Katria replied sheepishly.

Reena sighed. "No one understands my artistic genius." She hopped off her chair and hurried over to Katria, carving out the holes in a long, bamboo tube. "What are you working on?"

"It's a bansuri of my own." Katria blushed. "I want to learn how to play. I think it'd be really fun if we–Ouch!" She frowned at the drop of blood forming on her finger, then gasped at the carving tool poking through the bottom of her bansuri. "Oh no!"

Mona hurried over and examined the wound. "It doesn't look too bad. There's some healing salve in a medical kit down the hall, second door on the left. That should patch you up in no time."

"Thank you, Mona," Katria answered, examining her ruined instrument. "I can't believe I messed this up. I've been working so carefully for the past hour."

"Accidents happen and you can always make another one. You should be more relieved you didn't slice through your finger," Mona retorted.

"That's true." Resigned, Katria stood and hurried out the room, examining her wound. *All my hard work and my only accomplishment is a pricked finger. Maybe I'm not cut out for these kinds of arts. I should just stick with–*

"Woah, excuse me, ma'am." The blue-haired Magi dressed in white rodes hurriedly stepped aside, nearly bumping into Katria.

"Oh, my goodness!" She gasped. "I'm so sorry! I got lost in my own thoughts and didn't see you there."

"No harm done. Have a good rest of the night." He smiled at her, bowed, then hurried away.

I really am a klutz. She hung her head and noticed a silver ring on the floor, shaped like a little dragon curled around a sapphire. "Excuse me, sir," I think you dropped your–" but the Magi had left. Curious, she picked it up.

A wave of nausea washed over her body. Her skin burned and her vision blurred as she sprinted back to the art studio. She tripped and fell unconscious before she hit the floor.

A younger version of the Magi in white robes stood beside a silver roc wyvern adorned with cyan plumage. He laughed as it licked his face and he scratched behind its feathered ears. The ring told her the man's name, Soital, who had been newly recruited to the Watchers, whatever that meant. The scene shifted into an open cavern, larger than anything she had seen before, illuminated by thousands of torches. A skeleton of a colossal, winged beast lay buried in the rock. A strange machine sat atop a stone altar. Then the scene changed again. A sister ring had been forged at the same time, its dragon grasping a radiant ruby, gifted to Soital's twin, Satial, from their parents on their tenth birthday. Each twin also received a large white egg.

Katria slowly opened her eyes, taking in her surroundings. She sat in a comfy white cot in an unfamiliar room, divided by screens. Achyut sat at the foot of her bed, fast asleep, his head resting against his arms. "Prince Achyut?" she mumbled, still half asleep.

Achyut's eyes fluttered open. "My sweet Katria, you're awake! We were all so worried." He stood and hugged her gently, kissing her forehead.

"Where am I?" Katria asked.

"You're in the medical bay. Mona found you unconscious in the hallway. Thankfully, you didn't hit your head or anything, just a small cut on your finger."

"I found a ring. I had a vision. There was a man with a blue and white dragon and a giant skeleton in a cave, a Magi in white robes, something called the Watchers."

Achyut frowned. "Mona never mentioned a ring but the Watchers are a religious group spread across Reighja. They have long since been allies to the royal family. Actually, a few members of the crew belong to the group. I could introduce you to them if you'd–" Achyut smiled as Katria slept peacefully in his arms. "Get some rest, my dear." He kissed her once more. "We can always talk tomorrow."

***

The little loyal swift flew fast and true to Illadina, carrying Nuhir Rakiba's message to Padishah Angem and King Dabesh. It followed the Hayi River to the red walls of Illadina, flying over the citadel and through a palace window, landing on the marble lectern outside the throne room doors.

An elf with silver hair, dressed in white robes, curiously watched the loyal swift with a small metal canister around its neck. They were unremarkably ordinary in every way: gray eyes, average height, and enough muscle that showed they exercised regularly but only to stay healthy. Their silver hair was drab and shapeless and had lost most of its shine in the later years. It fell past their eyes and shoulders, not unkempt, but definitely unattended to, and resembled a wet mop. In fact, the only remarkable aspect of the silver-haired elf was a black tattoo of a small dragon that clung to the sunken skin around their left eye and cheek. Its long, winding tail converged with their square jawline and dropped off into a point on their chin.

One of the royal paragons outside the door, took the tin canister off the swift's neck and added its message to the ever-growing pile of documents and letters for the rulers of Lamaru to read after their scheduled meetings. Its mission successful, the swift flew back out the window for a well-deserved meal and rest.

The other paragon flipped through the parchment pages of a large, leatherbound book, until he found the correct appointment. "Dracona Cassio Naebuella of the Watchers for a 2:30 appointment with Padishah Angem and King Debesh?"

"That is correct," answered Cassio.

"You're early. The Padishah and King are still in their previous meeting. As such, we cannot let you into the throne room. You are, of course, allowed to wait here until their business is concluded."

"I will wait," replied Cassio and so they did, standing silently in front of the doors. "Is there a problem?" Cassio asked as the other guard stared at them through curious eyes.

"Are you *the* Cassio Naebuella, the famous fashion designer from the Wild Lands?"

"I am."

"I mean no offense, your brand is known across all of Reighja, but I always thought you'd be more... lively."

"My designing career comes second to my position as a leader of the Watchers. My responsibilities require more of me, and therefore, require more of my attention than old hobbies."

They heard movement inside as the doors opened outward. A heavyset man dressed from head to toe in soft, beautifully colored silks stepped out of the room. He mumbled profanities under his breath as two more paragons escorted him down the stairs and out the palace.

"Dracona Cassio Naebuella, you may now enter," said one guard.

"And I hope you'll be able to start designing again soon," added the other.

"Thank you, gentlemen. I'm always pleased to meet fans of my work." Cassio bowed their head and stepped into the rectangular room. Palm desks lined the long sides of the chamber, parallel to an emerald rug that led up to the base of the central and larger of the two thrones. The Royal Counsel sat behind the desks, dressed in jade and amethyst-colored silks. They wrote on paper, chalked-up slates, and ordered messengers and servants in and out of two hallways behind their desks on either side of the room. A massive window sat atop both side exits and warmed the room with sunlight. The colored lights from the glass danced on the rug and stopped short of the stone tiles at the base of the throne.

The ruler of the Dynasty of Lamaru, Padishah Angem, sat poised upon a throne encrusted with purple and green gemstones. She wore a floor-length jade abaya embroidered with gold, and her long black hair was curled in a way that resembled flower petals. Her husband wore a similarly elaborate amethyst kurta and sat in a second slightly smaller but still splendid and sacrosanct seat off to her side.

Dracona Cassio genuflected and walked to the edge of the jade carpet.

One of the Padishah's councilmen unrolled a short scroll and cleared his voice. He spoke in a formal but jeering tone as he read aloud the premise of Cassio's royal audience: "Cassio Naebuella, member of the Watchers and one of the nine in the organization to obtain the highest rank of Dracona, you stand in the presence of Padishah Angem and King Debesh, descended from House Adhikar of the Eleven Families of Lamaru, reigning monarchs of the Dynasty of Lamaru, to ask for a significant number of greater minna stones for a project of unknown design to 'fulfill the primary purpose of the Watchers and usher in peace and prosperity for the continent of Reighja' as you have so stated. Is this statement accurate?"

"Yes," replied Cassio.

The Padishah and King looked at Cassio and each other curiously. This was the first time they had been asked for an audience without knowing its purpose.

"Dracona Cassio, the Watchers have always backed the royal family, especially in times of crisis," began Padishah Angem. "Your Order has been responsible for our long years of lasting peace and your shared insights into minna theory have also advanced our own research in the fields of minna fusion, replication, and medicine. However, you must understand that such allocation of resources, and in such oddly specific quantities, is not only unlikely due to our longstanding, nearly completed, terraforming initiative, but I refuse to hand out such substantial resources without knowing their purpose."

"Your Majesty, allow me to clarify now that we are face-to-face. I know there are those among your court who see the leaders of my organization as your political rivals, as the Watchers were founded by another of the Elven Families. The nature of my project and proposal is also one of utmost secrecy. I dared not reveal the truth behind our acquisition when my audience could be swayed by non-believers or political idealists."

"You may speak freely, Dracona Cassio. My response to your proposal will be the King's and my opinion alone."

"Thank you, Your Majesties." Cassio bowed. "As you have stated, we of the Watchers are researchers and scientists yearning to uncover the secrets of minna; where it came from, why it exists, and how the ancient dragons of Reighja were able to harness it so masterfully, even as far as to bring sentience and life into the world in the form of the Clystudines and the various maiamorph clans. Long have we searched the continent for the lairs of any surviving dragons to ask for knowledge and beg for forgiveness for the crimes we committed against their kin in ages past. We were only a fledgling species at that time."

Padishah Angem shifted uncomfortably in her throne. It was true that the Watchers publicly supported the crown and nourished the growth and advancement of the Dynasty of Lamaru, but their obsession with dragons and their role in Reighja's past left her and many citizens of the kingdom uneasy. Some, on the fringes of the organization, even claimed their true purpose was to return control of the land back to whatever dragons still survived, not in terms of state or country, but through religious fervor. Many if not all the Watchers believed that dragons should be worshiped and thought divine for their longevity and the wisdom they accrued with it, immeasurably more than what mere humans could ever conceive within their short and fragile lives.

"I have spoken with the other nine Draconas, and we unanimously agreed to come forward with our findings. It is the official position of the Watchers that we have made recognizable strides in the fields of minna replication pertaining to the facets of *Sensu* and *Namal*. Our research has borne fruit. We have discovered the formula, in theory, and the correct quantities of minna needed, along with additional factors, to create the foundation of a reanimation ritual."

The room turned silent. All eyes rested on Cassio. Everyone understood the weight of their words.

Sensu and *Namal*.

Life and death.

The two most abundant facets of minna, yet the most difficult to harness for rituals or artifice. Their existence alone mocked and undermined Lamaru's vast understanding of how minna functioned and its place in the world.

"Dracona Cassio," the Padishah hesitated. "Do you swear on your fidelity to the ancient dragons that this information is correct? The implications of your words are graver and more important than you seem to realize."

"I swear on my devotion to the ancient gods of our lands. That is the purpose of my audience with Your Royal Highnesses today. Our organization would love to begin our research's testing phase, yet we lack the proper resources."

Whispers and murmurs drew forth from everyone in the room. Was this reanimation ritual possible? Had this dragon-loving cult found the path to immortality? What did they mean by the testing phase and what was the scope of the implications for individuals, societies, and Reighja as a whole?

The Padishah and King rescheduled every other appointment that day. They talked among themselves for three hours as Dracona Cassio stood quietly, and when they announced their decision, they decreed that not a word of this was to leave the chamber. Anyone who broke that rule would be severely punished. In fact, it would be the last mistake they ever made. Even the Watchers were forbidden by the Padishah to never speak of their findings or this meeting ever again.

***

A small skiff, a fraction of the size of the Prospector, sailed across the saffron sand in the northern desert of the Dynasty of Lamaru carrying only a skeleton crew and cargo. Dracona Cassio stood alone on the bow. The amber sun slipped under the horizon as they recounted the day's events and the decree from the Padishah and King.

"As Padishah of Lamaru, I hereby decree, to all persons in this room, regardless of position or background, that this revelation be never spoken of again. The power to control life, to bestow upon another, or to bring back a loved one, is too great a power for any species, much less our flawed societies, and civilizations. We will not disrupt the flow of nature, nor suffer its consequences, good or bad.

"Any and all of this ritual's research will be purged from all records, including those of the Watchers. Anyone found in possession of such findings will be detained, tried, and found guilty of treason against the crown and country. None of the past will be reborn, neither human nor dragon. Dracona Cassio, your request for resources has been denied. This is my irreversible decision on the matter. You are dismissed."

Fools, thought Cassio. *Even if our research it abandoned in its entirety, one day, it will be rediscovered and the circumstances surrounding it will be out of our control. Padishah Angem, by denying our proposal and funding in uncovering this paramount mystery, perhaps the only mystery worth solving in all of existence, you have cast aside your responsibility and role as a good and just leader and subjected yourself, your descendants, and everyone else in existence to the whims of fate. But as a devout follower of the ways of the past, and as one striving for a better future, I will not cast aside my research and integrity, even if it may one day cost me my life.*

The shrill shrieks and screeches of winged wyverns shook Cassio from their thoughts as their great, long shadows darkened the skiff. Three pairs of gray and green wings passed and flew further ahead, spiraling closer and closer to the ground, where a handful of torches illuminated the clump of sandstone buildings against the growing darkness of the night. A sailor with the same tattoo as Cassio on the opposite side of his face walked up the stairs from the underdeck. He held a wooden chalice filled with wine in one hand and a decorative, wooden box in the other and stood at attention until Dracona Cassio acknowledged his presence.

"Do you have something to report?" Cassio asked in a monotone, baritone voice, their mind preoccupied elsewhere.

"Yes, Dracona Cassio. I've just received orders from Dracona Zevulun. Those were his scout wyverns that flew overhead. He is prepared to receive our ship and requests that you begin the blood rite now so that you may depart for the dig site the moment we drop anchor. We're to arrive in ten to fifteen minutes."

Dracona Cassio took the cup of wine and set it on a barrel. They cradled the box in their hands.

"Thank you. You are dismissed." Cassio set the box next to the cup. They unclasped the silver chain around their neck and palmed the small, silver key shaped like a dragon's skull, and unlocked the box.

To the untrained eye, it was a random assortment of items: a ruby knife, a yellow sponge in a golden tray, a stamper, a vial of blueish-green blood, and a few cloth wraps but to a skilled Magi, this was everything needed to perform a blood ritual.

Cassio took the knife and slit their palm, not even wincing at the pain, immune to it after all these years. They picked up the sponge and squeezed it, staining it red with blood. After wrapping the shallow wound, Cassio uncorked the vial of blue blood and poured it onto the sponge, then mixed the two with the stamper until it became an unnatural, sickly purple. Satisfied, they took the stamper, held it to the sponge, and pressed it against their chest. They took the cup in their hands, gulped down the wine, and prayed.

"Oh, draconic Omnipotents of old, grant your humble servant the power to subdue your lesser kin once more. Grant me the power to make them understand my will as your own and I will bring wisdom, honor, and glory to your lost, divine names. Bind my heart and mind to yours and let me see with unclouded eyes."

The stamp glowed with an eerie light that danced through the colors of the rainbow and darkened to black. Cassio grabbed onto the barrel and ground their teeth as warm and strange sensations washed over their body. Tendrils spread from the stamp across their chest and down their arms and legs, weaving intricate designs. Cassio took slow deep breaths. The rite was done. They locked the box, handed it to another sailor, and demanded another cup of wine.

The skiff slowed to a halt beside a wooden ramp erected for Cassio and their crew. The encampment was busier than the last time they had visited, though that came as no surprise due to their recent discovery.

Humans and maiamorphs of all shapes, sizes, and backgrounds, all tattooed with a dragon on their body, bustled about with their daily tasks. Some prepared food and drink for the others and the six gray and green wyverns napping in the shade of a sizable enclosure. Some designed new buildings while others laid sandstone bricks and mortar. The crew hurriedly unloaded the crates of supplies from Cassio's skiff and distributed their contents to members of Watchers who sat at their assigned workstations and tinkered with strange devices, ancient tablets, and conducted minna experiments.

A man in his thirties, dressed in the same white robes, stood at the bottom of the ramp. He had short black hair and tawny skin and spread his hands in a welcoming gesture. Cassio walked down the ramp and glanced him over. He too had performed the blood rite.

"You've lost weight, Dracona Zevulun."

"Well, of course, Dracona Cassio," responded Zevulun. "Building an outpost in the middle of the desert will do that to anyone. I would have preferred to be on the slopes of the mountain, under the shade of camu berry trees, but a damned ragamauhfaki has claimed the pond and I'm tired of losing bodies and resources." He looked at the markings on Cassio's body and into their emerald eyes, complete with slender red pupils which resembled a serpent's. "I see the rite went well. But more importantly, how did your audience with the Padishah go, hmm? When will they send us the mountains of minna stones and declare our Order as the saviors of existence?"

"They rejected our proposal."

"I knew it!" Zevulun jumped up and down for joy. "Our names will be forever enshrined in history, the ancient dragons will—" Happiness and excitement fled from his face. He stood slack-jawed, as if the tiny rodent on a wheel that powered his brain died of a heart attack then and there. "W-wait! They *rejected* our proposal?"

"That's what I said before you began your incessant babbling."

"Bu-bu-bu-bu-but that's complete lunacy! Our research is correct! If they throw away this opportunity, who knows when someone else with worse intentions will rediscover it!"

"I am aware of the implications. Furthermore, the Padishah has decreed we halt our research at once. All of it is to be burned away and purged from our minds, lest we willingly admit treason against the Crown."

Zevulun's face resembled that of a baby whose favorite toy had been snatched away and replaced with a cactus.

"NonononononoNONONONO!" He fell to his knees, doubled over, and held his head in his hands. "My life's work... my research... my dream! All of it will be shattered! Lost into the abyss! My life is pointless! Existence is nothing but pain!"

"Stop your morose lunacy this instant." Cassio kicked him hard in the side. Zevulun looked up at his elvish friend dazed, confused, and in quite a bit of pain.

"Unless..." The glimmer returned to his eyes as he immediately stood. "We're to continue our research?"

"Of course. The Watchers have always acted from the shadows when the prevailing governments proved ineffective. This is a momentous setback to be sure, but it is not the end of our way. We will acquire the minna stones through a more inconspicuous method."

"Praise to you, Cassio! Praise to your commitment to the cause! And those in the Order who oppose us will be given the chance to reaffirm their beliefs. I need more test subjects for my reanimation ritual. Come, my friend, let's be on our way! There is much to show you and less day to show it in!" Zevulun giggled, giddy as a schoolgirl.

Cassio sighed and followed him through the camp. "I'm curious to see what you've found. Hopefully, this is the right one."

"Oh, I wholeheartedly believe it is. I've never seen one this size before and the caves below the mountain's peak give credence to our theory."

They stopped outside the large, gated-off enclosure where the six wyverns rested and waited for the attendant to meet them. She too had the rite markings all over her body. She scanned both Cassio and Zevulun with a handheld device and confirmed the rite had taken full effect. She chanted multiple incantations and lowered the defensive wards and barriers around the wyverns' temporary home. Lastly, she undid several locks with a multitude of strange keys and opened the iron gate.

Each of the six roc wyverns alone was a sight to frighten away all but the bravest, most foolhardy, and most skilled Magi or hunters, resembling towering walls of feathers and scales; their black forelimbs adorned with beautiful plumage in every shade of green and ending in two dagger-like talons. Their plumage continued across their bodies, some feathers the length of longswords. Their back legs were long and skinny, curled beneath their bodies as they slept. Their tails wrapped around their chests and had been meticulously cleaned after digging a body pit in which to rest. Two bright green plumes stuck up from their triangular heads and designated the social hierarchy of the flock.

None of the six wyverns seemed perturbed by Zevulun or Cassio's presence or even attempted to turn them into a tasty snack. The rite ensured they thought of them as oddly-shaped, wingless parents. Cassio approached the largest wyvern. Zevulun affectionately rustled the feathers of the second largest. The flying steeds stomped their feet and cooed in excitement as both Draconas placed heavy, leather saddles upon their backs and stored their satchels in chests for it was time to stretch their wings and fly.

Zevulun and Cassio each took a slab of raw meat and threw it into their mounts' mouths as a reward for being patient. They secured their wyverns' bridles and headgear along their necks and fastened their leads and reins. They led the wyverns out the back gate of the enclosure and climbed onto their backs, pressing their palms against their mounts' necks while speaking in draconian tongue. The two wyverns spread their feathered wings and soared into the black sky.

***

Prince Achyut sat in the crow's nest, unable to sleep, unable to enjoy his own melodies as he racked his brain for any logical deduction from Katria's vision. Even more disturbing came the revelation from

Captain Tanoy that two of the crew had gone missing the night before, both members of the Watchers.

Their disappearance has to be connected to Katria's vision. They must have fled after she fainted, but what could they be hiding? Were they so paranoid of what she saw? Have they been plotting their escape since our battle with Vitra and Magri? Would they betray Lamaru for a high position among their Order?

His breath hastened as his mind raced faster and faster, each of his thoughts giving way to countless more. *What if I've brought Lamaru to ruin? Vitra said he would seek vengeance against my people and I would be to blame. Yet would I have done anything different had I known what I know now? No, I would have stayed my course. Had I not, so many more would still be enslaved and I would have never met Katria. Still, are Vitra or Magri related to the skeleton that Katria saw? What is that strange cult even doing with such a relic? How long ago was that vision from the ring? Where did it take place?* He held his head in his hands and pulled at his hair, trying and failing to quiet the storm raging in his mind. *There's too many unknown variables. How am I supposed to come up with an answer or reason for any of this?*

"I thought I'd find you up here." Katria's sweet voice calmed the storm of his mind as if the eye of a vicious hurricane. Achyut looked up, dark circles under his eyes. Katria smiled at him.

"Katria, you're awake." Achyut sighed in relief.

"And feeling as good as new." She climbed up the ladder and sat beside him, wrapping her arms around his waist and resting her head on his shoulder. "The nurse let me out early for good behavior. They couldn't find any negative effects or lasting symptoms. I'm here and safe in your arms, so what's bothering you, my darling?"

"Since hearing your premonition, I can't help but worry I put Lamaru in grave danger. We know the events you saw have already happened, but because of the lack of context and timing, I'm worried they weren't as long ago as I'd hoped. Two members of the crew are missing. I would bet my life one of them was the Magi with the ring. Why would they flee, unless the Watchers are planning something they want to keep secret, some goal the Padishah could stop them from achieving."

He wrapped his arms around her waist and rested his head on hers. "I'm scared that because of my actions, Vitra and Magri will seek vengeance against Lamaru. Even if we repel their attack, I'm worried people will die because of my actions. It may be unprincely for me to admit, but I've been having nightmares since you passed out... about Lamaru's future, about the dragons, and about losing you."

"There's nothing unprincely about admitting you need help. In fact, I think you're very brave and wise for recognizing when you need a little extra love, and I'll do whatever I can to bring you peace of mind. I promised I'd never let you go." She snuggled into his arms and closed her eyes. "You told me we'd face whatever misfortune my curse will bring together. I'd be a bad girlfriend if I let you face your nightmares alone."

"Then would you sleep with me in my cabin tonight? I know I'd sleep better with my arms wrapped around you."

Katria blushed a deep crimson. "Of course."

***

By the time Cassio and Zevulun reached their destination, the sky had turned pink as dawn creeped across the sky. The sprawling network of caves and tunnels deep within the Omah Mountains had remained so perfectly hidden, the Watchers had lost innumerable days and lives to simply find the fabled entrance.

Zevulun guided his wyvern to a large, flat, stone outcropping. She landed with a loud 'thud' and let out a screech of accomplishment. "Oh, yes you are such a good girl!" He kissed her head, scratched her neck, and dismounted, then took two raw, heaping steaks from a storage chest and tossed them to her. The wyvern cooed affectionately as it ripped into the raw meat and swallowed whole chunks the size of his hand.

Cassio dismounted and fed their own steed, though objectively less affectionate than Zevulun. They were met by twelve guards in heavy white capotes and thick, furred trousers all armed with swords, lances, and bows. All also had dragon tattoos. The leader of the group pulled back her hood. Her red hair whipped back and forth in the frozen wind. The tattoo of a dragon wrapped around her neck as if a young drake slept peacefully on her right shoulder.

"Dracona Zevulun, it's good to see you again." She bowed politely and smiled affectionately at him then turned her stardust eyes to Cassio. "And of course, Dracona Cassio," she said in a much more neutral and professional tone that suited them just fine. "I am the newest appointed to the rank of Dracona, Satial. I'm sure you're anxious to see the dig site. Please follow me."

Cassio nodded. Satial dismissed her soldiers who returned to the mouth of the cave and set their arms aside. They drank hot beverages, threw dice, and shuffled hands of cards as they lazily guarded the cavern. Each of them knew their job was pointless. Only the most prominent of the Watchers knew anything about the dig site, and only Dracona Zevulun and his two trusted lieutenants knew the path into the mountains from the desert encampment below.

Satial led them deep into the central cavern where the only light came from flickering torches and bored light spirits trapped in tiny, metal cages. Cassio looked around in awe. The tunnel was so big that light grasped at the top of the stone walls but came up short and faded into inky blackness. They knew the tunnels and caverns had to be magnanimous in order to accommodate the largest dragons that ever roamed Reighja yet the endless caverns humbled Cassio immensely as they contemplated their own minuscule existence.

Cassio didn't say much during their two hour-long trek down into the depths of the mountains to a subterranean graveyard where the bones of ancient legends were supposedly buried. Zevulun and Satial brought each other up to speed on recent events and complained about the problems they faced with their respective assignments. They flirted with one another to which Cassio simply rolled their eyes and ignored their childish behavior.

Retired from a long and lucrative career of designing, Cassio's only goal, their own driving motivation was the mission of the Watchers: to guide all of Reighja, elvish, human, maiamorph and Clystudine alike, back to the age ruled by the superior race of dragons. Even compared to elves, Cassio understood all species remained infantile compared to the existence and lives of dragons. They longed for the yesteryears when their own kind worshiped their ancient gods and knew that only with their benevolent aid would they all return to a righteous path and reach their full potential as a species.

They crossed a wood and rope bridge over a dark and dismal abyss, where the only indication the chasm didn't stretch into the eternal depths was the sound of running water far below from a subterranean river underneath the mountain.

"Both of you please watch your step in this last room. The ground is unstable due to our digging," warned Satial as the tunnel opened into an even larger cavern, which stretched on like a gray stone ocean. Illuminated by pinpricks of light, two hundred archaeologists and Magi excavated the skeleton of an ancient, colossal dragon. Satial led Cassio and Zevulun to a cliff overlook with an elevator system that brought tools or rations down to the workers and relics or rubble up from the dig site.

"He's beautiful," murmured Cassio as they gazed upon the skeleton of what had surely been a god of the ancient world.

The rib cage alone dwarfed Lamaru's largest sandship. An average-sized elf equaled only the smallest phalange bone in one of the dragon's massive talons. A small palace could fit inside the skull and the bones in a single wing must have totaled at least a mile in length. Yet even for its massive size, the skeleton remained half-buried in the rock and earth where it had laid undisturbed for hundreds or thousands or millions of years.

"This way, please." Satial guided them to a rough, stone staircase hewn from the cavern walls itself. "We've found hundreds of smaller skeletons surrounding this large one, presumably kin or sacrifices buried along with her."

"Her?" repeated Zevulun. "I thought the ancient one was male."

"As does every other man who worships an amorphous or androgynous god," Satial rolled her eyes. "But *she* is definitely a *her*. We can tell by the bone structure compared to that of other remains, scaled up a few thousand times of course. The texts we gathered and deciphered from across Reighja all mention prayers to 'the mother'. We thought they were referring to the 'Mother Earth' or 'Mother Stars' similarly to many prehistoric or extinct religions, but after this discovery, it seems they may have been referring to the mother of dragons; the progenitor of the greatest dragons that ruled the continent even before humans permanently settled Reighja."

They reached the end of the stone stairs.

"Of course," Satial continued, "Even after her skeleton is fully excavated, we still have the problem of the restoration ritual."

"I thought you deciphered the correct runic order and minna capacity of our reanimation ritual." Cassio glared at Zevulun. Zevulun laughed nervously. Cassio was not amused.

"In theory, yes, but I'm not convinced of the scope of my test results. Follow me. I'll show you what I mean. I built a replica of the altar we'll need to construct to revive our sleeping deity." Zevulun led them across the excavation site, back toward the ledge and elevator.

A square stone altar had been built on top of three raised platforms in an alcove. A strange, spidery widget with twelve long, mechanical arms hung above the altar. Each had multiple slots where the greater minna stones would be placed. A metal, concave tendril stood on each of the four corners of the lowest square platform, again with slots carved out for minna stones. The entire contraption was covered in Magesep runes traced over with charcoal and liquidated, precious metals.

"My Magi have worked endless days and nights but have only had limited success. We can mend broken bones, close lacerations, and even regrow the tissue of damaged organs. We've reanimated small mammals, mostly rodents, and plants sacrificed on the altar.

"We've pushed the time frame of resurrection as far out as twelve hours after the subjects were proclaimed dead but it's impossible to revive anything deceased longer. Theoretically, it will work, but the amount of minna the ritual consumes is exponential. We aren't even close to the resources we need to revive something killed a few days or a week ago, and the amount of minna needed to bring back something hundreds or thousands of years old is astronomically larger."

"Is it possible to tighten the ritual so it consumes less minna?" asked Cassio, not the least bit disheartened.

Zevulun nodded. "But I need more data to figure out which runes and words can be combined. One wrong step and we revive a crazed, soulless, bloodthirsty monster instead of a wise and noble being. Without additional resources, our testing phase has ground to a halt."

"What about that individual who recently claimed to be a soulseeker? The one gaining power and influence in Banjiha? Would she be able to give us what we need?" Satial asked the other two Draconas.

Cassio and Zevulun made looks of disgust.

"She's much more likely to become a threat rather than an asset," Cassio remarked. "The woman named Lilith and her brother, Uriel, wholeheartedly believe in human virtue and superiority. Lilith plans to secede Banjiha from Lamaru and create a new nation, free from the 'unnatural, feral, and subhuman' maiamorphs. I'm not sure how many actually believe her lunacy but the Padishah and King have yet to pursue action against her."

"That's insane." Satial crossed her arms over her chest and scowled. "Our ancient gods created the maiamorphs. They have the same, if not a greater, right to life than we do."

Zevulun nodded. "The world should be rid of that scum and her bigoted views. I'd love nothing more than to see her and her followers banished from Lamaru."

"Indeed," agreed Cassio. "And with the support of the other Draconas, I've recently acquired a sandship, the newly christened Dragonfang, stationed in Thaniana. Should war break out between

Banjiha and Lamaru, our aid in quashing Lilith's rebellion might be enough to sway the Padishah's short-sighted judgment."

"And until this supposed war erupts?" asked Zevulun.

"We will do as we've always done: observe how this conflict evolves from the shadows and influence its players as we see fit. Then, when the time is right, we will aid the Crown and win over the loyalty of Lamaru's people."

"Ironic that the Padishah deemed our research hazardous, yet we cannot continue, even behind their backs, unless we aid them first," retorted Zevulun.

"It is not our way to question our path but simply seize whatever opportunities it brings us. That is what it means to have faith."

Zevulun nodded. "Then we must pray that Lilith strikes swiftly and with enough force to unnerve the Padishah. I'm anxious to continue my research."

End Part II

Part III

12

Interlude

Year 149 A.D. (After Demotion); present day

"Again," commanded Padishah Lila. Naemin sighed. He rubbed his head, stood up, and dusted himself off. He looked at his mother with big, pouty eyes.

"Come on, Momma. I'm tired of trying. I wanna give up for today. We've been working on this cantrip for almost an hourrr."

"And I'm surprised you still have so much energy left. If you put half as much effort into harnessing minna as you did complaining, I'm sure you would have equaled both Jiian and your sister by now."

Naemin blinked, utterly speechless. *I'd be as good as Jiian and sissy?* He glanced up at the northern end of the sandy arena where his father and Saffi's twin brother Jiian were completely engrossed in a sparring session of their own.

Jiian, a prodigy at harnessing water minna, effortlessly incorporated cantrip after cantrip into his unyielding assault, commanding water and ice as his blade danced back and forth. Yet King Jordan's fire was far from extinguished, and he perfectly countered Jiian's every cantrip, cut, spell, and slash despite the fact he had spent the last hour dueling with Saffi, both exclusively harnessing fire minna. He was the perfect mentor for the twin paragons and although the odds were stacked against him, Jiian battled on with a calm and confident smile, undeterred in the slightest.

Naemin smiled. He liked Jiian, who enjoyed conversation, unlike his sister, and indulged in all manner of games and good-natured chaos. The pair of them had already accomplished a plethora of misadventures around the castle. When Naemin turned ten, Jiian would become his retainer, just as Saffi was his sister's.

Then I can finally go on expeditions with sissy and General Gil. The young prince glanced toward the southern end of the arena where Amira stood, shamshir in hand, completely encased in her self-created, earth-minna shell. She quickly struck down four minnaquins, minna-powered automatons, whose swords and lances bounced harmlessly off her arcane armor. A wall of stone rose up from the ground and shielded her from General Gil's next bombardment of complex cantrips from the miniature minna orb thirty yards away.

"As good as sissy..." Naemin repeated absentmindedly. He looked up at his mom and frowned. "How? She knows so many different cantrips. All I can do is make this stupid air shield, and I can't even do that right half the time."

"Oh, my sweet baby boy, don't be so hard on yourself." Lila knelt beside her son. "You are a natural when it comes to harnessing wind minna, and you have the best Magi in the kingdom as your teacher." She booped his nose playfully.

Naemin giggled and smiled back.

"However, I want you to listen carefully to what I'm about to say. There are two kinds of people in this world: those who are naturally gifted, like you, and those who have to work much harder to master certain skills, like your sister. But even with a natural head start, the gifted almost always fall behind because of their lack of consistent training. Your affinity for wind minna is exceptionally high, but your sister spends at least three hours a day practicing. Can you imagine how much more quickly you would master these cantrips if you dedicated the same amount of time as she does?"

Naemin remained silent and curiously watched his sister. *Did sissy really struggle with harnessing minna? I thought she could easily do it... I thought everything came easy to her.* Amira's movements were fluid and precise. The earth and sand answered her beck and call whilst her sword struck as swiftly as an arrow. *Was I wrong? Is that why she spends so much time studying?*

"Your mother is right, as always," added King Jordan as he, Saffi, and Jiian joined them. "Talent without training is wasted potential. Even if you know the right way to react, it doesn't do you any good if your body can't keep up. Your sister knows that strength alone doesn't always win battles."

Naemin frowned. "But I don't like fighting. I don't want to hurt anyone."

"And I pray the day never comes that you have to use this training to defend yourself," retorted Jordan. "But it's better to be a warrior in a garden than a gardener in a war."

"Huh? But why would a gardener have to go to war? That's not their job in the first place."

Lila sighed. "Naemin, your life is more important than you realize. Even if you're not next in line for the throne, you're still a prince of Lamaru and my son. The world is such a fun and grand place, but it can be cruel and scary too. You will meet people who don't want what's best for you. I need to know you can look after yourself, especially since you want to join your sister and Sir Gil on their expeditions. I need to know you'll be safe."

"But I can always rely on Jiian to protect me. He's so good with a sword and water minna." Naemin's eyes lit up. "He's just like Prince Achyut in the story! Ooohh, instead of training can we keep reading? Pleeaaassee! My arms hurt."

"Alright, son, I'll make you a deal. If you show me you've actually been training with your mother by blocking one of my spells, we'll call it quits for today and continue reading the story."

"Yaaay!" Naemin clapped his hands and jumped joyfully.

"But," continued Jordan, "if you can't block my attack, then we train for another hour. Even Prince Achyut knew the value of practice."

"I'll do it!" Naemin crossed his arms and puffed out his chest.

Jordan smiled. He walked twenty paces away and gathered minna in his hand until his black glove burned brightly with white fire.

I can do this. I can do this, Naemin told himself over and over again. *I'll be better than sissy and Jiian. I'll work hard and join their expeditions! I'll show Momma I can defend myself. I am Naemin, the Gale Prince of Lamaru, descended from Prince Achyut the Gallant!*

"Ready or not, here I come!" Jordan hurled the fireball at his son. Naemin watched as it zoomed closer and closer. He couldn't sustain his shield for long and quickly realized his failure for not taking his lessons seriously. Therefore, the only option was to have perfect timing.

"Closer… closer… closer…*Naotanidurih!*" He threw up his arms and felt the winds whip around his body as he released all the minna stored in his focus. A bronze cyclone engulfed him. The fireball struck and dissipated. He was untouched!

"I did it! I actually did it!" Naemin laughed with triumphant glee.

"I'm so proud of my little prince!" Lila clapped her hands together.

"Well done, my son," lauded Jordan. "You see what you can accomplish with persistence and the right attitude?"

"Yes, sir!" Naemin grinned from ear to ear, exuberant that his efforts had finally borne fruit. "Now I can be just like Prince Achyut!"

"My, my, congratulations Prince Naemin! If you keep up this pace, you might even surpass my sister and me! Isn't that right, Saffi?"

"Hmph. If he outpaces you, then you've grown weak as his future retainer," Saffi retorted with a cheeky grin. Jiian rolled his eyes.

"Congratulations, little brother." Amira and Gil joined their circle. "I always knew you had it in you."

"Indeed. I have no doubt in my mind you'll become a powerful Magi, just like the other members of your family, as long as you keep your head up and keep pushing forward," added Gil. "Perhaps you'd like to try for two-for-two?"

"Nuh-uh! That's way too much effort way too soon!" Naemin scrunched his face up. Everyone laughed. He didn't understand what was so funny.

"Hey, hey," he pulled at his dad's robes, "you promised we'd hear the rest of Prince Achyut's story!"

"That I did, that I did. Well then, shall we head back over to the bluebell gardens?"

"Yeah!" Naemin, Amira, and Jiian all cheered and even Saffi couldn't hide her enthusiasm. Lila took her husband's arm as he led the procession back to the gardens. Gil brought over an extra bench for Jiian and Saffi. Lila sat beside Jordan with their son in her lap and their daughter by her side.

"Here you are, as promised." Jordan handed the hefty volume to Gil.

"Thank you, my liege. Alright then, is everyone cozy? Good, good." Gil sat back down in his rocking chair and flipped through its pages. "Let's see, let's see. The next entry takes place four months after Prince Achyut and Katria's close encounter with the bandits." He skimmed the next few pages, thought for a few moments, and cleared his throat.

"Prince Achyut stood on the bow of the Prospector, Katria in his arms, as the ship sailed past the great red walls outside An'ard. Something felt wrong in the sprawling port city yet he couldn't explain his reasoning...".

13

Illadina

Year 0: The Collapse

Prince Achyut stood on the bow of the Prospector, Katria in his arms, as the ship sailed past the great red walls outside An'ard. Something felt wrong in the sprawling port city yet he couldn't explain his reasoning. The Prospector sailed down a sand canal that cut through the city and joined the shores of the Hayi River, which ran from its headwaters in the western mountains all the way across southern Reighja and joined with the sea on the eastern coast. Boats of various sizes and shapes sailed up and down its course, which stretched three miles from bank to bank, shuttling passengers and cargo between Lamaru's great cities. Eight massive cranes overlooked a widened part of the canal where three other sandships rested in a sandlot near a wooden dock on the river's edge.

"Darling, what's wrong?" Katria wrapped her arms around Achyut's neck and pulled his head down, meeting her gaze. "You've been staring at every passenger ship since we entered the city. Are you looking for someone?"

"I'm not looking for anyone. I've got my most important person right here." He kissed her soft lips.

She melted into his arms until he pulled away and rested his head atop hers.

"It's just, something doesn't feel right. No ships are leaving the city. The docks are much more crowded than usual, and almost all the passengers are exclusively maiamorphs. I have a bad feeling that all this is linked to the increased security we saw entering the city."

The Prospector slid neatly in line just as the crews of the closest ship departed for the large, open-air bazaar and cultural center that overlooked the river; a place where sailors and civilians could relax while their ships were repaired or stocked or configured to travel across land or water.

"Alright, everyone, stick close and follow me. No wandering off," called Captain Tanoy as he, Mona, and Joseph herded all of Lamaru's new citizens toward the gangplanks.

"Come on, let's help them out. The sooner we get everyone off the ship, the sooner we can explore the city, and I've got a special surprise for you, my dear." Achyut smiled mischievously.

It was slow and arduous work herding everyone off the Prospector while ensuring none were lost among the city streets. They reached the closest embassy and waited while every new citizen's concerns and questions were answered. Once Prince Achyut decided they were no longer needed, he, Katria and Mona walked around the open stalls.

Katria had never seen so many people and new sights in one place and asked question after question about everything that piqued her interest. Achyut and Mona happily answered, surprised at how the once mousey maiden had grown into a confident and curious woman. They stopped at several different food stalls and ordered a bit of everything. Katria especially loved the unleavened bread Achyut called roti, torn into strips and dunked in a sweet curry while they sat on a bench and listened to street musicians play.

Prince Achyut studied every customer and passersby. His brows furrowed as his earlier observation crept back into his mind. Two families of urosi and foxtail maiamorphs waited in line for food, clutching their luggage close to their chest. A small flock of avian maiamorphs flew overhead; all of them carried wooden crates and supplies. A pair of city guards offered blankets to a group of elkan and sika children. The various maiamorphs were far from any oddity in any of the major ports and cities in the Dynasty of Lamaru, yet there had always been roughly the same number of maiamorphs and humans. Now, however, he estimated five or six maiamorphs for every human in the crowd.

"Hey, Mona, have you noticed anything strange since we arrived?"

Mona nodded. "There're so many more maiamorphs around than usual and all the civilian ships and transports have exclusively carried maiamorph passengers."

"But there aren't any special holidays or celebrations or festivities going on."

"So why has everyone gathered here?" finished Mona.

A loud brass bell rang out somewhere in the city. Prince Achyut looked down at his watch.

"Oh, it's almost time! We've got to get back to the Prospector! You won't want to miss this." He grinned and pulled Katria to her feet. "Coming, Mona?"

"You two go ahead. I'm going to talk with the city officials. I'll meet you back at the ship when I'm done."

Achyut nodded then led Katria to the dock overlook just as two of the massive cranes descended and wrapped their claws around the hull of the Prospector. Katria watched in awe as they hoisted the ship up and suspended it in the air. Its keel unhinged from the edge of the ship, fell downward, and latched into place. The long wheels and treads flattened and became flush with the hull. Two smaller cranes pressed rounded hulls against the supporting frames on either side of the ship and converted them into air-filled buoys with the wheels and treads trapped inside. The cranes swung slowly over the river and lowered the ship into the water beside another wooden dock. A gangplank fell against the dock. Down below, Captain Tanoy and the crew loaded everyone back on board.

"That's amazing!" exclaimed Katria. "What took four days by hand only took an hour with those giant cranes!"

"That's the power of harnessing minna," Achyut replied proudly. "The first leaders of Lamaru knew the country could only ever be as good as its infrastructure and spent innumerable days and even more resources to ensure the cities had room to grow and grow properly in all directions. I've lived here my whole life and I still get excited every time I see our magnificent widgets in action." He held Katria's hand and kissed it. "And once we're aboard, the journey to Illadina will only take three or four days, then you'll see the full majesty of your new home."

"My new home?"

"Of course! You're to live in the palace with me and Mona and Reena. I wouldn't have it any other way. I can't wait for you to meet the rest of my family."

"Your family? Including your parents? A-as in the Queen and King of Lamaru?!"

Achyut nodded.

"That seems a little overwhelming," muttered Katria. "I'm not opposed to the prospect, just a little nervous." She looked out over the river. "Meeting royalty again..."

"Hey." He took her hands in his own and held them to his chest. "I know you had a rough life back in Yaand, but I swear that's not how all royalty works. My parents are good people and soulseekers have always had an aptitude for leading our country justly. They're gifted with incredible levels of empathy and a perspective that allows them to help everyone. I know they'll love you. Especially after I announce you as my bride-to-be."

"What? Wait a moment! B-bride?! Darling, do you seriously mean that—" Katria's face turned chili pepper red. She only grew more flustered as she tried to speak. "I, um, well, uh, that's not something you should tease a lady about."

"Who said I was teasing you?" Achyut pulled her into his arms, the enticing aroma of her perfume filling his nostrils as he savored the taste of her sweet lips and the warmth of her body pressed against his.

Katria's heart raced like never before. Her body shook with excitement and longing as she kissed him again and again. They had known each other for so little time. She wasn't of noble birth or even properly educated. Even as the implications of her curse bubbled up in the back of her mind, she knew that should he ask, her only response would be 'yes'. More than anything else, she wanted to stay by his side. He had pulled her from her darkness. She thought so little of her time before she joined the Prospector's crew, for this was when her life truly began.

Achyut could barely pull away from her tight embrace. He knelt on one knee and pulled out a box hidden in one of his kurta's pockets.

"Katr—"

"Yes! Yes, I accept!" she replied before her name left his lips.

"I didn't even get a chance to ask you yet." Achyut laughed warmly. "Still, I have your answer and that makes me the happiest man in the world." He took the ring out of the box and slipped it onto her finger. Katria looked down at the white stone in pure ecstasy.

"Oh, my darling, it's absolutely wonderful. This is the most precious gift I've ever received. I love it and I love you so very, very much. Ah, I'm so happy! I promise I'll always treasure it, and I'll never take it off. I'll be the perfect wife for you." She giggled and kissed him again.

"Prince Achyut!" Mona called as she ran through the crowd. "Prince Achyut! We need to depart as soon as possible! I've heard terrible news from the city of Banjiha! Another soulseeker has— why are the two of you smiling like idiots?" She glanced between Achyut and Katria.

"Oh Mona, it's the best news ever!" Tears of happiness brimmed in Katria's amber eyes. She held out her hand with the ring on her finger. "Prince Achyut asked me to marry him! The two of us are engaged!"

Mona stared slack-jawed for a good minute, unable to simultaneously process what the city officials had told her along with this most excellent news. Achyut and Katria were getting married! She stepped toward them and wrapped her arms around the newly betrothed couple.

"Ahh-haha! I'm so happy for you both! We'll have a huge feast tonight and you can announce your engagement. Oh, Prince Achyut, your mother and father will be thrilled. It goes without saying that you both have my blessing."

"Thank you, Mona, that means the world to me." Achyut hugged her back.

"And I as well," added Katria, who returned Mona's embrace. "Afterall, you're my family too. Oh! Was there something you wanted to tell us? You seemed rather frantic a moment ago."

"It can wait till tomorrow. Tonight is a night of merriment and celebration."

The next four days went by quicker than Katria would have liked, yet they were the happiest she had ever been. She still spent every moment with Achyut that she could— meals and studying, combat training, and especially the warm and wonderful nights in his cabin. She knew in her heart they would be together forever and each night fell into a peaceful slumber with her arms wrapped around his chest as visions of wedding dresses danced in her head. Yet the night before they reached the capital, she awoke again and again from her fiance's fretful fidgeting.

"Darling, what's wrong?" she asked sleepily as she pressed her body against his and entwined his legs with her own. "You've been lying awake for the past few hours. You need your rest for tomorrow."

"I'm sorry, my dear." He wrapped his arms around her waist. "And I apologize I keep rousing you from your rest. I'm just having trouble contemplating what Mona told us the other day. To think a soulseeker would be born outside the royal family and that they would seek to establish their own nation. It's unheard of. Banjiha has always been a bustling center of commerce for Lamaru and if this debacle isn't handled properly, it will result in bloodshed. Rakiba and I will be on the front lines. To be separated from you right after our engagement; the world has a cruel sense of irony indeed."

"You won't be separated from me." She tilted his head down and pressed her lips to his, stroking his cheek as she slowly pulled away.

"Do you remember what I told you the day we left the Bale? That no place has ever felt like home to me? That changed after meeting you. My place, my home, is by your side. I'll be with you wherever you go. After all, what's the point of going through Mona's grueling training if I'm not able to protect my beloved?"

"Katria… I'm honored by your kindness and devotion, but the battlefield is no place for civilians. I don't want you to get hurt."

"There is absolutely no way I'm letting you out of my sight," she replied firmly. "I can help. I know I can. With Nuhir Rakiba's ability to soulshare, your kindness, and my divination, we'll end this conflict before it comes to bloodshed."

Achyut gazed lovingly at her and smiled. He remembered their first real conversation on the moonlit docks. She had grown into one hell of a woman.

"What are you staring at dummy?" She wiggled under their blanket and covered the tops of her breasts. "You're making me blush."

"You've grown so much since I met you. You were such a timid, little thing, and didn't even care about your own life."

"That's because I had no reason to live, no friends or family, and only believed I could bring ruin." A bright smile crossed her lips as she stared into his eyes. "Yet now I'm surrounded by people who love me. I want to make all of you smile and to give you the happiness you've given me." She gently grasped his face in her hands. "I'll be with you, forever and always, even through the very end." She kissed his lips and laid her head on his chest. "I promise."

Achyut smiled as he played with her copper hair. A wave of serenity washed over him. He suddenly felt very sleepy. Somehow, he knew everything would turn out all right. It had to. He couldn't afford to fail his friends, his family, his country, nor the woman of his dreams. Soon enough he drifted off to sleep with Katria in his arms.

The next morning, the newly betrothed couple showered, ate, and donned their royal appeal. Prince Achyut wore his dark blue kurta and dark-brown dhoti. Katria wore a cream-colored saree with an emerald green border and a jade, silken shawl which denoted her association with the royal family. Even Mona wore a more traditional and conservative crimson outfit to meet Nuhir Rakiba and the royal paragons at the dock and greet the citizens of Illadina during their procession to the citadel and palace.

By noon, the Prospector reached the red clay walls surrounding the capital city. Achyut, Katria, Mona, and Reena all stood on the bow. They passed under a sturdy gate, the sides lined with multi-level platforms and minna orbs. They waved happily at the guards who waved back and sounded large brass gongs and horns which signaled the return of the young prince.

Hundreds of ships sailed back and forth across the blue central lagoon of the city. Smooth sandstone roads cut through rows and rows of stacked houses and shops. Colossal clay towers rose between the shopping districts and subdivisions. Even before the anchor dropped and the safety lines were tied, a seemingly endless sea of people had gathered. They played cheerful music and danced throughout the city streets as a battalion of paragons calmly parted its citizens and cleared a path for the crew to safely disembark.

Nuhir Rakiba stood at the end of the dock, dressed in lavishly decorated ceremonial armor; their jade, knee-length cape fluttered in the light breeze. Amarak sat patiently beside them, frantically wagging his tail. Rakiba scratched his massive head and floppy ears as Achyut and the others disembarked.

"Mmm... so many people..." Katria whined as she clung to Achyut's arm.

"It's tradition to welcome the members of the royal family when we return to the palace." Achyut smiled and waved at the crowds as they departed the ship and walked up the dock to meet Rakiba and Amarak. "All aboard the Prospector will process up to the palace for a grand and glorious feast this evening. We'll talk with my parents first then have the afternoon to relax before the festivities begin."

"I guess so," replied Katria. "Though I'm a bit worried—"

"Reena will be fine," reassured Mona, who walked behind the pair. "Joseph and the rest of the crew are leading the new citizens off the ship right after us. Captain Tanoy will make sure everyone makes their way to the palace."

"Well, that's a relief," Katria sighed. "You know how rambunctious she can get."

As they reached the city streets, Rakiba smiled at the three of them and spread their arms in a warm, welcoming gesture. "Prince Achyut, Lady Mona, it does my heart well to see you've returned safely from your voyage."

"It's wonderful to be home." Prince Achyut bowed before his older sibling. "I see you and Amarak are in good health."

The great golden wolf barked and wagged its tail.

Achyut smiled. "It's also my greatest pleasure to introduce you to Katria Konners, an oracle from Yaand and my betrothed."

"You're betrothed? Well, little brother, you've certainly been busy! A pleasure to meet you, Lady Katria."

"It's, um, it's a pleasure to meet you, Nuhir Rakiba." Katria blushed as she curtsied.

"I look forward to learning more about you and your engagement this evening. I am certain that you are exactly the kind and wonderful woman my little brother deserves." They smiled affectionately. "To be honest, I'm a little jealous knowing you've had such a grand and fruitful adventure. My trip to Banjiha was utterly exhausting and our parents have been bogged down with their own political duties. I returned early this morning and still haven't seen them."

"I can tell, you look like you haven't slept in days," Achyut teased.

"And you continue to speak oh so elegantly and respectfully," Rakiba retorted with a smile. "Still, I'm thankful for your early return."

Their paragons continually created their path up the long, smooth, sandstone streets that stretched toward the Citadel. They passed through the stone gates and fence that surrounded the palace grounds and followed the winding path fringed with desert flowers and cacti. They arrived at the polished sandstone stairs that led to a pair of sturdy palmwood doors and marked the main entrance of the gigantic structure that sat on a hill and overlooked the lagoon and city.

Two guards took up posts and opened the doors of the magnificent palace. Katria stared in awe at its decorations and splendor as they walked through the labyrinth of halls and open-air gardens until at last they reached a pair of palm doors that led to the throne room. Two more guards stationed by the doors bowed and ushered them inside.

Padishah Angem and King Debash sat in their thrones as Prince Achyut, Katria, Lady Mona, Nuhir Rakiba and Amarak all entered, genuflected, and stood on the edge of an emerald rug. Angem glanced curiously at the copper-haired woman nervously clinging to Achyut's arm and smiled faintly before she addressed her son and his retainer.

"Prince Achyut, Lady Mona, welcome back to Illadina. We are most thankful for your safe return from your expedition investigating the northwest coast of Reighja. Please inform the King and myself of your findings and introduce us to this young woman."

"Yes, your Majesty," replied Prince Achyut. "Our initial expedition was met with little success. We found very few islands off the western seaboard, and none worth our colonization efforts. The islands and atolls are scarce with resources, with little information or resources we can sell to the Seafarer's Guild or Merchants of Jatharir. We then visited the newly formed Clystudine Confederation and met with the Enlightened Rakriliox of the Bale on our return to Reighja proper. In exchange for our assistance in aiding their reclamation efforts of stolen land, they released three-hundred and sixty-nine captured slaves from Yaand into my care. This is one of those freed, Lady Katria," He wrapped his arms around her and smiled proudly. "She is also my betrothed."

The royal council let out all manner of gasps and cheers and congratulations. Dabesh smiled proudly at his son. Angem used every ounce of strength not to break her queenly composure.

"I see," replied Padishah Angem. "Welcome, Lady Katria, to the palace of Illadina, and congratulations on your engagement to my son. The two of you will accompany the King and me on a walk once this audience is adjourned."

She took several deep breaths and then addressed her oldest child. "Nuhir Rakiba, have you any updates from the region of Banjiha?"

"Yes, Your Majesty," Rakiba replied, their expression calm but grave. "Unfortunately, we were unable to reach a peaceful settlement. Lilith has publicly declared she will not pursue violent action against the rest of Lamaru as long as we do not interfere with her reign, but from one soulseeker to another, I do not trust her words. Her supposedly peaceful relocation of maiamorph citizens turned violent the moment some opposed her, claiming self-defense. Many of the ships that fled Banjiha are also unaccounted for and Kinnari has been unable to ascertain their whereabouts. Even the avian flocks have been forced out of the Ironwood Forests. If Lilith remains in power, I'm convinced she will invade the province of Mutaedun once all of Banjiha is secure." They took a deep breath and continued their report.

"Lastly, I've made contact with Captain Karascotia of the Longevity and Captain Cassio Naebuella of the Dragonfang in Thaniana. Both have pledged their forces to my attack group should we choose to retake the city."

Padishah Angem sighed. "Then it seems our worst fears have been realized. For the second time since its founding, Lamaru lies on the brink of civil war."

Their counsel muttered curses and lamentations under their breath.

King Dabesh rubbed his eyes. "Nuhir Rakiba, I had hoped it would not come to this, but if Lilith and her leaders will not accept a peaceful reunification, we must retake the region by force. It pains me to say this, but as a soulseeker and heir apparent of Lamaru, you must lead this campaign."

Padishah Angem nodded. "I agree. You will depart for An'ard in one week and rendezvous with the Longevity and Dragonfang. Lead your task force to the heart of Banjiha, retake the city, and capture their leader. Prince Achyut, you will remain here and help advise us on the situation as it develops."

"Yes, your Majesty." Rakiba's face was stone-cold and emotionless. They already knew it would come to this. It was best to bear this burden with stoic dignity and grace.

Prince Achyut stood slack-jawed as his eyes flitted back and forth between his mother and sibling. Rakiba had told him the situation with the soulseeker was difficult, not that Lamaru would declare open war. Even worse, if Rakiba could not claim a quick, decisive victory, hundreds or thousands of citizens could be swept up in the chaos. He quietly clenched his jaw. He knew he couldn't stand around and wait it out. They had the same responsibilities, both as royal children and citizens of the country. He had to help.

Here we go again. Mona sighed as she watched Achyut's pained expression.

"Padishah Angem, King Dabesh," interrupted Prince Achyut. "With your permission, I would like the Prospector to join Nuhir Rakiba's task force to retake Banjiha."

"Prince Achyut," King Dabesh stared blankly at his son. "I understand your willingness to lead and your wish to help our people and country, but we will not allow you to take such a risk. Nuhir Rakiba is more than capable of leading our forces, and should the worst befall them, you will survive to take the throne." Yet they knew their son's moral compass was incorrigible.

"Then let me go with Rakiba to maximize our chances of winning. The Prospector's crew has faced danger time and time again and we've always come up strong. You can't deny the advantage of bringing an extra sandship."

"My son, some advantages, are too costly," argued Angem, "And with your engagement to Lady Katria, you cannot afford to gamble away your life."

Katria shyly raised her hand. "If I may add something."

"You may speak freely, Lady Katria," reassured the Padishah.

"I would also like to join Prince Achyut and Nuhir Rakiba in this endeavor. I may not know much about combat, but my powers as an oracle would give Lamaru's forces an unprecedented advantage. You see, I can recount the history of any item I touch as if the item itself could use its senses." Katria lowered her eyes and the faintest glimpse of a smile tugged at the corner of her lips.

"Honestly, I used to think my powers were a curse. My life was constantly threatened because people valued my insights more than my existence but when I met Prince Achyut, he loved and loves me for me. He's protected me and shown me I can use my powers to protect others. I now understand that even on our darkest days, when we're lost in thoughts and all alone, life is still too precious of a gift to be taken lightly." She raised her head and spoke with confidence and poise. "I want to give hope to those that have none. I want to teach them that their lives do matter. Prince Achyut pulled me from my darkness. I want to do the same for your people."

A member of the royal council stood and clapped. Then another and another and another joined until all the court stood and applauded Katria's words and bravery. Both Angem and Dabesh sighed.

"I love you," Achyut whispered in her ear and wrapped his arms around her waist. His lips brushed against the back of her neck and tickled her skin.

"I love you too." Katria giggled.

"Eh-hem," the Padishah coughed at their unwarranted public display of affection yet on the inside she couldn't be prouder. Katria was a fine woman indeed.

"Lady Katria," she continued, "your offer and your words are most honorable. While it is still my current decision that you and my son remain at the palace, I cannot deny your bravery nor the invaluable information your powers would provide our offensive. However, we shall save discussion of your offer and of our trials and tribulations for the day after tomorrow. Tonight, we will celebrate Prince Achyut's return, your engagement, the lives of the Prospector's crew, and the lives of the newest citizens of Lamaru. The feast will begin at six o'clock sharp. I declare this audience adjourned. Prince Achyut, Lady Katria, please join the King and myself for a stroll around the palace. Nuhir Rakiba, Lady Mona, Amarak, the three of you are dismissed."

"Thank you, Your Majesties," Rakiba and Mona answered in unison. Amarak barked in agreement.

Achyut and Katria followed Angem and Dabesh out of the hallway at the far end of the throne room that led to a walkway atop the inner palace walls. They silently strode across a sandstone bridge that overlooked one of the palace courtyards until they were in the middle of the bridge, out of earshot of anyone.

"Oh, my goodness! My little boy is getting married!" Angem threw her arms around her son and hugged him tightly. "And to such a lovely and brave young woman! Oh, come here Katria, let me give you a hug as well."

Surprised, Katria embraced her mother-in-law. It made sense when she thought about it; out of the public eye, the Angem was a regular person with feelings and emotions just like her. Right now, she was simply a proud mother thrilled with her son's engagement.

"To think so much would come out of your simple expedition." Dabesh hugged Achyut tightly. "I couldn't be prouder of you, son. You've grown into a fine man indeed."

"Thank you both, but about the matter of joining Rakiba's fleet—"

"Oh, shush," interrupted Angem. "I told you we'll talk about that later. Right now, let me enjoy being your mother. I want to know everything about my future daughter-in-law. Where did you meet? How did he propose? And please don't take my son's occasional arrogance to heart, he always means well, even if his way of expressing it is sometimes rather odd."

"Mom! Stop! You're embarrassing me," hissed Achyut. Katria and Dabesh laughed.

Angem doted Katria and her son, who told them everything about their adventures. Achyut's fight against the dragons was met with mixed feelings of awe and admonishment. Katria demonstrated her powers as an oracle. Both Angem and Debesh showered her with praise and spoke to her as part of their family. They asked about her past, listened intently to all of her thoughts and opinions, and asked everything they could to ensure her stay in the palace would be comfortable.

Katria had so much fun getting to know her new relations, she felt surprised at how quickly and effortlessly their time together passed. An hour before the feast began, Angem joyfully clasped her daughter-in-law's hands and they hurried off to her chambers to freshen up and dress for the night's affairs.

The palace brimmed and overflowed with extravagant music and cheerful voices accompanying the grand and joyous celebration. Everyone dressed in exquisite, formal clothing. Dabesh, Rakiba, and Achyut each wore a collared long-sleeve button-down coat called a sherwani and dhoti adorned with the symbols of the royal family, both woven from the finest silks, and dyed in colors associated with their preferred harness of minna. Angem, Katria, and Mona each wore traditional garad sarees with a bright-colored border and stripes that also matched their elemental flairs.

Couples danced in a large circle overlooked by the high table where the royal family and guests of honor sat; all except Prince Achyut and Katria, who mingled with the crowds of people who congratulated them on their engagement.

Katria clung to Achyut's arm, intimidated by the sheer number of people who approached her, yet nonetheless deeply appreciative and grateful for their warm wishes. The young couple danced until their feet were sore before they returned to the high table covered in bowls and plates stacked high with the best foods from all of Lamaru's six major regions. Mouth-watering aromas wafted from a multitude of curries, fried vegetables, flatbread, and sweets.

Rakiba stood before they could take their seats. "Ah, dear brother, Lady Katria, let me introduce you to Captain Zatizimak of the King's Wrath, and Captain Iyushi of the Queen's Salvation. I'm sure you've already heard of their exploits and services to our country."

"Of course! It's an honor to meet you, Captain Zatizimak." Achyut grinned and offered his hand to the man with orange-tinted skin and a mane of fire-red hair. Two black horns protruded from his forehead that matched a pair of black, leathery wings folded neatly against his black jacket. Achyut's eyes fell upon the long, barbed tail that flicked around the man's legs.

"Aye, my eyes are up here, laddie," chafed Zatizimak. "Though I'm surprised my tail is what snared your attention. Usually, people can't get past the horns. They think I'm some sort of fire djinn."

"That's absurd," replied Achyut. "You've clearly the noble heritage of a manticore, not a fire djinn."

Zatizimak grinned a toothy grin. "I like this one, smart as a whip, and with such a lovely lass as well. Your hair is absolutely beautiful, ma'am." He offered his hand to Katria who blushed and returned the gesture. "I heard you two want to join us on the front lines! Why don't we share a drink or three? I'll do what I can to convince the Padishah and King to let you join us. After all, the battlefield is the great equalizer, a true test for the bravest and fittest!"

"Don't give him the wrong idea, Zatizimak," scolded Captain Iyushi, dressed in a dark purple saree. "This isn't one of our little war games. That soulseeker wants Banjiha to secede from Lamaru. Our job is to take her down, dead or alive. But I digress, Prince Achyut, Lady Katria, I'm honored to make your acquaintance, and congratulations to both of you on your engagement." The three of them exchanged another round of handshakes and then sat while more and more plates of food were served.

Zatizimak leaned over and whispered into Achyut's ear. "Captain Iyushi might not say it out loud, but I bet she's itching to blast those xenophobic scumbags. Her husband is of maiamorph ancestry and the both of them take pride in his culture and Lamaru's traditions. She's living proof we can all get along. Our differences are to be shared and celebrated. That's what makes our country such a magical place."

"I couldn't agree more, Captain." Achyut smiled as he looked out over the hundreds of dancers that filled the Great Hall. Each wonderful being had a life of their own, stories to share, wisdom to give, and experiences to learn from. "I couldn't agree more."

14

Reparations and Preparations

Masami Joruka stood in the shadows with her back against the wall, arms crossed over her chest. She wore a scowl on her lips as her husband pawned off more of their family treasures and valuables, just to pay the monthly rent for a cheap, rundown hole-in-the-wall house where their family and remaining staff lived. Her family deserved so much better, and their situation left her absolutely livid. She knew she was exceptionally attractive by human and maiamorph standards and had all the right womanly charms and mannerisms of a lady of court, yet even in Illadina, the capital city of the Dynasty of Lamaru, there were those who looked down on her and her children simply for their heritage. A cloak of overwhelming guilt suffocated her thoughts and covered her heart. Semoru's reputation had shattered. His rich family history, their home, their wonderful life in Banjiha— all gone. All because he had married a maiamorph. All because of her.

Even now, in their new life, she only caused trouble for her husband and family. The old clock tower hadn't even struck ten and yet the city paragons had already told her off twice for punching two different noblemen for badmouthing her, her husband, and their lovely children.

"One more disturbance and you're out of the market," yelled the guard who shoved his fat fingers in Semoru's face. "No coming back until you've proven you can keep *her* under control. *Hmph.* Go buy a leash and muzzle," he muttered as he walked away.

Even the guards think I'm nothing but a savage animal! She clenched her fists and took slow deep breaths. *Those wretched men are fortunate I used my fists instead of my claws. I hope their broken noses will remind them to hold their tongue when addressing the next woman they come across. Dammit!* Bitter tears fell from the corners of her eyes. *Everything is ruined! All because of me, all because I simply exist! Oh, Semoru, my darling, I never meant to cause you so much pain... if I ever get the chance, I promise to show the world I'm worthy of your love and name.* Her black tail flitted back and forth in frustration. *Just one chance. Please, just let me show them I'm supposed to be here.* She closed her eyes and took two more deep, calming breaths. She had to compose herself and return to Semoru's side. Their sales were much more profitable whenever she giggled and flashed a dazzling smile.

"Masami, darling, come quick." Semoru's warm voice cut through the distant sounds of the marketplace, and her own dark thoughts like the summer sun after a harsh thunderstorm.

"If it's alright with you, dear, I'd like to calm down a bit longer. I've not exactly recovered from earlier."

"Please, love, I'd like to introduce you to our next customers. It's quite the unexpected surprise."

"Semoru—" She looked up with a frozen scowl that instantly melted his goofy smile. It was impossible to stay mad when her husband was as giddy as a child during the midwinter festival.

"Fine, fine. I'm coming." Resigned, she stepped out of the shadows and glanced at their three customers, curious as to who could possibly get her husband so excited other than herself. The first was a young man with dark skin and dreadlocks, dressed in a dark blue kurta and cream-colored dhoti. A woman in a bright yellow sundress with long copper hair clung longingly to his arm.

Ah, young love. Masami smiled. The last woman wore a crimson qipao dress adorned with armor plating, obviously the chaperone of the young lovers.

"May I introduce to you Prince Achyut of Lamaru, his fiancée, Lady Katria, and Lady Mona, former Champion of Thaniana! This is my lovely wife, Masami." Semoru held her waist close to his side and pointed across the street. "And those are our little pups playing tag in the park."

"Pleased to meet you," answered Achyut as he gently shook Masami's hand. "I was mortified when I heard about what happened in Banjiha. I know my words cannot do much, but I hope this will help ease your burdens." He placed a small drawstring pouch in her palm.

Curious, she opened the bag and gasped at the treasure trove of coins and minna stones, more than enough to remedy their living situation and buy food for a few months. She stared at Achyut in awe and bewilderment before she finally found her voice. "Th-thank you, Prince Achyut. Bless you and the royal family. If there's anything we can do to repay you—"

"Nonsense. It's a leader's job to take care of his people. I'd be a poor prince if I didn't help those in need. Your husband and I were discussing the possibility of getting your little ones enrolled in Illadina's school system. It might be a bit late in the semester but I'm sure—"

A big brass bell in a high tower rang ten times.

"Prince Achyut, I don't mean to interrupt but we need to leave the bazaar if we're to be on time for the audience with the Padishah and King," reminded Mona.

"That's right. There's no way they'd let us join the campaign if we can't even arrive promptly for the briefing. I apologize, Mr. and Mrs. Joruka, we must be going now."

"It was lovely to meet you." Katria bowed her head and smiled.

"Wait, the campaign? You're actually going back to Banjiha?" Masami's eyes flitted between Prince Achuyt and Mona.

Achytu nodded. "We're to retake the city, capture Lilith, and have her stand trial for her crimes against Lamaru," the prince announced as if it were a simple matter.

"Please, Prince Achyut, you may think this a sudden and foolish request, but let me come with you."

"Masami?! Darling, what's gotten into you?" asked Semoru.

"I want to prove the Joruka family's and foxtails' loyalty to Lamaru. I need to show to that soulseeker Lilith and her followers that we do belong," she proclaimed.

Achyut smiled. "You are a courageous woman, Masami Joruka, and your offer alone is proof enough of your loyalty to this country, but a battlefield is no place for the untrained."

"I can learn," she retorted. "I'm quick and stealthy and my claws are as sharp as any sword."

"Masami, please, I can't lose you too," pleaded Semoru.

"Prince Achyut, we have to leave. Now," Mona stated matter-of-factly.

"Thank you for your offer, but we must be going." Achyut bowed politely and turned to leave.

Masami stood silently as the young prince walked away. Once more she had failed to make it up to her family and herself. She clenched her teeth. *No. Never again.*

"Prince Achyut! You'll need a guide to lead you through Banjiha's streets. I know them better than anyone!" She touched the peridot necklace she wore, a gift from her beloved on the night they were engaged. She closed her eyes and pictured the city streets; the countless maps she had studied whenever Semoru worked long nights and fit the pieces of her cantrip together in her mind. She knelt and touched the sandstone road. A shockwave pulsed out from the ground and covered her in a cloud of dust. It knocked over carts and stalls. People yelled and cursed in confusion.

Achyut watched and waited for the dust to settle and as the air cleared around them, a near-perfect replica of Banjiha filled the entire street.

"Please, allow me to go with you," Masami panted. "I'm begging you."

Prince Achyut, Katria, and Mona were stunned as they took in the details of the miniature replica of Banjiha. Achyut crouched and examined the hundreds of tiny stone houses and shops. It was like nothing he had ever seen before. He looked at Mona and smiled.

"No," Mona replied bluntly.

His smile grew into a toothy grin.

"Absolutely not." Mona crossed her arms over her chest and glared at him.

***

Masami gasped in awe as she entered the lavishly furnished sandstone palace Prince Achyut called home. Soft, dark red rugs lined the floors and massive woven tapestries hung from its impressive and sturdy walls. Busts of previous rulers, heroes, and other important figures of Lamrus's history lined the hall in pairs. She followed the prince, his beloved, and his retainer up a grandiose staircase with relief carvings of Lamaru's history etched into its sides while he regaled them with the story behind each work of art. He led them down another long hallway that opened into a bright and sunny garden and over a wooden bridge that arched over a pool made of shimmering, colored stones.

She licked her lips as she stared at the many strange and colorful fish swimming through the clear water below. They crossed onto a rounded, central island where the path diverged into multiple bridges and passageways that led back inside the palace. Achyut led them over another bridge, up more stairs, through another small garden, and up to one final set of stairs where Rakiba and Amarak waited outside the palmwood doors that lead to the throne room.

"Ah, there you are! I almost thought you'd miss our meeting."

Achyut grinned. "Even I know when it's necessary to be on time. Our parents would never allow me to join your forces if I showed up late today of all days."

"Oh? It looks like some of my royal demeanor is finally rubbing off on you. It only took a decade longer than I expected." Rakiba smiled, turning to greet the others, when their eyes landed on Masami. "Mrs. Joruka? It is you! Oh, thank goodness. I'm so glad to see you again! Is Semoru here too? Your pups? The rest of your staff? I'm so sorry I was unable to help you escape."

"There's no need to apologize, Your Majesty, and yes, Semoru and all of our family arrived in Illadina a few days ago." She smiled at them. "I'm glad to see you safe as well."

"Wait, you two know each other?" Achyut's eyes shifted curiously between Rakiba and Masami.

Rakiba nodded. "They graciously gave me shelter and helped me escape Banjiha after riots broke out across the city." Rakiba's lips curled into a smirk. "Little brother, don't tell me you've forgotten. Semoru used to live in the palace. His father was the first Magi to teach you basic minna theory."

"I um, well, I guess I was too young to remember." Achyut blushed and let out a forced laugh. *Damn. If I had remembered, I would have offered much more than a small bag of trinkets. I'll have to apologize to Semoru next time I see him.*

Rakiba turned to Masami. "Although thankful, I'm surprised to see you attending our war meeting."

"I met Prince Achyut in the bazaar this morning, and he told me you were going to retake Banjiha," answered Masami. "I want to help you in whatever way I can and right the wrongs my family has endured because of me."

"Semoru is lucky to have you. We'll do whatever we can to get back your old lives. Friends of the royal family will always be loved and appreciated, regardless of their heritage or upbringing."

Amarak barked in agreement.

"Prince Achyut, Nuhir Rakiba, and company, you may enter." The two guards pulled the doors open.

Prince Achyut and Nuhir Rakiba genuflected and walked to the edge of the emerald rug that stopped at the base of the throne. Mona,

Amarak, Katria, and Masami all stayed further back and stood quietly until addressed, while the royal family discussed their plan of action.

Masami listened intently to their discussion, how they weighed the pros and cons of each choice and kept the bickering to a minimum. It reminded her of how the foxtail clan chiefs discussed business and how she and Semoru conducted their own affairs.

She smiled faintly. Under all the pomp and grandeur, this was a family, just like her own, with a worried mother and two eager children who sought to carve their names into the stone of history.

After some time, the Padishah addressed Masami who shared her own story and reasons for wanting to join the Banjihan campaign. She recreated the replica city of Banjiha, at which Angem was most impressed. Although she hated to admit it, she could no longer deny the usefulness of Katria's talent, Masami's knowledge of the city, and the firepower of an additional sandship.

"So be it." The Padishah sighed, resigned to her decision. "Prince Achyut, I will allow you and the Prospector to join Nuhir Rakiba's forces. The sooner we can put an end to this conflict, the sooner we can return families to their homes and reunite those separated. Nuhir Rakiba, I will allow for your complete discretion during this operation, though I implore you to capture Lilith and her leaders alive."

"Yes, Your Majesty," answered Rakiba. "Your will and wishes are my own."

Angem nodded and turned back to her younger son. "Prince Achyut, you are under the direct command of Nuhir Rakiba for the duration of this campaign. I will not tolerate any insubordination on a matter this delicate. They are your commanding officer. Their words are my words and my law."

"I understand," Achyut replied. "I will not question my commander's orders nor act without permission."

The Padishah nodded. "Nuhir Rakiba, are you still on schedule to depart within two days' time?"

"Yes, Your Majesty."

"Prince Achyut, will you, Captain Tanoy, and the Prospector's crew be prepared to depart alongside Nuhir Rakiba?"

"Yes, Your Majesty." Achyut did his best to suppress his excitement.

"Then I bid you both safe travels and timely success. The future of Lamaru lies in your hands. I declare this audience adjourned."

Prince Achyut and Nuhir Rakiba stood, bowed, and left the throne room in silence, followed by their accompaniment.

"Well, that went better than I expected! Two royal leaders and their allies on the front lines of history! Oh, the songs and stories they'll tell about our victory! I'm so excited I might burst!" Achyut kissed Katria who giggled and playfully swatted away his assault. Mona rolled her eyes. Masami smiled.

"Congratulations, little brother, you passed our test with flying colors." Rakiba smiled mischievously.

"Our test?" Achyut repeated.

"Mother wasn't too happy about it when I, she, and father talked at length about your involvement, but she couldn't deny the potential advantages. We convinced her to let you and the Prospector join only if you managed to be on time for this morning's audience and hold your tongue while they 'discussed' the pros and cons of your participation"

"You mean all of that was just a setup to test Prince Achyut?" asked Masami.

"Not all of it, but a good majority. However, none of us expected him to bring an additional companion, nor one who knows Banjiha's streets so well. I have no doubt your presence alone placated our mother's remaining fears, and for that, I sincerely thank you."

Masami smiled. "If my children had to face such a difficult situation, I would want to give them every advantage I could think of."

"That's a very impressive cantrip, Mrs. Joruka. Is it something you've been working on for a while?" asked Mona as the group slowly made their way back to the palace entrance.

"A few years, give or take a month or two. As a professor of theoretical minna studies, my husband was very eager to teach me minna, even before we started dating. I was always fascinated by what you humans accomplished with it, and I loved hearing Semoru talk for hours about its imaginative uses.

"You see, many maiamorphs prefer to hone their natural strength instead. It certainly isn't frowned upon by the rest of my clan, yet as we successfully hunted with teeth and claws, we didn't see much use for it." She smiled proudly. "But this one goofy and charming man not only shared my awe of minna but held a deep such a deep determination and passion to understand its secrets and better the world. He's so selfless and purehearted, I couldn't help but fall for him."

They came to the front doors of the sandstone palace where Achyut, Katria, and Mona departed to inform Captain Tanoy and the crew of their news. Rakiba called for an irrivir and carriage to bring Masami home. They worked out the logistics of bringing her on as hired help and informed her of the generous pay for her services. With her tail wagging and a bright smile on her face, Masami bid farewell to Rakiba, scratched Amarak's ears, and stepped into the carriage.

The two days passed quicker than anyone would have liked and soon enough it was time for the battlegroup to depart. The crews loaded the last of the supplies onto their three sandships and bade farewell to their loved ones on the docks outside the citadel.

"Please be careful." Reena hugged Katria tightly, who returned her warm embrace and ruffled her hair.

"We will Reena. We'll be back before you know it, okay?"

Reena nodded and smiled up at her big sister.

Masami hugged her children and reassured them she'd be safe on their journey and, if possible, would bring them their requested items from their house. She kissed each of them then stood up and kissed her husband.

"I wish I could go with you," he mumbled as he held her in a loving embrace.

"I know, babe, but things will be dangerous, and not to brag but I am stronger and quicker and stealthier than you," she teased. He rolled his eyes. She kissed him again.

"After all, you're only human and someone has to look over the kids."

"Just make sure you come back to us. I can't lose you. There's no shame in a tactical retreat if you're outmaneuvered."

"I'll keep that in mind." She kissed him one last time as the gongs sounded from the three sandships, signalling the time to depart. The gangplanks of the Prospector, Queen's Salvation, and King's Wrath were raised, and three ships began their journey up the Hayi River. They left the safety of the city; the red clay walls quickly vanished in the distance as the open desert sprawled out before them.

After four days, Rakiba's fleet reached An'ard where they were met by the Clystudine merchant, Karascotia, and Dracona Cassio Naebuella, captains of the Longevity and Dragonfang respectively, who had traveled from the city and region of Thaniana. They departed in high spirits to Banjiha.

***

Over the next few weeks of travel, Nuhir Rakiba, Prince Achyut, the five captains, and their entourage devised, debated, and discarded plan after plan to retake the city. Their information on Lilith's forces remained dubious at best, and with no way to confirm her numbers without moving close enough to the city and to provoke an attack, slowly but surely, morale sank. Rakiba and the ships' captains realized this would not be the quick and easy victory they had hoped for.

Strategy meetings lagged on for hours as few feasible solutions became fathomable without great risk or intentional sacrifice, something both royals would never consider. In only a matter of days, they'd reach Banjiha's walls, yet still no solution had shown itself to the weary fleet. Exhausted and exasperated, Rakiba held their head in their hands, rubbing their tired and sunken eyes.

"Drink up," Kinnari ordered, placing a cup of cold water in front of Rakiba. She handed out drinks to everyone else. "If you're going to sit in the sun all day, at least make sure you're hydrated."

Rakiba took the cup and drained it, the cool clean water refreshing their body and spirit. "Thank you, Kinnari. I truly appreciate your–"

"Nuhir Rakiba, we've visual sight of a large shadow moving across the plains," announced Captain Iyushi. "Do you have immediate orders?"

"Captain Tanoy, would you please investigate? Let's find out what this is before we take action."

"Of course, Your Majesty." Tanoy stood from their table, maps and battle plans strewn across its wooden surface, and stretched. He hurried over to the mounted telescope and peered through its lens at the shadow that grew larger and larger across the horizon. Slowly and surely, it split into tens, then hundreds of distinguishable smaller shadows.

"Why, it's a flock of avian maiamorphs, the largest I've ever seen!" reported Tanoy.

"What?" Bronze light flooded the main deck as Kinnari dropped her tray of drinks and transformed into a giant raven. She beat her wings and took to the sky, flying as fast as she could.

"Send up the signal to stop the fleet," ordered Rakiba.

Captain Iyushi sent up a show of red sparks. The other four ships replied in the same fashion.

"There aren't any migratory groups that pass through here this time of year." Mona crossed her arms over her chest and watched cautiously as the flock veered toward their fleet.

"Maybe they're from Banjiha?" answered Achyut. "We could use the reinforcements if they're willing."

"And even if they aren't, it's our duty to help them however we can," added Rakiba.

The battlegroup slowed to a crawl then a stop. Within minutes, their fleet was engulfed in a sea of colorful feathers from birds of every shape and size. Some clutched barrels and crates in their talons. Others wore enchanted backpacks that changed size to accommodate their avian or humanoid form. Most of them landed on the ground beside the gargantuan sandships, weary and worn out from their banishment from Banjiha.

"Aquilo? Eravil?" Kinnari called as she flew between the hundreds of avians displaced from the Ironwood Forests. "Aquilo! Eravil!" She cawed again, her eyes darting in every direction as she flew circles around the central mast. "Aqui–"

"Oye, Kinnari, no more screeching. I heard ya the second time," muttered a slender charcoal-colored bird with light blue plumage slouched against the wall of the crow's nest. A bronze light enveloped his body; his wings separated into human arms and vestigial wings sprouting from his spine.

"Eravil!" Kinnari dove out of the sky, changing mid-flight and tackling the blue-haired man stretching his toned legs. "You're alive! You found us!"

"Heyhey, easy there, kiddo." Eravil patted the top of her head. "I don't need you breaking my ribs. The journey's been rough enough. We've spent weeks flying around looking for food and water and shelter."

Kinnari sighed. "Even so, I'm glad you're safe."

"You too. When we saw your ship getting chased out of Banjiha, we feared the worst. I knew you'd be safe, but your humans don't last long in the desert without their fancy ships."

Kinnari relinquished her hold on him. "Is Aquilo here too?"

"Yeah, the idiot's probably resting on the ground. He'd be in better shape if he didn't fight every wyvern we encountered along the way. At least he's protecting the rest of the flock."

"Can you take me to him? Please, I'll even carry you if you need to rest."

Eravil laughed. "I may be starved and parched, my left wing muscles aching, my right wing muscles pulled, my body sore from sleepless nights, my talons strained from heavy lifting, my feathers unpreened, my eyes full of dust and sand, my…"

Kinnari glared as he rambled on.

"…But I'd rather break my own wings than be carried by another avian warrior." He stood and balanced himself against the railing as bronze light enveloped his body again. They soared to the ground, landing amid a group of avians in their humanoid form, all battered and bruised, their more serious wounds wrapped in clean white cloth.

"Hold still. The more you move, the longer it takes to wrap your arm!" ordered a petite woman in an emerald dress, her long black hair tied into two braids.

"I'm trying, promise," grumbled a veritable giant, the muscles in his arms tensing and relaxing, his long blond hair tied in a ponytail, swishing back and forth as the woman poked and prodded at his wound. "You keep wrapping it too– hey! Kinnari!" Aquilo stood up, much to his doctor's annoyance, as Kinnari rushed him for a gentle hug.

"Aquilo! What the hell happened to you?" Kinnari's eyes swept across his sculpted chest, marred by abrasions and claw marks.

"Just a few scraps with the local roc wyverns. It looks a lot worse than it feels, promise, but my proud warrior spirit is without blemish! I am as the legendary phoenix, rising from the ashes of my–"

"Sit down and let her dress your wounds!" Kinnari scolded.

Aquilo did as she instructed, grumbling under his breath.

"Much obliged," answered his doctor, continuing his treatment.

Eravil snorted. "Hopefully, he'll listen now that we're all together again. Care to tell us what you and your humans are doing out here?"

***

Rakiba and Achyut looked up as the shadows of two giant birds descended upon the main deck of the Queen's Salvation. Bronze light enveloped Kinnari and Eravil, regaining their humanoid forms and supporting Aquilo between them.

"Nuhir Rakiba," Kinnari began, "let me introduce Eravil and Aquilo, commanders of the Blue and Gold Feather Squawdrons respectively."

"It's an honor to meet you, Your Majesty." Eravil bowed. "You are considered a benevolent and honorable warrior among your kind. I hope you will extend such kindness to us. Our flock is in desperate need of food and water. We've traveled for weeks with meager resources, forced to flee our homes. Many of us are sick from dehydration and starvation. The least fortunate were preyed upon by desert beasts and roc wyverns. It is not in any proud avian to beg, but our situation is dire."

"Peace, friend," answered Rakiba. "We've heard of the atrocities committed against you and will do whatever we can to aid your flock. Although we must travel with haste toward Banjiha, I would be honored to let you rest with us for a day or two and replenish your rations before we must continue on."

"Thank goodness." Aqulio sighed. "I wasn't sure how much more I could take." He closed his eyes and collapsed, his brave facade faltering, his body unwilling to move.

"Aquilo!" Kinnari gasped.

"I told you not to push yourself like this. One of these days, you'll push too far and..." Eravil's voice drifted further and further away until it faded altogether.

Aquilo awoke in a strange but not uncomfortable human bed with no idea of how long he had been unconscious. He struggled to raise his head, enervated from the countless days of travel. The beds around him were filled with his kin, all resting, their wounds tended to, water and food beside them. He ate what he could, but sleep pulled at his eyelids and he drifted off into a deep and dreamless state.

The next morning he roused himself from his bed just as the sun peeked over the horizon. He quietly trudged up the wooden steps, examining his healed wounds. Even their scars had begun to fade away. He pushed through the doors onto the main deck, inhaling the cool morning air and stretching his arms and wings.

High above the fleet of sandships, the proud warriors of the Ironwood Forests practiced drills and formations. He transformed and flew up to join them. Kinnari and Eravil flew out of formation and the three soared in circles around the Queen's Salvation.

"Look who's finally awake," chided Eravil. "Maybe next time you'll listen when I tell you not to push yourself too hard, hmm?"

"I only wished to protect the flock."

"You can't protect them if you're dead," he retorted. "You've got to stay alive until you find a moment worth dying for."

"I apologize." Aquilo bowed his head. "How long have I been asleep?"

"Since you so rudely collapsed on Kinnari's ship yesterday afternoon," clacked Eravil. "I took over negotiations with Rakiba and the others. You'll rest today and continue leading the flock north toward Thaniana tomorrow."

"Neither of you are coming with me?" Aquilo's eyes shifted between Eravil and Kinnari.

"I vowed to see this to the end alongside Nuhir Rakiba," Kinnari answered proudly.

"Blue Feather Squawdron is joining their attack group," Eravil added. "The sooner that wretched woman is brought to justice, the sooner we can return to our forests where we belong. However, there are those among us who wish to avoid further conflict. You should lead them to Thaniana."

"Me?" Aquilo blinked in astonishment. "But we vowed to stay together as a flock."

"The Magi healed your wounds but your body still needs rest. You aren't ready to fight and this is a battle we cannot afford to lose. If we do fall, they still have someone to rely on." Eravil nodded toward the countless avians, resting on the ground—new parents and children, the sick, the elderly, and those who's limited avian ancestry prevented them from soaring through the skies.

"I... I understand. I shall inform Lamaru's leaders." Aquilo sank down to the top yard of the Prospector on defeated wings. He looked back to Kinnari and Eravil, who had returned to their proud warriors and resumed their training. *To be separated again so soon, to hide my tailfeathers and fly away in shame... No, not shame, but I must do what is best for the flock, even if it goes against my personal wishes. This is for the best.* He jumped down to the helm where nine distinct individuals sat on barrels or stood around a round table covered in maps. All eyes turned to him.

"Nuhir Rakiba, Prince Achyut, first and foremost, thank you for tending to my wounds. You are of the best character, to offer such supplies on the eve of battle. Yet there are those among us unable or unwilling to fight and I must take responsibility for their lives. After careful consideration, I... I... I have decided to join your efforts in retaking the city."

"Oh?" Rakiba replied in slight dismay. "Eravil informed me you would be leading the rest of your flock north to Thaniana. We even partitioned our supplies to ensure you have enough resources to make the journey."

"That soulseeker destroyed the honor and livelihood of my kin and countless maiamorphs. She took everything from us. I could not live with myself if I cast aside my responsibilities to reclaim what was lost. Allow me to help you right her wrongs. Those in our flock who wish to abstain from conflict will wait outside Banjiha's walls."

"We're honored for you to join us." Prince Achyut grinned. "In fact, I've already through of your first special assignment, provided you were willing to join our cause. Your friends, Kinnari and Eravil, said you were the best of the best."

"The heart of a warrior is inside every avian, though there are those among us, myself included, who were gifted the stamina and skill to make the most of it." Aquilo smiled. "I gladly accept this mission if it aids you in defeating Lilith."

Rakiba stood from the table and grabbed a small, round widget hanging from a golden chain. "We've nearly planned our assault on the city, but we're missing one crucial piece of information: the size and location of her sandship fleet. It's too risky to attack without knowing the enemy's numbers and position, lest we are outflanked or fall into a trap. Fly around the city and find those ships." They offered the widget to Aquilo. "Any information gathered will be stored on this widget once we've activated it. Then we'll analyze their positions and finalize our plan."

"My skills and warriors are yours to command, my liege. You have no idea how much I desire to bring that foul woman to justice."

Captain Zatizimak laughed loudly. "Ye can fight with me and mine anytime, brother!" He gave Aquilo a toothy grin.

Rakiba fixed the amulet around Aquilo's neck and muttered an incantation. The stone in the center warmed and gave off a faint, golden light. They stepped away and Aquilo transformed once more, spreading his powerful wings and soaring into the bright blue sky, Banjiha's red clay walls on the horizon.

***

The sun had nearly set when the shadow of the massive eagle came into view once more. Everyone gathered on the bow of the Queen's Salvation, eager to know what Aquilo had found out about their enemy. He flew lower and lower and landed smoothly on the ship's deck. A burlap sack hung around his neck.

"Nuhir Rakiba, I've done as you've asked. Lilith has four sandships in total, all of which are docked outside the northern wall of the city," he squawked in rough, human speech.

Rakiba nodded. "This information was absolutely vital. Thanks to you, I am much more confident in our chances of success." They glanced curiously at the sack. "May I ask what else you've found on your scouting mission?"

Aquilo lowered his head. The bag slid off his neck and onto the deck.

"Woof!" Amarak bounded from his master's side, sniffing the bag and wagging his tail hard enough to shatter glass.

Two, small, garden snakes slithered out and glowed with a bright green light. Their serpentine bodies grew, sprouting arms and legs. Their flat, triangular heads thickened and sprouted ears and hair.

"Doggy! You're okay!" Netheli shouted with glee and wrapped her arms around his neck.

Rakiba sprinted to Netheli and Nadia, falling to their knees and hugging them both. "Nadia, Netheli, you're alive! You're both safe!" Tears brimmed in their eyes as they all embraced. "I'm so sorry I abandoned you. Please, forgive me. I thought if I could lead them away, you'd be able to escape."

"It's not your fault." Nadia buried her face into their chest, barely holding back her own tears. "You did what you could to keep us safe. We got away just like you hoped and fled into the forest."

"These children were also banished and forced to survive on their own?" Katria clung to Achyut's arm, nearly crying herself.

"In Lilith's eyes, a maiamorph is a maiamorph, regardless of age or station. Show no mercy, show no hesitation. Deal with one the same as the rest," mumbled Mona.

Achyut held Katria in his arms, resting his head on top of hers. "And that's why it's up to us to end her terrible rule and restore as many lives as we can."

"I found the two of them scrounging for scraps outside Banjiha's walls," Aquilo reported. "They have asked to join our campaign and are able and willing to provide valuable information."

Rakiba's mouth dropped. "No. You two have already risked your lives associating with me. I will not allow you to take any more unnecessary risks."

"Nuhir Rakiba, please," Nadia begged. The sooner this is over the sooner we can see our mothers again!"

"Absolutely not," Rakiba reiterated. "I won't allow children to fight their parents' wars. You must live for the future, for hope. You bear no blame nor responsibility to fix our shortcomings."

"Our parents are imprisoned because of Lilith!" Nadia's nostrils flared, her gaze unflinching as she met Rakiba's. "We have every right to help, even as kids, even if we can't fight! We'll show you an unguarded entrance into the city through an old sewer pipe. Please! We'll never see our parents again if you don't defeat Lilith."

"Yeah, we wanna help too!" Nadia grinned and hugged Amarak, who barked in approval.

"Rakiba, they might be onto something." Achyut gazed curiously at the two naga children and scratched his chin. "We'd waste precious time and resources forcing our way through their minna wards and barriers. As long as you are girls confident in your decision, I think I know exactly how to defeat Lilith's forces." He nodded with a smirk on his lips.

Mona sighed. "Why do I have the feeling your idea is both extremely dangerous and probably insane?"

"Because all of my dangerous and insane ideas have worked in the past." Achyut turned to Rakiba and grinned. "If there's a sufficient enough distraction to draw Lilith's forces out of the city—"

"Then she'll be left with minimal protection within its walls." Rakiba nodded, fully aware of Achyut's plan. "You want us to send a strike team into the city to capture her and force surrender before the fighting becomes too fierce."

"It's extremely risky," noted Captain Iyushi. "If the strike team isn't successful, they could easily be killed, or worse, become hostages for bartering."

"But if the strike team succeeds, we could end this with minimal casualties and damage to the city," reasoned Dracona Cassio. "I agree with Prince Achyut. "Five against four sandships is not a guaranteed victory, and even if we are victorious, we'd still have to secure the city before Lilith and her followers flee. Using the battle as a diversion is the best ploy to ensure she stays put."

"And how do we know she'll take the bait?" argued Captain Karascotia. "What's to stop her from doubling down on her defenses and forcing us into a siege?"

"Lilith knows she can't win the long game," answered Rakiba. "Lamaru has supperior resources and military power but if she wins this first engagement, she'll gain an indispencible amount of time, morale, and legitimacy. I've seen inside her mind and understand her tactics. She won't be able to resist such a prize."

"We still have no idea where she's hiding inside the city," retorted Karascotia. "Sending in a strike team blind is almost certainly sending them to their deaths."

"Not necessarily." Captain Tanoy stroked his beard. "I would bet my entire ship Lilith and her leadership are garrisoned in Banjiha's embassy. Not only is it a defensible position, but it gives her access to

Banjiha's security and public address systems. Even if she's not there, if we take the embassy, we should be able to find her before she flees the city."

"I say we do it." Captain Zatizimak crossed his arms over his chest. "The strike team can disable her eyes on their way to the embassy. We won't get another chance to take her by surprise. One quick, decisive blow—that's the best way to win a fight."

Iyushi sighed. "Even if we find someone foolhardy enough to lead the strike team, they'll still need soldiers and a way to make it to the embassy undetected. We'll need an updated map of the city as well."

"Umm, Captain Iyushi, I believe we already have the answers to our problems," Katria replied as she clung to Achyut's arm. "It's already late, but I don't think we'd need more than a day of preparation. Just make sure you give us ample time to get into the city and capture Lilith."

Mona's jaw dropped. "You're kidding." She stared at Katria in bewilderment. "Really?"

Katria blushed and nodded.

Achyut grinned from ear to ear. He broke into a fit of giggles that grew louder and louder until he laughed as boisterously as a madman. He pulled his beloved into his arms and covered her face and neck with kisses. "I thought it was my job to volunteer to risk our lives for the common good!" He smiled at her with renewed reverence.

"Maybe your way of thinking has rubbed off on me." She smiled and kissed him back. "Just a bit."

Rakiba glanced between Achyut, Katria, Mona, and the two naga children, weighing the pros and cons of the plan. *So much could go wrong, so many more innocent lives destroyed, and here I am, once again, forced to choose between my family and my role as a leader. Only a fool wishes to govern, the wise never pursue such predicaments.*

Rakiba sighed and smiled, accepting their choice and whatever fate may come of it. "My little brother, it pains me to send you so far behind enemy lines, but if there's anyone brave enough, strong enough, cunning and gallant enough to bear the weight of this mission and see it through successfully, it's you. You'll have tomorrow to assemble your team and make your final preparations. We cannot risk Lilith repositioning her fleet, so unfortunately, we cannot delay any longer than that."

"I understand, Nuhir Rakiba." Achyut straightened his shoulders and met their steady gaze. "If that's all the time I have, so be it. We'll depart before dawn once your fleet is in position."

"I look forward to your return with Lilith in chains. The dawn after Lamaru's darkest day is already on the horizon. Godspeed, Prince Achyut." Rakiba bowed.

Achyut bowed back then turned to Nadia and Aquilo. "If you two would please join me, I know exactly how we'll pull this off."

15

The Battle for Banjiha

"Are you nervous?" Rakiba patted their brother on the shoulder. Amarak licked Achyut's hand. All three stood on the bow of the Prospector, the red walls of Banjiha and Lilith's fleet hidden somewhere in the darkness beyond.

"Nervous, hah, why would I be nervous?" Achyut forced a smile. "We're only about to fight hundreds of our people, who hate our family enough to destroy hundreds more lives just to prove a point."

"Good." Rakiba smiled. They put their arms behind their back and stood beside their younger brother. "I'd be worried if you weren't. It's the natural response. I could barely hold my lance the first time I routed a group of bandits. All the training in the world couldn't prepare me for the bloodstains and snapping bones, the overwhelming stench and horror after my adrenaline faded away."

"You know, you really aren't helping." Achyut glared at his older sibling.

"Of course I am. I'm the one who taught you how to get out of bad brain."

"Yeah, well, your approach doesn't have to be so... graphic." Achyut shuddered.

"As your older sibling, I'm supposed to bully you; it builds character."

Achyut rolled his eyes. "And trauma."

"Only the character-building kind. And while I'm always willing to push you through a rough patch, as your commanding officer, I need to know you're up for the job. Once you're behind those walls, I won't be able to help you."

"I know, I know," Achyut shot back. "And it's almost sunrise. I need to get going. It's just, well..." For once he was at a loss for words.

"It's difficult fighting our own people, when our role in society is to protect them. But those farmers, bakers, blacksmiths, researchers, and doctors, neighbors and friends who took up arms have decided their way of thinking outweighs another's life. Once beyond that mental barrier, it isn't so easy to turn back."

"And that's why we must meet force with force, to protect those who cannot protect themselves," Achyut added.

Amarak woofed in approval.

"Now you sound like my little brother." Rakiba smiled. "I know you'll lead them well."

"It's all so surreal, isn't it. All of those war games, all the make-believe we played as kids, except now we're gambling with other people's lives. When I lost or failed my soulshare training before, I could just quit and give up, but now, if we fail, the only way we're getting home is in a coffin."

"Then it's a good thing you've both been learning to lead from such a young age; not just physically, no, this is why training your mind is so important." Achyut and Rakiba turned around as Captain Tanoy tore his eyes away from the ship's minna orbs and his gaze landed on the two royal children, now fully grown and dressed in shining armor.

"Don't worry, Prince Achyut. We'll do all we can to handle the bulk of their forces. If we're lucky enough, you may not even need to draw your sword, and we'll be headed home by sunrise with Lilith and her cronies in chains."

"And what of our people?" asked Achyut.

"Captains Iyushi, Zatizimak, and Karascotia will stay behind and restore peaceful leadership in the city. They have special orders and equipment from the Padishah to help ease post-battle tensions."

"You see? We've taken care of everything," quipped Rakiba. "All you have to do is get into the city. Should be a piece of cake compared to a couple of dragons."

"And to celebrate your success, I'll teach ya a new cantrip I've just finished." Captain Tanoy winked at Achyut. "I promise it's unlike anything you've ever seen before."

"Now that sounds exceptionally enticing. Thank you, both of you." Achyut smiled, bowing to his captain and commander, both his mentor and his family.

"Prince Achyut!" Mona hollered from the main deck in her oh-so-familiar no-nonsense tone. "Come on, we need to go! The sun's about to rise!"

Achyut glanced over Tanoy's shoulder. Katria waved at him, dressed for battle, standing beside Mona along with the rest of his strike team and three magnificent, giant birds.

"I'm coming, I'm coming," Achyut called, taking one last look at Rakiba, Amarak, and Tanoy before he left on his mission.

Rakiba waved goodbye and watched as Achyut and his strike group took to the skies, approached the red clay walls, dove to the ground, and vanished among the underbrush outside the city. "And there they go. Well, at least we've got the numbers advantage." They turned their attention to the opposing fleet of sandships that held the city of Banjiha hostage.

"Numbers or not, this will be a tough battle and it'll only get tougher if they've stacked the deck in their favor." Tanoy crossed his arms over his chest and frowned. "We can't deny the possibility that there might be reinforcements hidden throughout the city."

"If there are, we need to draw them out quickly. My brother doesn't have the numbers to take on a whole legion. We're supposed to be the distraction."

"Then let's get their attention." Tanoy smiled as the first rays of sunlight warmed his skin. "In service to the Crown and country; Joseph! Send up the signal. We'll begin our assault."

"Aye, aye Captain!" Joseph closed his eyes and gathered minna in the palm of his hand. He flung a shower of green sparks high into the air which detonated in a beautiful but chilling emerald blast. Similar signals detonated above every other ship of their fleet.

Captain Zatizimak stared at the brilliant display with the same awe and excitement as a child on New Year's Eve. He let out a loud, hearty laugh as the emerald flares dissipated in the wind and his eyes fell to the fleet of sandships across the open desert. The child in him had grown into a man whose eyes burned with passion and war.

"And so the game begins. Alright you lazy louts, charge the minna orbs! Load the cannons! I want a full round of defensive spells pre-charged before we're breathing down their backs!" he howled off the bow of the King's Wrath. "Let's give these bastards hell!" He kicked the brake levers and his sandship lurched toward the enemy line.

Far across the open desert, Uriel stood on the bow of his flagship, the Mourning Star. He watched the green flairs pitter out in the air above the enemy fleet. *They choose to fight after all. Interesting,* he mused to himself, *I never thought Nuhir Rakiba would be so brash.*

"Captain! Prepare our forces for combat! Make sure to stay within range of the city's defense network. We only need to draw them in close enough for the batteries to obliterate their fleet."

"Yes sir," replied Uriel's captain. His first mate launched a green flair into the air as their ship crawled forward.

The King's Wrath took point of Lamaru's forces. The Prospector and the Queen's Salvation followed closely behind. The Longevity completed their diamond formation while the Dragonfang sailed straight south and prepared to flank Banjiha's forces. The crews of every vessel held their breath and waited to see which side would make the first daring move.

Five fireballs, each the size of a small barn, launched from Banjiha's flagship and into the air. They hung momentarily like stars in the sky, then plummeted back toward the earth below.

"Bow defenses, on my mark!" Zatizimak watched the fireballs fall closer and closer to his ship. "Now!" Five maelstroms materialized above the King's Wrath. The fireballs smashed into the sudden curtain of swirling water and cloaked the ship in dense fog.

"Orbs one through six, I want a stoneslide concentrated on their flagship. Orbs seven and eight, prepare preemptive tether! All else, prepare defenses!" Zatizimak ordered with nothing short of glee in his rough voice. The King's Wrath emerged from the fog and launched six greenish-brown vortexes of minna which hung in the air on either side of the Mourning Star. Tendrils broke through the earth below, latched onto the ship, and held it in place just as a few hundred tons of rock and earth spilled out of the vortexes above.

Hundreds more tendrils sprouted from the deck of the Mourning Star and spread upward like the branches of an overzealous tree. The falling rock crowned the tree's branches with leaves of earth as the tendrils split and over and over again. Not a single stone made contact. With a loud, leaden groan, the great tree leaned back and catapulted the earth back toward the King's Wrath.

"Launch comet strike!" ordered Captain Tanoy.

"Bow defenses! Again!" commanded Zatizimak. A second set of whirlpools appeared above the bow of the ship and drowned out the first few hundred tons of rock. Stone and earth piled higher and higher until the weight was too great and the whirlpools shattered like glass. Before the King's Wrath and its crew were buried alive, a hailstorm of small comets materialized overhead and melted the earth into ash that fell like fresh snow. Then the ships were in range of small arms fire and all hell broke loose.

***

Kinnari, Aquilo, and Eravil dropped Prince Achyut and his team into the underbrush then landed outside the city walls. Achyut dusted himself off and stood, his eyes glued to the horizon as flashes of minna filled the open sky. The Battle for Banjiha had begun.

"Prince Achyut." Mona tapped his shoulder and pulled him from his trance. "This is no time to be distracted. We've our own mission to accomplish."

"R-right." Achyut tore his eyes from the spectacle and faced the mass of humans and maiamorphs; thirty-six soldiers and volunteers had agreed to risk their lives under his cockamamy plan. He would lead them to the best of his abilities— no, better.

"Nadia, Netheli, the next part is up to you. Lead us to the sewer entrance." The naga sisters nodded and took the form of little garden snakes. They slithered toward the wall as Achyut and the others followed, concealed by the leafy tree limbs until they reached the lip of a massive pit filled with murky brown liquid.

"What an incredible smell we've discovered." Achyut coughed and clenched his hands over his nose and mouth. The other members of his team did the same. Yet the naga sisters slithered onward, around the pit of filth, to the end of a large, hollow, metal tube where a lovely brown waterfall trickled into the putrid lake below.

"Ooohh... I hate sewers, I hate sewers, I hate sewers, I hate sewers!" Masami barked as she clutched her fluffy, black tail against her chest. Although she had tried her best to avoid it, the tips of her fur had the slightest tinge of green.

"I thought they smelled bad on the outside but this is ridiculous! How can you humans stand to live with so much waste right below your streets?"

"Because we don't crawl through them to move about the city," replied Mona matter-of-factly. Masami growled at her. Achyut and Katria stifled their chuckles as they marched on through the muck and filth for at least another hour.

"Did you two make this trek in and out every day?" Katria asked the naga sisters.

Netheli nodded, splashing through the sludge.

"We had to," answered Nadia. "There isn't much food in the desert and the forest was filled with too many people. We may be part serpent, but we never had to hunt or forage. The walk is annoying but it's easier to sneak into the city and steal scraps."

"It's like hide and seek!" Netheli giggled. "We slither around and grab food while avoiding BEN."

"Who's Ben?" Katria asked.

"The Banjiha Eye Network, BEN for short," informed Mona.

"That's the prototype security system you'll be looking for once we reach our destination," added Achyut as he kissed Katria's hand. "The widgets aren't difficult to find, they're just glass balls that look like, well, eyes."

"I love hide-and-seek!" repeated Netheli. "We're really good at it! We haven't been caught yet!"

"Nadia, what happens if you're caught?" Katria glanced worryingly at the oldest child, who bit her lower lip and looked away. Katria felt cold. A rush of memories from her time in Yaand and the Bale flooded her mind and the weight of their mission settled on her shoulders.

"You poor dears," she uttered. "To think children would have to live like this. It's horrible."

"We got used to it after a few weeks." Netheli shrugged her shoulders, an extremely impressive feat for a naga.

They reached the ladder that led up to Banjiha's commercial district. Katria touched the ladder and closed her eyes. Everyone else gathered around Prince Achyut as he detailed the next step in his plan.

"Nadia, Netheli, once Katria confirms the location of the nearest eyes, you two will slither up and slip through the cover." He grabbed a handful of small orange balls of putty from his backpack.

"Each eye has a blind spot at the base of its column. Stick these to their bases and slither back here as quickly as you can without being seen. Mona will harness just enough minna to short out the eyes and freeze them on whatever images they're already collecting. Then the rest of us will climb up and out. Masami and Katria will lead us and reveal the location of the other eyes. We'll short out every eye in our path until we reach the central embassy then reboot BEN and use it to find Lilith and her leadership. We know she's still somewhere in the city. Lastly, no harnessing any unnecessary minna or we might set off traps or defensive wards set up around the city.

"Do I assume correctly that if one or more of these 'eyes' see us, our numbers and location will be reported directly to Lilith's forces?" asked Eravil.

Achyut nodded.

Kinnari and Aquilo shifted their weight uncomfortably.

"We have to keep the element of surprise," Achyut continued. "If we're caught before we reach the embassy, Aquilo, Kinnari, and Eravil, you'll have to fly us out. We'll rejoin Rakiba and come up with a new plan. Masami, can you make a map of the embassy and surrounding streets?"

"Of course." She stepped away from the group, closed her eyes, and created a minna miniature of the area.

"If we reach the embassy undiscovered, you three will fly out here, here, and here." Achyut pointed at their minna map. "Lilith will realize we're in the city and send forces to investigate. That should further thin her personal guard. Gather all of your warriors and fly back here while we storm the building. I'm counting on you to provide backup once we're sealed inside the embassy."

Aquilo, Eravil, and Kinnari nodded.

Achyut glanced at everyone around him: loyal soldiers to the crown, friends and allies, family and loved ones. A lump rose in the back of his throat. *How many of us will live to see the next day?* He thought about everyone else, already fighting and dying on the front line just to give them this opportunity. *I've no time for doubt. We have to win.* He took a deep breath and swallowed his fears.

"Stay together and stick to the plan. They won't know we're coming until it's too late. If everything goes well, we'll take the city swiftly and force their surrender before the day is done." He forced a smile on his lips. "Our kingdom may be splintered by hate, but this is still our home. Today we fight for the lives of our friends and family so that all can return to a time of peace and prosperity. We can do this. We will do this. We must."

"We wouldn't be here if we thought this plan would fail," added Katria. "I have the utmost faith in you, my prince." She smiled at the rest of their company. "And in all of us."

"Well said." Mona rested her hand on Katria's shoulder. Her lips curled into a hunter's smile, eager and confident. "Now, let's get out there and crack some heads."

"Right!" Katria nodded. "My darling, I've found the three closest eyes and the next few in our path. The city is also on lockdown so we shouldn't run into any civilians."

Achyut nodded. "Masami, if you could please create another map. My dearest, point out the locations of the eyes, and we'll get going."

***

"Hold your defenses! Do not falter in the face of terror!" ordered Nuhir Rakiba as their Magi and paragons held their shields and endured a hailstorm of spells, buckshot, and arrows. The Prospector's minna orbs spun round and round as they launched spell after spell on a broadside attack on the Steel Heart. A beam of ice sliced through its front mast. Giant boulders flung from the Prospector's sides only to be pushed back and onto their own by powerful streams of fire. Strands of lightning struck the port side of their ship. White flames licked at the Steel Heart's bow only to be flash-frozen by a miniature blizzard. Three Magi in the crow's nest solidified the long shadows the Prospector's masts cast upon the Steel Heart.

"For our kingdom, for the Padishah! Charge!" Rakiba leaped onto Amarak's back and raised their lance above their head. They summoned shields of earth and stone and sheltered Amarak and their paragons as they raced across the shadow bridge and onto the deck of the Steel Heart. The heavy and constant clashing and clanging of metal-on-metal droned out the whirl of minna orbs and screams of fallen soldiers. The smell of burning wood and blood hung in the air. Two Magi on the Steel Heart severed the shadow bridge and a company of Rakiba's paragons fell onto the sand below. They gathered up the wounded and bored through the ship's ironwood armor while archers and Magi took potshots from above.

Rakiba pushed further through Uriel's ranks. A bomb made of a white, sticky substance detonated off to their right and sealed the crew's reinforcements below deck. Rakiba leaped from Amarak's back and the pair fought their way to the helm of the ship. They grunted in pain as a handful of arrows pierced armor and skin. Rakiba fell to one knee, tore the arrows from their flesh, then stood and continued fighting. A rejuvenating wave of minna washed over their bodies and closed the wounds on the spot, leaving nothing more than a few stains of blood.

Amarak moved as a living battery ram. He knocked Uriel's soldiers aside and tore flesh from the unlucky few close enough to his sharp teeth. He caught a spear in his jaws as it flew overhead and brandished it back and forth, clearing the way for Rakiba and their paragons. Rakiba and Amarak pointed their polearms at the captain's neck who threw his hands up in surrender.

"The ship is ours!" Rakiba proclaimed. Their paragons cheered as they tied up the stranglers and forced them below deck. "Magi, take up the minna orbs! I want defensive wards around the entire ship before we commence our counterattack!"

Uriel leered at Rakiba from the bow of the Mourning Star as his ship and the Kingslayer exchanged spellfire with the King's Wrath and Queen's Salvation. While he deemed Rakiba's skill and tenacity impressive, their little victory meant nothing.

"Captain, the Steel Heart is lost. It's time we reveal our secret weapon." The captain nodded and ordered the first mate to send up their special flare. Immediately, the Steel Heart became engulfed in purple smoke that choked Rakiba and marked the target of the newly mounted minna batteries. Light flashed atop Banjiha's walls. Soldiers on both sides shielded their eyes as a low and distant hum grew louder and louder. Within moments, countless spells rained upon the ship and overwhelmed their defenses. Burning flames, crackling lightning, globs of poison, and corrosive mud pelted Rakiba's soldiers and tore through the hull of the doomed vessel.

"Abandon ship! Abandon ship!" Rakiba's wards and barriers failed. "Amarak, come!" They hastily took shelter behind a cracked mast. Soldiers from both sides jumped overboard without hesitation and landed on sticky nets and soft, billowy clouds conjured above the ground. Rakiba sighed in relief as the last of their own jumped to safety just as an explosion of dragonfire detonated and swept them and Amarak into the air like loose leaves in a hurricane.

***

The sounds of explosions and spellfire shook the ground and sky as Lilith stared out the reinforced, glass wall on the third floor of the Banjiha's capitol. Uriel had fired the weapon. The battle would be over soon, or so she thought, before her eyes caught the unwanted sight of a giant eagle that spread its wings and flew toward the city walls. She ground her teeth and glared at the bird but the sound of hurried footsteps overtook her attention. She turned, sword in hand, as two of her soldiers rushed up the stairs.

"Sovereign Lilith! An avian maiamorph just appeared in the city and flew over the eastern wall!" The first blurted out as he caught his breath.

"What? I just saw another flying toward the northern wall!" added the second. "We hit it with a few arrows, but it flew out of range before we could bring it down."

"That makes three in total," Lilith mused aloud. "Not enough force to take the city, but enough to spook our guard." She looked back out the window. "I do believe someone has infiltrated my lovely city in a feeble attempt to ambush us, but how did they get in? Bah, it doesn't matter. They're already here."

"Should we send out the city guard to intercept before they reach the embassy?" asked the first soldier.

Lilith considered her options. "No. I have a better idea. You two, come with me." They rushed down the stairs to the lowest level of the building, where a portly man with short blond hair slouched in a comfy, plush chair in front of a wall of magic mirrors that collected and presented all of BEN's visual information.

"You there! Enhance the images from the eyes on King's Corner. Play the images back frame by frame," commanded Lilith.

Startled, the man jolted upright and quietly followed the Sovereign's orders as all four watched the empty streets.

"Look at the clouds. They stopped moving, noticed one of the soldiers."

"Someone must have hacked into BEN to cover their tracks," added the other.

"Continually reset the next four eyes between King's Corner and the embassy. If an intruder is in fact headed here, we'll catch them as they pass by."

"Yes, ma'am!"

The four of them held their breath and watched as the mirrors blinked on and off again until one of the eyes caught a sight that made Lilith smile. There couldn't have been more than twenty, thirty, soldiers at most, both human and maiamorph, yet what intrigued her was one man near the front of the charge. He rode a giant black fox beside a woman in red and another with copper hair.

"Well, well, well, it seems we have a royal visitor. Prince Achyut, thank you for volunteering to be my hostage. I'm sure your parents will give in to my demands to see you returned safe and sound. Rally every soldier we have in the city–on or off duty. Tell them to report immediately to the embassy. Let's give our uninvited guests the royal welcome."

"Yes, Sovereign Lilith!" The two men hurried back up the stairs.

"You, continue to monitor the situation from here. I want a detailed report of their numbers and weapons on my desk within fifteen minutes. If you fail my request, consider yourself out of a job— permanently."

The man gulped audibly and nodded without a word.

Let's see if this assassin from the Hunter's Guild was worth the price we paid. Lilith calmly walked up the stairs of the embassy. She opened the door onto the open-air roof and sauntered over to a cloth tent where a man dressed in all black tended to a small fire and a giant pan filled with meat, carrots, and onions, and topped with a layer of steamed rice. He silently looked up at her approach.

"A strike group of humans and maiamorphs led by Prince Achyut has infiltrated the city and are likely on their way to the embassy. I need you to kill as many as you can while keeping the prince alive. Can you do that for me?"

The man nodded and doused his fire then donned a bandolier filled with glass vials and knives of various shapes and sizes.

"I hope your reputation is well earned." Lilith smiled. "My soldiers will join you as backup. You have the right to use them as you see fit. Happy hunting, Boris."

Boris pulled his dark hood over his face. He walked to the edge of the building and stepped off as naturally as a leisurely stroll through the woods. Curious, Lilith peered over the edge, but the bandit was already out of sight, hidden among the shadows in the streets below.

***

A cloud of purple smoke detonated around the Longevity. Barely visible blades of air sliced through its masts. Molten rocks rained down from above and crushed the cannons, minna orbs, and crew. Flashing lights blinded everyone on the main deck while steady streams of boiling water and acid melted through the ship's hull.

"Keep your defenses up! We must endure!" ordered Captain Karascotia from the helm. Lightning struck overhead. She retreated into her shell only to be flung from the deck by a second explosion and into the second mast of the ship. She staggered up and spat out blood. Both her shell and fighting spirit had cracked.

"Captain Karascotia, what are your orders?" The crew anxiously awaited her reply.

She looked upon their terrified faces. Although they stood their ground, everyone knew the ship wouldn't survive five more minutes of heavy spellfire. The end was here. "Dammit all. Get the injured below deck. I want every ounce of minna left in every focus harnessed for defensive cantrips only. We need to buy enough time to open the main hatch and evacuate the ship." *And pray that luck is on our side.*

She glanced around her ruined ship, her life savings and legacy. The masts were cracked, the rollers damaged beyond repair, the floorboards twisted and burned and splintered to pieces. Nearly all her crew were badly injured. Another wave of spellfire rained upon the deck. They were out of time. The last fragments of the minna shields shattered, their wards cracked, and their barriers failed.

Karascotia closed her eyes and held her breath as she waited for the end. Seconds felt like years. Minutes passed as slowly as a millennium, yet strangely enough, the next assault never came. She opened her eyes and sighed in relief as countless protective barriers launched from the Prospector and the Queen's Salvation. Yet as Lamaru's forces protected their own, Uriel's unoccupied ships, the Kingslayer and the People's Will, opened fire on the now defenseless vessels.

***

"Ahh, shit," cursed Achyut as seventy or so soldiers rushed out from the steps of the embassy armed with bows, spears, swords, and shields. He clutched onto Masami's fur and held Katria close as the first volley of arrows rained down upon them. Mona drew her aruvel off her back and held it above her head. Tiny vipers made of lightning bit through the arrows as Masami and her riders charged on ahead.

"Everyone, stay together! Take up defensive positions and don't let yourself get surrounded!" Achyut ordered as his paragons pushed into the plaza and courtyard outside of the embassy. "Mona, we need to find cover or close the gap. There's no way we'll win a war of attrition out in the open!"

"If that's all we need, this will be a piece of cake," Mona answered with a wolfish grin. Her sword crackled with sparks and glowed red-orange. Two walls of fire suddenly sprang up and divided Lilith's forces in half. Masami sprinted through the surrounding sea of flames up to the steps of the embassy while Mona, Achyut, and Katria protected her from unfriendly spells and arrows.

A man dressed in all black stepped out of the shadows and stood alone on the steps. He took off a leather band embossed with runic symbols. Suddenly he grew four, eight, twelve feet taller. He sprinted toward Masami and hurled two greatsword-sized daggers.

Masami nimbly dodged both daggers only to be kicked in the stomach and launched into the air. Achyut, Mona, and Katria were flung from her back and landed painfully on the stone tiles. Mona and Masami were the first to stand. Boris blocked the steps of the embassy and waited for his opponents to make their next move.

"This guy? Really?" Achyut dabbed at his busted lip and spat out a few drops of blood.

"You two go ahead," ordered Mona as she helped Katria to her feet. "Find Lilith. Keep her occupied. Masami and I will create an opening for you to slip past, deal with him, then back you up momentarily."

"Are you sure you two can take him? We don't know what other tricks he has up his sleeve." Katria glanced back and forth, her eyes filled with worry.

"Hey, now's not the time to get mousey and mushy. He got in one lucky shot, that's all." Mona rolled her shoulders and cracked her knuckles. White flames licked her boots and gloves. Her aruval crackled with lightning. "But since he thinks he's so strong, I won't hold back at all."

"We will succeed," Masami growled.

"Be safe out there." Achyut smiled weakly at Mona.

"You too," she replied with a confident smirk. "I'll see you in a few minutes." Mona climbed onto Masami's back and rode off to battle without another word.

Achyut and Katria waited on the far side of the courtyard while the battle raged on all around them. Two of their urosi soldiers smashed apart a set of storage sheds and rebuilt them into a ram-shackled barricade. A manticore whipped her tail around her wings and fired off a volley of toxic spikes. Lamaru's Magi and paragons huddled behind wards and barriers as more of Lilith's soldiers poured out of the city like an unstoppable rising tide.

Achyut tore his eyes away from the scene and back to Mona and Masami who charged Boris once more and pelted him with spellfire. She forced him away from the steps as Masami bit and clawed at whatever she could reach. Achyut held his bansuri to his lips and waited. Mona leaped from Masami's back. Boris took two more giant steps away from the embassy. Achyut stood and played. He and Katria sprinted toward the side of the embassy under the cover of his illusions. Katria closed her eyes and touched the massive, stone walls.

"Eight humans on the ground and second floor, none on the third and fourth, four on the fifth, and three in the basement. I doubt we'll be able to waltz through the front doors."

"You don't think they'd like my music?" Achyut teased. He looked up at the square, stone walls of the building. "Any chance we could scale up?"

"No," Katria shook her head, "There are wards set up outside of the second floor and higher. Touching them for more than a few seconds will trigger some sort of alarm and building lockdown. Wait. I've found a maintenance shaft further down this side that leads up to the second floor."

"That'll work. We'll climb inside, barricade the stairs going down, then fight off the remaining guards."

"What about Mona and Masami? They'll need to join us somehow."

"Don't worry." He grinned and kissed her cheek. "Mona will know exactly how to bring it all down once the ground floor is secure." Katria nodded.

Achyut took one more glance at the structure and tapped his lips thoughtfully. "So many wards and barriers, I bet there's all kinds of useful equipment as well. My dear, let's take a closer look and cook up a few extra schemes before we go in. We won't have time to plan like this once we're inside, and if we're not careful, we could have to fight two on twelve. I'm good, but not that good."

"Come on, you worthless shits! Come get some!" Mona summoned a lance of fire and flung it at Lilith's soldiers, but Boris caught the fire in one hand and snapped it like a twig. He grabbed and smashed another vial from his bandolier which quickly healed his burns. He pointed the tip of a timber-sized dagger at Prince Achyut's strike team and their barricade. Lilith's soldiers understood. They rallied from the giant's side and engaged Lamaru's troops. Boris stared down Mona and Masami on his own.

He lunged at Masami but she feinted away from his kicks and skirted his attacks, howling and snarling with unbridled rage. Boris did not fall for her distraction. He spun on his heel and blocked with his giant daggers just as Mona leaped into the air and plummeted down from above. Her aruval crackled with electricity as she slammed her sword against his daggers to no avail. Masami flanked him from the right. Boris smashed another vial against his skin. Masami scratched and bit at his calves, but his skin became hard and leathery and the wounds she left were minor.

Boris focused on Mona, hacking and slashing at the tiny woman who blocked each strike with her sword and minna shield. She rolled out of range and wiped the sweat from her forehead. Boris charged. Mona held her ground and slashed upward at his forearms. Blood welled up from his thick, tree-like arms. Masami lunged at him once more, but Boris caught her by the scruff of her neck and flung her across the plaza.

***

Aquilo, Kinnari, and Eravil flew as fast as they could over the walls of Banjiha, back to the Ironwood Forest where the avian soldiers prepared for battle. The proud warriors donned helmets, chest plates, chausses, and talon gauntlets. They attached lightweight scythes and other bladed weapons to their forelimbs and made their wings as deadly as their beak and claws. By the time the avian chieftains arrived, their warriors were armed to the beak and preemptively divided into three battle groups.

Aquilo perched on the lowest branches of an ironwood tree, dressed in his own tailored armor, painted to match the royal gold plumage of the Eagle Chieftains before him. Kinnari and Eravil stood on either side of him, similarly dressed in the crimson and azure armor of their predecessors.

"Listen up!" Aquilo's voice rang through the trees. "Today we fight for more than our own. We fight for our way of life, our right to exist! Our kind has seen the rise and fall of many leaders of Reighja, long since the days of draconic rule, yet time has not broken our alliance with the humans of Lamaru, the Magi of the desert who have always respected our way of life. Now our glorious history and honorable alliance are endangered by this rogue soulseeker who desires to rid the world of our kind. Well, I say if she wants to fight, we'll fight!"

Shouts and squawks chorused up from the crowd.

"Let's show her why we've lived so long! Let's show her a single avian with a sharp stick is worth more than twenty of her soldiers! Come, my comrades and kin, take flight! To battle!"

Aquilo let out an ear-shattering war cry as he soared high above the ironwood trees, Kinnari and Eravil by his side; the rest of their flock rallied behind them. They flew higher and higher into the air, far above the city of Banjiha and out of range of the sandships' spellfire.

Eravil watched as the Longevity was engulfed in purple smoke and took heavy fire from minna turrets mounted on the city's northern wall. Their allies wouldn't last long under such sustained fire. Time was almost out. "Kinnari, I'm changing the orders for our squawdrons!"

"You mean you aren't going back to aid Prince Achyut? What if his forces are in trouble?" cawed Aquilo.

"Lilith's capture won't mean a thing if we lose the battle outside the walls," retorted Eravil. "Lead Gold Squawdron back as Achyut's reinforcements. I'll lead Blue Squawdron and destroy those minna turrets. That ought to buy Lamaru's forces more time. Kinnari, take Red Squawdron and swarm Lilith's sandships. Break their masts, tear out their eyes and sails and aid Nuhir Rakiba however you can! Good luck! We'll celebrate when this is over!"

Eravil screeched and tucked in his wings. He fell out of the sky like a meteor, followed by the rest of his proud, azure warriors, who descended upon the northern wall. They tore into the Magi and turrets with their beaks and claws as Lilith's forces fended off the surprise attack. Ever vicious and valiant, Eravil and his warriors fought on outnumbered two-to-one. Lilith's forces slowly pushed back his assault. Their feathers became soaked in blood; some from Lilith's forces, but mostly their own.

"Keep fighting! We won't let a bunch of flightless jealous little humans get the best of us, will we?"

"Eravil, below you!" shouted an azure hawk. Eravil looked down just as hundreds of tiny icicles pierced his feathered chest and knocked him from the sky.

Kinnari whistled loudly as her squawdron of crimson-tipped black birds fell out of formation and followed her to the desert sands below. Ravens and crows swooped and strafed Uriel's sandships. Grackles carried soldiers, both wounded and ready to fight, between the remaining vessels. Unable to fend off the smaller, quicker maiamorphs, the tides of battle shifted in Lamaru's favor as Kinnari's forces easily read and dodged the clunky humans' movements.

***

"Nuhir Rakiba, wake up! Nuhir Rakiba, please!" Rakiba's eyes fluttered open, yet they could only see out of their left. A stinging, burning pain flooded their right side. They cried out in agony. Amarak whimpered and licked his master's face.

"Keep them steady," called another medic. "We've got to clear the debris out of the wound before we can seal it. Someone keep pressure on their eye before we lose it permanently!" The six medics worked tirelessly on Rakiba's wounds while six more Magi shielded them from attacks. Although Rakiba's will was strong, their body felt broken, their ears ringing with too many voices and sounds. Their senses quickly faded away.

Captain Zatizimak bit his lip as he watched Cassio's medics through his spyglass. He could do nothing to protect the young Nuhir. The King's Wrath had been horribly damaged from its firefight. All but one of its minna orbs were destroyed and the windsails and arcane engine that powered the sandship had nearly met a similar fate. He watched the flock of avians that descended upon Banjiha's north wall. He watched them fight and fall, one at a time, to countless arrows and spells. The walls were too well protected. They would likely perish before all the turrets were destroyed. Banjiha's forces would renew their attack. Lamaru's ships and the battle would be lost.

Zatizimak considered his options carefully and surmised the only surefire way to eliminate Banjiha's encampments.

"Abandon ship! Everyone, abandon ship! Make toward the Prospector and Queen's Salvation!" Bewildered, his crew nonetheless leaped off the King's Wrath or were picked up and carried by the avian warriors who just recently came to the ship's aid. Captain Zatizimak adjusted the windsails and turned the ship around for one final gambit. The most loyal of his crew realized his plan and rushed to meet him at the helm.

"Captain Zatizimak," called a young woman who Zatizimak had rescued from a pirate vessel many moons ago. "You're not actually thinking of ramming the wall, are you? There's no way the Wrath would survive that impact!"

"Aye, if those turrets don't fall, the battle is lost. This is the nature of the great equalizer and the honor of knowing when sacrifice is more worthy than participating in the next combat."

The woman sighed and frowned. She knew her captain was right yet he wouldn't be able to guide the ship properly by himself.

"In service to my country and my captain, allow me to aid you. If we can ensure victory, it'll be a glorious end." She saluted him and smiled.

"Aye! If the ship is to be lost, let's go down fighting!" called another crewman.

"The King's Wrath to the very end!" proclaimed another as shouts and cheers erupted from the few left on board.

"I too would be honored to serve on the King's Wrath's final mission," called a charcoal-colored avian, recently recovered from the sands. His bloodied back was wrapped in loose bandages; his azure wings hung bent and useless by his sides. "I doubt I'll last long with my wounds. Please, allow me to aid you however I can; for Lamaru and my kin, who sacrificed their lives, a warrior's death is by far the most deserving."

Captain Zatizimak smiled. "Thank you, Eravil, everyone." He wiped a single tear from his eyes. "Thank you for fighting with me until the end. I'm honored to have served with such a wonderful crew. May your descendants live long lives and may history never forget our names. Now! Man the sails! Hold her steady and shove as much minna into the bow orb as you can! We've a wall to bring down!"

"Aye, Captain!" they yelled in unison.

"Let's show these traitors why we're named the King's Wrath! Set a course straight for the city! Hahahaha!"

"Captain, the King's Wrath has changed course!" shouted Iyushi's first mate. "They're heading straight for Banjiha's wall!"

"What?!" Iyushi hastily grabbed her spyglass. Captain Zatizimak stood at the helm and laughed maniacally. He waved at Iyushi and gave her a proper salute and grandiose bow.

"Captain Zatizimak, we'll never forget your heroic sacrifice." She saluted back. "Thank you for your service, my old friend. Rest easy."

The explosion from the King's Wrath captured everyone's attention. The sandship became engulfed in flame and wind and enough magical energy that its impact alone vaporized the nearest sections of the wall. Cracks crawled up the remaining structure and spread like lightning. More and more sections crumbled to dust. The entire northern wall collapsed in spectacular fashion, like a house of playing cards suddenly caught in the winds of a ferocious desert storm. The avians above flew out of range as the minna stored in the turrets detonated and set off a second chain of explosions that lit up the sky with shimmering light, vivid colors, and enough heat that the desert sand turned to glass and exposed the heart of the fortified city.

16

Two Royals, Two Visionaries

Uriel stood on the bow of the Mourning Star, unable to process what had just happened. Rakiba and Cassio stood on the bow of the Dragonfang. They closed their eyes and bowed their heads in respect and lamentation at Zatizimak's sacrifice.

"Dracona Cassio, set a course straight for the Mourning Star and engage at point-blank range."

"Nuhir Rakiba, our foci are cracked and our minna stores are nearly depleted. We won't last long in direct combat."

"We don't have to last forever, just long enough for Amarak and myself to storm the deck. I'll take Uriel myself."

"You're in no state to fight alone." Dracona Cassio frowned at Rakiba's bloodied, white armor and black eye patch over their right eye.

"Captain Zatizimak gave his life to protect our fleet from further destruction. He's crippled the enemy's morale. If we strike now, we can end this. I will not let a second of his sacrifice go to waste."

"Very well," sighed Cassio, knowingly unable to change the young royal's mind. "Give me a few moments to prepare, and I will join you. We'll take him captive and end this battle before any more lives are lost."

"Thank you, Dracona Cassio." Rakiba smiled. Amarak barked and wagged his tail.

The Dragonfang sped toward the Mourning Star and broadsided once more. Its minna orbs roared to life as Magi on both ships poured every ounce of power left into one final strike. For better or worse, this was the beginning of the end.

Cassio's medics and members of the Watchers did everything they could to hasten Rakiba's healing. They provided potions and elixirs, closed the breaks in their armor where they could, and surrounded both Rakiba and Cassio with minna barriers and wards. Uriel's forces did the same.

The Sovereign-elect's right hand and next heir of Lamaru glowered at each other across the empty sands. The shadow from the Dragonfang's first mast crossed the deck of the Mourning Star and solidified into a passable bridge.

"Come on, bud, one last battle, then we can rest." Rakiba jumped onto Amarak's back and scratched his ears. Amarak let out a long and ferocious howl as he raced across the shadow bridge.

Uriel met them, greatsword in his left hand and lance in his right. He slashed at Rakiba, who leaped from Amarak's back and knocked Uriel's weapons aside. Rakiba twirled their own lance around their body in an impenetrable defense and forced Uriel away from Amarak to give him space to eliminate Uriel's bodyguards.

Dracona Cassio closed their eyes and summoned a swirling mass of dragonfire complete with horns and wings. It opened its toothed maw to chomp down on Uriel but the man simply raised his sword, which glowed a sickly purple and sucked the fiery beast into the aether. He spun on his heel and redirected the spell at Rakiba who barricaded himself behind a stone palisade not a moment too soon. The dragonfire melted his defenses and left a perfect hole.

Uriel charged through the opening. Their lances crashed and clanged together. Uriel brought his sword over his head and slammed it against Rakiba's armor, forcing them to yelp in pain and step away. He swung his lance around his body and stabbed toward Rakiba's chest but they knocked it aside and closed the distance between them. Rakiba thrusted their lance toward the man's head. The blade missed by inches. Uriel knocked Rakiba's lance aside, trapping its blade under his greatsword. He stomped on Rakiba's kneecap and brought them to the floor. Uriel towered over Rakiba, raising his lance to deal a deadly blow.

A clamorous shriek pierced the air. Without warning, Kinnari dove from the skies and flung Uriel him from his feet. He sailed across the Mourning Star and slammed into one of the ship's three masts. He roared in agony as a second blast of dragonfire burned holes in his armor like parchment. Dracona Cassio's Watchers and Kinnari's warriors held back Uriel's reinforcements as Amarak rushed to his master's side. He pulled Rakiba to their feet and licked their face.

"Thanks." Rakiba wiped the sweat and blood from their forehead. "Let's end this here and now." They charged Uriel together, determined to bring him to justice.

***

"Darling, now!" Katria yelled as Achyut summoned a second whip from his bansuri and wrapped it around the shelf above the top of the stairs. He pulled with all his might and toppled its contents; boxes and crates and bundles of stacked paper dropped upon the guards' heads and knocked them off balance. Katria burned through the stair fastenings. She pushed with all her might and with Achyut's help, the two of them toppled the stairway to the ground floor.

"Only four left." Katria clutched the top railing and steadied her breath.

Achyut sighed and smiled at his beloved. "That went better than I could have hoped for. I didn't know Mona taught you so mu—" He gasped. "Katria, you're hurt!" He gingerly took her arm.

She looked down at the long line of blood on her forearm, not too deep but painful all the same. "It's just a scratch, I-I'll be fine." She winced as he wiped the blood and grime from her wound.

"That is not 'just a scratch' my dear. I'll close it up as best I can. We have to be careful. Lilith is surely waiting for us and it's never wise to underestimate a soulseeker." Strands of cold, blue water dripped from Achyut's fingertips, wrapped around her arm, and expelled dirt and metal from the wound.

"Ah!" Katria shut her eyes and clenched her teeth as Achyut healed her as best he could.

"I'm sorry I can't do more." He temporarily closed her wound and kissed her gently. "This will have to do. Now to find something to wrap it."

"There's a first aid kit in the storage room down the hall, second door on the left." Katria opened her eyes, which shifted back from black to amber. "We should be safe for a little bit longer, as long as we're quiet. I don't sense anyone on the floor above us."

"Okay. You stay right here and rest. I'll be right back." He tilted her head up, kissed her soft lips, then sprinted down the hall. "Second door, second door... here." He jiggled the handle, but the door was tightly locked. He pressed his palm against the keyhole and closed his eyes. Water flowed from his hand and into the keyhole, pushing and pulling until he heard the gentle click of each of the lock pins. He froze the water into ice and opened the door with his makeshift key then dug through the disorganized mess until he found the red and white clay box filled with medical supplies. He hurried back out of the room and down the long hallway.

"Don't worry, my love, we'll fix you up right as... rain." His eyes grew wide in shock and fear. Katria was nowhere to be found. Her sword lay at the foot of the stairs alongside her silver ring and a set of bloody footprints that led up the stairs. He gathered minna in his left palm, clenched his sword in his right, and sprinted up the stairs ready to unleash hell on the damned soul who dared hurt his beloved.

"Who would have thought such a little mouse would cause so much trouble, even after I went through all that effort of masking my presence and silencing you," complained Lilith as she dragged Katria behind her, bound and gagged with minna as she limped up the stairs to the roof of the embassy. "You must be very special to the little prince for him to bring you this far into my city."

Katria struggled to scream or shout but no sound came from her lips. She kicked and thrashed and slammed her legs against the stairs and walls all to no avail. *What do I do? What do I do? Think, Katria. There has to be a way out of this. I'll blind her with my cantrip and run back down the stairs. No, my hands are useless right now and even if I could, I can't speak the evocation.* All she had was her wit and her curse... but perhaps that could be enough. *My love is coming to rescue me. I need to buy him as much time as I can.* She looked around for anything that could help her, and her eyes fell upon the strange and beautiful sword the woman wore on her side. Its blueish-gray blade struck something in the back of her mind, something she remembered from one of her lessons aboard the Prospector on her journey to Lamaru. All she needed to do was touch it, if only for a moment.

Katria slammed her legs into a desk and knocked a picture of a young man in a suit and a young lotor maiamorph in a wedding dress onto the floor. Before her capturer noticed, she kicked the broken frame into Lilith's path.

"Dammit!" Lilith howled in pain as the glass cut into her already bloody foot. Her sword swung wildly as she jerked around in pain.

"Ooohh, you'll pay for that, little wretch." She cursed under her breath as she removed the glass. "Just wait till we get to the roof. I'll grab my boots and kick you till you bleed!"

Katria paid no mind to Lilith's howls and threats as she silently scooted across the floor, entirely focused on Lilith's sword. She closed her eyes and winced in pain as it struck across her forehead but for a brief and beautiful moment, visions from the sword coursed through her mind.

Venkati! That's what the metal was called; a rare and resilient alloy that could break through cantrips and nullify minna. In an instant, Lilith's silencing spell shattered. She could fight back!

No, she quickly thought to herself. *If I fight back now, I'll be put back into the same position as before, yet Lilith will know I know how to break her spell. I have to be quiet. No grunts or moans or painful gasps to give me away, not until my beloved is here. Then we can fight back together.* She thought back to the days of Yaand and the Bale, when she only wished to be unseen and unheard, and held her tongue as Lilith dragged her up one more set of stairs.

Achyut threw open the door onto the roof, his sword held at guard, surrounded by swirling orbs of water and dagger-sharp icicles. He stared at Lilith, standing on the far side of the roof, clutching Katria in her left hand and her sword in her right. Katria's head hung limp, her arms dangling by her sides.

"Lilith! Return Katria to me now and I might let you live!"

"Prince Achyut, what a wonderful surprise. You honor me with your appearance. Though I'm afraid I can't let her go. How about an alternative: surrender to me now and I'll let her live. You see, she's taking a little nap right now and is completely at my mercy."

Achyut snarled and took two steps toward the wretched woman.

"Ahahah, you're too hasty, young prince." Lilith held her blade to Katria's throat.

Achyut froze, panic in his eyes. He stared longingly at Katria, only wishing for her to be safe in his arms once more. Then he blinked, unsure of if what he saw was real. He looked deep into her beautiful amber eyes. She winked at him. She was awake! It took every ounce of restraint not to show the relief that spread through his body. He exhaled calmly and returned his gaze to Lilith. "Tell me what you want, and I'll listen."

"First, dispel your minna constructs. Then drop your sword. I want it out of your reach."

The floating orbs and icicles vanished in an instant. Achyut slowly placed his sword at his feet, kicked it away, and adjusted his kurta to hide his bansuri.

"Good boy. I have a contract that will finalize the terms of Banjiha's succession and you're going to sign with a blood pact. My nation will be protected from Lamaru's greedy hands, and your life will be forfeit should your parents think otherwise."

"Fine. Just don't hurt Katria."

A victorious grin spread across Lilith's lips. "You're much more reasonable than Rakiba. I'll drop the contract and you'll sign it. Any movement toward your sword and the girl dies. Let's end this pointless conflict, and you and your woman can return safe and sound before the day is done."

***

Mona rolled in front of Masami and harnessed whatever minna was left in her aruval. Boris swiped and slashed at them with oversized daggers. Mona bared her teeth and held her ground as small cracks appeared and grew in her blade and shield. Masami staggered and stood up weakly. Flecks of blood coated her silky black fur, her eyes cloudy and distant.

"Come on, Masami! Stand up! You've got more fight left in you. I know it! Think of your kids, your husband! This is no time to fall!" Mona let out a fierce and guttural yawp. She unleashed all her harnessed minna into a single, brilliant explosion that knocked Boris off his feet and flung him across the plaza. She fell to her knees and steadied herself on her sword.

Dammit, she cursed as she steadied her breath. *He's tough. At this rate, I'll run out of minna before I can land a killing blow.* She bared her fangs and stood. *Like hell I'm giving up.* She reached into her satchel and pulled out a small vial filled with a dark blue, viscous liquid. She bit off the cork and downed its contents.

Power surged through her body as she felt her senses heighten tenfold. The flames on her boots and gloves glowed white and violet. The cracks in her aruval filled with raw, crackling minna and made the weapon whole once more. Mona charged at Boris, faster than any human could feasibly move. She twirled her blade around her body and slammed it against his daggers. Thunder and fire erupted from every strike.

Boris blocked as best he could, but Mona was too fast. She nipped and nicked at his body. Blood spurted from countless cuts. Burns formed far faster than he could heal with his own potions. Boris grunted in pain as he fell to his knees.

Mona gasped for breath as the potion's effects faded. Her muscles grew tight and sore. Her sweat evaporated the moment it formed on her skin. Boris lunged toward her in a desperate attack. His dagger pierced her armored shoulder. Mona howled in pain. She grabbed the dagger with her free hand and flooded the weapon and their bodies with electrically-charged minna. Once more, Boris flew across the plaza. He stood up shakily, his head spinning, his body all but broken. Mona lunged toward the giant. With a powerful stab, her sword pushed past his guard, inches from his chest.

Masami howled as she leaped onto Boris from behind. She slammed into his back with all her might. Mona's sword slipped further. The tip of Mona's blade pierced Boris's chest, yet his own blade rested inches from her neck. Masami jumped again. Boris grabbed her by the throat. He caught his breath as he strangled the foxtail.

"Masami!" cried Mona as she held her ground. The giant was too big. She couldn't move, lest she risk being impaled herself. Boris pushed Mona's blade further away. He drew a drop of scarlet blood from Mona's neck. An earsplitting shriek sounded high above.

"Look, in the sky!" called one of Achyut's lieutenants. A storm of eagles descended over the city walls. "It's Aquilo! The eagles are here! Come on everyone! For the Crown, for Lamaru, for Prince Achyut!" He rallied his soldiers against Lilith's forces as the eagles swarmed over the plaza. Swords and spears and claws and fangs pushed back against the unrelenting tides of men. Beaks and talons tore past armor and rendered flesh from their bodies. Unsuspecting soldiers were flung from their feet as the eagles strafed low to the ground and smashed through Lilith's ranks like a tidal wave through a small village.

High above the plaza, Aquilo searched in vain for Prince Achyut. Yet he spied Mona, locked in combat with a ferocious giant, Masami held limply in his grasp. He let out another fearsome shriek, tucked his wings close to his body, and dropped like a feathered boulder, smashing into the giant from behind.

Boris grunted in pain. He shuttered and dropped Masami, who fell to the plaza and lay still. He looked down at the woman's sword, buried in his chest. Blood trickled from the deep wound and formed a puddle at his feet.

Mona howled. Her aruval shattered as she poured fire and thunder from her body into a single concentrated blast. She punched Boris hard in the chest. The man flew high into the air, consumed by sparks and flames, and drew the eyes of all in the plaza. He smashed through the stone wall of a building beside the embassy.

Silence.

Boris the bandit was well and truly dead.

Immediately after the giant's demise, Lilith's forces threw down their weapons and raised their hands in surrender. The sudden arrival of the avian warriors dealt the final, crushing blow to their ranks. Now they only wished to escape with their lives.

Aquilo stood and shook his feathers. His head spun from the sudden impact.

"Aquilo, go to the embassy. Help Prince Achyut," ordered Mona through labored breaths as she rushed to and knelt by Masami's side. "The battle here is won. Make sure he and Katria are safe."

"Of course, Lady Mona." Aquilo spread his wings and took to the skies.

***

"It's over, Uriel, surrender and your life will be spared." Rakiba pressed the tip of their lance against Uriel's neck. Amarak growled. Cassio stood behind them, sword in hand, while another being of dragonfire and Kinnari slowly circled above them.

"I yield." Uriel dropped his weapons. They clanged against the ship's deck.

"Call off the rest of your troops."

Uriel slowly raised his left hand above his head. He gathered a small amount of minna which shot upward and radiated into crimson sparks above the Mourning Star. The same sparks erupted above the

Kingslayer and Peoples' Will. Slowly but surely, the spell and cannon fire subsided. Uriel's remaining forces dropped their weapons and held up their hands in surrender. Rakiba's paragons let out shouts and screams of joy. Captain Tanoy, Iyushi, and Karascotia breathed a collective sigh of relief. The battle was won.

"Dracona Cassio, prepare a cell on the Dragonfang for our special guest. I want enough wards and countermeasures that any attempt to harness minna knocks him out cold."

"Very well, Nuhir Rakiba." Cassio turned to their crew. "You heard the Nuhir—get that cell ready then tend to our wounded and round up the rest of these traitors."

"Yes, Dracona Cassio," they replied wholeheartedly.

Uriel glared at Rakiba. "I may have lost the battle, but the people have made their choice. The power of the crown is fading. The old ways will die."

"You're wrong. You led my people astray and into darkness. Their loyalty will rekindle once you and your sister are tried and found guilty of treason against the country."

Uriel smiled. "Is it really justice to preemptively assume my guilt? It is that exact attitude that originally bred their discontent. You should kill me now, say I died in combat and safeguard your lies from revealing the people's true will." Invisible to the naked eye, Uriel gathered minna in his open palm and formed a sleek and vile dagger.

"I will not stoop to your level. The people's loyalty will remain to those leaders who are just and compassionate. The fault of this bloodshed is yours and your sister's alone."

"I wonder, little royal, how long will your words hold true?"

"I will stand by my principles until I no longer draw breath."

"Honorable indeed, but you will soon learn that power left unchecked is a weakness to be exploited!" With one quick movement, Uriel grabbed Rakiba's lance and threw it aside. He plunged the minna dagger toward a hole in their chest plate.

"Nuhir Rakiba!" Dracona Cassio's eyes grew wide with horror. Rakiba's paragons drew their weapons and lunged at Uriel.

It was too late. His dagger pierced flesh. Rakiba's eyes fluttered as they staggered back, looking down at the slender blade. Blood dripped from the wicked wound.

"No... Amarak, Amarak!"

The great golden dire wolf collapsed on the deck of the ship.

Rakiba's soldiers tackled Uriel and bound his hands and legs with minna-dispersing cuffs. Uriel howled with laughter as Rakiba dropped to their knees. They held their friend in their arms as two medics rushed to Amarak's aid. His fur stained red with blood; his eyes grew cloudy and distant.

"I'm here, Amarak. I'm here, my friend." Rakiba rubbed his ears and lightly stroked his soft fur. Tears formed in the corners of their eyes. "You did so well. You saved my life. You're such a good boy; the goodest of good boys." Amarak's tail wagged limply.

"Nuhir Rakiba," one of the medics began in a soft, trembling voice. "The wound was imbued with some form of toxic minna. It's spreading too quickly. Even our most intricate spells can't save him, only prolong his life."

"He's dying?" croaked Rakiba. Amarak let out a despondent sigh.

The medic nodded. "The best we can do is give him a sedative to ease his pain until the end."

"Very well." Rakiba looked down at his lifelong friend. Tears fell into steady streams. "Please, do whatever you can."

"Yes, Your Majesty." They hurriedly administered a sedative.

Amarak whimpered and leaned against his best friend and master.

"Shhh, it's okay, bud." He gently stroked the golden wolf's fur. "When you wake up, you'll feel so much better. I'll give you a nice, fat, juicy, tapi steak as soon as we get home."

Amarak sighed. His breathing slowed.

"I know you must be tired now. It must hurt so much. It's okay to sleep. I'm right here with you. I'll always be by my best buddy's side." Rakiba kissed Amarak's head.

Amarak closed his eyes. His breathing slowed and slowed until it stopped altogether. Rakiba looked to the medics for some kind of hope or reassurance, but their silent expressions explained everything.

"You should have killed me when you had the chance." Uriel smiled.

Rakiba glared at the man with hatred in his eyes. They gently moved Amarak's body aside and stood. They picked up Uriel's greatsword and hefted it in their hands, shaking in anguish and rage. "Maybe you're right. Maybe you and all your followers should be executed for treason; the matter dealt with here and now. Then the rest of us can live on in peace. You... you deserve death!" Rakiba held the sword high above their head and brought it down with all the strength they could muster.

The hilt of the sword smashed against Uriel's helmet and knocked the man unconscious.

"But I believe in justice for all, even scum like you, and I will stand by my principles now and as future Padishah of Lamaru." They dropped Uriel's sword which clattered against the deck, the sound cutting through the silent crowd stronger than any strike. "Take him away."

"Yes, Your Majesty."

Rakiba knelt beside Amarak and wept.

***

"And you think I'll just trust you to keep Katria and I unharmed, even if you win the battle outside the walls? No chance." Prince Achyut crumbled Lilith's contract into a ball of parchment. "If you want me to sign your blood pact, you have to include in your terms that no harm will come to either of us, lest you forfeit your own life."

"You don't seem to get it, do you little prince?" Lilith spat in frustration. "I hold all the cards here! You don't get to bargain or parlay or demand anything from me! You've lost!"

Achyut laughed, loud and boisterous. "I've lost? Really? I've lost?" He tossed the crumpled ball up and down in his hand. "If I die, your sick dreams will never be realized. My parents will stop at nothing to bring you to justice, and they won't be as forgiving as Rakiba or me. You can't win."

Lilith eyed him suspiciously. Clearly, he was stalling. But for what? He faced her alone with no weapon in his hands. Did he know something she didn't? She glanced at the copper-haired woman behind her. *Is she communicating with him behind my back?*

"Hey, I'm not done talking to you." Achyut threw the balled-up contract which bounced off Lilith's head and into the streets below.

Lilith wasn't amused in the slightest. Her scowl became a grimace that could cut diamonds. "Look here, you obnoxious-little-royal shit, I'm not playing your game! You're lucky I have a copy of my contract, otherwise, she'd be dead! You'll sign now or watch her die." She took a second metal tube from her bag and tossed it to Achyut's feet, sauntering over to Katria and holding her sword against her neck. "You have thirty seconds before I cut off her head."

Acyut picked up the tube and took out the second piece of parchment.

"Twenty."

He had to think of something, some way to distract Lilith and buy just a few more minutes. He knew the avian warriors were on their way, they had to be. He just needed more time.

"Ten."

The ground shook as if an angry ancient creature had been ill-roused from its rest. A horrendous sound tore through the air that made both Achyut and Lilith wonder if such a demon or evil god had in fact been released. The air around them became unfathomably hot. Suddenly Banjiha's northern wall was engulfed in colored lights that blinded them both and filled the sky. When the noise and lights finally subsided, the entire northern wall was gone; reduced to nothing, and both fleets of sandships were put on display for the entire city to see.

Prince Achyut immediately drew his bansuri. He summoned a length of rope that wrapped around the hilt of his sword and whipped the weapon into the air and toward Lilith, who stood with her eyes glued to the gargantuan hole, filled with unbridled rage and dismay as to how the wall and minna batteries had been reduced to nothing.

"Katria, get down!"

Katria pushed herself away from Lilith and fell toward the roof, just as Lilith regained her understanding of the situation at hand. Yet Katria was already out of reach. Lilith knocked his blade away only to hear the voice of the young maiden on the ground.

"*Caecus lux e nar!*" A flash of light and heat erupted from the woman's hands.

Lilith shielded her eyes and summoned her own invisible wards. She brought her sword down upon where the woman should have been only to be met with the sound of metal scraping against the stone roof. She snarled and turned around as the blinding flash faded. The prince lunged at her in barbaric rage. His sword caught her own and she parried his strike away only to be bashed in the shoulder by his bansuri. Lilith stepped back and lunged at Achyut, her strikes a furious, dancing, flurry of metal yet his sudden assault had bought enough time for Katria to rise and retreat to safety behind her lover's sword.

Achyut blocked as best he could but Lilith continually gained ground. Cuts and nicks turned red as blood oozed from his surface wounds across his body. Then from out of nowhere, he heard Katria scream. She lunged between the two of them, a red-hot metal tentpole in her arms. She swung wildly around and forced Lilith to back away from her prince.

Invisible power coursed through Lilith's open hand as she swiped at Katria. With two quick slashes, she cut Katria's weapon into three. With a third slash, she nearly severed Katria's head from her body, but Achyut jumped in front of his beloved and blasted Lilith at point-blank with a solid mass of ice.

Lilith was thrown off her feet and smashed into the far side of the roof. Even before she could stand, she heard the young prince close the gap between them. She quickly rose, drew her sword once more, and parried Achyut's strikes. She rolled out of the way of his next strike and grabbed a piece of the cut tent pole. She came to her feet, feinted to her left, then smashed the pole against Achyut's side. Before he had the chance to recover, she kicked him hard in the gut.

Achyut spat up blood as he fell to the ground. He placed his weight on his bansuri and rose to his feet. Lilith hefted the rod in her hands and grinned. Shockwaves blasted from her palm and sent the pole speeding toward Achyut. Achyut's breath froze. He braced himself for pain, but the pole only grazed his shoulder and flew past his head.

"Hah!" He raised his sword in defiance. "You need to work on your aim!"

Lilith's grin doubled in size. "You weren't the target, little prince." She jeered back.

Achyut turned around. His eyes grew wide in fear. A cold wave of numbness washed over his body.

Katria coughed up blood. She fell back against the broken wall and stared down at the metal rod that pierced through her chest.

End Part III

Part IV

17

Light in the Dark

"Katria!" Achyut screamed, desperately rushing toward his beloved, but Lilith hefted a second piece of the pole and launched it toward him. This time it pierced Achyut's left arm. He dropped his bansuri, howled in pain, and fell to one knee. He glared over his shoulder, eyes full of hatred and rage.

"Nu-uh-uh, you're not done playing with me," Lilith taunted. "You better hurry, who knows how long she'll last. If you were smart, you'd surrender now. Give into my demands and I'll let you save her."

Achyut dug the tip of his sword into the stone roof. He pushed himself up and held the blade in front of him, letting out a blood-curdling yawp and rushing Lilith with raw, primal fury.

Lilith parried his first few swipes with ease. She knocked his blade aside and kicked him hard in the gut. Achyut fell to the ground. He spat out more blood and stood once more. He gathered what minna he could in his left hand and rushed her again. Again, Lilith parried his first strike, then his second, and his third. Achyut's torso was left wide open. As Lilith slashed at his shoulder, Achyut shaped his gathered minna into a water whip which wrapped around her blade and closed the gap between them. He shoved his sword through her right arm.

Lilith shrieked. She blasted Achyut back with another shattering shockwave. She drew his sword from her arm and pointed them both at the young prince, sprawled out and weaponless on the stone roof.

"I was going to take you hostage, but you're making me regret my decision. Perhaps killing you will send a stronger message to your family after all!" She sprinted toward him.

Achyut quickly snatched up the last two poles and held them over his chest. Lilith's swords clanged loudly against the metal. She struck again and nicked Achyut's right shoulder, plunging her second blade down upon him and missing his neck by inches. Achyut raised the left pole in his hand and smashed it against the side of her head. Lilith dropped like a stone. Achyut rolled away from her, came up to his knees, and bashed the second pole against her kneecap. She yelped and cursed. He rose and towered over her.

"I'll make you pay for hurting Katria! I'll make you pay for everything you've done!" He smashed his right pole against her other knee and knocked his sword from her open palm with the left. Lilith rolled toward him, covered in blood, sweat, and dirt, and slashed at his leg with her own sword. Achyut blocked and was suddenly thrown from his feet by another burst of her powerful shatter minna. His pipes were torn from his grasp and clanged loudly against the roof as they rolled out of reach.

I... I can barely move. He gasped through labored breaths. *Everything hurts. I... I can't hold out much longer. Is this the end? Everything is so dark, so cold...* His eyes grew heavy and the world turned dark.

"Prince Achyut! Get up! Please, you have to get up!" He heard a sweet and oh-so-familiar voice from somewhere far away.

"Katria?" he mumbled.

"You have to get up! You can't falter now! Think of Rakiba, Mona. Me! We need you! Please, you can't give up now!"

He opened his eyes and winced in pain. *I can't give up. Everyone... is depending on me. Everyone...* He rolled onto his stomach and shakily pushed himself off the ground. *Come on body, move!* He raised his head.

Even with both her kneecaps shattered, Lilith crawled across the roof, pipe and sword in hand, murder in her eyes.

MOVE! Achyut pushed himself onto his knees.

"Oh no, you don't! I'll kill you first!" shouted Lilith. She gathered minna in her left hand, released it, and slammed Achyut flat against the ground. "You die here, little prince, then I'll make your wench suffer!" A wicked smile crept across her lips.

"Dammit all! I won't let you touch Katria!" Achyut roared and forced his body to move. "You'll never hurt her again!"

"Why won't you just give up? Save yourself the trouble and surrender while I still offer you the chance!"

"I'll never give up! If I can still punch you, I can still fight!"

"I'll cut off your arms, boy."

"I'll kick you to death!"

"I'll cut off your legs!"

"I'll bite you!" He locked eyes with Lilith.

Blood leaked from four of her separate wounds. He guessed he didn't look much better. His body hurt like hell, his heart pounding in his ears. It took every ounce of willpower just to move, but his determination to save his beloved and his hatred for this woman stoked the flames in his heart. He reached for the nearest tent pole and used it like a crutch to make his broken body stand. He wanted, no, needed to make her bleed. Forget his orders, forget her trial, this would be a fight to the death.

A piercing shriek cut through the air and a massive shadow covered the rooftop. Aquilo swooped down from about and purposely crashed into Lilith. Before she could react, his talons pinned her arms flat against the roof, his sharp beak inches away from her exposed neck.

"Move and you're dead," he commanded.

Lilith tensed her body and gathered minna in her palms.

Aquilo pressed his beak against her skin. A trickle of blood ran down her neck.

"I... I yield." She dispersed what little minna she had gathered and lay limp under the eagle's talons. Even if she had time to strike, it would not be enough to kill the abhorrent creature before he killed her.

"Prince Achyut, the fight is won," proclaimed Aquilo.

Achyut sighed in relief, his pain dulled by adrenaline, but this was no time to rest.

"Aquilo, go down to the second floor. There's a first-aid kit by the base of the stairs. Bring it here!"

"Yes, Your Majesty. What should I do with her?" He gestured at Lilith.

"Keep her contained. If she tries anything, kill her. Now go! Katria's life depends on it." Aquilo nodded, though somewhat shocked by the prince's ferocity. Still, he understood the young man's pain. He transformed back into his humanoid form and pressed Lilith's sword against her neck. The Eye of Eruber cracked.

"Come worm, you heard the Prince's orders." He hauled her to her feet and hurried down into the embassy. Prince Achyut hobbled to Katria's side.

"Katria, we did it. The battle is over. We won." He scooped her cold body gently into his arms. "Katria, please, please, say something. Just hang on a little longer. I'll save you, I promise."

"Prince... Achyut..." she whimpered through wispy breaths. "It hurts. It hurts so much. Yet..." She opened her eyes and smiled weakly at him. "To die in your arms, to see your face at the end of all things, I couldn't have imagined a better death."

"No, Katria. Don't leave me, please hold on. I'll save you. I promised I'd save you!"

"Darling, you already have." She reached up and cupped his face in her right hand. "You've saved me countless times, from teaching me how to stand up for myself, through our travels across Reighja, and in giving me the chance to help others. I've known your kindness and love since we first met, and for that, I'm eternally grateful. You gave my life value and meaning when I couldn't find it myself. These last few months have... have meant more to me than anything in the world. I wouldn't trade them for anything. I'd rather live and die by your side than live a long and lonely life."

"Katria... I-I love you so much. I'm so sorry. I wasn't quick enough. I wasn't strong enough to save you." Silent tears rolled down his cheeks.

"Shhh. Don't say that, my love." She wiped away his tears. "The future isn't promised to anyone. We both knew the risks of coming here. I'll find peace knowing you'll live to see tomorrow."

"But how am I supposed to live without you by my side? I won't have the strength to carry on. Oh, Katria... I wanted to build a future with you. I wanted to make you smile for the rest of your days."

"I'm smiling now, aren't I?"

Achyut nodded without a word.

"You lived before you met me, you'll continue to live after I die. You must keep living, for both of our sakes. Live a long and happy life without regrets. Promise me you won't give up, no matter how rough it gets. Promise me my death won't change who you are. Your country and your people need your kind heart just as much as I need you."

"I promise. I'll strive to be the man you saw in me. I won't give up, ever, and I'll find a way to bring you back, even if it takes the rest of my life!"

Katria giggled faintly. "Now, now, don't make promises you can't keep. As long as you look back on our time together with fondness and love, that will be enough."

"We did have a lot of fun, didn't we?" Achyut wiped away his tears but the steady rain from his eyes returned too quickly and blurred his vision.

Katria held his hand and kissed it. She closed her eyes and took a deep breath. "If I could have one last request, I want to see you smile before I go. That would mean everything to me." She smiled at him weakly. The light had nearly faded from her eyes.

"Of course, my dear." Achyut held her hands in his. An unbearable weight crushed his chest. His heart and lungs felt tight, crippled by pain. He wanted to cry and scream and slam his head against the wall until it shattered, yet as he gazed tenderly at his beloved, he couldn't help but smile. She had made his life so much more fulfilling. Even after she left, nothing would blot out his love for her, not even his own sorrow.

"I love you so much," he whispered.

"I know." She smiled and closed her eyes. "I love you too... and when the time comes for you to join me, after a long and happy life, you'll see it too, and I'll see joy upon your face once more."

"See what?" asked Achyut.

"White shores, a blue sea, green rolling hills, and the most magical sunset ever. We'll build a small house right on top of this hill and live here for the rest of eternity."

"You know, when you put it like that, dying doesn't sound so bad. Tell me more about our house on the hill. Will we have a garden? Pets? Children?"

Katria fell silent.

"Katria, please, tell me more. Tell me anything. Just let me hear your voice again. Don't leave me... don't leave me." He touched his forehead to hers and cradled her limp body in his arms.

"Prince Achyut! I've found it!" Aquilo sat by his side.

Achyut cradled Katria's body, using every tool and bandage to treat her wounds, but she remained silent. Despite their best efforts, Achyut knew he would never hear her sweet voice again.

Grief gripped his heart like never before. All he could feel was pain. The most unbearable pain he had ever felt in his life and the woman who caused it lay mere feet away from him, still alive— bound and gagged, beaten and bloody, but alive, nonetheless. There was no justice in the world.

Achyut closed Katria's eyes and kissed her forehead. He stood and picked up his sword.

"You!" He glared at Lilith. "You did this... You did this to her!" He ripped off her gag as roughly as he could. "Tell me, are you happy now? Are you finally content with your reign of destruction? The lives you ruined? Answer me!" He pressed the tip of his sword against her neck. "Choose your words carefully. They may very well be your last."

"You're the one who attacked me," replied Lilith calmly. "You couldn't let my new nation prosper on its own. You had to interfere. All I wanted was peace for humankind, a home that was ours alone."

"Peace? Peace?! How dare you speak of peace after all the lives you destroyed! Your peace was only brought about through the suffering of others! Your peace is a lie that you told yourself so you could play the role of the hero; so that you wouldn't have to feel their pain, the pain I feel right now!"

"I've felt more pain than you'll ever know! I watched my parents die! I lost my lover and my child, but I'm not weak, like you. I did something about it! I used my pain as fuel and created a world where humans could be free from the pain I've felt all my life! Who cares if a few abominations die in the process? That is the way of the world, Prince Achyut: eat or be eaten, fight, win, or be killed!"

Achyut's fists shook with rage. "If that's what you truly think, I'll create a better world as well!" He punched her hard in the face. "One where you no longer live!" He smashed the hilt of his sword against her skull. "This is the way of the world is it not?!"

Lilith smiled as she coughed up blood. *Even when I die, I will be remembered; a martyr for those who stand against the tyranny of the Crown and the maiamorph abominations. My vision will still come true.*

"Answer me! Or I'll forever wipe that wicked smile off your face!"

Lilith closed her eyes and said nothing.

"Fine. Have it your way." Achyut raised his sword high above his head.

"Prince Achyut, please, this isn't the way! Don't prove her right, you're not a monster like her!" Aquilo's efforts to soothe him were all for not.

Prince Achyut's morality was broken and cast aside. At that moment, he cared for nothing but to watch Lilith die. He brought his sword down with all the strength he could muster. The blade cut through her neck and severed her head from her shoulders.

"This is what I think of your way of the world." He kicked her head off the side of the building and into the empty streets below.

***

Rakiba scooped up Amarak's body and gently laid it in an empty coffin; another among the hundreds, where the fallen of the battle would sleep for all eternity. They wiped fresh tears from their face and picked up their lance, trudging down the steps of the Dragonfang to the brig where Uriel was being interrogated by Tanoy and Iyushi.

Captain Tanoy sighed and rubbed his eyes as the door above opened and Rakiba entered.

"Apologies, Your Majesty, we've tried everything to make him talk, but he hasn't told us anything about Lilith's grand ambitions nor how many of her faction's leaders were in the city or spread about the other regions of Lamaru."

Uriel lifted his head. "I will speak to Rakiba, alone."

Rakiba glared at the man who had taken the life of his best friend and the lives of so many more. "Fine. I'll talk with you. And when my brother returns with your sister in chains, you'll tell us everything if you wish to ever see her again."

"But of course." Uriel smiled.

"Captain Tanoy, Captain, Iyushi, please leave us. I'll call for your assistance should I need it."

Iyushi and Tanoy shifted hesitantly but ultimately obeyed Rakiba's orders. They closed the door as they left, and the room became silent as a tomb. Rakiba opened the brig door and studied Uriel's appearance. The man's white armor had bent and scratched, its sheen lost to a thick layer of dried blood, dust, and scoring from combat. His blond hair cut oddly from the close shaves of their duel. His skin was covered in scratches and burns, but the man showed no sign of pain, discomfort, or weakness. He bore his injuries with pride and purpose and met their unflinching gaze with his own.

"Are you proud of what you've accomplished, Uriel? Have you met your sister's expectations?"

Uriel didn't speak.

Rakiba narrowed their eyes and frowned. "My best friend, my paragons, even the citizens of Banjiha you conscripted into your ranks, so many of them are dead because of your cruel and failed leadership."

"They are dead because you attacked us; another act of tyranny by the jaded Crown of Lamaru." Uriel retorted calmly. "All we wanted was to create a safe haven for humankind— a place where none would suffer the burdens we carry from the wretched existence of maiamorphs."

"A place where humans would suffer all the same injustices you claim to be victims of. The maiamorphs were only your scapegoats; someone different to label as an enemy and rally against. Tell me, after you purged your country from one group, which would be next? Perhaps those of different hair or skin? Maybe people with a binding or shatter minna flare would become your next heretics."

"We would have no need for such atrocities. There would have been no civil strife in our great nation. We would have peace."

"Really? Then what would you do with all the people like you? The troublemakers, those who believe your new regime is flawed? If justice is brought about through vengeance, then vengeance will rise to take its place. No one stays in power forever. Someone will try to overthrow your rule, just as you tried to overthrow ours."

"The threat of retaliation from the maiamorph clans would be enough to keep solidarity between our people. As long as one of those creatures lives, we will rally together against them."

"You're a coward who can only rule by fear."

"And the Crown only rules through fanciful lies and empty covenants. Your hubris alone makes me gag. You take from the citizens of Banjiha and Thaniana and Mutedan and promise them untold riches and technology, yet only the capital grows and grows. I do not care if you kill me. I only wish to live long enough to watch your terraforming ritual fail— to watch you falter in such a splendid fashion that the people's loyalty is stripped away once and for all."

"The people will remain loyal once we expose your lies and treachery. Your beliefs will be stripped away, layer by layer, until nothing remains of your twisted ideology. Then, when you die, no one will follow you. No one will sing your praises or mourn your loss and the pages of history will remember you for what you are: a twisted, evil, self-serving bigot."

"Big talk from a pampered royal who can't even kill their rival."

"You are not my rival; you are a jingoistic zealot. I don't have to kill you to prove myself."

"Then your little pup's sacrifice was all for naught. Maybe his meaningless death will enlighten yo—"

Rakiba pressed their lance's blade against Uriel's throat.

Uriel smiled. "Are you going to kill me after all?"

"I would certainly like to, after everything you've done, but I won't follow down your depraved path. I will break your cycle of hatred and let true justice run its course. No one else will suffer the way you made others suffer, not while I draw breath." Rakiba stepped out of Uriel's cell, locked the door, and ascended the stairs without another word.

Uriel heard Rakiba slam the door shut, leaving him alone in the silent darkness of the brig. *Hmm... not as corruptible as I had hoped. It doesn't matter. Sister, our vision will come to fruition. We will create our paradise in due time. The people's emotions are turbid; their loyalty shaken. Although we've lost this battle, our war, our freedom, is just beginning.* Uriel closed his eyes and rested on his wooden bed.

Rakiba stared off into the empty horizon and waited for Achyut and the others' return. Although they wished to ignore Uriel's words completely, they couldn't refuse the grain of truth planted in the fields of deception that had sprouted and grown into a harvest of problems. *Discontent alone does not breed war. They chose, willingly, to follow Lilith and Uriel. I fear our kingdom has more cracks deeper inside its foundation than those discernible from its surface. I wonder...*

"Nuhir Rakiba, pardon my interruption. Would you be willing to confer with me a moment?"

Rakiba glanced over their shoulder and bowed politely as Dracona Cassio approached, dressed in the formal, white robes of the Watchers.

"Of course, Dracona Cassio. I welcome any and all conversation. It can be rather tedious living with my own thoughts for too long. Speak freely, my friend."

"Thank you, Your Majesty. I-well, I'm finding it rather difficult to come to terms with all of this. So much needless bloodshed, so many lives cast aside and shattered. Although this was our victory, there is still much work to be done; trials will be held and the concerns of Banjiha's citizens will have to be addressed if we're to protect our kingdom's integrity from the next fanatical revolution."

"I agree. We've stopped the fighting here, and I pray my brother has met similar success. Still, we must mediate this problem entirely if we're to move forward as a unified kingdom. We must remember all the lives we lost, for if we fail, then they died for nothing. I for one will not let their sacrifice be in vain."

"What do you mean, Your Majesty? Their sacrifices were in vain. How do we make up for their lost time, the dreams our paragons held in their hearts? How do we come to terms with the lives lost on behalf of the living?"

"In all honesty, we can't. Death itself is not an honorable thing but rather the end of a road we all must travel when the time comes. Whatever dreams our soldiers carried died with them on the battlefield. Whatever plans or ambitions we sought means nothing when we die." Rakiba's eyes held nothing but sadness, yet the smallest smile formed on their lips, as if remembering countless, wonderful moments with friends and family long gone.

"But that is why it is up to us, the living, to ensure their sacrifices have meaning. They died knowing we would push on in their stead. They entrusted the future, their dreams, and their ambitions into our hands. Their lives have meaning because we refuse to forget them and must carry on. When my parents eventually pass into the next world, I know they will believe their successor—that I will hold fast to their lives and memories and do what is right. Because they taught me to leave this world a better place than how it was gifted to us."

Cassio smiled. "Your kindness and wisdom will serve you well in the future, Your Majesty, yet wouldn't this world be a happier place without the shadow of death bearing down upon us?"

"It would, for certain, but I also believe that death, and with the same reasoning, the infinitesimal amount of time in which we live our wondrous lives, is what makes our existence so precious. The sooner we come to the realization that tomorrow isn't given, the sooner we learn to live for others as well as ourselves. Our children, our legacies, the wisdom and knowledge we chose to leave behind, whether it be in book or song, house or deed, is what becomes important and the driving force that betters us as a whole."

"But, theoretically speaking, if you could somehow find a way to rid ourselves of the cold embrace of death's arms, wouldn't we be able to learn and create much more, to progress even further and at a much quicker pace? To never mourn the loss of a parent or child... or even Amarak?"

Rakiba stifled a small chuckle. "Dracona Cassio, you remind me so much of my old teacher in my earliest days training to be a soulseeker. She always said 'there's no use in a great body if one's mind withers away in the process'. I must admit, if that power did exist, the thought of endless joyous days with Amarak and all of those we've lost is enticing, seductive even. However, even if this power was gifted to me by the gods themselves, I would not subject Amarak, nor anyone, to that fate."

Cassio frowned. "Forgive my questioning, but I cannot understand the reasoning behind your answer. You stand with nothing to lose and everything to gain. Would you humor me and extrapolate further?"

"I don't mind at all. The purpose of discussing such theoreticals is paramount in understanding another's perspective. I would not revive Amarak because that is the way of the world. All things that begin must end, even if they can begin anew. I will miss my companion dearly. I most certainly know that when my adrenaline fades, I will weep for the loss of my oldest friend and will always remember his sacrifice so I may live. In fact, I've decided I shall thank him every morning and every night in my daily prayers, as he gave his life, like so many others here, to protect my own, and to protect those who cannot protect themselves."

Rakiba continued, amused at Cassio's bemused expression, "Do you not think it cruel and selfish to drag one back from eternal peace, just so they can suffer further among the living? When the day comes for me to join him on the other side, I will not wish to come back to the mortal world. I will miss those I leave behind, but all will eventually join me in everlasting happiness. As long as I treasure Amarak's life and the good times we shared, he will live on inside of me. My memories will have to tide me over until we are reunited in the next life."

"A very interesting take on the mortality of this world." Cassio studied Rakiba with curious eyes. Their mind seemed elsewhere and far away, almost disappointed, until a requisite smile crossed their lips.

"You are as wise and noble as you are kind, Nuhir Rakiba. You will make an exemplary Padishah and I pray to the ancient dragons to live long enough to see the glorious days of your reign."

"Thank you. Your words bring me joy in this time of darkness and suffering."

"I am honored to aid, my liege." Cassio bowed. "And thank you for answering my silly questions. If you will excuse me, there is much I still have to ponder on my own, and of course, much paperwork to be done, not only for our campaign, but for the Order of the Watchers as well." Dismissing themselves, Cassio began to walk away but stopped and turned around instead. "Oh, and, Nuhir Rakiba, would you please inform me when Prince Achyut arrives? I would like to speak to him."

"Of course," replied Rakiba.

***

It was late afternoon when Aquilo and his warriors soared over the broken walls of Banjiha and reunited Prince Achyut and his strike team with Nuhir Rakiba and the sandship fleet. News of Lilith's death spread quickly throughout the city. Rakiba welcomed Achyut with open arms in celebration of their overwhelming victory, but their heart shattered as they saw their little brother cradling Katria's body, wrapped in cloth, in his arms.

No words broke Achyut from his stupor, who simply walked below the main deck of the Prospector to his private quarters. He locked the door and wept. Time lost all meaning and only emptiness and pain resonated with his broken heart.

"Prince Achyut, I know you're in there, come on, open this damn door and talk to me. I brought you some warm soup and bread. You have to eat something." Mona rapped her knuckles against the wooden frame.

"I'm sorry, Mona, I'm not hungry. I just want to be left alone. Thank you."

Mona took slow, deep breaths and rubbed her temples. "You don't have to suffer alone. You aren't the only one who misses her. She was the closest person I had to a sister and now that she's gone... I can't rid myself of this void in my chest. But destroying your own health through grieving won't bring her back. Your solitude is worrying us."

"I won't be alone much longer, perhaps a day or two more, that's it, I promise."

"I'll hold you to it," replied Mona gruffly. "I'm leaving this soup outside your door. Promise me you'll at least attempt to eat it."

"I promise."

Mona set the bowl down and rubbed her eyes. She felt tired, sore, and helpless. It was a horrible feeling and something she never wished to experience again.

True to his word, Achyut spent the next full day locked in his room. He felt the lurching of the sandship and knew they must be on their return journey to Illadina, where they would tell the Padishah and King their tale, and funerals would be held for all the fallen— both from Banjiha and of Lamaru. His time with Katria grew ever shorter. Soon she would be buried, along with his heart, and he would have to press on, just as he promised her.

His next visitor was Captain Tanoy, who also brought him food from the kitchens. He set the bowl of rice and curry next to the untouched bowl of soup and knocked on the door.

"Prince Achyut, lad, this isn't healthy. You cannot sacrifice your wellbeing to satisfy your grief, especially since that hole may never be filled."

"I appreciate your concern, Captain Tanoy, but you don't understand what I'm going through."

"Aye, I do lad, even more so than you realize. I doubt I've ever told you the truth about why I joined Lamaru's navy, but... it was to search for my husband and daughter, taken by pirates long, long ago."

Achyut glanced up at the door, a puzzled expression on his face. Tanoy had never spoken of his past before joining the crew of the Prospector. He had no idea the man had once had a family, and that they had likely met an early demise.

"I- I'm sorry to hear that, sir. I had no idea."

"It hurts, doesn't it? It hurts like hell knowing you'll never see them again, knowing you'll never hear their voice or laugh or feel the warmth of their skin under the shining sun. The weight is almost unbearable."

"It is," replied Achyut. His eyes brimmed with tears.

"But you have to pull yourself out of this stupor, not only for your health but because those you've lost would hate to see you in this state. You have to persevere for their sake."

"Captain Tanoy, if I may ask, what happened to your husband and daughter?"

"I searched and searched, seeking vengeance on that wretched man and his crew. Eventually, we did find their hideout, and I gutted the vile creature who took away my family... yet it still didn't heal my pain. The only thing I accomplished that day was murdering the parents of a little girl and leaving her without a family."

Achyut was silent.

"I've often wondered what became of her, if she survived and grew strong or died at a young age. The cycle of loss and hate is not easily broken. Perhaps she'll seek me out and cut me down for my deeds. It's up to us and the people we trust to break us away from that lasting pain. After all, that's what family and friends are for. I'm not going to force you to come out of your room, but there are many here who love you and share your grief. In all my years of loss and travel, I've found the best way to lessen your own burdens is to share them with the people you love and trust." Without another word, Captain Tanoy walked away.

The sun had long set when Achyut stood up from his bed. He took the bowl of rice and curry and ate hesitantly. Yet after only the first bite, hunger overtook exhaustion. He wolfed down the rest of the meal and the cold soup left the day before. Still his stomach grumbled for more, and he crept out of his room, a lonely shadow in the night, searching for solace from his sorrowful existence.

Unsatisfied by food alone, he wandered the empty halls of the Prospector, memories of Katria washing over his mind like gentle waves on a beach. A light flickered on the main deck and Mona and Rakiba's voices broke through the eerie silence of the night. Achyut drifted toward them, praying they could provide some form of comfort.

"I don't know what to do, Mona. I fear I'm destined to always be torn between my duties as the next heir and my relationships with my friends, family—everyone." Rakiba sighed and rubbed their face. "I know the right course, but it is far from an easy path, yet action must be taken."

"Nuhir Rakiba, I understand how driven you are by your sense of duty, perhaps more than anyone else, but is now really the time to burden him with such knowledge? He's already suffering so much. Are you truly capable of such cruelty at a time like this?" asked Mona.

"While I will never forgive Lilith for her crimes against our country, and I will never forget the pain and suffering she caused so many others, at the time of her capture, she was an unarmed prisoner. I heard everything from Aquilo. To cut down a defeated foe and go against my direct orders, my brother must face the consequences of his actions, whatever the Padishah decides."

Achyut's heart stopped, unable to process Rakiba's words, his lungs unable to hold more than a puff of air. Sweat dripped from his forehead as his knees shook, barely able to hold his weight. *That's right. I forgot. In my rage I... I...* He sprinted back to his room, slammed the door, and fell to his knees and wept.

"Did you hear something?" Curious, Mona turned toward the stairs. Rakiba shook their head. "Only the wind."

⁂

Achyut's body shook. Rivers of tears flooded his face as he realized the painful truth. *I cut her down in cold blood. I'm no better than either of them. Nothing more than a failed prince, too weak of body to save my beloved, too weak of mind to save my ideals.* A wrenching sensation gripped his heart. Fresh waves of pain pounded in his chest. His arms became too heavy to lift and his nails cut deep into his palms. Blood welled from his wounds and stained his hands. *She was a murderer. She deserved to die. I did a service to the world by silencing her hateful lies!*

But Rakiba's words echoed in his mind as his brown eyes shifted to an unnatural and encompassing black. *She was an unarmed prisoner and murdering her makes you nothing more than a common criminal.*

Liar! I did what had to be done!

Didn't Lilith say the same?

She didn't deserve to live.

Just as you were never deserving of your station, never deserving of Katria's love.

Lies, lies, lies, lies! He slammed his head against the floor over and over and over again until his vision blurred and his skull felt fuzzy and warm, a pleasant numbness lulling him to sleep. *If only I could have saved her... everything would be right....*

18

Paradise Lost

The cheers and shouts from the crowd felt distant and alien when the Prospector and the Dragonfang returned to the royal docks of Illadina. Nuhir Rakiba did their best to smile and wave and appease the masses, but the loss of Amarak, Katria, Captain Zatizimak, and the countless soldiers weighed heavily on their heart. Mona and Achyut departed the vessel in somber silence. They did not smile or wave but stared blankly down at the sandstone tiles that lined the road as the procession marched up to the citadel and palace. When they reached the royal audience chambers, Rakiba, Tanoy, and Cassio did all of the talking.

Angem and Dabesh's composed facade faltered as anguish fell upon their faces at the sight of their son, silent and sepulchral. Almost immediately, the Padishah adjourned all further meetings until tomorrow.

With Lilith dead and Uriel in chains, her children and their allies had vanquished the threat of Banjiha's secession; and now, in this moment, her responsibilities as a mother mattered more than those of a queen.

The castle staff cleaned and dressed the bodies of the fallen. The heroes of Banjiha lay in glass boxes atop marble catafalques in the Great

Hall. The doors of the palace opened to the public so all could mourn and look for a sliver of solace together.

Mona stood in a corner of the Great Hall, the sounds of weeping and wailing echoing throughout. She dug her nails into her palms as she ambled up and down the seemingly endless rows of the dead. Friends, soldiers, sparring partners, and rivals— death was the great equalizer for them all.

"Lady Mona, might I trouble you for a word?"

Mona glanced over her shoulder. Nuhir Rakiba stood alone, dressed in a solid black knee-length kurta and trousers.

"None of your words could trouble me more than this sight, Your Majesty. Please, speak freely."

Rakiba made the smallest attempt to smile. "Even in this darkness, I must commend your stalwart nature. It's about my brother. I daresay you know him better than anyone, myself included. Have you seen him since our meeting with the Padishah and King this morning?"

"Only for a short time. He left his chambers and told me he was going on a walk to visit Masami, now that she's made a full recovery. Why? Is something the matter?"

"I don't know," admitted Rakiba hesitantly. "I hoped he was breaking through his solitude, but he's been even more distant since we arrived at Illadina. It almost feels as if he's avoiding me. He's never acted this way before."

"Avoiding you?" Mona frowned. "Why would he do that?"

"That is precisely the question I wished to ask you. I wondered if perhaps you could provide insight I cannot see."

"I apologize, I cannot think of any reason why he would avoid you. He always sings so highly of your deeds." A faint smile crossed her lips. "In many ways, I think he wishes he was more like you."

"Then perhaps only guilt and paranoia plagues my nerves." Rakiba bowed. "Thank you, Lady Mona. Your words put my heart at ease. If you'll excuse me, there is much I must attend to, with funeral preparations and in regards to the terraforming ritual."

Mona watched Rakiba hurry across the crowded hall, addressing three Magi dressed in black, then leaving. *That's right, even with everything that's happened, the ritual is supposed to take place in a week. Perhaps the good news will distract everyone from this loss and pain, at least temporarily.* She smiled as she remembered the Padishah's promise. *The deserts will turn green and bloom with flowers while rivers and lakes spring forth from barren ground.*

She walked down the rows of the dead and stood in front of Katria's body, dressed in her lovely yellow qipao dress, her copper hair tied in a crown braid, a few loose strands resting on her shoulders. *She looks so peaceful, almost as if she's in a deep sleep.* Mona bit her lip and stiffened her shoulders. It took every ounce of pride and willpower to not break into bitter tears. *I need to find Prince Achyut.* She wiped away a few stray tears and hurried out of the hall only to be stopped by a pair of familiar faces: Joseph, dressed in a light yellow kurta and dark brown trousers and Reena, wearing her favorite yellow dress and pink knit hat.

At the sight of Mona, Reena sprinted toward her, wrapping her arms around Mona's legs and bursting into tears.

"I know, kid, I know." Mona patted her head.

"Why? Why did she have to leave us behind?" Reena whimpered.

Mona knelt to the ground and hugged Reena tightly, unable to answer her question, unsure of what she could say to help soften the blow of the hardest lesson life would ever teach the little girl.

"I want you to train me like you trained Katria. I want to be strong, just like my sister. I'll become strong enough and, and never lose anyone ever again!"

"Reena... I admire your resolve, but getting stronger won't prevent you from losing others. I'm sorry, I don't have time to take on an apprentice right now."

"Please!" she begged, pulling away and meeting Mona's gaze. "I know I can help when I'm older, just like Katria. I promise, I won't let you down. Even if I fail over and over again, I won't stop until I'm as strong as you!"

Mona glared at Joseph, who merely shrugged his shoulders. She sighed. "I'm not a nice teacher. I'll be hard on you. You'll be sore and covered in bruises."

"I don't care. I'll do it," Reena shot back.

"How can I be sure you won't quit on me?"

"Because it was Katria's dream to get strong and help people!" she replied with fierce determination, "It's not fair she didn't get to fulfill her dream so... so I'll do it for her! That's my job, as her friend and as her sister!"

"You're job as her sister, huh?" Mona smiled. With her hair hidden under her hat, Reena almost looked like Katria, yellow dress and all. "Alright, I'll train you. Katria is my sister too, so as you say, it's my job to help you fulfill your dreams and hers. It won't be easy, but if you keep at it, you'll grow strong too."

Reena gasped, her face brightening up ever so slightly. "Really?"

"Really really." Mona patted her head and stood. "We'll start lessons after the terraforming ritual."

"Thank you, Lady Mona, thank you! I promise I won't let you down!"

Joseph stood behind Reena and offered her his hand. "Come on kiddo, I'll buy you an ice cream on the way home."

"K." Reena wiped her nose and took it.

"Home?" Mona asked, looking between the two of them.

Joseph's lips formed the faintest smile. "Well, you see, after everything that's happened, I thought it best if–"

"Mister Joseph adopted me," finished Reena. "He's my new papa."

Mona eyed Joseph and smirked. "I never took you for the domestic type."

"What can I say, the kid grew on me." Joseph beamed back. "She's got a lot of spunk."

"She's gonna need it if she wants to be my protégé. I'll send you a message after the ritual, and we'll figure out a training plan. I apologize but I really must be going. Still, I'm glad I ran into both of you. I'll see you soon."

Joseph nodded. "Sounds good to me, boss."

Even with the prospect of a new apprentice, the next two days were some of the worst in Mona's life. She grew tired and restless, and worried about Achyut, fearing some truth behind Rakiba's words. No matter where she looked or turned, Achyut was always one step ahead. She spoke with Angem and Debesh, both of whom also had little contact with their son. Achyut locked himself in his room for hours at a time, and when one of the royal family found him roaming around the halls or stopped by the guards at the gate, he insisted he was merely on a walk into town, to visit Masami or get some fresh air.

Mona quickly grew weary of his obtuse answers and early the next morning, before Achyut had time to leave the palace, she woke to visit Masami herself. She walked down the streets of Illadina with a slip of paper in her hands: the Joruka family's new address after being rewarded quite lavishly for Masami's role and bravery in the Battle for Banjiha.

She opened the gate into a flower-filled garden where two children chased each other round and round a pair of giant desert willow trees. The sound of the gate opening roused their attention.

"Ms. Mona! Ms. Mona!" They laughed and cheered as they wrapped their paws around Mona's legs; their tails flitting back and forth.

"Hello, you two." Mona patted both their heads. "Is your mother awake? I need to talk with her about something."

"She's with Dad in the study," they answered. "They've been tinkering with her map cantrip and a couple of weird-looking widgets."

"Come on, we'll show you the way!" They grabbed Mona's hands and pulled her into the house, up a flight of stairs, and into a large room filled with books and maps sprawled across many tables. Masami looked up from a giant leather-bound tome and smiled the moment Mona and her children entered the room.

"Why, Lady Mona, it's good to see you again." She stood up and curtsied in her short, green sundress. "To what do we owe this wonderful visit?"

"Actually, there's something that's been troubling me about Prince Achyut. I was hoping to speak with you... *alone*." Mona didn't even say the last word, Masami knew from her eyes that this was a private matter.

"Semoru, darling, would you please bring Lady Mona a cup of tea and some snacks from downstairs? Oh, and get the kids something as well. They must be hungry from playing all morning."

Semoru's eyes flitted between his wife and Mona. "Ah, yes. Of course, my dear." He nodded in understanding. "Come on, kids. Let's go see if those cookies are done. And even if they aren't, I see no reason why we can't sample our fine desserts."

"Yeah!" they cried in unison.

Semoru quietly closed the door on their way out.

"Is something wrong with Prince Achyut?" Masami asked worriedly.

"I was hoping you'd be able to tell me," replied Mona. "He's become even more distant lately, very short with his words. His family have all confessed they feel like he's avoiding them. During his visits, has he confided in you?"

"His visits?" Masami tilted her head to the side. "I haven't seen Prince Achyut since we returned to Illadina. It still breaks my heart to know how distraught he must feel over Katria's death."

Mona blinked. Her mind stopped. She knew she wasn't crazy. He had told her time and time again that he was going to visit Masami and her family.

"You're one-hundred percent sure you haven't seen him since?"

"Yes, Lady Mona. But why would Achyut lie to you? He told me many times he considers you to be part of his family. Besides, isn't it taboo to lie in Illadina's culture? Any soulseeker can easily find the truth of the matter in mere minutes."

A cold, numbing wave washed over Mona. Rakiba had been right all along. Achyut had been avoiding his family, and purposely at that. But what was he hiding?

Masami crossed the room. "Would you please sit down for a moment? You look frighteningly pale." She took Mona's arm and guided her to a plush chair.

"I, yes, um, thank you." Mona sat down slowly. She closed her eyes and steadied her breath.

"I think a cup of tea and some sweets will do you very well."

Mona nodded. "However, I'm afraid I can only stay for a few minutes. I have to find Nuhir Rakiba immediately."

***

It was the first night Mona could remember where sleep eluded her entirely. She had followed her bedtime routine, the same as every night, yet still her mind remained restless, unable to find comfort in her soft, downy bed. She sat up and stared at the clock on the wall, illuminated by soft, red, candlelight.

1:30 a.m.

"Damnit." She laid back down and pulled the covers over her head. She had been awake for four hours. *Why tonight of all nights? I've slept in much worse sleeping arrangements before. Am I anxious about terraforming ritual? No... I already know why....* Sleep wouldn't come until she knew Achyut was okay. She stood up and donned her pink slippers and soft, crimson robe then slipped silently out of her room.

She walked down the long halls of the palace, illuminated by the light of a full moon through the open windows. A cool breeze fluttered the tassels on her robe and playfully swung her long, dark hair like the pendulum of a regal grandfather clock. She journeyed to Prince Achyut's quarters in near solitude, only stopping to let two squads of paragons on nightwatch patrol pass uninterrupted. She reached the prince's room, held up her hand to knock, and hesitated.

What am I doing? Surely, he's asleep by now. Is it worth it to wake him from his rest? No, I have to do this. Not only for my sake but for his. She knocked gently on the door.

"Prince Achyut? Are you awake? It's Mona. I know it's late, but I'd like to spend some time with you, if you don't mind of course."

No response.

He's merely asleep. She reassured herself. *The cooks did say he went to bed instead of dinner. We can discuss all of this tomorrow.* Still, she couldn't shake her uneasy feeling. Her instincts were always right and neither her nor Rakiba nor the Padishah had seen him all day. She knocked once more.

"Prince Achyut, please, I really need to talk with you. I'm worried about your health and it's not just me, but Nuhir Rakiba and Reena and Masami as well." Still no answer. She bit her lower lip and stared at the doorknob. Her choice to enter any of the royal quarters without permission, especially at this hour, weighed heavily on her mine, her behavior ridiculously unbefitting of her station.

Still, if she could abate her fears for the night, perhaps they could have a heart-to-heart talk in the morning. Keenly aware of her uncouth actions, she tried the doorknob. Flummoxed, she opened the unlocked door and peered into the room.

"Prince Achyut, I apologize for waking you at this unseen hour, but I—" Her words fell short. She frowned as she looked around the empty room. The clean and untouched bedsheets and the fluffed and pristine pillows worried her. The empty marble support which usually held his bansuri frightened her to the core.

Mona closed her eyes and summoned a white wisp of fire, which she held in her hand and illuminated the empty room. She knelt beside the door and waved the mote just above the floor. Slowly but surely, the heat imprints of someone, presumably Prince Achyut, appeared and formed a trail that led back down the palace halls. She tightened her robe and set off at a brisk pace. She followed the dissipating heat trail to the ground floor of the palace and into the Great Hall where the bodies of the fallen heroes of the Battle for Banjiha were housed.

"Prince Achyut? Are you here?" she called aloud only to be met with the echoes of her own voice. She walked slowly up and down the rows of coffins.

"Please, I just want to talk. I miss her too. I desperately wish she was here right now, for all of us. I understand the pain you feel right now must be unbearable but you don't have to go through this... alone."

Mona stopped and stared at the glass box. She blinked and rubbed her eyes then read the plaque at the base of the box.

"Katria Konners; beloved fiancée of Prince Achyut & honorary soulseeker." Mona looked up at the glass case, even more befuddled and bewildered than before. It was empty except for Prince Achyut's bansuri that lay atop a bundle of white cloth. She walked around the case, her fingers pressing against the cool glass. She unlatched the sides and lifted, touching the soft fabric of her old shawl and Achyut's bansuri.

Why did he take her body and leave behind his prized possession? She summoned another wisp and expanded its search radius around Katria's casket. The heat signature burned much stronger. She had just missed him. Breaking into a full sprint, she followed the trail outside of the palace, out past the walls of the citadel, out into an open, empty field that stretched all the way to the outer city wall and caught the sight of flickering lamplight.

"Prince Achyut! Prince Achyut! Wait! Dammit, get back here!" she yelled as she chased after the orange glow. The light stopped moving. Mona sprinted as fast as she could and soon enough came upon a lone irrivir that pulled a simple wooden cart.

Prince Achyut walked beside the bird, dressed in a dark cloak and well-worn boots. "Mona? What are you doing out here? You should be asleep." Achyut's voice sounded gruff and incredulous.

"What am *I* doing here?" Mona's nostrils flared. "What are *you* doing here? Why the hell are you skulking around in the early hours of the morning, dressed and packed for a long journey?"

"Because I'm going on a journey," he replied in a matter-of-fact no-nonsense tone.

"No, you aren't! I know these last few days have been a living hell but running away won't solve anything. Come on, we're heading back to the palace."

"I'm not going back. I have something I need to do. Something I need to do by myself."

Mona stared at him in disbelief. She glanced at the wooden cart which carried Achyut's rucksack, three large barrels, and something large, wrapped in cloth. "Where are you going with Katria's body?"

"I'm sorry Mona, I can't tell you. I don't want you to be at risk."

"Prince Achyut!" She took two steps toward him.

He drew his shortsword and held it between them. "Don't come any closer. Please, just go back to the palace and go to bed. Everything will be better in a few days."

Mona stared at the silver blade. "Prince Achyut... please. I've already lost my little sister. Don't make me lose you as well. Don't push me away."

"I'm sorry, Mona. This is the way it has to be. There are some burdens we must carry alone. You are my family, as much as Rakiba and my parents. I don't want you to suffer for my choice."

"I'm already suffering! I'm worried about you, dammit! Rakiba is worried! Your parents are worried! Your friends are worried!"

"I'll be back soon, I promise."

"No." She glared at him in anger and anguish. Tears welled in the corners of her eyes but instantly evaporated from the heat and flame that surrounded her clenched fists. "I don't know what you plan to do, but as your retainer and friend, my job is to protect you, even from yourself. I don't want to fight, but I will do what I must."

She slid her left foot back and brought her flaming fists in front of her face as she stared down her liege and the closest person she ever had to a brother.

He glared back. There was something different about his eyes: they were cold and distant, unflinching and unafraid to fight. This wasn't the Achyut she knew, but he was buried deep inside this imposter, under unimaginable layers of grief and pain, and she would free him. She would bring him back, even if she had to knock him out and carry him herself.

The wind stood still, the night silent, except for the crackling of Mona's fire. Achyut returned her steady gaze. He didn't speak. He didn't move.

"Fine," he uttered after an eternity had passed. "Fine. I'm in no condition to fight you, nor would I ever want to."

"You're coming back to the palace. We're going to speak to Nuhir Rakiba immediately. Understand?"

"I understand." In one quick motion, he sheathed his sword. He sighed, deep and weary, picked up his lantern, and tugged on the reins of his irrivir. "Let's just get this over with."

They walked back across the field. Mona eyed Achyut suspiciously, but he was silent and sullen and only stared at the ground beneath their feet.

"I understand." She sighed as they passed under the first gate. These feelings are horrible and this grief will be part of us for the rest of our lives. I don't know what the hell has gotten into you, lying to everyone, stealing Katria's body; I know you're better than this."

"All my life, I always felt the need to prove myself, against you, against Rakiba and my parents. I always needed more... but when Katria was by my side, I finally felt complete, content. Her love made me feel alive and proud of who I am, more than any great deed I've accomplished or any song I ever wrote."

"That doesn't make what you're doing right and you better have a sincere apology and damn good explanation for your behavior." Mona turned to walk up the stone stairs leading to the citadel. Something heavy and metallic smashed against the back of her head.

"She's the reason I'm doing all this and why I'll stop at nothing if there's even the slightest chance I can bring her back. I'm sorry."

Mona's senses faded as she fell to the ground, unconscious.

Achyut picked up his lantern, pulled his hood over his dreadlocks, and turned away. He walked further and further into the darkness until he was beyond anyone's reach.

***

"Lady Mona, Lady Mona! Are you alright?"

A gloved hand shook Mona's shoulder as her senses slowly returned. The warm rays of the rising sun kissed her skin as she opened her eyes and a dull, throbbing pain returned to the back of her head. Dazed and confused, she looked into the face of a helmeted paragon, presumably on patrol, when her memories rushed over her like a cold waterfall and cleared the fog from her mind.

"That little shit!" She punched the ground, jolted around, and glared out over the field, but there was no sign of Achyut or his cart.

"Lady Mona, is everything okay? What hap—"

"I'm fine!" she shot back at the paragon who quickly reeled away. She closed her eyes and took a deep breath. "Sorry, I've had a really bad night. I need to see Nuhir Rakiba immediately. Where are they?"

"T-they should still be in their chambers."

"Thanks." Mona gruffed as she stood, dusted herself off, and stomped off.

The palace was ablaze with activity as staff and Magi bustled back and forth and finished their final preparations for the terraforming rite. No one gave Mona a second glance, which suited her just fine. She reached Rakiba's chambers and banged on the door.

"Nuhir Rakiba, it's Mona. I need to speak with you immediately. It's about Achyut."

"Achyut? Please, give me just a moment."

Rakiba opened the door, dressed in ceremonial armor, with their helmet in their left hand and a beautiful and deadly lance in their right. They glanced over Mona's disheveled appearance, still dressed in her nightgown.

"What happened?"

Mona bit her lip. She clenched her fists as she tried to find the right words. "Prince Achyut... he's... he's gone. I couldn't stop him. I'm sorry."

"Gone? What do you mean gone?" Rakiba frowned.

"He's gone. He left. He went away, left the city, cleared out, vamoosed, vacated the premise! How else do you want me to say it?!" She glared at them, holding back tears then took a deep breath. "I'm sorry. I just... he just—"

"Whatever happened, it's not your fault. Please don't blame yourself."

"No. I deserve whatever punishment you see fit. I failed in my duties as your brother's retainer."

"I disagree. There was only so much that could be done, given his position. Come with me. We'll figure something out." They hurried through the palace to the king and queen's private dressing chambers.

"Mother, Father?" Rakiba rapped their knuckles on the sturdy palm wood door. "I need to speak with you. I'm here with Mona. It's about Achyut."

"Achyut? Is everything okay, my dear? I didn't see your brother at breakfast this morning," answered Angem from the other side.

"It's best if I tell you in the privacy of your chambers," replied Rakiba.

Silence.

"Very well," answered King Dabesh after an eternity. "The two of you may enter."

Rakiba opened the door. Racks on racks of tailored clothing covered one of the long sides of the rectangular space. A complete barbershop with two chairs and hundreds of specialized widgets placed opposite the door. A wall of mirrors hung from a rail on the ceiling and could be pushed around the room so that any king or queen could view their ensemble from any angle.

Padishah Angem sat in one of the hair salon's chairs where one of her attendants quickly and quietly snipped away at her long, black hair. Kind Debash stood in front of a wall of mirrors as he chose from a plethora of coats and kingly jackets. Immediately, their eyes fell on Mona, still dressed in her crimson nightgown covered with smudges of dirt.

"Sitara, please leave us for a moment. I believe this is a matter to be discussed only among the royal family," Angem commanded with kind but firm authority.

"Of course, my liege," the young woman replied. "Please send for me whenever you wish to continue your treatment." She bowed and left the room without another word.

"Padishah Angem, I take full responsibility for my failure as Prince Achyut's retainer," confessed Mona the moment the four of them were alone. "I was unable to convince him to stay nor ascertain any reason for his actions. Whatever punishment you deem fit for my failures–"

"Peace, Mona," King Dabesh interrupted. "We all know of your loyalty to the royal family. I will not have you punished for my son's actions. Do not ask for retribution, just calmly explain the situation."

Mona opened her mouth to speak but her voice was lost among her memories.

"Is this about what you told me yesterday?" Rakiba asked calmly. Mona nodded.

Angem bit her lip. She looked up at her husband, her eyes full of worry.

"I believe this matter would be best resolved by soulsharing," answered Dabesh.

"I agree," added Angem. "Mona, please give me your hands. I swear not to pry into anything unrelated to this matter."

Mona did as instructed. Padishah Angem took her hands in her own, closed her eyes, and took slow, steady breaths. She opened her charcoal eyes and peered into Mona's memories and soul.

Although the soulshare took merely a minute, Angem watched the events of the last few days play out in real-time through Mona's own eyes. She painfully understood the torment and anguish in her soul, the rage and disbelief as her youngest son drew his sword on his lifelong friend. She saw Katria's body nestled among Achyut's things and heard him promise his eventual return. Angem closed her eyes and they regained their regal dark brown color, the soulshare now complete. She sat in complete silence.

My baby boy... how much pain and suffering you must feel. What are you planning to do with your beloved's corpse? Why did you leave in the dead of night, as if your actions would be deprecated by your own family? We love you more than anyone in this world. Eventually, Angem found her voice.

"Although my son is no longer under your protection, I will not disown you or your clan. I know I speak for all of us when I say we consider you to be part of our family."

"Thank you, Your Majesty."

"As for my little Achyut," Angem continued, "we must trust in his judgment. He is kind and wise and his love for his country and his people knows no bounds. If he states he will return soon, we must believe him and carry on in his absence."

"And the terraforming ritual?" asked Rakiba.

"We will go forward as planned. Our people are scared and our country remains splintered. I have no doubt in my mind this ritual will bring them both together again. When Prince Achyut returns, we will have the most beautiful and bountiful lands in all of Reighja. Nuhir Rakiba, you will give your speech as planned and we will tell our people their prince hasn't recovered from his grief and wishes not to be in the public eye."

"Yes, Your Majesty," answered Rakiba.

"We must trust his judgment." King Dabesh crossed his arms over his chest. "That is the role of family in difficult times. He is still the young man we love, and when he returns, we will do whatever we can to abate his grief."

Yet beneath the King's reassurance and Padishah's smile, doubt and fear lingered in Mona's mind. There were few reasons she could imagine as to why he would take Katria's body and silently prayed to whatever gods would listen that he would be safe.

***

Around two o'clock on the day of the terraforming ritual, in the tallest tower of the Citadel of Illadina, the thirty most powerful Magi of Lamaru; scholars and soldiers, adventurers and widget tinkerers, stood around the most complex minna-powered machine ever created. They triple-checked the massive, octagonal machine with four stone pillars embossed with sparkling gems and hundreds of runes and glyphs set in the four cardinal directions. A metallic structure rose up from the center of the machine and pointed upward like talons on the claw of some gigantic creature.

Satisfied with their work, the Magi brought up sacks and sacks filled with minna stones, dumping them in the center of the machine; the predetermined amount for the titanic ritual, all of which had been securely stored in a massive vault, only accessible by the royal family. Lastly, they plastered the stone walls with hundreds of pages of pre-harnessed spells from tomes.

In the city of Thaniana, thirty more of the most powerful Magi concluded the same careful preparations, for the ritual proved too complex and the area of effect too expansive for a single, fixed epicenter. It was nearly three o'clock when they began.

Loyal citizens, both maiamorph and human, had traveled from all six regions of Lamaru and filled every street corner, rooftop, and ship at the docks or afloat in the central lagoon to hear the glorious speeches from the royal family who promised this magnanimous occasion would breathe new life into the most desolate and barren regions of the kingdom.

As Nuhir Rakiba finished their speech, they gestured toward the tower that housed the arcane engine, just as the machine whirred to life. It shot a single beam of white light high into the sky. People gasped and shouted and cheered in excitement. The machine's whirring grew louder and louder; its low faint rumble echoing throughout the city. Swirling black and white clouds poured out from the beam of light and spread like ripples in a pond.

A sphere of midnight-colored fire engulfed the top of the tower, the arcane engine, and the thirty Magi performing the ritual. The fire swooshed down the stone spire, forcing itself free and launching the weakest bricks and stones like cannonballs out of its path. Tendrils of raw, shimmering minna oozed out of the openings and cracks and smashed through anything in their path. The black and white clouds merged into an unrelenting gray mass.

Colored lightning split the sky as everlasting night fell, blotting out the sun. The ground shook and broke apart more violently than a paper house in a hurricane. The desert outside the city walls tore open as magma erupted, covering the clay and sand. Across the central deserts of Lamaru, putrid puddles of a brownish-black sludge bubbled up from the most fertile fields and largest oases, consuming any and all living beings unfortunate enough to disturb its growth. Otherworldly spores appeared, flourished, and multiplied faster than anyone could fathom, assuming chimeric forms of their devoured prey to expedite their hunting and harvest of more unfortunate souls.

Throughout the cities of Illadina and Thaniana, translucent vestiges of departed souls appeared before their descendants and loved ones, their utterance and warnings drowned out by a horrific and ethereal sound, consisting of only a few discernible words:

"...the emissary for... tortured souls... wasted away... their anguish and rage...will bring this world to ruin!"

19

Interlude

Year 149 A.D. (After Demotion); present day

"And that is the end of our story." General Gil closed the hefty book.

Amira and Naemin squinted at their teacher through incredulous eyes.

"That's it? That's the end of the story?!" A plethora of emotions rattled inside Naemin's body; bleakness, bitterness, bewilderment, bamboozlment and countless other feelings he couldn't even begin to describe. "He steals Katria's body, vanishes without a trace, and then the ter-terafurmation—"

"Terraforming," corrected King Jordan.

"The terraforming ritual fails and the Collapse destroys all of Lamaru? That's his connection with the Collapse? What a crappy ending!"

"Well, not all of Lamaru was destroyed," corrected Gil. "Our cities of Thaniana and Illadina, the epicenters of the ritual, were immune to the rot and decay that claimed the rest of our kingdom. Additionally, the province of Mutadun, over which your uncle presides, was relatively untouched, perhaps due to its distance from the other regions. The most extreme damage and most frequent Withered attacks occurred in the area between the spell epicenters."

"So that's why the region of Banjiha was designated a restricted area, save for properly equipped salvage and reconnaissance teams," Amira mused aloud.

"The Ravaged Basin." Saffi nodded with newfound understanding.

"But what about Prince Achyut? Where did he go? And what about An'ard?" asked Naemin. "The port is fine and the sandships even use the cranes to travel across the desert."

"It seems someone hasn't been keeping up with his history lessons," teased Jiian. "Your great, great, great, grandfather, the son of Padishah Rakiba, led a very successful campaign to fight off the Withered and reclaim the region. He knew if Lamaru was ever to rebuild its former stature we would need safe passage through the desert and fresh water from the Hayi River."

"Oh..." Naemin replied sheepishly. "I didn't get that far in my readings."

"So maybe now you'll start to appreciate the value of studying?" asked Amira.

"I guess so," answered Naemin. "And with stories like these, studying history doesn't seem as boring as before."

"As for Prince Achyut," added Jordan. "I told you this was one of Lamaru's unsolved mysteries. We can only use historical evidence to speculate what happened on that fateful day many years ago."

"Still, it is a rather abrupt ending to an otherwise thrilling tale... but that creepy voice and ghosts," Amira shivered. "Sir Gil, you better not have included them just to scare me."

"Nuhir Amira, I would never intentionally alter a tale such as this in order to tease or frighten you," Gil replied with a shifty smile.

Amira rolled her eyes. "It would be far more beneficial to my studies if you included information about Ecarima's establishment following the Collapse instead of silly ghost stories at my personal expense."

"Ah yes, the dastard Uriel escaped from prison and fled with his followers across the ravaged landscape at the peak of Lamaru's destruction and Withered attacks. Pursued by Nuhir Rakiba and Lady Mona, he was banished from the central desert and forced to live atop the frozen, inhospitable peaks of the western mountains in the Wild Lands. Such a riveting and harrowing tale," answered Gil with a twinkle in his eyes. He held up the volume and pointed at its golden title.

"Remember Nuhir Amira, this record contains only Prince Achyut's final adventure to retake Banjiha, not anything after, nor can it answer how or why he vanished from history without a trace."

"However, if both of you continue studying hard and harnessing minna, I'm sure your father and Sir Gil would love to read you another story, my dears." Lila ruffled Naemin's hair and smiled at her daughter.

Naemin crossed his arms over his chest and pouted. "I'd love to hear another story but I'm still mad about how this one ended. He had to have gone somewhere!"

"But where?" added Amira, just as riddled and ruffled as her brother. "And why did he steal Katria's body instead of burying her in the citadel's memorial park?" She ransacked her brain for ideas but only came up with more questions instead of answers.

"No one knows for sure. The past guards its secrets carefully and with no record or sighting of him from across all of Reighja, the possibilities of what really happened are all an enigma." King Jordan looked up at the setting sun. Pink and orange clouds lingered across the horizon.

"We aren't even sure his disappearance and the Collapse are linked, although, our scholars and historians believe there's too much concurrence between the two events to be mere coincidence. How could countless years of research, two decades' worth of planning and construction, and far more powerful widgets than what we have today fail in such spectacular fashion? Was the Collapse the pinnacle lesson about the hubris of man or simply the worst luck in the history of existence?"

"Are there any other texts about Prince Achyut's life and his adventures?" asked Amira. "This one is titled *The Definitive Expedition.*"

Lila nodded. "Of course. All of our family's history is kept safe in journals just like this one. You're more than welcome to read as many as you can. In fact, I encourage it. Although they're likely a good bit drier than the tale your father told."

"I can't take all of the credit, my dear. Sir Gil has become a master storyteller in his own right, but I thank you for your praises nonetheless." Jordan chuckled and kissed his wife's hand.

Lila blushed and leaned her head against his shoulder. She pulled Amira close and wrapped her arms around her darlings. "And one day, far, far away, a journal just like this will be written about your father and I, and another will be written about the two of you, my dearest children, and of course their gallant retainers."

Amira, Naemin, Saffi, and Jiian all grinned at Lila's praise.

"Indeed," agreed Jordan, "who knows what wonderful and exciting lives you've yet to live, what friends you'll meet along the way, and what you will choose to accomplish with the time you're given. But for the present, how about we all enjoy a nice warm meal? And I'll happily answer whatever questions I can about Prince Achyut and his adventures."

"Yeah!" cheered Naemin and Jiian. They stood up and stretched, along with Gil, Jordan, and Lila, and turned to leave the gardens.

Naemin glanced over his shoulder at his sister, her eyes transfixed on Achyut's story. "Aren't you coming, sissy?"

"I'll be there in a minute. I want to look at this a little longer."

"Of course." King Jordan smiled. "We won't start without you, but please don't take too long."

"Yes, Father."

Gill, Lila, and Jordan all made their way to the dining hall but Naemin, ever curious, tottled back to the clearing, Jiian at his side. They sat on a bench opposite of their sisters.

"Nuhir Amira, do I surmise correctly that you're curious about the nature of strange runes this record is written in?" asked Jiian.

Amira nodded. "If these runes truly react to a person's mental state and 'allow the reader to see into the past with unclouded eyes' as Father stated, I believe it best to try to read it while Achyut's story and its lessons are still fresh in my mind."

Amira closed her eyes and steadied her breathing. She touched the amulet around her neck and gathered minna in her other hand, placing it on the ancient cover. *This time I'll get it right. I can see Achyut's story clearly: his bonds, his driving purpose, his hardships. As the future leader of Lamaru, I have to learn all I can to lead this kingdom and my people into prosperous times and happiness.* She opened her eyes and smiled.

The journal glowed with the same light it did when her father began Achyut's story. She picked up the book and opened it as Naemin, Saffi and Jiian watched in curiosity and awe.

The runes began to shift slowly, and Amira could almost make out words, sentences, paragraphs. Excitement swelled in her chest only to be replaced with bitter disappointment. The runes shifted back into an incoherent form.

"Ugh, what's wrong with me?" She sighed as she slumped on the bench. "It's the same problem with my soulsharing. I can almost get it, I'm so close, and then every attempt ends in failure."

"I wonder if these runes are affected by a person's intentions along with needing the correct headspace," pondered Jiian.

"All I want to do is learn and become the best Padishah I can when I take the throne." Amira pouted. "How is that a bad thing?"

"Maybe it requires a more selfish aspect? Like accumulating knowledge not to share, but merely preserve it for future generations," reasoned Saffi.

"But then how was Dad able to tell us the story?" asked Naemin. "Is it like a one and done thing? You read it once then you can read it whenever?"

"Not likely. A ritual or spell with that level of complexity would need an additional focus and minna stones to recognize each individual and activate over and over again," added Jiian.

Naemin stood up and looked at the book. He flipped through its pages, forward to back, back to front, right-side up and upside down.

"What if you aren't missing anything… but instead have something you don't need?"

"What do you mean?" asked Amira.

"Well, Dad said Achyut's ending was a great mystery. What if you can't read it if you're trying to solve that mystery?"

Amira, Saffi, and Jiian all exchanged glances.

"You might be onto something, little bro, but why would the author chronicle Achyut's story with no intention of finding the truth or how it ended?"

"I dunno. Why does any author write anything?"

"It could be for a variety of reasons: to teach, to entertain, to preserve knowledge, to understand oneself, to communicate abstract ideas…" Jiian blathered more and more reasons but only one stuck with Naemin, the same one that captivated his mind since the book landed on his head back in the library.

"For fun." Naemin looked up at his sister.

"For fun?" Amira repeated. Gazing upon the hefty book, she mentally rattled down her list of reasons to read and continue reading Achyut's story. Fun had never even crossed her mind. Curious, she lifted the journal and opened its cover. The runes remained meaningless. She sighed. "I guess I won't know I'm ready until I'm ready."

"Maybe that's the answer," suggested Saffi. "Honestly, it could be any number of factors, even something we haven't thought of. Best not to dwell on it too much."

"Well said." Jiian nodded. "There is a time and place and a reasoning behind all things."

"Or I have to accept that there is no reasoning for some things and that all questions don't have answers," replied Amira, who gazed thoughtfully at the book. She flipped through its contents and paused. *Is my mind playing tricks on me? That passage looks legible!* She peered closer at the page, but the runes shifted back into incomprehensible nonsense.

"Did you see something? Can you read it?" asked Naemin, his voice full of awe.

Amira smiled. "No, not yet, but that won't stop me from trying, and one day I'll know the secrets of every book in our library."

"I hope so! You can teach me and I can write about my adventures! The Tale of Naemin, Gale Prince of Lamaru. Chapter One: Naemin and Jiian fight Magri and the Withered! Ooooh and I'll write a better ending for Prince Achyut as well, one where he and Katria live happily ever after!"

"Now that sounds like a worthy endeavor of both your time and skills." Jiian tapped his cheek thoughtfully. "And a perfect opportunity for you to practice writing in Magesep runes. I'll ask Sir Gil to give you that assignment tomorrow."

"Hey! You're supposed to be on my side!" Naemin glared at Jiian, who responded with a sly smirk. He wanted to groan and moan about his self-imposed work, but unlike last time, the assignment didn't feel too troublesome.

In fact, he felt strangely excited to write a story of his own, to take the threads of history and weave them into something new—something he could share and be proud of. "Fine! I'll do it!" proclaimed Naemin triumphantly, much to everyone's surprise. "And it will be the best story you've ever read!"

"Oh yeah?" teased Amira. "Then you'll have to study hard, otherwise I'll steal all your ideas. Amira, Padishah of the Sands, and Saffi, the Blue Flame, will destroy the Withered, defeat the evil dragon Vitra, and restore Lamaru's glory. We'll travel across Reighja, righting wrongs, solving mysteries, and of course, meeting lots of handsome men." She giggled to herself. "Don't worry, Saffi, we'll also find your perfect match."

"That's... not necessary." Saffi blushed and looked away.

"Oh, come now, surely you trust Nuhir Amira's matchmaking abilities," Jiian quipped. "I bet she could even find a suitable partner for you, Prince Naemin."

"Ewwe." Naemin scrunched up his face. "No mushy stuff."

"Then we should probably head inside before Mother convinces Father to let her help with dinner."

Suddenly overcome by an onslaught of giggles, Naemin fell back and rolled on the ground. Even Jiian and Saffi couldn't hide their smiles.

"Come on." Amira stood, picked up the book, and offered her hand to her brother. "And just this once, I'll race you to the dining hall."

With eyes sparkling like gems, Naemin took his sister's hand.

"Oh no, not this again." Saffi sighed.

"Come now Saf, this'll be fun. Nothing wrong like a light jog before dinner." Jiian stood in front of them, his handkerchief held above his head. "Ready? Set? Go!"

Amira and Naemin took off toward the palace, just as the sun's last rays vanished over the horizon. The night was cold and dark but warmth and love permeated its ancient halls and all was right and good in the city of Illadina, the last shining light of the Dynasty of Lamaru.

20

Frog at the Bottom
of a Well

Year 0; The Collapse

Price Achyut stood on the bow of a sandskiff as it crossed the desert north of Lamaru. He studied the dull, monotonous landscape as it stretched out before him; an ocean of sand with rocky islands scattered across the horizon. It had been years since he explored these parts of his kingdom, yet the desert remained as it always had been. He wondered how it would look after the terraforming ritual. Would there be trees and forests? Orchards and farmlands? Perhaps his parents would carve out a vast lake and build a new city for the region.

A single raindrop fell on his nose. He looked up as dark clouds gathered and the gentle pitter-patter of rain fell against his skin. The rain fell harder and quicker, the low rumble of thunder sounding in the distance as wispy strikes of lightning flashed across the sky.

He smiled. *How I've missed the rain.*

He thought back to the days of his childhood as he played in the palace courtyards during the sudden downpours. Perhaps he loved it because of his elemental flair, or because it was something rare and often unexpected to be enjoyed, or perhaps he loved it just because. One didn't exactly need a reason to love something.

Memories of rainy days washed over him, recalling the time he tripped and nearly fell face-first into the palace courtyard's well. As he stared into the watery abyss, he heard the low, deep croak of a desert bufon—a small, four-legged amphibian that hid under rocks during the sweltering days and came out at night and ate lightning bugs, which gave the bufon incredible electrical resistance.

The brown bufon clung onto a rocky ledge. It tried to hop to a higher stone but the walls were too slick with rainfall. Each time he fell back into the water, struggled back to his starting ledge, and tried again. Bufons were only good swimmers when they were young. They traded their tails and fins to survive better on land.

"Hey! Mr. Bufon! What are you doing in the well? You really got yourself into a tough situation. Here, let me find something to haul you out before you drown!" Young Achyut called to the creature. Then he took off running. He looked for a broom or a stick or spade, something he could use to help the poor guy out. Lightning crackled in the sky above. Achyut looked up and gasped in amazement, never having seen such sparks in the sky! In the rain no less! He stood for a good while, distracted by the strange phenomenon. Only too late did he realize he was wasting time. He quickly resumed his quest, found a large shovel, and returned to the well.

"Don't worry, Mr. Bufon! I brought Mr. Shovel to help! Now, let's get you out of the—" his eyes brimmed with tears. The bufon lay belly up, dead in the well. The water had risen too high and washed him from the safety of the ledge. How long had he struggled before he died? Prince Achyut didn't know. He only knew he had doomed the poor creature the moment he stopped and watched the light show. He ran inside and into the safety of his mother's arms, hugging her tightly as she consoled him, telling him over and over again it wasn't his fault.

Later that night, as she tucked him into bed, he asked her why the bufon was down there in the first place. Surely he knew he wouldn't be able to make it back out if it rained. Why risk it?

"Perhaps he was hungry," his mother replied. "Lots of tasty, flying bugs live near still water. Maybe he hadn't eaten in days and saw a big tasty feast all to himself."

"But why, Momma? Why would he put himself in harm's way?"

"Because he saw something he wanted and decided it was worth the risk. As you grow older, and have to make more difficult choices, you'll learn what is worth the risk and what is best left alone. Sometimes you'll find the thing you wanted wasn't worth the price you paid. Actions and words are not easily taken back and if you act on your impulses alone, you may regret it later in life."

A piercing shriek high above shook Achyut from his thoughts. He instinctively clutched the hilt of his sword as a pair of gray and green roc wyverns flew over the ship but paid them no mind. He sighed in relief at his apparent luck.

"Don't be alarmed, Prince Achyut," remarked Dracona Cassio as they joined him on the bow of the sandskiff. "Those are the trained scouts of Dracona Zevulun, another leader of the Watchers. We find it best to conduct our research in secrecy and have taken the proper precautions to ensure as much."

Achyut eyed the elf suspiciously yet understood that any talk of the reanimation ritual was kept secret, even before his parents outlawed their research entirely. Then his eyes fell on the small wooden box engraved with gold that Cassio cradled as carefully as a newborn child. He turned his eyes back to the wyverns which had flown further and further away and now circled something far in the distance. Slowly and surely, a cluster of sandstone buildings rose up off the horizon.

"So that's where you've been conducting your research. I never knew there was a settlement this far north of Illadina. How do you supply it with the proper resources?"

"Harvesting moisture from the air and snow from the mountains secures our need for water, which we use to grow a few hardy crops. We are few in number and this is not a permanent settlement, more like an outpost for our actual base of operations. Of course, a bulk of our food and widgets must be shipped in, a secondary purpose of these sandskiffs," Cassio answered nonchalantly as they placed the box on a wooden barrel. They took a small key from a chain around their neck and opened it.

Achyut looked over their shoulder at its contents: a ruby knife, two yellow sponges in two golden trays, a wooden stamper, a vial of blueish-green blood, and a few cloth wraps.

"A blood ritual. So that's how you control the roc wyverns and use them as scouts," he concluded.

"Indeed. Unfortunately, it is not a permanent solution, but the dragons of old and their descendants today were never meant to be tamed, such is the will of our gods. You will have to partake if you desire to see the reanimation ritual through to its end."

"I didn't come this far to hand over the minna stones and wait."

"A wise decision. This is a momentous occasion." Cassio took the ruby dagger, slit their palm, and offered the hilt to Achyut before squeezing one of the sponges, turning it red.

Achyut stared at the ruby dagger. *So much blood has already been spilled, what're a few more drops, especially to see you smile again? Hold on, my love. I will save you. I promise.* Without hesitation, he slit his palm and squeezed the second sponge. Cassio handed him a roll of cloth wraps to dress his wound. Then they added a few drops of wyvern's blood to both their and Achyut's sponge, mixing it into a sickly purple.

"I will now stamp your chest so that the blood ritual can take effect."

Achyut nodded and pulled open his kurta. Cassio stamped his chest. Then they cleaned the wooden tool and stamped their own chest.

"We are ready to begin. My wine please."

A sailor stepped forth and handed Dracona Cassio one of two chalices of wine. "Here you are, Your Majesty, a little booze goes a long way." He handed Achyut the second cup. "The sensations are a bit odd if you're not used to them."

"Thank you, sir," replied Achyut.

Cassio raised their hands to the heavens. "Oh, draconic omnipotents of old, grant your humble servant the power to subdue your lesser kin once more. Grant me the power to make them understand my will as your own and I will bring wisdom, honor, and glory to your divine names. Bind my heart and mind to yours and let me see with unclouded eyes." They drained their cups in two or three gulps.

A moment after Cassio finished praying, Achyut felt a tingling sensation from the stamp that radiated across his chest and down his arms and legs. The strange feeling grew and grew until his entire body shook and ached, as if every nerve in his body frantically fired over and over again, warning him of danger. He dropped the cup and doubled over, clutching his stomach as waves of red-hot pain consumed his very being. He grunted and groaned and screamed loudly.

Suddenly, the sensation stopped. His body, bathed in sweat, his breathing irregular, yet he felt more alive than ever before. He looked down at his chest. Strange markings had appeared all over his body, which felt warm and unnatural, yet his senses felt sharper than ever.

"You've done well to stay conscious." Cassio's voice echoed from somewhere far away. "Most new recruits aren't able to do so. Clearly, the spirits of the ancient dragons are with you, young prince. This is a most excellent omen."

The sandskiff slowed and stopped beside a crude wooden dock where Dracona Cassio introduced Prince Achyut to Dracona Zevulun, who bowed and assured the distraught prince that he had carefully reviewed everything and was one-hundred percent certain of the ritual's success. Two of Cassio's men carefully carried Katria's body and the sacks of minna stones Achyut provided. The five of them made their way to a massive, covered enclosure where six roc wyverns slept. A woman with the same markings on her body scanned them with a strange widget, disarmed the barriers, and opened the gate.

A brief flicker of hope and amazement flared within Prince Achyut's heart as the faintest smile reached his lips. *This is amazing, I'll actually ride a roc wyvern! Oh, I can't wait to tell Mona and Ka...* then the moment passed. His smile became a frown, then a scowl. The woman he loved lay in the box the two men loaded onto a wyvern's back. *No, she'll be able to ride back with us. She has too, otherwise I... I...* Any further thoughts were unbearable. He jumped on his mount's back and took off into the dark sky.

Cassio, Zevulun, and Achyut flew closer and closer to the mighty Omah Mountain range that divided Reighja into the lush plains of the north and the dry deserts of the south. The yellow sand gave way to rolling green foothills dotted with lakes and ponds. Rock and stone built upon itself until it became steep, gray cliffs where only a handful of pine trees broke up the landscape. Soon the trees all but vanished and the dark slabs of rock became capped with white drifts of snow and everlasting, celeste glaciers. They reached into their bags and pulled out brass cylinders connected to rubber tubing and a mouthpiece. Each bit their mouthpiece, pinched their nose, and turned the knob on the cylinder for the air above the mountains was thin and frozen.

They flew over the gallant peaks, which stretched on for endless miles, until the two Draconas pulled on the reins of their wyverns and began their slow descent. Cassio and Zevulun guided their wyverns to a large, flat stone outcropping outside the mouth of a massive cavern. Achyut's wyvern followed their lead.

As Achyut dismounted from the roc wyvern's back, the three men were met by an armed guard of twelve, and a man and woman in the same white robes as Cassio and Zevulun.

"Greetings, Your Majesty, my name is Saital, the newest to reach the rank of Dracona in our organization. I'm the woman in charge of our operations at this archeological site."

Achyut recognized her name from Katria's vision. *Her brother is the one who fled the Prospector. This must be the hidden tomb Katria saw. If she had visions of this place, was she destined to come here in the end?*

"It is also my great honor to introduce you to Dracona Meruyk, the oldest and most prominent of the living nine. He's traveled all the way from Yaand to observe the reanimation ritual."

"Welcome, Prince Achyut, we've been expecting your arrival." Meruyk bowed. "Although you are still young, simply by being here you have proven your wisdom, foresight, and aptitude as a good ruler. Your patronage to the Watchers will be forever memorialized in our records; the strides we make here today will be done in your name."

"Thank you, Dracona Meruyk, although I prefer the accolades to be saved until after the ritual is complete."

"Of course. I'm sure you are anxious to have this woman returned to you. However, before we begin, there is the matter of an official statement, just for our records."

"I understand," Achyut nodded. "Should this ritual prove successful, I'll secretly fund whatever resources the Watchers need to continue the research. When Rakiba takes the throne, I'll publicly support all of your endeavors and become a devotee myself."

"Splendid." Dracona Meruyk smiled as one of the guards wrote down Achyut's statement. He handed the parchment and a feather quill to the young prince who signed his name.

"Let's proceed inside. The altar is deep within the mountain." Saital led them into the central cavern where the only light came from flickering torches and bored light spirits trapped in tiny metal cages.

Prince Achyut looked around in awe. The tunnel was so big that light couldn't reach the top and the stone walls simply faded into inky blackness. They crossed a wood and rope bridge over a dark and dismal abyss where the sound of a rushing subterranean river echoed up from far below the mountain. The tunnel opened up into an even larger cavern which stretched on like the desert, illuminated by pinpricks of light where hundreds of archeologists and Magi excavated the skeleton of an ancient, colossal dragon.

They walked down stone steps hewn from the cliff wall and across the expansive cavern to a small hollowed-out alcove where a square, stone altar had been built atop three raised platforms.

A strange, spidery widget with twelve long, mechanical arms hung above the altar. Each had multiple slots where minna stones could be placed. A metal, concave tendril stood on each of the four corners of the lowest square platform, again with slots carved out for minna stones, and the entire contraption was covered in Magesep runes traced over in charcoal and liquidated precious metals.

Achyut examined the strange widget above the altar, his mind racing in realization, his blood pumping in anticipation. *This is the altar Katria saw in her visions but why would she see a vision of this... unless the ritual was a success? Yes! That must be it!*

"Beautiful, isn't it?" Dracona Zevulun beamed at Achyut's apparent awe of his machine. "The shadow of death will be banished from our world forever more. Dracona Meruyk gathered fifty of the most skilled Magi from the far corners of Reighja to ensure our ritual's success. Here, I'll show you where to put the minna stones."

Prince Achyut did as instructed and placed each of the minna stones in their designated slots in the spidery, mechanical widget that hung above the altar. He placed the remaining stones at exact intervals around the machine until his sacks were empty. Then Zevulun lowered each of its twelve arms into position. Lastly, Achyut placed Katria's body on the altar.

"Don't worry, my love, we'll soon be together. I promise you." Achyut stroked her copper hair and touched her cold cheek. He hurried off the platform as the fifty Magi took their places.

Zevulun closed his eyes and began the incantation. One at a time, the Magi joined him until they all chanted in unison; their separate voices joined as one in this cathedral of a cavern. Colored sparks erupted from one of the minna stones. Colored lightning crackled from one arm of the machine and jumped to another and another with thunderous reverberations until all twelve arms were connected by a ring of fractured light. The mountain shook as the Magi chanted.

Zevulun lowered the visor on his helmet and stepped onto the altar. He held a twisted, bone scepter in his left hand, adorned with raw minna crystals and ancient runes Achyut didn't recognize. He held a collection of loose wires made of compressed minna stones in his right, a conduit of pure magical energy that would have instantly charred anyone without the proper barriers and precautions in place. He carefully attached the first wire to one of the machine's arms and leaped away as it glowed and crackled with deadly power.

He touched the bone scepter to the end of the loose wire and held it against the left side of Katria's slender neck. He muttered an incantation in an unknown language, the words rough and guttural, and linked Katria's body to the strange machine. He repeated the process until all but one were attached to her body. He held the last wire with his bone scepter and touched it to her heart.

Katria's body seized uncontrollably as immense amounts of magical energy circulated from the arms of the machine into her corpse and back into the machine again. Cracks appeared in both the minna stones and the altar. The cavern shook like a volcano that had just erupted in raw, blazing fury. Black and white smoke rings emanated from the machine, like ripples in a pond, until they congealed in a mass of thick, gray mist. As if from nowhere and everywhere at once, Achyut heard Katria's voice, faint and enigmatic— whispers from another realm.

"Please, please, my love, you have to stop this! I'm already gone! You must accept this! My curse remains even in death. I don't want to hurt you! Your promise to me is already fulfilled!"

Prince Achyut turned away; a steady stream of tears fell down his face. He couldn't watch and no longer wished to hear the echoes of her voice. He knew she was already gone, that she couldn't feel the pain of the machine, yet some part of him believed she actually called out to him, that her spirit remained by his side. To give that spirit a physical form, to hear her sweet voice, to hold her within his grasp, he'd have stolen the terraforming ritual's minna stones a thousand times over.

Dracona Meruyk and Dracona Saital watched from the safety of the raised platform at the mouth of the megalithic cavern. Ominous and unnatural wind howled around them. Stalactites crashed to the floor. Two of the machine's arms shattered and crashed against the altar. The sound of a thousand pained, otherworldly screams overtook the Magi's chanting.

"Keep going!" Zevulun shouted. "We have a heartbeat! We're almost through!"

The unsettling wind and otherworldly screams grew louder and louder. Three more of the machine's arms exploded. The blast flung Zevulun off the altar and slammed him against the cavern wall. His body crumpled against the floor, still alive but badly injured. Cassio rushed to his side.

"Stop it! Stop it! That's enough!" ordered Dracona Cassio.

Slowly, the Magi stopped chanting. Their eyes turned to Cassio who had gathered up Zevulun's broken body and helped him stand. From the eerie silence across the cavern, Achyut heard faint moans and coughs from atop the shattered altar. He rushed up the stone steps to where Katria lay. He gently touched her shoulders and held her body in his arms.

"Katria! Katria, please, can you hear me? Are you alive?"

"Prince... Achyut," she mumbled, her voice barely above a whisper, "I told you... your promise was fulfilled. Please, leave me. It's not too late... to save yourself."

"Shh, rest now my love. It's not too late, you're back in my arms. We can be together again."

She opened her eyes and smiled at him. "Your soul... you look as beautiful as when I left you so very long ago... or maybe it was recently. I don't know. Time feels so fuzzy to me." She lightly touched his lips. "My prince, my Achyut."

"I missed you so much." He slipped her ring onto her slender finger. "I need you by my side." He clasped her cold hands in his own.

"I-I need you too." Her voice grew rough and wispy. "So beautiful... so succulent." Katria's body shuddered. "I... I must have it." Her grip tightened on his hands.

"Ah!" Achyut yelped in pain as her grip became tighter and tighter. He felt the bones in his fingers crack. Blood spurted from the wound.

"Give... give me your soul and I will be whole again. Come, my prince, complete your lover's existence."

Achyut yanked his broken hand from her clutches. He hurriedly backed away, his eyes wide with absolute terror and disbelief.

"Come here, my prince." Katria sat up from the altar and stretched her limbs, her movements spasmodic and irregular. Her neck cracked as she rolled her head from side to side.

"You wished me to live again, yet I am incomplete! Give me what I desire!" She coughed and spat out drops of black blood. "This vessel is incomplete. I feel s-so cold, so empty." She touched the hole in her palm left behind by the minna-wire and summoned a black, wicked flame that closed her wound.

"Please, my lover, we'll be together forever. Isn't that what you wanted?" Her soft smile turned tainted and toothy as she stared down the remaining Magi. "I guess I don't have to take your soul, although it is the most desirable, any of these louts will do. The more I consume the stronger I will become. Help me. Feed me their lives, and we'll bring back the Katria you so desperately love. We're so close!" She giggled and trudged awkwardly toward Achyut.

One of the Magi screamed and summoned long, jagged icicle.

"No!" cried Achyut as the Magi hurled his frozen spear toward Katria. The ice tore through her left arm which landed with a squishy thud on the stone altar.

Katria stared at the Magi. She reached up with her right arm and yanked a minna stone from the machine. She pointed her left stump at the Magi, instantly consumed by black bonfires.

"You will not interfere, none of you will! This is what you wanted!" Katria looked at her forearm. Fire sprouted from her stump and grew, the flames reshaping themselves into a new arm. She watched it flicker curiously before it solidified. She smiled.

Another Magi stood and summoned a bronze cyclone. She hurled it across the cavern floor while Katria stared at her new appendage. Before the spell made contact, Katria swiveled around with unnatural speed. Her arm expanded and caught the cyclone, crushing it in her palm as easily as an autumn leaf.

"Thank you for volunteering." An evil grin crossed her lips. The flames erupted from her arm once more and raced toward the Magi.

Two members of the Watchers summoned wards and barriers, but Katria's arm smashed through like an arrow through wet paper and wrapped around the throat of the woman who attacked her.

"Katria! Stop! This isn't right! This isn't you!" Achyut yelled in vain.

"Do not worry, my lovely prince. You and I will be rejoined once I regain what their ritual could not give me, and after I exterminate those who dragged me from my eternal peace. You and I will be bound forever." She giggled as she crushed the woman's throat and her body turned to ash.

Sheer, primal panic raced through the remaining members of the Watchers. Some of them tried to fight back and those who did were instantly killed. Others tried to flee but Katria melted the stone stairs with her midnight fire. She cackled with glee as it spread throughout the cavern and engulfed everything it touched.

Prince Achyut starred in silent horror as Katria murdered the Watchers. He closed his eyes and fell to his knees as she ripped a man in two and squeezed out his soul like juice from an orange. He heard Cassio and Zevulun's screams from somewhere in the distance.

What have I done? he thought as he clamped his hands over his ears in a vain attempt to drown out their screams. *This isn't what Katria would do, this isn't the woman I loved. I have to make this right.*

"You bastards wouldn't respect me in life, of course you wouldn't respect me in death! Now you face my judgment! I am the emissary for all of the tortured souls forced to join the ranks of the dead, our lives wasted away for your petty squabbles. I call upon their anguish and rage and bring them back with renewed purpose. We will bring this world to ruin! Death comes for all in the—" Katria's voice faded. "—end." She looked down at the sword that pierced her heart. She turned her head and frowned.

"Prince Achyut... why? Why would you... don't you love me?"

"I do love you, Katria, but this is wrong. You aren't the same woman you were before. This ritual, it must have done something to you. I can't, I won't stand idle and let you kill all these people."

"But... but they brought me back... that was the point of the ritual. I just needed more time, more souls until I could be made whole. We could have been together... forever."

"I'm sorry, Katria. I'd rather join you in death than live like this."

Katria fell to her knees. Achyut caught her and lowered her to the ground. A pool of dark red blood formed beneath her. She looked up at him once more and smiled weakly.

"Thank you, my darling. The pain, it's all fading away. Please, please let me rest."

"I will. I promise. I'm so sorry, Katria." Achyut's tears fell onto her cheeks as held her body in his arms. "I only wanted to hold you once more, to hear your laugh and see your smile."

"I know. I forgive you. I'll always forgive you because... I love you." She weakly wiped away his tears. "I'll wait for you on the other side. Remember that I love... you." She closed her eyes and fell limp in his lap.

Prince Achyut's heart shattered. To hold his beloved once more, to lose her again, the pain was even more unbearable the second time. He sat on the stone altar with Katria in his lap as more and more stalactites crashed to the floor around him. He looked around him at the bodies of the dead Magi, Cassio, and Zevulun. Dracona Meruyk and Dracona Saital had fled and sealed the entrance to the cavern with barriers and wards.

Without warning, the last of the machine's arms exploded and sent Achyut flying across the chamber. He felt a searing pain in his side and looked up at the skull of the ancient dragon. He stood, shakily, and pressed his hand against the open wound in his stomach. *I can still make it out. I can still make it home. I have to make it to the ledge. I know I can disarm the wards—*

One of the dragon's ribs broke loose and fell. It trapped Achyut beneath its weight.

I guess... I'm not allowed to leave. This will be my tomb as well, here with Katria. Achyut lay in a puddle of blood. He felt the cavern shudder all around him as more and more boulders fell from the ceiling. The faint lights above twinkled like stars in the distance, much too far for him to reach. Droplets of water fell from a pipe, smashed open from the falling debris.

It almost feels like rain. He smiled weakly. *And here I am, a bufon at the bottom of a well. How long before I drown?* A stone slab crashed and shattered beside him. *Perhaps another will fall and crush me first. Or perhaps I'll bleed out. I think I'd prefer the stone; quick and painless. Was that my undoing? Always choosing the quickest or easiest solution? Maybe there was something else I could have done to save Katria or maybe I should have accepted her death, like Rakiba with Amarak. Oh well, it's too late now.*

His stream of thoughts meandered like the Hayi River and deepened like the great sea beyond. He hoped Mona would be okay without him. He hoped his parents would weather the storm of his loss and that Rakiba would lead Lamaru into its next golden age; that Reena, Masami, the avian chiefs, and the naga sisters could all live peacefully with their families.

I only wish I could have died a hero's death instead. I wanted to do something so great, songs would be written about my feats, stories to tell my children and grandchildren. But no, I die in a pool of my own blood, here at the bottom of a nameless cavern, an ancient well, and a fitting tomb for my failure of a life. I only lasted so long because of the strength of others; I never had that strength myself. Rakiba, Mona, Mother, Father, Tanoy, my friends, and most of all, Katria. I'm sorry I failed you.

Achyut sighed and closed his eyes.

"Darling, don't talk about yourself like that. You did plenty of good in your life. It isn't fair to yourself to only remember your failures. You fought for what you thought was good and just. You freed countless lives from oppression, humans and maiamorphs alike. You protected your family and most of all, you loved, unconditionally. You gave me a life worth living."

Achyut could barely open his eyes, but he swore he had heard Katria's voice. The pain in his side was too great and he closed his eyes again.

"That's right, I'm here. I promised I'd be with you through the end. Once you cross over to the other side, we'll be together again, with endless adventures across the horizon. Death is only the next part of our journey. You'll see everyone soon enough." He felt the warmth of Katria's lips on his forehead, though in all likelihood, it was blood leaking further from his body.

The final load-bearing wall of the ancient cavern collapsed.

Endless adventures across the horizon... I like the sound of that; a second chance to see everyone; white shores... a blue sea. That doesn't sound so bad...
Prince Achyut lost touch with his senses and his mind faded to black.

The End

21

Epilogue

~3 years after the disappearance of Prince Achyut

Dracona Meruyk and Dracona Satial stood on a snowy clifftop overlooking the white granite buildings of Crater Lake City, the newly established capital of the Free States of Ecarima. Their white robes whipped about in the frozen wind as they listened to the shouts and cheers of celebration that rang throughout the city streets below.

Earlier that same day, the country's first election results had been tallied and announced. Uriel, hero of the Battle for Banjiha and leader of the mass exodus from the jaded Dynasty of Lamaru had been declared the first Sovereign-elect of the nation. Both Meruyk and Satial had attended his inaugural speech.

Uriel promised the people to build their human-run nation on the freedoms of the individual, and although they lacked much of the minna-based technology of Lamaru, they would prosper in their own way. They would not lust after the power that destroyed their homelands. In fact, Uriel challenged them to completely abandon their ways of the past and cast aside Lamaru's laws, customs, and minna itself.

"It's not surprising that they would abandon harnessing minna after what happened to Banjiha and the central regions of Lamaru." Satial crossed her arms over her chest. "Still, their belief in refusing to harness minna presents a unique problem for our future endeavors. I doubt we'll be able to recruit any of them to our cause."

"Nonsense," replied Meruyk. "There will always be those who rebel against the current way of the world. They will be drawn to our power and mystery, especially since the Dynasty of Lamaru banished our Order after the disappearance of Prince Achyut."

"Do you think the Padishah and King figured out what really happened?" Satial asked in earnest curiosity.

"Perhaps, but it is only a setback in our grand plans of existence. Our immediate concern is to muster our allies across Reighja and find a new way to purify and process whatever minna crystals Ecarima finds. They will no doubt trade the crystals for food, better weapons, and technology. We will have to provide for ourselves now that Lamaru is in shambles."

"And those horrible creatures, what did they call them? The Withered?"

Meruyk nodded.

"Do you really think they're tied to the reanimation ritual and that girl?"

"I do. The woman we brought back had an insatiable urge to kill. She harnessed minna like I had never seen before. Draconas Cassio and Zevulun never stood a chance. Without the prince to stop her rampage, I'm sure you, and I, and the rest of our Order, would have all been killed. She might have even escaped and consumed every living thing on Reighja." *Yet salvation has fettered our grand ambition.* Dracona Meruyk mused to himself. *The tomb is forever buried, lost under the Omah Mountains. The power within has vanished from our world.*

Satial shifted her weight uncomfortably. She bit her lip and twisted a strand of her own bright red hair around her fingers as she rocked back and forth on her feet.

Meruyk sighed. "If there is something you wish to say, say it. Our numbers are too few for us to hide secrets."

"I have my reservations about attempting the rite again. We don't have the members or resources. Should catastrophe befall us, as you say, it could mean the end of all life and our dream."

"Is that why you declined to lead the investigation to find both the elemental and alloy dragons from Dracona Soital's last report?"

Satial nodded.

"And you're sure you won't reconsider?"

"I'm sure. In light of recent events and more frequent attacks from the Withered, Soital and I have begun our own undertaking."

"What duty could be more important, now of all times?" Meruyk eyed Satial curiously.

"There are still many refugees, unable or unwilling to cross the desert to Ecarima, who are also dissatisfied with the Padishah's actions and the state of Lamaru. We've decided to gather these individuals and take ships far to the south, beyond Reighja's borders, watching over them and feeding them legends of dragons and of Reighja. I do not expect to see you again, but when the time is right, we will return."

"You're forming a contingency colony, should Larmaru fall and Ecarima not find faith with the dragons?"

"That's correct." Satial nodded.

"Then perhaps it is for the best that our Order disappears for now, working from the shadows and quietly influencing the way the world spins. I will ask the others to watch over Lamaru and ensure at least one of their cities survives. At the same time, I will guide Ecarima's hand and teach them the ways of the ancient dragons. I wish you and your brother a safe journey into the unknown. May the dragons of old watch over you and your endeavors. Do not forget the reason we exist."

"Of course, Dracona Meruyk." Satial put two fingers to her lips and whistled. A silver roc wyvern with crimson feathers took to the skies from a nearby peak and landed somewhat clumsily in the deep snow in front of her.

"One day, my descendants will return to Reighja. What transpired in the tomb was only a setback. As long as the Watchers exist, there is hope for a better age." She patted the neck of her wyvern, who beat her wings and rose into the sky.

Meruyk watched Satial's silhouette fly east over the rolling hills and yellow desert far beyond. Soon enough, she disappeared over the horizon.

"A better age indeed..." Meruyk mused to himself. He pulled his hood up over his head and walked back down the mountain, back to the shouts and cheers of Ecarima's people and the self-proclaimed fifth Pillar Civilization of Reighja.

22

A Prince's Edit

The REAL Ending to Prince Achyut's Adventure

(written by Prince Naemin & edited by General Gil)

A piercing shriek cut through the air as a massive shadow covered the rooftop. Aquilo swooped down from above and crashed into Lilith. Before she could react, his talons pinned her arms flat against the roof, his sharp beak inches away from her exposed neck.

"Move and you're dead," he commanded.

Lilith tensed her body and gathered minna in her palms. Aquilo pressed his beak against her skin. A trickle of blood ran down her neck.

"I... I yield." She dispersed what little minna she had gathered and lay limp under the eagle's talons. Even if she had time to strike, it would not be enough to kill the abhorrent creature before he killed her.

"Prince Achyut, the fight is won," proclaimed Aquilo.

Achyut sighed in relief, his pain dulled by adrenaline, but this was no time to rest.

"Aquilo, go down to the second floor. There's a first aid kit by the base of the stairs. Bring it here quickly."

"Yes, Your Majesty. What should I do with her?" He gestured at Lilith.

"Keep her contained. If she tries anything, kill her immediately. Now go! Katria's life depends on it."

Aquilo nodded, somewhat shocked by the prince's ferocity. Still, he understood the young man's pain. He transformed back into his humanoid form and pressed Lilith's sword against her neck.

"Come worm, you heard the Prince's orders." He hauled her to her feet and hurried down into the embassy.

Prince Achyut hobbled to Katria's side. "Katria, we did it. The battle is over. We won." He cradled her cold body in his arms. "Katria, please, please, say something. Just hang on a little longer. I'll save you, I promise."

But Katria said not a word. Tears brimmed and flowed from Prince Achyut's eyes. He laid his head against his beloved's chest and wept waterfalls. Then he heard a sound, the most wonderful sound he had heard in his entire life; fiercer than a dragon's call, more melodious than Katria's singing. He thought he was imagining. He steadied his own breathing and listened again. It was faint but definitely there; he heard Katria's heartbeat.

"Katria…" He glanced at the pipe that had pierced her heart—or so he had thought—but the pipe had buried through her shoulder, inches away from a fatal wound.

"Katria! Hold on! I'll save you!" He wiped the tears and snot from his face and poured every ounce of minna he held left into her body.

Aquilo sprinted back up the staircase with Lilith still in tow. He held the medical kit and rushed to Achyut's side.

"I'll save you. I'll save you!" Achyut yelled over and over again. The minna stones in his bansuri cracked and shattered. His prized instrument snapped in half as he siphoned whatever minna he could to save his beloved.

Aquilo sat opposite him and went to work, stabilizing Katria's wound with the kit and his own knowledge of avian medicine.

Prince Achyut wasn't sure when Mona had arrived; she had brought their best field medics to Katria's aid. It was hard and tiresome work but they dared not stop and risk failing.

By the time the medics stopped, the sun had set, Lilith and her followers had been taken away, and Achyut remained at Katria's side.

"That's everything we can do," one of the medics wiped the sweat from his brow. "Her condition is stable, for now, but she's lost a lot of blood. We need to get her back to the Prospector as soon as possible for better medical attention, but I do think she'll live."

"Thank you, thank you all." Achyut smiled and wiped his tears on his sleeve. "Did you hear that, my love? You're going to make it. We'll bo—" His head felt strange. His vision faded to black, and Achyut collapsed then and there.

He came to in a cot aboard the Prospector, his own wounds bandaged and taken care of. He sat up and called out Katria's name.

"It's alright, Prince Achyut, she's safe." Mona stood from her chair and sat on the edge of his bed. She nodded toward the cot beside him where Katria slept. "She's still unconscious, but the doctors said she'll make it." Tears brimmed in Mona's eyes. She threw her arms around him. "I was so worried about both of you. Thank the gods you're safe!"

Achyut returned her warm embrace. "I'm glad to see you're safe as well. What about everyone else? How are Rakiba and Masami and the naga sisters?"

"Nuhir Rakiba and Amarak were both bruised and badly hurt in their fight against Uriel but both are alive and even managed to kill that dastard. Masami was badly injured as well but her condition is stable. The naga sisters returned to their parents but they did leave you a gift: a brand new bansuri, along with their utmost thanks. Lilith is imprisoned and will go to trial for her crimes against Lamaru and our people."

"Then it's over. It's finally over." Suddenly, Achyut felt very heavy, exhausted, exasperated, and wanted nothing more than to sleep for the next few weeks, but then he heard a sound that breathed life and energy back into his broken body. Katria stirred in her sleep. He stood up with Mona's help and hobbled over to her bed.

"Katria! My love, are you awake?"

"Please, Prince Achyut let her sleep. She still has to recover from her wounds," pleaded Mona.

Achyut held his beloved in his arms and kissed her.

Katria's eyes fluttered open. "P-prince Achyut? Is that you? I'm not dreaming, am I?"

"No, my dear, you're here with me, exactly where you belong, in my arms and on our way home."

"I… I thought I died. Everything felt so cold but I wanted to see you again. I needed to see you. I couldn't give up."

Achyut held her in a warm embrace. Katria wrapped her arms around her prince. She looked curiously at her bandaged hand. "My ring… my ring shattered."

Achyut gently pulled away and examined her hand. He looked up at Mona who gasped in realization.

"You enchanted her ring with wards and barriers, didn't you? It must have used up every ounce of minna to save her and shattered during your fight with Lilith. Your love was stronger than Lilith's hatred."

Achyut smiled and cradled Katria, who had drifted back into a deep slumber. "So it seems."

When the Prospector returned to the city of Illadina, Prince Achyut and Katria were wed in the most wondrous celebration of life and love Lamaru had ever seen and everyone danced and ate and gave their blessings to the happy couple.

However, this was only the start to Achyut and Katria's adventures, as weeks later they would save Lamaru once again by thwarting the evil plans of Vitra and Magri, who had slipped into the city disguised as humans to mess up the terraforming ritual. Prince Achyut, Princess Katria, Nuhir Rakiba, and Lady Mona then sailed back up to the Bale and enlisted the aid of their Clystudine allies to take the fight to the accursed dragons, but that is a story for another time.

Needless to say, the newlywed couple, their friends and family, and the entire Dynasty of Lamaru lived in everlasting peace and happily ever after.

THE END

The Tale of Achyut the Gallant

Cast of Characters

~in order of appearance/mention~

- **Amira Adhikar:** The present-day Nuhir of the Dynasty of Lamaru, older sister to Prince Naemin. She's proud of her commitment to her royal duties and takes her studies seriously.
- **Saffi:** Amira's retainer and best friend. Jiian's twin sister. She has a quiet and reserved personality.
- **Naemin Adikar:** The present-day youngest prince of Lamaru with a mischievous streak and good heart. He prefers action and adventure over studying and other 'boring adult responsibilities'.
- **Lila Adhikar:** The present-day Padishah of the Dynasty of Lamaru, Amira and Naemin's strict and loving mother, wife of King Jordan.
- **King Jordan:** The present-day King of the Dynasty of Lamaru. A former educator and father of Amira and Naemin. His fabled skill with a blade has earned him the title 'The Sword of Illadina'.
- **General Gil:** A General of Lamaru's army and King Jordan's previous retainer, now Amira and Naemin's mentor. His unyielding ferocity has earned him the title 'The Axe of Illadina'.
- **Jiian:** Naemin's retainer when he turns ten, Saffi's twin brother. Calculating eyes lie behind his warm smile and smug attitude.

***

- **Achyut Adhikar:** A former prince of Lamaru and Nuhir Rakiba's younger brother. He has a mischievous streak and a good heart, preferring action and adventure over living in the palace.

- **Mona:** Achyut's retainer and former Champion of Thaniana, thanks to her mastery of the sword and harness of electrical and fire minna. She comes from a long line of serving the royal family.
- **Captain Tanoy:** Captain of the sandship 'Prospector' and Achyut's mentor in harnessing water minna.
- **Rakiba Adhikar:** A former Nuhir/Padishah of the Dynasty of Lamaru who takes their royal station very seriously. With their friend, Amarak, they have accomplished a great many heroic deeds.
- **Rakriliox:** 'Enlightened One' of the Bale and leader of the newly united Clystudine Confederation.
- **Griskrus:** Champion for Rakriliox, his shell is adorned with hundreds of victory pigments.
- **Magri:** An ancient alloy dragon who lives in the caverns under the northernmost mountains of Reighja. His scales are reinforced by black tungsten, his real name has been long forgotten by all.
- **Vitra:** A young elemental dragon who seeks to usher in a second age of draconic superiority. His mastery of ice and harness of water minna has warranted the title 'The Eternal Winter'.
- **Gerald, Sonyia, and Jennifer Miller:** Natives to the Queendom of Yaand forced into slavery by the Clystudine Confederation. They, along with 366 others, became citizens of Lamaru.
- **Katria Konners:** A shy and pessimistic native to the Queendom of Yaand forced into slavery by the Clystudine Confederation. She is a self-proclaimed oracle inflicted by a curse.
- **Joseph:** Member of the Prospector's crew who cares for the irrivir and harnesses earth minna.

- **Reena Shizuka:** Native to the Queendom of Yaand, forced into slavery by the Clystudine Confederation, who befriends Katria and thinks of her as an older sister.
- **Boris:** A bandit-for-hire and member of the Hunters' Guild.
- **Lilith Eruber:** A soulseeker and the newly-elected Grand Vizier of Banjiha. Her profound ambition and silver tongue have helped her amass a great following. Older sister to Uriel.
- **Amarak:** A great golden direwolf and Rakiba's companion. He loves treats, playing with children, and scratches behind his floppy ears.
- **Nadia and Netheli:** naga sisters living in the city of Banjiha. Their mothers are friends of the royal family.
- **Uriel Eruber:** Lilith's younger brother and second in command. A captain of Banjiha's paragons, he is praised for his superb harness of minna and survival skills.
- **Gunith:** A captain of Banjiha's paragons and Lilith's husband.
- **Masami Joruka:** A foxtail maiamorph and Semoru's wife who lives in the city of Banjiha with her family.
- **Semoru Joruka:** Professor of Theoretical Minna Studies at the University of Central Banjiha. Rakiba's childhood friend who lived in Illadina during his younger years. His father taught Rakiba and Achyut the basics to harnessing minna.
- **Angem Adhikar:** A former Padishah of Lamaru and mother of Rakiba and Achyut.
- **King Debesh:** A former King of Lamaru and father of Rakiba and Achyut.
- **Kinnari:** An avian maiamorph and leader of the fabled Red Feather Squawdron. She is a crew member aboard the Queen's Salvation and friend of Nuhir Rakiba.
- **Aquilo:** An avian maiamorph and leader of the fabled Gold Feather Squawdron. Bold and strong, he is always the first willing to fight to protect his flock.

- **Eravil:** An avian maiamorph and leader of the fabled Blue Feather Squawdron. His strategic mind is unmatched, rivaled only by his own vanity.
- **Captain Iyushi:** Captain of the sandship 'Queen's Salvation' and friend of Nuhir Rakiba.
- **Dracona Soital:** A member of the Watchers and Satial's twin brother. One of the Nine to be granted the rank of Dracona. He rides a silver and cyan wyvern.
- **Dracona Satial:** A member of the Watchers and Soital's twin sister. One of the Nine to be granted the rank of Dracona. She rides a silver and crimson wyvern.
- **Dracona Cassio Naebuella:** A member of the Watchers and One of the Nine to be granted the rank of Dracona. They are well-known across Reighja for their unique brand of elvish fashion. Captain of the newly-christened sandship, 'Dragonfang'.
- **Dracona Zevulun:** A member of the Watchers and One of the Nine to be granted the rank of Dracona. Obsessed with his research on minna theory, his colleagues describe him as 'endearingly eccentric'.
- **Captain Karascotia:** A Clystudine merchant and captain of the sandship, 'Longevity'. She retired exceedingly young and wealthy but deemed the call to adventure and profit more enticing.
- **Dracona Meruyk:** A member of the Watchers and the oldest of the Nine Dracona. No cost is too high, no sacrifice too great to prove his commitment to their cause.

Glossary

- **Age of Dragons:** the first age of Reighja, characterized by the immigration of the first humans, draconic rule, and the creation of the first maiamorph species
- **abaya:** a long, usually dark-colored cloak, worn by many women in the Dynasty of Lamaru
- **altrusynaptic acts:** one of the three classifications of minna, often referred to as mental minna, that draws power from memories, emotions, experiences, etc. Unlike blood or elemental minna, the caster uses their soul as a focus. It is the rarest and most unstable form of harnessed minna.
- **aruval:** a straight-edge machete-like sword tipped in a reverse-curve billhook. The weapon doubles as a grabbing tool and is often used to clear brush, lightly-wood paths, or cut coconuts
- **Banjiha Eye Network (BEN):** A network of connected camera-like widgets called 'eyes' that displays real-time information to a system of magic mirrors mounted inside the Banjihan central embassy.
- **bansuri:** a side-blown flute with six finger holes, covering two and a half octaves of music
- **bufon:** a small four-legged amphibian that trades its ability to swim to better survive on land. Their favorite food, lightning bugs, gives them incredible electrical resistance
- **camu berries:** a sweet red berry native to southern Reighja, it is chock-full of nutrients and often used in cooking
- **Champion of Thaniana:** title given to Thaniana's strongest warrior, won by defeating all other combatants in an annual competition testing raw strength, cunning, and survival skills

- **charrwood:** a species of tree native to northern Reighja. When properly treated, the wood blackens and becomes fire-resistant and hydrophobic
- **Clystudine (species):** the first experimental species created by ancient dragons in their attempts to hide from the territorial expansion and hunting from humans. They are semi-aquatic turtle-like reptiles preceding over Reighja's northern-western seaboard
- **Collapse:** a magically-powered environmental catastrophe caused by the failed terraforming ritual which marked the end of Lamaru's golden age; released the Withered across Reighja
- **Continental Navigation Assistant (CNA):** A widget used by cartographers to map lands and important geological features. Information collected through a pair of eyeglasses and stored in the CNA can be transferred to maps or other widgets for precise replication
- **dhoti:** common legwear in the Dynasty of Lamaru, this length of fabric is wrapped around the waist and legs then knotted in the front
- **direwolf:** a species of over-sized wolf, boasting higher strength, intelligence, and resistance to minna compared to their smaller cousins
- **djinn:** spiritual beings of extraordinary power that roam the continent of Reighja; they are masters of harnessing minna and often take a humanoid form in order to persuade others to do their bidding
- **dotara:** a rounded two-to-four stringed instrument with a long neck often used in folk music
- **dragons (alloy):** the largest and most common of all dragon species, alloy dragons boast superior physical strength and defense, taking on the color and characteristics of whatever ore or precious metal they consume during their early years. They live near ore-rich mountains and cave systems

- **dragons (elemental):** these midsize dragons have complete mastery over one of the six primordial facets of minna and usually preside over regions associated with their element
- **dragons (gemstone):** the smallest and rarest subspecies of dragon, they are masters of strategy and agility and most apt at harnessing non-elemental minna (such as altrusynaptic acts), taking on the color and characteristics of whatever gemstone they consume during their early years
- **Eleven Families of Lamaru:** the earliest still-surviving human settlers of Reighja, who spread their influence across the continent, resulting in the creation of three of the four Pillar Civilizations
- **Eye of Eruber:** an ancient amethyst and powerful minna focus, used by the Eruber family to subdue the area now known as Banjiha. It will crack in the hands of anyone unworthy of its power
- **Feather Squawdrons (Red, Blue, and Gold):** elite legions of avian warriors, masters of aerial and ground-based combat who share a mutual respect and understanding with the citizens of Lamaru
- **fire eels:** gigantic crimson fish capable of producing a plasma-like substance that instantly boils the water around them; often rode as aquatic mounts by Clystudine soldiers and merchants
- **Free States of Ecarima:** the human-centric self-proclaimed fifth Pillar Civilization following the Collapse and the subsequent mass exodus out west
- **garad saree:** a traditional dress of undyed silk with a bright-colored border worn by the women of the Dynasty of Lamaru for special occasions and formal ceremonies
- **Grand Vizier:** title given to the governor of one of the six regions of Lamaru, who reports directly to the Padishah and their council, electing their own cabinet to handle the region's internal affairs

- **Hayi River:** the largest river in all of Reighja, its headwaters are located in the Wild Lands where it flows east until it reaches the sea; the largest source of freshwater for the Dynasty of Lamaru
- **hellswood:** an endangered species of tree native to the Wild Lands with extraordinary fire resistance and often found growing on the slopes of active volcanoes
- **Hunters' Guild:** a shadow organization monopolizing organized crime across all of Reighja with their headquarters somewhere in the Wild Lands
- **ironwood:** a species of tree native to southern Reighja used in construction for its mixture of metallic and wooden properties. When burned, its blue leaves release a toxic gray smoke
- **irrivir:** a large, flightless bird native to southern Reighja used as a mount and beast of burden by the Dynasty of Lamaru. When threatened, it curls into a ball and stiffens its feathers creating a cocoon of spikes. Their flat feet allow them to run quickly over the desert sand.
- **jaracut:** a species of rodent whose small size, exceptional agility, and quick learning allow them to thrive across almost all of Reighja
- **korma:** a dish from the Dynasty of Lamaru, consisting of meat or vegetables braised with yogurt, water, or stock, and spices to produce a thick sauce
- **kudzu vine:** a creeping, climbing perennial vine that hunts both plants and small animals by ensnaring its victim and depriving it of essential resources
- **kurta:** a loose collarless shirt or tunic commonly worn across the Dynasty of Lamaru, being either simple wear or intricately designed for formal and special occasions
- **light spirits:** semi-sentient magical beings that wander across Reighja. Because they come in any color imaginable, large migrations are sights to behold, often accompanied by feasts and festivals

- **loyal swift:** a small species of bird native to southern Reighja domesticated as messenger birds for their keen sense of direction, memory, and ability to stay airborne for months at a time
- **Magesep:** an runic language with twenty-seven glyphs, each representing an emotion; the written and spoken language of harnessing minna
- **Magi:** a title given to those in the Dynasty of Lamaru who have shown a mastery of harnessing minna and continually strive to understand its applications in any related field. Magi may be scholars, explorers, widget tinkerers, soldiers, religious leaders, etc.
- **maiamorph (avian, foxtail, lotor, naga, sika, urosi, etc):** the general term for any member of the experimental species created by ancient dragons in their attempts to hide from the mass hunting efforts of early humans. Individuals of maiamorph heritage are grouped together in clans and able to shift between a humanoid and fully animalistic form.
- **minna:** a microscopic particulate substance found all across Reighja that allows for its inhabitants to practice magic through a scientific and creative process called 'harnessing'
  - **six primal facets of minna:** the six most basic aspects of minna, unable to break down further, that combine into every other facet; water, earth, fire, air, shatter and binding
  - **Facets of Creation:** The eighteen combinations of the six primal facets that form the building blocks of how any additionally added facet will behave or change
- **minnaquins:** minna-powered automatons that can perform basic movements and functions
- **minna focus:** a construct used to store pre-determined minna charges for later use in spells, widgets or rituals ie a tome, wand, staff, or enchanted item

- **naan:** leavened, oven-baked flatbread served in the Dynasty of Lamaru
- **nafsiyat whales:** a species of carnivorous whale that roams the open seas around Reighja. They have a black and white coloration and have evolved the use of low-level telepathy for communication and pack hunting
- **nosorogs:** a terrestrial quadrupedal species that roams the open plains and grasslands of northern Reighja. Their tough leathery skin resists most basic elemental forms of minna and are often used as mounts by Clystudine soldiers and merchants; related to the ragamauhfaki
- **Nuhir:** title bestowed upon the next heir apparent to the Dynasty of Lamaru; usually the oldest or first recognized as a soulseeker although some exceptions have occurred
- **Omah Mountains:** the largest mountain range in Reighja that divides the northern and southern parts of the continent
- **Order of the Watchers:** a cult that worships the knowledge and wisdom accrued by the ancient dragons and seeks to restore their power over Reighja through religious fervor
- **Dracona:** title bestowed upon the nine leaders of the Watchers
- **Padishah:** title of the current leader of the Dynasty of Lamaru; a powerful soulseeker who guides the kingdom's people and is responsible for handling executive and judicial duties
- **Pact of the Champions:** a Clystudine law enacted to settle political disputes and disagreements through nonlethal combat
- **Pillar Civilizations of Reighja:** the most sizable and most prominent civilizations on Reighja, who hold enough economic or political leverage to affect all others on the continent ie through exports of certain goods and services, military power, joint infrastructure, knowledge, or resources
    - ○ **Consortium of Jatharir:** a conglomerate of banks, guilds, and merchant companies responsible for most trade and commerce between the Pillar Civilizations. Their fleet

of sandships is famous for sailing across the oceans and returning with wondrous treasure

- ○ **Clystudine Confederation:** after years of infighting and civil strife, the Clystudine species have united into a single government, each region lead by an "Enlightened One" and renewed their status as a Pillar Civilization due to their export of ore and nafsiyat products
- ○ **Dynasty of Lamaru:** the largest and most economically powerful of the Pillar Civilizations, thanks to their mass production of widgets and export of fabricated minna stones and raw minna crystals. Their Magi's talent is legendary across the continent
- ○ **Queendom of Yaand:** A matriarchal monarchy who constantly clashes with their Clystudine neighbors. They are staunch allies of the Consortium of Jatharir and Reighja's largest exporter of valuable woods, crops, and commodities such as dyes and animal products

- **paragons:** Lamaru's order of knights, loyal to the Padishah, and trained to use a variety of weapons, combat styles, survival skills and basic minna defense
- **pitcher scorpion:** a species of gigantic stone scorpion that lives underground, hunting across the open deserts of southern Reighja
- **Pleb:** the common language spoken between all Pillar Civilizations
- **qipao:** a figure-fitting, one piece garment with a standing collar and asymmetric fasteners
- **ragamauhfaki:** a semiaquatic quadruped with powerful jaws. They are stocky, stalwart, extremely territorial, and resist most basic elemental forms of minna, related to nosorogs
- **retainer:** title and position given to skilled individuals who aid specific members of the royal family providing protection, council, and assistance completing various tasks and royal duties

- **roc wyverns:** a classification of wyverns with more bird-like characteristics
- **roti:** a round unleavened flatbread eaten across the Dynasty of Lamaru
- **sarong:** a long length of fabric with a multitude of purposes, often wrapped around the waist
- **shamshir:** a curved sword with a slim blade and little taper; best for slashing unarmored opponents
- **sherwani:** a long-sleeved, collared outer coat worn by men in the Dynasty of Lamaru
- **soulseeker:** honorary title given to those capable of performing altrusynaptic acts.
- **soulshare:** An altrusynaptic act that allows the seeker to see and understand the recipient's motives, memories, and core values and feel them as their own. The persuasiveness of the power is amplified if the seeker and recipient share common values
- **Sovereign-elect:** title given to the elected president of both the Free States of Ecarima and the Banjihan Autocracy
- **tapi:** a terrestrial quadrupedal species that lives near and around the jungles of southern Reighja. They are docile in nature and can be used as mounts or beasts of burden.
- **tricorn hat:** a triangular hat with a folded-up brim, worn by captains of sandships and their accompanying esteemed guests
- **turban:** a type of headwear in the Dynasty of Lamaru created by winding a length of cloth
- **widgets:** name for any piece of minna-powered technology made in the Dynasty of Lamaru
- **Wild Lands:** the predominately unexplored southwestern area of Reighja
- **withered:** gruesome amalgamations of hunted prey contorted into chimeras that serve the parent withermold. They have hunted across southern Reighja since the Collapse.

Jim Gill, photo by Cassie Flynn

About the Author

From Mos Eisley to the Shire, Hogwarts to Hyrule Castle, the Hidden Leaf Village to the Indigo Plateau, I've always loved stories that pull me into their own worlds, let me see through another's eyes, and provide perspectives and lessons that I can transpose onto my own experience. Everywhere I go I see a stories worth telling; people whose lives should be shared and celebrated and differences in culture and perspectives that have broadened my own horizons.

With a passion for environmental conservation and high fantasy, I created the rolling hills, towering mountains, and scorching deserts of the mystical and awe-inspiring continent of Reighja; a fantasy world to share with everyone, to indulge in stories that examine the human experience, and to provide occasional relief from our sometimes overbearing lives. I'm thankful for everyone who has supported my journey thus far and for the ability to share my stories with you and hope they help you to grow into the person your younger self would be proud of and needed.

I am a self-published author with a background in biological sciences who has flourished in a variety of fun and exciting careers including as a trained lifeguard and swim instructor, diver, animal handler and keeper, public speaker, showman, and teacher.

learn more at www.jimgillbooks.com